# HIGHLAND SURRENDER

# ALSO BY TRACY BROGAN

*Crazy Little Thing*

# HIGHLAND SURRENDER

## TRACY BROGAN

Published by Montlake Romance
P.O. Box 400818
Las Vegas, NV 89140

ISBN-13: 9781612186962
ISBN-10: 1612186963

*For my father,*

*who was born in Scotland,*

*and who told me when I couldn't sleep*

*I should make up stories in my head.*

# CHAPTER 1

Fiona Sinclair could not reconcile the irony of nature's twisted humor. For today of all wretched days, the sky should be burdened with clouds as dark and dismal as her mood. But the morning dawned soft and fair, mild as a Highland calf, and she knew that God himself mocked her. At any moment, Myles Campbell and his father, the Earl of Argyll, would pass through the gates of Sinclair Hall, unwelcome, yet unhindered by her clan. Soon after that, she must stand upon the chapel steps and marry a man she had never met, and yet had hated for all of her life.

Through her narrow bedchamber window, sounds from the bailey filtered up. The smithy's hammer tapped a mellow cadence as if this day were just like any other. Perhaps he shaped a horseshoe or a pointed pike. She smiled at the latter and imaged the heaviness of that same pike in her hand. Oh, that she had the courage to plunge it deep into the earl's heart, if indeed he had one.

She rose from the threadbare cushion on the bench and moved without purpose toward the stone fireplace. A low fire burned, warding off the spring morning's chill. From habit, Fiona slipped her hand into the leather pouch around her waist. She squeezed tight the silver brooch inside, its design and inscription etched as clearly in her memory as on the pin itself. A boar's head, symbol of Clan Campbell, with words chosen by the king himself.

*To Cedric Campbell, a true friend is
worth a king's ransom. James V.*

The brooch had been a gift to the Campbell chief, the man about to become her father-in-law. But he had left it behind nearly seven years earlier, pierced into the flesh of Fiona's mother so that all the world might know he had dishonored her.

The priest had found Aislinn Sinclair's lifeless body in a secluded glen outside the village, stripped bare and broken, marked by Cedric's lust and spite. Thus a feud, long simmering at the edges, boiled over. But today the king thought to put an end to it with this farce of a marriage between a Sinclair lass and a Campbell son. It would not work.

Fiona paced to the window, restless and melancholy. She leaned out to breathe fresh spring air, hoping it might lighten her spirits. The too-sweet scent of hyacinth clung to the breeze, along with the ever-present brine of Moray Firth.

Along the west curtain wall, more hammering sounded as masons worked to bolster the steps leading to the main keep. As if precarious stairs alone might halt the Campbell men from gaining entrance. But nothing would. Her fate as a Campbell bride had been declared the very day she drew in her first breath, and sealed when her father blew out his last.

The latch rattled, and her chamber door swung open. Her brothers had come to ensure her compliance once more. Simon, with hair and countenance both dark as the Irish Sea, entered first, for he was always in a rush. With their father now two months in the grave, he was also their laird. John followed close behind.

"Are you ready, Fiona? I'll brook no nonsense from you this day." Simon strode to the window and looked out, but just as quickly turned to stare her way.

She bit the inside of her cheek. She'd not cower beneath his stormy gaze, nor willingly abide by his commands. Laird or no, he was still her brother and she would defend herself.

"I'll not play pawn in your game of politics," Fiona said, holding her voice steady with some effort. "I've told you so. For years, we've lived in exile, forsaken by King James because father dared defy him. Yet suddenly he forgives and wants to draw us into his fold? It makes no sense." Her skin tingled with unease, yet she persisted. "The Earl of Argyll is his right hand, so why does James enforce a betrothal which benefits neither the Campbells nor the Crown? And why has Cedric agreed to it? We are poor and bring nothing to the table."

Simon scoffed, dismissive of her argument. "The Campbell chief agreed to it because he's nothing more than a royal whore. He'd bend over and bare his noble arse if the king wished it."

Fiona's heart pulsed jaggedly at his harsh words. The pointed little stabs made it difficult to breathe.

John set a gentle hand upon her shoulder. "It makes perfect sense, Fiona, if you've a mind to see it." Two years younger but a head taller than Simon, John had their mother's coloring, with sand-colored hair and eyes the same glittering blue as Fiona's. "The king has declared himself Lord of the Isles, but he knows we Highlanders hold no allegiance to the Crown. He thinks to seduce us into obedience by marrying his nobles to our daughters and our sisters. 'Tis easier than waging war, for what's the blood of a few virgin brides compared to that of Scotland's sons?"

Simon's blunt fingers curled into a fist, and he turned away and looked to the window again, but John continued. "The king well knows our ugly history with the Campbells, and so he proves himself our master. If we agree to the marriage, he can claim our loyalty. If we refuse, he will crush us, and none will rise to our aid."

Desperation filled the cavern of Fiona's chest. "If father were alive, he'd never allow this. He'd not hand me over to the Campbells to be abused as our mother was."

John's jaw clenched. The tenderness in his voice vanished. "Simon is our laird now, and we must follow him, Fiona. Your marriage to Myles Campbell will seal the truce and keep our people safe. Do not persist in this selfishness."

She reached out and gripped John's arm as if he dangled her over a precipice, for indeed he did. Where was the brother who had been her champion? 'Twas always John who interceded when Simon became too rough or harsh, but now it seemed he had abandoned her. Her gaze skittered from one to the other.

"That's it, then? Neither of you will raise a sword to protect me from these murderers or defend our mother's honor? Cedric Campbell choked the life from her and left her body in a stream to rot. What if they intend the same for me? What if this is just a scheme to trick me onto my back and you fools down to your knees?"

"If the Campbells wanted us on our knees, we'd be there." John's voice went rough as tree bark. "For years, we've fought to avenge our mother. You know that. Simon and I have both taken our turn against them on the field. Now the battle comes to you. Do your part as a Sinclair warrior. Wed the earl's son and buy us some peace."

4

His words fell like granite blocks, crushing her beneath their weight. Panic sharpened her voice. "Peace? You coward. You are selling my future to buy yours because you're not man enough to defeat them in battle!"

John's hand drew back, quick as an archer's, and let it swing. His open palm cracked against her cheek, the sound exploding in her ear.

Simon was the kind to strike, but not John. Never John. The shock stung as sharply as the blow itself. She covered her face with her own hand and drew up taller.

Simon stepped closer to them both. "We are all warriors in our own way, Fiona. John is right. This is your duty to our clan. Shirk from it, and we will have no choice but to offer Margaret in your place."

Fiona's breath went hot inside her throat. She sank to a bench along the wall. "You would give them our sister? She's but a child!"

Simon shrugged his thick shoulders. "She is nearly thirteen—plenty old enough to see herself wed—and I'm sure it matters little to Myles Campbell where he sheaths his sword."

John's slap was mild compared to the blow of Simon's crude words. Impotent rage rattled her senses. "You wouldn't."

"It's your choice," he said. "Do your duty or see Margaret take your place. Either way, the Campbells leave here with a Sinclair bride."

"'Tis time, Fiona. Enough wallowing. They're just outside the gate." Bess, the old nursemaid, strode into Fiona's chamber, her gnarled hands pulling a blue dress off the bed and shaking it. It was deep blue, trimmed in ermine and gold thread, but showed signs of age and wear. Once her mother's from her days at the Scottish court, it now belonged to Fiona.

"They're here?" Young Margaret had joined her sister soon after John and Simon left. With thick blonde curls cascading to the small of her back and a sweet smattering of pale freckles across her nose, Margaret was a bud about to blossom into full beauty. She moved toward the window, light as a sparrow. "What do they look like, Bess? Are they very horrible? And as big as they say?"

Fiona's gut churned as if it fought against bad mutton. She ran to the garderobe and retched up what little breakfast she had eaten.

Bess was quick to Fiona's side, wiping her brow with a damp cloth. "There, there, missy. It won't be so bad. You'll see. One man is much like the next when the fire is low."

Fiona stared at her homely maid for the briefest moment, wondering what the dear old woman could possibly recall of men in dim light, and heaved once more.

"Oh, Fiona, come see." Margaret gasped. "There are so many."

Fiona steeled herself and clutched the maid's arm a moment. Bess patted her and gave a reassuring nod. With trembling breath, Fiona stepped forward to pull her sister back. "Come away from the window, Marg. It's best if they don't see you."

"Why?"

"Because then they will covet you, for certain, and I cannot risk it. You must stay here, safe with Bess at Sinclair Hall." *Until our brothers betray you too.*

Margaret flung her arms around Fiona. "But if they take me too, then I could live with you, always."

Fiona blinked away a hot tear. "No, sweeting, you cannot. I will manage well enough amid our enemy, but I shall rest easier knowing you are not in harm's way."

For Margaret, she'd put on a brave face. For Margaret, she would offer herself to the Campbells to do with her what they may. But none of them would see her quaking in her slippers or shedding girlish tears. Hugh Sinclair had sired sterner stuff than that.

She kissed Marg's cheek and set her aside, walking toward the bed. "Bess, please help me don that gown. You're right. 'Tis time."

Fiona stood at the top of the staircase leading into the great hall. The room teemed with people, enemy and kin all eager to see if she'd be weeping and frail, defiant or obedient. How could they not? 'Twas a day in history when a Sinclair laid down weapons and embraced a Campbell.

Well then, let them ogle in their morbid curiosity. Let them gaze upon the virgin sacrifice her brothers placed at the altar of the king. She lifted the hem of her skirt with one hand, clenching the brooch in the other, and descended. An angel doomed to Lucifer's pit.

Simon extended his hand to guide her. She ignored him. In moments, he would no longer be her laird, the only blessing of this unholy mess.

The room hushed.

She searched the crowd, seeking the one who would be her husband. But how to know among so many strangers? There was a redheaded giant with a beard so thick one could scarcely tell if there was a mouth in there. *Please, Lord, not that one.* Next to him was another man, tall, broad of shoulder, but with hair halfway to silver. *Not him. Too old.* And yet another, so broad in the beam his saffron shirt could double as a tent at market. These tiny facts her mind absorbed while trying to block out reality.

And then she saw them.

Father and son, of that she was certain. They stood, heads nearly touching as one murmured to the other. With garments too fine to be practical this far north, they stood within the crowd, yet separated by some invisible barrier. The earl possessed an arrogant, regal bearing, like a peacock in full plumage, while his son had the dark look of a warrior, and one accustomed to having his own way. His broad hand wrapped around the hilt of his sword, and foreboding clutched at her like brambles of a thicket.

Her foot faltered on the last step as he turned and looked her way.

# CHAPTER 2

MYLES BARELY HEARD HIS FATHER'S WORDS FOR THE DIN IN his ears. The hall itself was not loud, but the pulsing of his heart muddled all other sound. They'd ridden without fanfare or mishap into the thick of the Sinclairs' nest, and now he stood amid men he'd sooner skewer through than dine with. He pulled at the neck of his shirt. It was the finest linen from France, and yet today it scratched like a peasant's rags.

His father squeezed his shoulder. "Easy, lad. The men will watch our backs and see no harm comes."

Myles said nothing. It wasn't a fight that had him rattled. In fact, he'd relish the chance to have at it and dispose of these Sinclairs once and for all. No, it wasn't a brawl that made him quake. It was the thought of her. His *bride.* The word choked, even inside his own mind. *Unjust* was the next word that came.

King James had promised him a tender mademoiselle. Odette was her name, a sweet bit of French fluff with skin like fresh cream, and lips plump and succulent as a strawberry. She wept when she learned the king had called him home from France. Myles promised to return, but instead, he was standing here, inside a pit of vipers, waiting for a coarse Highland wench with two surly brothers and a vendetta against his family.

The room hushed. A tiny movement caught his eye. There she was upon the step, wearing a threadbare gown well past its days. It was too small and nudged her breasts skyward in a most sinful way. She faltered and rebuffed her brother's outstretched hand. Her eyes sparked with defiance. No wilting miss was she.

The chasm between clusters of his men and theirs widened as she made her way toward him and his father. Her brothers flanked her on either side, the stocky, brooding one to her left and the tall, observant one to the right. As they approached, her eyes flickered over Myles, like a rabbit in a snare, and then settled upon his father. The tilt of her chin extended.

The earl's arm dropped from his son's shoulder as he turned to face them.

The dark one spoke first. "My lords, I am Simon, laird of the Clan Sinclair. This is my brother, John, and our sister, Fiona."

John nodded once in acknowledgment, his lips pressed tight.

But Myles's betrothed did not speak or nod or even blink. Her eyes bore into his father. Her chest rose and fell with rapid breaths.

With some reluctance, Myles tore his gaze from her tantalizing cleavage. She was lovely, his bride to be, and he had not expected that. He thought she'd be plain or freckled, but she was neither. Her skin was flawless, her blue eyes brilliant though rimmed red with recently shed tears, and her hair, so rich in hue it was nearly burgundy, wound round her head in braids with a few curls, defying an attempt to tame them, falling loose. He swallowed and gripped his sword more tightly.

"Greetings to you. It is our honor to be welcomed into your home," Cedric said.

Myles heard not a hint of sarcasm in his father's voice, though certainly the honor was entirely the Sinclairs'. This keep was a rickety pile of limestone and mortar held together by piss and mud. Why the king had sent him here to claim his bride, delicious though she appeared to be, was beyond his comprehension.

Cedric reached out his hands to Fiona's. "And you, my dear, how lovely you are. May the Lord bless and keep you."

She kept her hands fisted at her sides. "The Lord has abandoned me, sir, for had He not, you'd be this moment smothering beneath a pile of dung."

Gasps went round the room, followed by furious whispers. Her words struck Myles like a kick to the head. Not even the noblest of men insulted Cedric Campbell and lived to tell the tale. He turned to his father, expecting rage, but the earl smiled. Not a grand smile, but a genuine one.

"I see you've your mother's spirit," Cedric said, eliciting more whispers.

"A spirit set free too soon. How dare you mention her as if her death was not your doing!" She slapped the palm of her hand flat against his chest with all her apparent might and left in its place a silver brooch.

"This is yours, is it not?" she demanded.

Simon tugged her back roughly. "Fiona, have a care!"

"Is it not?" she asked again.

Cedric pulled the pin from the thick fabric of his garment and stared down at it. The lines of his face deepened and the smile faded from his lips. He flipped the pin to read the inscription. He raised his gaze to Fiona and then swept over her brothers.

"You know it is. But I swear to you, as I swore to your father for all these years, 'twas not by my hand she died. This is our chance to start anew."

Simon tugged her farther back and whispered in her ear. Her face blanched, and a tiny breath escaped her lips. John turned as well, to block her from view while the brothers plied her with hushed words.

Myles leaned toward his father. "This is going poorly. She appears to have a most disagreeable nature."

"Would you not expect a beautiful rose to have some thorns?" Cedric whispered back.

"Aye, Father. But this one has talons. Were she a man, I'd kill her for insulting you so."

Cedric shook his head. "She is impetuous, like her mother. But a spirited mare is far superior to a meek pony."

Frustration tapped at Myles. "To ride? Yes. To live with? That is another matter."

John stepped back into his place, and Simon hauled Fiona before them. Her cheeks were splotched with red; her lips quivered as she curtsied before them. "My lords, I beg you, forgive my imprudent speech. I was overcome with emotions. Have mercy and I shall prove a dutiful wife…and…daughter." The last of this she choked out in a whisper so soft only they could hear.

At her capitulation, Myles felt an uneasy twist in his gut. He was wholly offended by the insults she hurled, and yet her abject surrender and plea for mercy made him feel grotesque, as if he had somehow abused her. Someday he would ask what threats her brothers had used to bend her will, and the thought gave him a start.

She was to be his wife. He had understood that in the abstract, when her name was merely ink scrawled upon parchment and sealed with the king's insignia. But this woman would stand beside him all his days and nights forevermore. Suddenly, France and his little mademoiselle seemed very far away.

The marriage ceremony was her purgatory, a postponement of that final judgment condemning her to everlasting doom. Father Bettney, sanctimonious as ever, held the yellowed Bible in his equally yellowed hands. He wheezed the words of God in a nasal monotone. Fiona often thought if rats could speak, they would sound like this priest. He glowered at Fiona, as if he read her mind and judged accordingly. As if she were Eve in the garden and wholly to blame for this sacramental abuse instead of her brothers. Then Father Bettney spoke the words *love*, *obey*, and *cherish*, and she could not decide which of these was most offensive.

Simon and John kept close, no doubt afraid she'd flee or incite the Campbells to violence with more reckless words. But she bit her lip and kept a vision of her sweet Marg close to mind, as they had prompted her to do.

When time came for her vows, she recited her part, steady and clear, with head held high. She even managed to still the trembling of her hand when her husband slipped a gold-and-emerald ring upon her finger. It glimmered in the light but was a heavy shackle. Fear sliced a wide swath a moment later as she placed her pale fingers against the brown roughness of his own. His were killing hands, honed for battle. And soon enough they'd be on her.

Then her husband pressed his lips against her own to seal this bargain forged in the devil's own fire, and she wished she might have venom in her kiss, that he might perish in that moment. But he stepped away, alive. And she drew another breath and lived as well.

The crowd murmured its approval, but no cheering came forth. On this day, only whispers of sympathy and predictions of an uncertain future circulated among the congregation.

After the ceremony, the meal was served without the usual pageantry of a bridal feast. There had been neither the time nor the inclination to celebrate. Fiona sat beside her husband on the dais, with Simon to her right. Cedric, thanks be to God, was next to John, who kept him deep in conversation. What they discussed, she could not imagine.

Father Bettney gave the blessing, droning on about chastity and duty, though through it all he glared at her as if she were Pandora with one hand on the lid.

Next to her, Myles's nearness swirled like a hot vapor all around. She was torn between wanting to stare and take in every detail of him, and wishing he might burst into flame and turn to ash. He was tall—taller than John, even. His close-cropped hair was dark, his jaw broad, and were she feeling generous, she might admit his clean-shaven face was not repulsive. His eyes were disconcerting, though. Too bright to be natural, an icy sort of green, like a frosted glen in the early spring.

From the trencher before them, Fiona ate little. A few almonds and figs, a slice of apple, but it all tasted of wood pulp in her mouth. It was expected for her to select the choicest bits of food for her husband, but instead, she kept her hands to herself and eyes in her lap. Her disregard appeared to have little impact on his appetite.

"You're not eating much. Is the meal not to your liking?" he asked at last. At her continued silence, he leaned over so that his lips nearly touched her ear. She felt the warmth of his breath as he whispered, "How pleased and fortunate I am to have such a silent, docile wife."

She snapped her head in his direction. *Silent and docile?* Then she saw his smile. He had set the bait, and she had scooped it up.

He laughed at her expression and stuffed a piece of veal into his mouth. "Not so docile after all, aye? I wondered where that chit hurling slurs in the hall had gone. Now I see you've just tucked her away." He nodded once. "Good."

Fiona's pulses raced. He'd duped her, and how easily she'd fallen. Fine. If he'd a mind to know her nature, so be it. "'Tis the company which turns my stomach sour. The stink of so many Campbells has ruined my meal."

He laughed again. "Is that what I smell? I thought it was you."

Her face flamed with instant heat. Her brothers pinched and taunted readily enough, but little did she think to get the same from her enemy husband. "I'll roll in manure each day if the stench will keep you away from me," she said.

He took another bite and let his eyes rove over her in the most obscene way, as if she were more harlot than bride. He sucked a bit of gravy off his finger.

"It won't," he said at last.

Her senses thrummed. What peculiar assault. His words flicked like a feather and yet sent tremors of unease licking at her limbs. She suddenly felt naked beneath his gaze, and the certainty of this night's events clanged inside her head like the bells of Saint Andrews. No foul stench, or pointed dagger, or field of loyal men would keep him from his purpose. She was both the prize and the prey.

She looked at her hands once more, her ears burning as he laughed again.

# CHAPTER 3

No ladies escorted Fiona to her bedchamber. Her mother lay cold in the grave, and Fiona's only aunt was a nun who, for years, had made her home at a convent near Ludlow. So it was scrawny, dependable Bess who led Fiona from the hall when the feasting ended.

"Come along, miss," she whispered. "No sense dragging your feet. It'll be all but over in twenty minutes. Not much a strong girl like you can't put up with for that brief time, aye?"

A vision of her mother, gray with death's pallor, her arm twisted about at an unnatural angle, seeped into Fiona's mind like a fume. *How long had that assault taken?* Twenty minutes could be an eternity.

Bess helped Fiona remove the blue gown, quickly replacing it with a linen shift embroidered at the neck with tiny seed pearls, and all the while muttering awkward encouragements in her gravelly voice. Tonight her words grated rather than comforted.

This room had been Fiona's since she'd left the nursery. In that bed, she had wept a child's tears of grief over her mother's death, but also giggled under the covers with Marg, playing silly games, hiding from the cold, and from their brothers. With Margaret, she had told stories and held her little sister through nightmares and illness. In this room, she had lived her life and dreamed of a future. But never had those dreams looked anything like this.

The bed loomed large, a trap baited with pillows and velvet. The stone walls of the chamber bent in at a sinister angle, shrinking the room. It would feel smaller still when her enemy husband came through the door. Fiona plucked a hairbrush from her table, anxious for a task. She ran the brush from scalp to tip, pulling roughly at the curls and snarls, relishing the pain for the distraction it offered.

Bess moved toward the bed, pulling the coverlet down and plumping the pillows, just as she had done so many nights before. The old nurse rubbed her hands down the front of her tunic.

"Fiona, you've saved souls this day. Nothing can bring back the ones we've lost, Lord bless them, but you should be a mite proud of your sacrifice."

Vulnerability sprang forth at the maid's words of kindness. But she could not let that weakness in. She must face this night, and every night forevermore, with the strength of ten Sinclairs. She'd show them all she was the warrior they sought her to be.

"Thank you, Bess. You may leave me now."

"Are you certain? I could stay until your husband arrives."

Fiona shook her head. "No."

The nurse nodded and kissed her charge's smooth cheek. "God keep you, Fiona." And then she was gone.

Alone, Fiona paced, to the window, to the fireplace. Anywhere but near the bed. He'd come soon, expecting her to be in it, but she'd not sit there like some marzipan upon a plate. She pulled a silk shawl from a bench where Bess had left it, and wrapped it around her shoulders. 'Twas more for protection than warmth, as if the thin fabric were her mother's safe embrace. Fiona stared into the fireplace and saw Cedric dancing with the devil amid the flames.

A log crumbled, sending flecks of fire upon the hearth. She jumped like a cat at the noise and then jumped again as the latch rattled in the door.

It opened and Myles appeared, stopping short at the sight of her. After a pause, he stepped inside the chamber and shut the door, securing the lock.

"You need not lock it. Where would I go?" She strove to keep her voice bland, untainted by the fear pulsing in her temples.

He looked her over, his intense eyes a darker green in the firelight. "Even if you left, I have men on watch outside the door."

"To keep me in?"

"No, to keep your brothers' men out. You Sinclairs have a cunning nature and a will to see me dead."

"If you believe that, why agree to this alliance? Surely the king would free you, had you but asked."

Myles's chuckle was without humor. He crossed the room to where a jug of wine and cups sat on a table. "The king does not grant favors lightly. Or keep promises. If he did, I'd be in France right now instead of the godforsaken Highlands." He splashed wine into two cups.

Fiona bridled at his insult. "My sympathies for all you've suffered."

His shoulders rose and fell with a sigh. "There is no pretending either of us would have chosen this end, Fiona. You are not the only marionette dancing at the end of James's strings."

He held out a cup of wine toward her.

"Is it poisoned?"

"Only if your people poisoned it." He glanced down at his own cup, brows furrowing.

"I don't want any." She pulled the shawl more tightly about her shoulders.

He raised the cup higher. "Drink. It will make things go more easily for you."

"Or for you, perhaps?" she snapped. "Is that how you like your women, Campbell? Soused and unresisting?"

He stared at her so long her skin began to prickle, and then he shrugged. "Upon occasion." He set her cup on the table and drained his own, refilling it again, as if to sustain him. But what had he to be nervous about? He was twice her size, and a man. He had a distinct advantage. Tomorrow, he'd go on about his life with little difference, but she would be forever altered, in body, at least, if not in spirit.

Against her will, her hand snaked out and snatched the goblet up. She drank the wine in gulps and held the cup out for more.

He smiled at her weakness.

They stood together in silence, drinking, staring into the fireplace, until at last he said, "I do like my women willing, Fiona. I've never taken one without consent."

A derisive snort rasped through her nose. "Then you must be as virginal as I." She waited for his strike, but there was no need.

His lips curved into a smile instead. "My wealth comes in handy at times."

She'd sought to taunt him but missed her mark. "So, you've bought them, then? I have a husband tarnished by whores?"

His smile broadened. "Not tarnished, my sweet. Tutored. You should count yourself most fortunate." He took another gulp of wine.

She gasped at his implication. "Fortunate? I'm not some tavern trollop to be swayed by coins and honeyed words."

"Hardly honeyed words. 'Tis simply fact. And needling me will not change our course." He set the cup down on the table.

"Fiona, I understand you have a warrior's spirit and a fierce pride. I can even admire it. But only a fool keeps fighting a battle which is already lost. I am no longer your enemy. I am your husband. The sooner you yield to that, the better this will be for us both."

If he had struck her, she'd know how to respond. If he railed and threatened and made accusations, she could return as much in kind. But against this quiet manner, she had no weapon, save her will.

"I shall never yield."

He nodded and ambled slowly round her, as if she were a sculpture to be admired. Then he stopped behind her back and slid his warrior's hands up along her arms. His voice was low, like the hum of honeybees around the hive.

"I cannot change your heart, Fiona. But I promise, if you will but meet me halfway, I will be a good husband. Submit to me, and I'll not hurt you."

His hands were like velvet ropes, binding her to him.

"You haven't the power to hurt me." The lie was delivered in a husky whisper.

He tugged at her shawl. "Yes, I have. I could crush you in a hundred different ways. Or caress you in twice as many. Surrender to me, and I'll show you mercy such as you've never imagined."

His voice moved like cool water over heated skin, leaving her muscles weak and her thoughts jumbled. He was nothing of what she'd expected.

"Surrender, yield, submit—those are cursed words to me," she whispered.

"I know. It is your nature to fight, but we are wed now. Lower your defenses. Let me show you that—in this battle, at least—surrender and victory are one and the same."

He gave the shawl a final tug and she let loose her grasp. It fell to the floor like a lover's whisper, and his arms encircled her, the heat of him like a forge fire.

She didn't struggle and could not for the life of her imagine why. The wine had gone to her head. The strain of the day had left her empty inside, with no strength left to fight him.

"What do you intend?" she heard herself asking.

He pressed warm lips against her neck and murmured, "I intend to seduce you."

His overconfidence reawakened her drugged senses, and the full force of her distaste returned tenfold. "Oh!" she gasped, and drove her elbow back with all her might, plowing him in the abdomen.

He let out a woof of surprise. His grip loosened and she scrambled from his embrace.

"You conceited boar. Do you think I am so easily won?"

"I had hoped you might be." His tone was wry as he rubbed his stomach.

"And you call me the fool?" she gasped.

He raised his hands up toward the ceiling, as if looking to God for guidance. Then he met her eyes with his own, his tone laced with the impatience of one speaking to a wayward child. "Fiona, this is the circumstance we are faced with. We have…We have a task to complete."

She crossed her arms. "I know that. I'm not a dolt."

He shook his head and stomped back to the wine. He filled his cup and drained it with one swallow. "You object when I perfume it with flowery words. You object when I state it plainly. Is there no pleasing you?"

"Nothing you do or say will ever please me."

Every sign of his good humor faded. "Christ, woman! You try my patience. I have tried all day to win your good graces, and yet you meet me at every turn with derision and scorn. But I am done with it. You are my wife. Do you hear me? I had hoped to make this at least tolerable for you, but if you prefer pain to pleasure, so be it. Get in the bed."

He yanked off his doublet, then turned away and pulled his shirt up over his head. At the sight of his broad, naked back, Fiona's heart fell to the floor, and the rest of her nearly with it. She had goaded him on purpose and made him angry. Perhaps she was the fool after all.

Good Lord, the girl was infuriating! He had teased and cajoled, been stern and direct. Nothing worked. She was determined to despise him. He'd never been faced with this situation before. His women were willing, paid or not. Some had even begged for his kisses and moaned beneath his touch. How he longed for that encouragement now! He'd sooner bed a pincushion than this churlish wench.

He pulled his remaining garments off in rapid succession until he was naked as the day of his birth and climbed into the bed.

His wife, however, remained rooted to her spot, eyeing him like a doe and twisting her fingers in knots. With the firelight behind her, he could see clear through the thin shift. His anger softened the slightest bit. She was young after all. And free of guile. Every emotion she had showed on her face like paint. And right now she was the very picture of fear.

He softened his tone. "Come here, Fiona."

After another brief hesitation, she approached, and he was pleased his scolding had made an impact. She seemed resigned now. Not dejected as she'd been in the hall after insulting his father, but reconciled.

He bit back a smile as she stared at the bed as if it were some great, mysterious loch—dark, forbidding, and certainly nothing to dive into. He nudged aside the covers and patted the space next to him. "Lie down. I promise not to bite. Too hard."

Her expression brought him to laughter. "You have the face of an angel, you know. A very angry, misplaced angel."

She sat gingerly upon the mattress, facing him, and clutched the front of her garment. He reached out and physically turned her around so that she must lean back against the pillows and next to him.

"We are a pair, are we not?" He pulled one hand away from her chest and held it in his own. "Do you like this ring?"

She glanced down at the emerald. It was large, set in gold and surrounded by tiny garnets. "It's heavy," she replied.

"It's been in my family for four generations. James II had it made for my great-grandfather. And now it's yours."

She pulled her hand from his clasp. "You should not have given me such a ring. It's meant to be worn by a Campbell."

"You are a Campbell now."

She swallowed and folded her arms in front of her breasts again, closing the drawbridge of her own impenetrable fortress. She seemed done with verbal attacks for the moment, but remained rigid as marble, and as cold. If she were a simpler wench, he'd be halfway to his release by now, but this Fiona was a skittish mare, and one he'd need to coax before mounting.

He rolled to his side and propped his head on one arm. With the other, he pushed the hair back from her face. She did not flinch. A minor victory.

"Tell me something about yourself," he prompted softly.

A tiny noise escaped her throat. "What?"

"Just any little something so I might know you better." Female chatter typically grated on him, but he would welcome a bit of conversation from this statue in the bed. Anything to draw her out and open her up.

"There is nothing of me to remark upon." She plucked a loose thread on the edge of the cover.

A chuckle bubbled in his throat, for if ever a lie were told, that was one. "On the contrary, I'm sure there are a great many fascinating things about you. But if you're feeling shy, I'll go first." He readjusted the pillow, moving closer to her. "I don't like hawks."

She turned her head and looked at him with some curiosity.

He pulled her hand into his again and gently toyed with her fingers. "Never have, never will. Hawks are too cunning by half and always glaring like they'd sooner peck your eyes out than do your bidding. Falcons too. They're even worse."

She gave a small laugh, if indeed he could term it as that. But at least it was a noise of interest and amusement.

"Have they married you off to me because you are a simpleton?" she asked.

His own laughter caught him off guard. This wife of his bore a sense of humor—when she'd a mind to share it. "Perhaps. Do you like hawks?" He let her hand fall to the bed and ran one finger along her forearm.

"I never thought about it. We haven't had any in quite some time. None trained, at least."

"What happened to them?"

She regarded him a moment. "Our falconer died during a raid."

"Ah, I'm sorry for him. Whose raid?"

She gave a tiny shrug, making the sheet rustle from her movement. "The Grants, I think. Maybe the MacPhersons. Any ally to the king is an enemy of ours. It keeps us busy." She tried to fold her arm back to her body, but he followed with his hand, sliding it along her collarbone.

"Then this marriage is a good thing for the Sinclairs. The raids should stop now that you've the might of the king's army behind you."

She stared at the canopy above them, but her pulse was rapid beneath his fingers as they traveled along the column of her throat. "The king is far away in Edinburgh. Even his arm cannot reach this far north," she said softly.

"Times are changing, Fiona. The king plans to sail around the Isles from Oban to Inverness, gathering oaths of fealty from the Highland chiefs. Those who refuse will feel the wrath of his army. But his friends will be rewarded." He nudged at the neckline of her shift, slipping his fingers underneath the fabric. "Tell me something about you now."

She let out a deep breath. Her voice was small when at last she spoke. "I had a pony."

"And?" he prompted when she said no more.

"Her name was Gwynlyn. She was a lovely soft gray with a white blaze and boots, and she would come when I whistled."

"And where is she now?" He plucked lightly at the top ribbon tie of her shift.

"She died when I was fourteen. Father never gave me another one."

His heart twisted in a way most unaccustomed. She'd lost much in such a short life, for she was little more than seventeen. "Dempsey has a fine stable full of mares. You may have your choosing."

She frowned. "I did not tell you such so you might offer me a gift."

"I know. But I offer one nonetheless." The tie came undone, and he almost with it. It was such a small matter, the offer of a pony, and yet it seemed to distress her. She saw a trick where there was none. What a combination she was, at once fierce and

25

fragile. Her hair, in the firelight, glowed like the garnets of her ring. He wanted to feel the weight of it and twist those tresses between his fingers. Bedding her would not be such a chore, after all, if she stayed sweet like in this moment. He leaned over and pressed a kiss against her shoulder.

She gasped at the contact. His mouth on her skin seared like a brand. "Must you do that?"

He looked at her, surprised. "What?"

"Kiss me. Is it…necessary?"

His head crooked, along with his smile. "Necessary? No. But it's my preference."

She didn't like it. Not one bit. It singed, and not just where his lips met her skin, but other places too. "Well, it's not my preference. Could you proceed without it?"

His laughter was rich, a deep rumbling sound like faraway thunder. "I could," he said. "But the kissing…helps."

Why? It seemed most distracting to her. Everything about him was bewildering. He was her enemy sworn. A cruel, detestable, violent Campbell. And yet, tonight, this man in her bed seemed none of these things. None of those things that she needed him to be to stoke the fire of her anger. Instead, he was gentle and inquisitive and patient. And naked, stoking another kind of fire entirely. Her mind, which all day had been assailed with unpleasant thoughts, was now roaming to places it had never conjured previously. And she was awash with the shame of it.

"Fiona, do you understand what must occur between us?" He twisted the second tie of her nightdress loose.

Fire lit her cheeks like cinders. "Of course. My nurse explained it."

He laughed again. "Your nurse? You mean that old sack of bones who hovers around you like a fly? What did she tell you?"

"If you don't know, than I shan't enlighten you." She pulled the covers up higher and tried unsuccessfully to push his hand away.

Instead, he tugged the covers farther down and nudged her jaw with his thumb, turning her face toward him. "Did she frighten you?"

"Not as much as you do." Her answer was out before she could pull it back, yet how she wished she could. Hugh Sinclair must be turning in his grave at her admission. Myles might think only a fool fought a battle already lost, but her father would say only a coward gave up before he was dead. So what was she to do, really? Was it more courageous to fight him until death? Or live, and perhaps win the war another day?

She thought of Margaret and knew her answer.

Fiona's heart felt like ice in her chest, brittle and cold as she stared back at her husband. Something about his gaze seemed almost familiar, but of course it would, for he had been staring at her all day, pulling her toward him with an invisible string.

"You can trust in me, Fiona."

This was it, then. No more talk of hawks and ponies and unnecessary kisses. She heaved a sigh from deep within. "I don't know what to do," she said, more to herself and God than to her husband.

Myles rolled closer. "Let's take off that shift, and I will teach you."

# CHAPTER 4

S HE WAITED FOR LIGHTNING TO STRIKE FROM HEAVEN AS AN-
gels came to rescue her, but heard only the common crackle of the fire and her husband's shallow breath.

His hand slid down her body and caught the hem of her
garment, raising it slowly, pushing it into a bunch about her
waist. Reluctantly, she shifted, granting him access while trying to evade any additional contact. But his hands skimmed
along her skin like petals blowing over water and her lungs
fluttered inside. She sat up and turned her back, raising her
arms. He tugged the last of the shift over her head, and the
fabric slipped away and floated to the floor, along with all her
defenses.

She fell back against the mattress as if pushed, and closed her
eyes tight, wishing him away. But he leaned closer and ran a fin-
gertip down her face, between her eyes, and over her nose, letting
it linger on her lips. One finger joined another and another as he
traced the soft curves and tiny valleys of her ears and jaw and
throat. Her pulse thrummed, like the flap of a thousand swans
leaving the surface of a loch.

When his lips brushed, feather soft, against the corner of her
mouth, she nearly bolted upright. But she fought the urge to flee,

and instead lay unresponsive as he trailed tiny butterfly kisses following the path where his fingers had explored.

A sweet, unexpected torment.

And always, he'd come back to the edge of her lips, never kissing her full-on. She flushed with heat and nearly turned her mouth toward his just to end the teasing. But she could not. Would not. A Sinclair could withstand any torture, no matter how it was delivered.

She felt the moisture of his lips on her skin and the cool aftermath as the night air continued the kiss. She tried to think of Margaret or her father, or anything besides the sensations swirling within her. She should hate this, despise him, writhe away from his grasp. To find pleasure in his touch would be her ultimate defeat.

But his hands traveled lower, growing bolder and more firm, sliding over her shoulder and along one arm, then back to cup her breast. Her eyes popped open then, and she caught him by the wrist, trying to still his ministrations. But he persisted, gently squeezing the fullness of it and rubbing his thumb over the tip. It sizzled like fire from his fingers. She gasped and would have begged him to stop had he not chosen that moment to at last kiss her mouth. Traitorous relief flooded through her.

This was no chaste peck like he'd given her upon the chapel steps. That kiss had been for God and for the priest, but even in her innocence, she knew this kiss was for Myles himself. He pressed firm, teasing her mouth with his own. His lips were soft, so much softer than she expected, and felt at delicious odds with the scrape of his jaw. He smelled of wine and cloves and leather, a scent mingled with the fragrance of her own body, creating a potent mixture.

He bent his head lower, gently nipping at her skin and then soothing away the tiny injuries with his tongue. She moved to escape the tender assault, but he followed and pressed his leg between her own, pushing them apart. She felt unraveled. Adrift. Disloyal. He was a despicable Campbell, but somehow her body had forgotten and overruled her mind. She grabbed at his arms in useless defense, for with each movement, he somehow melted closer, like hot wax, conforming to her every peak and valley. His hand caressed her hip, pulling her tight against him, then pushing her back so he might slip his hand between them.

Her face turned toward the wall as his fingers sought out her most feminine folds, but a shameless whimper betrayed her shock of pleasure as he easily slipped within them. Faithless, perfidious limbs, useless now when she needed her strength. This enemy had tapped her will like sap from a tree, but with all she had left, she brought her leg up, pushing against the mattress to twist herself free. To no avail. Her pitiful actions only granted him more generous access to her very core.

"Ah, God, Fiona," he murmured against her breast and drew his tongue across its center, "what perfection."

She tried to push his head away, but his close-cropped hair beneath her fingers felt of mink, enticing rather than repelling. Oh, what a traitor she was, giving up all Sinclair thought to simply *feel* beneath this Campbell's touch.

She was sweet as a peach and ripe for the plucking, her skin silky smooth and pliant beneath his hands. As he savored each kiss and caress, the reckless urge to take this coupling to its completion assailed him. He had sought to woo her, to gently introduce her to the ways of sin and sacrament, but her body was primed, slick with want as she twisted against him. She was as eager as he to take this journey onward. He could tell by the flush of her skin, the pant of her shallow breath. Awash with need, he felt the last of her resistance give way to invitation.

He caught up the back of her knee with his hand and found his mark, piercing into her tender flesh and claiming her as his own. 'Twas a swift move, meant to make the initial pain pass quickly, but Fiona gasped at his intrusion, pushing against his chest as he tore through the delicate barrier of her virginity. He felt a moment's remorse, for he would have spared her that discomfort, but it could not be helped. 'Twas the cost for maidens. Soon he'd soothe her with his touch and show her all the pleasures of this union. He moved against her, slowly, hoping to carry her with him, but she was hot, surrounding him with such tight sweetness. He'd been weeks without a woman, and his will evaporated in a misty haze of desire.

His pace increased. She moved upward, her legs pressing against his own in glorious surrender. She was with him, his bride, ready to receive his full measure, and soon his senses overtook reason. He plunged with his full might. She rose up again, a willing partner. His mind went blank as instinct and need claimed sovereignty over patience. Fast and bold, he thrust, until his taut nerves reached their zenith and he erupted into her, spilling himself in joyful release.

He collapsed in utter relaxation, breathing as if he'd run to the crest of Ben Nevis and back. But this summit was so much the sweeter. Closer to heaven than the tallest mountain. She had welcomed his attention, sending through him a jolt of bliss. He'd left her behind at the last, true enough. But he'd make it up to her. She was untutored after all, and surely maidens required more guidance. Still, this woman, his woman, might not make such a bad wife after all.

He lifted his head and smiled down at her, his body gratified, his soul content.

Fiona lay motionless, stunned. Confused. Was that it? She felt suddenly bereft and uneasy, as if she'd been struggling to remember something that was very nearly there, but then dashed away again. Myles had set her body afloat, tingling in the most delectable manner. But then he'd speared her with his manhood, crushed her with his bulk, and shouted in her ear.

She couldn't breathe. He was too heavy. The hair on his chest and legs, which only moments before had been so enticing, suddenly chafed against her skin. Their legs were tangled, his hands twisted in her hair, pulling even now.

But worse than that, he'd made her forget herself. He'd made her wanton. He'd made her a Campbell.

She shoved against him.

"Get off me," she croaked, for want of air in her lungs.

He lifted his torso, grinning down at her like an idiot.

Dear Lord, they *had* married her to a simpleton. She filled her grateful lungs with air and then pushed at him again, kicking at the back of his legs with her feet. "Get off me, you hulking brute."

His smile faded, and he let her extricate herself from the jumble of their bodies and the bedding. Once free, she scuttled to the farthest edge of the bed.

"Fiona? Did I hurt you?"

Tears popped from her eyes, and she swiped them away. "Of course you did. You are Cedric Campbell's son. Your very existence hurts me. God, how I despise you."

His expression traversed from confusion to anger, the angle of his jaw hardening, his eyes going black in the dim room.

"You have no right to be angry, woman. I took care with you. If you weren't ready, you should not have spurred me on so."

"Spurred you on?" she spat. "I did no such thing, you conceited boar. I just wanted it over with." She pulled the covers around her. "Give me my shift. I can't reach it."

He glared at her for another moment, and she thought he might refuse. But at last, he reached down and plucked it from the floor, tossing it at her face.

"Women!" he said, and then flopped over on his other side, done with her.

Fiona stared at the thick muscles of his back and fought her tears. He hadn't hurt her, in truth. It was her own traitorous nature that caused her pain. How could she have found delight in his kisses? What type of woman was she, to fall over on her back for the fiercest enemy she'd ever known? She could not betray her parents in such a way. It was one thing to submit to one's husband, but quite another to relish his caress. Self-loathing overwhelmed her.

Myles's breathing steadied. When it was rhythmic and deep, she gathered a blanket and went to make a bed down by the fire. She'd not rest next to him if she had an ounce of will to resist it. She laid her head upon the cold floor, certain sleep would never come.

But come it must have, for after a while, she felt herself being lifted up in strong arms and tucked into a soft, warm place. A gentle voice whispered in her ear, "Come sleep in the bed, you silly girl. You're safe from me."

"Fiona is none the wiser, and the better off for her ignorance, John," Simon whispered as they sat in the hall, long after the last of the guests had fallen asleep. "She would betray us without even realizing."

John rubbed a tiny scar along his jaw. "Do you think he'll kill her when they learn what we're about?"

Simon drained his goblet of wine. "Perhaps. But she'll not last a fortnight if she doesn't keep civil that tongue of hers. He may silence her for that alone."

John's brows pinched together. "How easily you jest about our sister's destiny."

Simon sighed with impatience. "Yes, I jest, John. Would you have me keen and wail like the women? We must behave as though we have accepted this. If the Campbells smell deceit, we are done for. We need time, and we need their trust."

"Still, if Fiona knew her days with them were temporary, she could steel herself and not lose hope."

Simon shook his head. "We cannot risk it. It will take months to band together the Highland chiefs and prepare for an assault. As distasteful as it is, it's better for Fiona to believe we have given her over to them." He took another draught of the wine, spilling some on his tunic in his haste. He wiped his sleeve across his mouth and handed the glass to John. "Drink, brother. Today we have cut in half the number of our enemies."

John took the wine. "Until we double them again by attacking the king."

# CHAPTER 5

THE NEXT MORNING, FIONA RODE AWAY FROM THE ONLY home she'd ever known.

Her green cloak dulled the wind's fierce bite, but did nothing to ease the cold piercing from the inside out, like icy waves breaking on the shores of Moray Firth. Her good-bye with Margaret had been cut brutally short by Cedric's declaration that they must depart after the morning meal. But perhaps, after all, that was best. She sought to show only a brave face to her little sister, but the effort had drained Fiona like a bloodletting.

The brevity of her farewell to Simon and John troubled her less. Their inquisitive, falsely sympathetic gazes stirred no forgiveness within her, nor did it bring moisture to her eyes. She did not weep when her brothers and the Campbell chief examined the bedsheets, seeking evidence of her lost virginity. But now, outside the village walls, away from her people, she let the tears flow, hot and bitter, scalding away her Sinclair identity. She was a Campbell now, wedded and bedded, and all but banished from her homeland by her brothers' shortsighted cowardice.

How long would this truce hold? A week? A month? A year, perhaps? Simon and John were gullible as sheep if they thought peace would spread as easily as her thighs. How long before

Cedric's lust for twisting his blade into a Sinclair heart surfaced and the feuding erupted once more? In the end, she would have been sacrificed for nothing.

The wind spun again, sending up the musky scent of horses on the move. The steady clip-clop of their hooves mixed with the chatter of the traveling party. Both man and beast seemed glad to be heading homeward. Of course they were. They left satisfied, having obtained what they came for. She left as nothing more than spoils to the victor. The gray-speckled palfrey she rode upon held more worth than she in these men's eyes.

She rubbed away those tears at last and stared ahead, for there was no looking back now. She was a fallen leaf, adrift upon a sea of Campbells. At the front of the procession, Myles and his father rode side by side, their equally broad shoulders swaying in unison with the tide of their men. When father turned to son, their profiles were so physically alike her gut gave a violent churn. That face—Cedric Campbell's face, so much like her own husband's—was the last vision her mother had ever beheld.

Yet last night, Fiona had lain beneath Myles, timid as a field mouse when she should have roared like a lion. The memory of her acquiescence—nay, her encouragement—scorched in the light of the day. A true warrior would've faced the morning with a bloodied lip and blackened eye, for if she'd fought as a Sinclair should, surely he would've struck her and she could parade her injuries, bold and proud, before her brothers. But she had not fought back.

No, far worse than that. She'd quivered and sighed like one of his paid whores, and today, shame burned her at its stake.

"I've little fondness for riding, miss. You tell that graceless brute to find me a cart." Bess rode up beside her, on a nag so old and rheumy they nearly looked related, both swaybacked and toothy.

"You should not have pleaded so to come, Bess. You sacrifice too much. You were supposed to stay and care for Marg," Fiona said to her old nurse. "And what good will come of it? You think you can protect me with those scrawny arms of yours?"

Bess held out one arm to examine it. "No, but I can bear witness to all I see. And they know that." She nodded, triumphant at her faulty wisdom.

"You'll see nothing but the inside of a pit if you cross them."

The woman's well-intentioned meddling had gone too far. This morning, the sweet, old ninny had knelt at the foot of the Campbell himself and asked if she might come along to see to her mistress. She'd nearly tripped him with her eagerness.

"Don't be peevish, girl. 'Twas your welfare I was thinking of. Margaret will be fine. She's stronger than you give her credit."

"She's a child."

"But she's not your child. You've coddled her too much since your mother died, and it's no wonder. But soon you'll have a babe of your own to care for, and you'll realize Marg can fend for herself."

A child of her own? Her senses reeled, nearly toppling her from the saddle, and for the second time in as many days, she fought to keep her breakfast. With a fist pressed hard against her belly, she sent up a silent prayer to the God who had forsaken her, begging for a barren womb.

A Campbell babe inside her? How could she not despise it? Just one more thing tying her to Myles. And to Cedric Campbell.

As the traveled distance grew, so burgeoned Fiona's nauseating fear and the certainty that destiny was hers alone to shape. Like a tiny seed, an idea germinated. As the miles passed, she nurtured it, as she would never nurture any child of the Campbell bloodline. And as they stopped in a glen next to a stream to make camp for the night, Fiona knew what she must do.

Myles stretched his back and tried to rub the tension from his neck. 'Twas near dusk when his father reined in his own mount and instructed the men to make camp. With military precision, each Campbell dismounted and went to his duties, assembling a tent, building fires, or tending to the horses. They were a troop of twenty brawny lads, each hearty and hale. Men he'd taken into both battle and brothel. Men he trusted with his life. Someday he'd be their laird, and they would serve him well, as they had the earl. He swung a leg around and climbed down from his destrier, stiff but glad to be away from Sinclair holdings. A great, gaping yawn escaped as his feet landed on the soft forest floor. His uncle Tavish cuffed him on the shoulder and laughed, the sound muffled in the depths of a thick red beard. "Not much sleep last night, aye, lad? 'Tis one disadvantage of marriage. But there are advantages aplenty."

Myles grimaced with the memory of Fiona's bitterness. "Advantages or disadvantages, I've yet to see which carries greater weight."

Tavish laughed again, scratching his head as he nodded in Fiona's direction. She and her maid were still perched on their ponies, looking exhausted and bewildered. "Eh, don't worry about that one. She'll come around, once she sees we're not the butchers she's been led to believe."

Myles tilted his head to crack his neck. "Any ally of King James is an enemy of hers. I am guilty simply by association. I fear there will be no swaying her."

His uncle spit on the ground. "That's women's logic for you. I suppose if I fart, she'd blame you for the stink?"

Shallow laughter came from Myles. "'Tis apparent she blames me for a great many things I had no part in."

Tavish leaned against a tree trunk, scratching his back against the bark like a playful bear. "Aye, this business about her mother is an unholy mess. I'll flay from beard to bollocks any cur who says your father had a hand in her death. I'd bet my eyesight the bastard who started that wicked lie just got put in the ground."

"You mean Fiona's father?" Myles cracked his neck in the other direction.

"Aye, Hugh Sinclair. Bad blood between the two of them ever since their days at court."

Myles had heard those stories often enough. When James was but a boy, Scotland was ruled by a board of regents, with the queen's husband, Archibald Douglas, at the helm. 'Twas a time when Hugh Sinclair and the earl had shared friendship and an equal measure of power. In a show of solidarity between their clans, Myles had even been betrothed to Fiona.

But as greed and politics are often wont to do, allies became foes. Sinclair sided with Douglas in holding the boy king captive, but the Campbells sought to free him, and succeeded.

"Sinclair chose the wrong side," Tavish said. "If he'd joined your father in helping the young king escape to claim his throne, things would now be different."

"Not so very different," Myles said. "I'd still be married to Fiona." It seemed fate had cast his lot, and the ploys of men swayed little. "And if Aislinn was still murdered, we might be in this spot once more."

Tavish plucked at his ample waistband and pulled out a flagon of wine. He took a long draw from it and wiped his lips with the back of his hand. "Aislinn's murder set much askew, but as sure as I'm standing here, it wasn't a Campbell who struck the life from her. She was a lovely thing at court. I cannot fathom who might wish her harm."

"Father never speaks of court. Or his thoughts on Aislinn's death. What more do you know of it?"

Tavish looked to the ground, kicking at a thick, knobby root embedded in the ground. "If you've questions on it, ask the man himself." He nodded over Myles's shoulder.

Cedric approached, his gait stiff. The ride had been arduous enough for Myles, so surely his father's bones must be set to rattling, though anyone saying so risked finding his blade to their throat.

"Father, are you well?"

Cedric nodded and took the wine from his brother. "I will be if Tavish shares his bounty." He drank and then passed it to Myles, nodding at him with a wink. "Your bride held up well today. Once she stopped crying."

Her tears had been an embarrassment. She'd kept them silent, but for a mile or more, they'd streamed down her face and left her nose bright red in the sunlight. He'd not abused her in any way, yet she acted as if he'd dragged her behind the pony instead of letting her ride on one. Tomorrow, he'd put her and that scarecrow maid in the back of a cart. Let them bounce about in one of those for a day and she'd have something to cry about.

"Thank you for letting her bring the maid, Father. I'll make sure they don't slow down our travels."

The earl nodded again. "'Tis slow enough on rocky roads with these carts, but with a few good hours in the morning, we should reach Inverness and the boats. Help young Darby with your women now. They look ready to keel over. Oh, and you and your bride may have the tent."

Myles looked toward Fiona, who had at last dismounted with the aid of his squire. Smudges of exhaustion were dark against her pale face. She was dusty and disheveled, but ever defiant as she shook away Darby's offer of further assistance. Myles had avoided her much of the day, preferring the pleasant company of his uncle and father to her forlorn sighs and red-rimmed eyes. But he'd face her now. Exhausted or no, she was his wife and his responsibility.

Her body ached like joints pried apart with fire tongs. But Bess was even worse for wear, her arthritic hands bent as if they still held the reins. Fiona rubbed Bess's back lightly, trying to ease the woman into standing straight.

She ceased when her husband approached.

"'Twas a long day in the saddle, ladies. But tomorrow, we reach Inverness. From there, we'll take barges down Loch Ness and the traveling will be easier."

Faster, he meant. Today had been harsh, but at least she'd had the open Highland air to breathe and a fool's chance of riding away into the mountains. And every mile brought her plan closer to fruition. But tomorrow, if she boarded a boat, all her scheming would come to naught, for by the time they disembarked she'd be too far away.

"Will there be food soon, or is it your plan to jostle and starve us to death?"

Her husband stared a moment; then his lips quirked into a smile and he turned to the wide-eyed squire. "Darby, get the women something to eat while we set up camp."

"Yes, Lord Myles."

Myles rubbed his hand across his jaw. "And see to it that the old maid has a thick pallet near the fire, and an extra blanket."

"Yes, my lord," the boy said again and scampered away.

Unease prickled over Fiona's skin. "And what of me? Am I to have no pallet near the fire?"

"We'll be in the tent. I shall keep you warm myself."

No, no, no. That wouldn't do. Her plan would not work if she must lie with him throughout the night. There must be another solution.

Myles chuckled. "You needn't look so distressed, Fiona. Appreciate my offer of a soft bed, if not my affection."

"But my maid is stiff from riding in the cold. I'd rather sleep near her, to offer my warmth and ease her sore muscles." What a fast and clever liar she could be.

"You show an unusual concern for your maid."

Oh, not so clever after all. She could tell by his tone she'd not duped him. "She's old," Fiona protested further. "Only the heartless would refuse comfort to an old woman."

Myles crossed her arms. "Very well. She may join us in the tent."

"No!" Fiona's voice was sharp as a dagger, but little could she alter that now.

Her husband's expression hardened.

"I could not have her with us. I…" she faltered, looking up at the trees and pressing her lips tight. "No. I refuse."

His eyes widened for the briefest second, then narrowed with a deep frown. He leaned forth to murmur in her ear so only she might hear. His breath was warm, his words hot. "Do not test me, girl. I'll not stand here bickering in front of my men. You sleep with me inside the tent. The maid sleeps by the fire. Press this issue further and you'll find yourself in a storm of regret." He turned and strode away.

She'd been a fool. Of course he'd want her next to him so he might paw and thrust and stain her with his touch. He was his father's son after all. What respect would he have for her dignity? He'd think nothing of molesting her with only thin tent walls to muffle her complaints. It looked as if her plan would have to wait.

# CHAPTER 6

M YLES'S TEMPLE ACHED AT HER REACTION. 'TWAS PURE generosity, the offer of the tent, but she'd come at him, growling like a badger and making demands. As if she had a say in how this night went forth. As if her tears were not humiliation enough. Already, his father and uncle were winking at one another as if he were some green lad with no idea how to woo a wench. That was absurd. He'd pleased women aplenty. Why, he'd half a mind to drag her into that tent this minute and kiss her senseless. And this time, he'd be sure she reached that sweet oasis. There'd be no complaints from her after that.

He ripped off a chunk of brown bread. Thankless girl. She had no idea how gentle he'd been. Or how grateful she should be that they'd let her bring that scrappy maid. Yet she'd not said one word of gratitude about the beautiful palfrey she'd ridden today. Or that he'd ordered one of his best men to ride an edgy old gelding so she might have a fine mount. No. From her? Nothing but scorn.

Well, enough was enough. He'd not chase his tail like a crazy dog. This woman would learn her place. Maybe he should let her sleep with the crone, out in the cold air and on hard ground. He took a bite of bread and chuckled to himself.

Darkness descended and sounds of the forest filled the air as some woodland creatures settled in for the night and others awoke. The fire crackled near the men's feet as Myles, Cedric, and Tavish finished their evening meal and the other men bedded down.

"Father, thank you again for the tent."

Cedric scooped up a bit of gravy with his bread. "Of course."

"Shall I take first watch?"

Tavish, sitting on the other side of him, rumbled with quiet laughter, but his father smiled. "That won't be necessary, son. I think you'll have your hands full enough for tonight."

Myles bristled at the innuendo. Did they think he could not handle her?

One simple wench?

Well, not so simple, but still, there was just one of her. He ripped another bite from his bread.

His father clamped him on the shoulder. "I would not think to keep you from your bride. You may not see it yet, but the king did you an honor."

He could not help the wistful tone from slipping into his voice. "You never saw Odette, Father. She would have been an honor."

His father nodded knowingly. "And I'm sorry for that. 'Tis no easy thing, giving up a woman you love. But the politics of men often overrule the politics of love, though both are equally complex." He chuckled at the last. "Give this girl a chance, though. She's frightened still, but not so rough. Her mother could cut diamonds with her speech."

Myles saw his opening and plunged forward.

"How well did you know Aislinn, Father? Until this journey, I've rarely heard you speak of her."

Cedric poured himself more wine and a cup for Myles. "We were together at court when King James was still a boy. You knew that."

"I think I'll see to the horses," Tavish said, hoisting his expansive girth up from the log where he'd been sitting, leaving father alone with son.

Myles took a sip of wine and spoke carefully. "I imagine there were lots of people at court."

Cedric drained his cup and stared into the fire, saying nothing.

Fresh curiosity tingled at the base of his spine, piqued by the earl's long silence. "I don't mean to be impertinent, Father, but surely you've heard the rumors surrounding you and Aislinn Sinclair. It gives me cause to wonder why the king chose this bride out of all the families in the North he could've bound us to."

"You were betrothed to Fiona the day she was born."

"Aye, seventeen years ago when our clans were allies. But much has occurred since then."

"Leave it alone for now, lad. Go make peace with your bride."

Myles waited, hoping his father might relent and tell him more. But Cedric returned to his food and his silence, and Myles knew he'd get no answers this evening.

"'Tis the only way," Fiona whispered to Bess as they sat together, heads close.

The maid's thin lips puckered. "You're a fool, and likely to perish in the trying. But I'll do my part if your mind is set."

"It is set, Bess. And better to die by my own hand than a Campbell blade."

"Shh, quiet, girl. Your husband approaches."

They peered at Myles from their seats on an old log, dinner cold and forgotten on their plates.

"Say good night now, Fiona. 'Tis time for bed," he said.

Bess started to rise. "I'll assist her."

Myles put a hand on the old woman's narrow shoulder, ceasing her movement. "No need. I'll see to her myself."

Fiona's insides quivered with fear and an odd anticipation. In one way or another, she meant to free herself from him. She rose, pulling her green cloak tight. "I'll see you in the morning, Bess."

Bess nodded, ducking her head and staring fixedly at the ground.

Myles led Fiona to the tent and held open the flap. It was unadorned inside, small but dry, with a decadent pile of colorful blankets, animal furs, and pillows. It would indeed be a soft place to lay her head, if she had a mind to rest.

To one side sat a basin and pitcher, along with a washing cloth. No Campbell luxury could be more tempting. The longing to bathe her face and hands proved overwhelming. She dropped her cloak and crossed to the basin, dipping her fingers in the fire-warmed water.

He watched her as he removed his belt and scabbards, laying them near the door, but she closed her eyes to the vision of him and let the cloth scrub away some of her tension, along with grit from the road.

"Are you sore?" he asked.

Her eyes opened. Given the circumstances, she could not decide if the question was solicitous or rude.

But he added, "From the riding. On the horse."

She set down the cloth and turned to face him, surprised he had the decency to blush at the innuendo. "I stopped being sore somewhere near Dornoch. Now I am raw. Does it matter?"

He looked perplexed for a moment and then sighed, folding his hands in front of him. "If it didn't matter, I would not have asked. In spite of what you think, your comfort is of concern to me. And to my father. Thus, the tent." He spread his arms out wide and circled around. "I could've let you sleep on the ground like a serving wench, but instead, here you are, in a nest of pillows and softness."

"I'd sooner sleep on rocks than next to you."

He tilted his head. "So, we're back to that again, aye? Let me save us time. You hate me. I'm starting to dislike you quite a bit as well. Now lie down on your belly and pull up that skirt."

His words slapped, hitching breath painfully in her lungs.

But her husband turned his back, relaxed as a cat, and walked to a small trunk in the corner of the tent. He knelt down and lifted the lid, shuffling the contents until he pulled out a vial. "Ah, here it is."

He turned back to her with no malice in his expression. "Do you need help with that dress? If I tear it, there'll be no one to fix it until we reach Dempsey. Come over here and lie down, I said."

He sat down and patted the blanket, just as he'd done the night before, only this time he gestured with the container in his other hand.

She could articulate no protest, though several raged inside her mind. The wood of the table where the basin rested dug into her palms as she clutched it. His intent seemed plain enough, and yet his demeanor was benevolent, as if he offered some sweet bit instead of more callous treatment.

"What's in the vial?" she asked at length when he said no more but simply sat and stared.

A smile crooked his mouth. "Salve. For your backside."

"My backside?" She could not contain the gasp.

Her husband's smile broadened, and she knew he laughed at her expense. "Aye. I don't imagine you're accustomed to so many hours in the saddle. This will ease the ache."

"You keeping your filthy hands off would ease me more."

"Ah, but where's the fun in that? Come here, now."

The teasing lilt softened his command, but command it was. She saw the glint in his eye. He'd not be defied. And if her plan was to work, she needed him sated and deep in slumber. It was a small price to pay. One more night of abuse for an eternity of freedom.

She walked to the bed of blankets and lowered to her knees, keeping her gaze on him. He tipped his head, gesturing to the pillows, and slowly, she sank, until her belly was flat against the surface. She folded her arms up near her face and shut her eyes, praying fervently that her deaf God might finally hear her.

That went more smoothly than he'd anticipated. Though her thick-lashed eyes were wary as a doe's, she'd done as he asked with little complaint. And now she lay on the blankets, still as a tree stump. He eased her skirt up toward her knees.

"Ack, no muddy boots in my bed." He took his time unlacing her boots, brushing away the dirt that crumbled and fell to the covers. He slid his hand up farther, easing down her hose and pulling them off with her boots. Then he bent down and removed his own soiled boots, setting them next to hers, side by side, like two pairs of old mares pulling a wagon.

And still she didn't flinch or protest. He almost missed her banter. So silent and motionless was she, he finally asked, "Fiona, are you sleeping?"

"Yes," she mumbled.

He chuckled at her coy response and then turned his attention back to her legs, which he'd not taken the time to appreciate last night. Her calves were slender and peachy pink. A languid sensation warmed his blood as he imagined those limbs rubbing against the back of his thighs, or better yet, caught up on his shoulders. Breath shot like a spear into his lungs, and he coughed once and tried to blink the thought away. 'Twas not his purpose to seduce her. Yet.

Instead, he gathered the hem of her gown and slid it up, over the curve of her bottom, until she was exposed from heel to hip. Bruises dotted the backs of her thighs from jostling in the saddle, and a welt, bright red against the paleness of her skin, ran along one leg where it had rubbed raw against a strap. A stab of remorse slit through his veins.

"Ah, Fiona. You should've told me."

Then, on one thigh, he saw them. A pattern of four tiny oval marks, more faint than the rest, yet causing him more distress than all the others. They were made by his own hand, from where he'd grabbed her leg the night before and hitched it round his own. He had sought to leave his mark upon her body, but not like that. His chest ached from it.

He opened the vial and tapped some of the pungent ointment into his palm, warming it between his hands before sliding them over her battered skin. He took the greatest of care, but a tiny noise escaped her throat. Fear? Pain? He couldn't tell.

He knew only that, somehow, wounds on her created scars on him.

The calloused pads of his hands scraped like a cat's tongue on her skin as he massaged ointment over her raw bottom. His caress caused little pain against her bruises, but the humiliation of being bare under his perusal slapped like the sail of a ship in strong wind. She willed herself to lie steady, lulling him with false compliance. His sword lay forgotten, taunting her and just out of reach, his dagger, with jewels glistening in the hilt, next to it on the floor. Her hands itched with the urge to snatch it up and plunge it into his side. But like a true hunter, she waited. It would not do to be hasty, to bash and thrash and act without forethought. No, she must bide her time.

He finished rubbing the liniment into her heated skin and pulled her dress down. That surprised her. She thought for certain those hands would find their way to her center to torment her further. But he nudged her limbs aside and got up from the bed, washing his hands in the basin and putting the vial of ointment back into the trunk. She watched as he paced around, wondering at his purpose. He blew out all the lanterns and lay down next to her, both of them still fully clothed. Pulling up a blanket, he rolled her onto one side so her back was pressed to his broad chest. He wrapped an iron arm around her middle and pressed his groin against her bottom, scorching it more than his hands had, even through the layers of fabric.

His breath sucked in deep, then released like a fire bellow. "Go to sleep, Fiona. We've another long day before us tomorrow."

She said nothing. Only waited. Surely there was more to come. Soon he'd push her skirts aside and plunder her with his lips and tongue and worse. But he didn't. He just breathed, in and out, in and out, ruffling the hair near her ear with exhalation, his chest pressing close and then retreating.

She'd been ready for a fight. Had stewed all day about how to give enough, just enough, to placate him, yet not be distracted and give in to his touch. She'd let loose no more careless whimpers or wanton sighs. She'd have no more accusations of spurring him on! Indeed, the very thought galled her. He could take her body, but she'd make certain he knew she wanted no part of it. No part of him.

But he was…doing nothing, save breathing. The steady rhythm of it annoyed her agitated senses. What a numbskull he was, to fall asleep so easily, relaxed as an infant in its mother's arms. The lack of threat she apparently posed was insulting. She moved abruptly under the guise of resettling herself into a more comfortable position, but she made sure to whack him in the jaw with the back of her head. A mistake, for his jaw was like castle rock. He grunted softly and pulled her closer.

She pushed his forearm lower, farther from her breasts, but he moved it up again without bothering to comment or open his eyes. Another moment passed, and she flopped around once more.

"If you continue to fidget so, perhaps you'd be more comfortable sleeping without your gown." His voice was low, warm against her ear, and stilled her motions like a slice to the throat. She must remember her purpose. A wise warrior knew patience. Fiona let loose her breath in one last huff and willed her limbs to be still. She must wait until the moment was right.

# CHAPTER 7

M YLES WILLED HIS BREATH TO STEADY, THOUGH HIS HEART clamored in his chest at the restraint. She was soft and pliant in his arms, and even a day in the saddle could not erase the smell of vanilla that lingered on her skin. He wanted to press his face into the mass of deep-red tresses now tickling his nose. That damn hair of hers may as well be tickling his balls, for the sensation shot straight to them like an arrow. Her every wiggle was like a stroke to his prick. The girl obviously had no notion what it was like to be a man.

His mind galloped toward lust. He could take her, still. 'Twas well within his rights. She was his wife after all. But the bruises haunted him. They'd ridden hard today, hoping to clear both Sinclair and Fraser land before nightfall. Campbells were unwelcome this far north, and any party, even one as well armed and well trained as his, was at risk from opportunistic marauders. Some would be after their coffers, but as many would attack simply to eliminate a Campbell from their woods.

Fiona moved again, and he considered pulling her astride so he might ease into her and take his pleasure without more damage to her tender backside. But a horse nickered outside, and another answered. The quiet murmur of the men seeped through the tent walls. She'd not be silent if he pressed his advance. And in truth, he didn't trust his own ability for discretion while undertaking such an ardent endeavor. It was one thing to have his men hear him with some tavern whore, but Fiona was his wife. And as much as he'd like to teach her a lesson in obedience, he'd not do it now. Not here in a tent, surrounded by twenty pairs of interested ears. Tonight, both his bride and his overeager cock would have to wait.

The harsh screech of an owl awoke Fiona with a start. At first uncertain of her surroundings, her mental fogginess cleared, and she remembered. She'd not meant to fall asleep. But there she was, curled up in a ball with her husband snuggled up behind her, like cozy kittens in a box. His quiet breath was soft and rhythmic. She straightened and turned, just enough to see what she could of his face in the pale light, and agitation scoured away any remnants of her slumber.

Torches lit the camp outside, and the fire, tended by the night watch, still burned bright. She could see its illumination through the tent walls, and though the hour remained a mystery, beyond the firelight, darkness beckoned. Her time had come.

Slow and silent as the moon rising, Fiona slid from under her husband's arm. The blankets rustled like a whisper, but clanged like cathedral bells in her mind. Sweat prickled under her arms and down her neck as she moved from the makeshift bed, slithering like a snake from under a rock. When she at last reached the edge of the covers, out she came, reborn and free from his grasp. She picked up her shoes and hose and then stepped toward the tent flap.

Myles breathed deeply in his sleep and rolled to the spot she'd just vacated. Fiona froze in her tracks, waiting for him to wake up at her absence, but he merely stretched his long leg out and sighed with slumber.

She offered up a silent prayer of thanks, and on the chance her neglectful God might indeed be listening, she offered up a second prayer, asking forgiveness for the sin she'd soon commit. With one eye on her husband's inert form, she reached down and gripped the handle of his dagger. The blade scraped the scabbard's side with a metallic hiss as she pulled it loose. And still Myles slept. Leaning farther down, she scooped up her green cloak and swung it round her shoulders. Then she stood, and with one final glance at the body in the bed, she stepped outside the tent.

The moon was a sliver in the sky, a mixed blessing, for any light could be a boon or a curse, depending on her immediate circumstance. The big red giant, sitting several yards away and near the fire, rose from his seat and stared at her. He must be the watch. She pulled shut the cloak, tucking the dagger inside.

"What are you about, lass?"

She stood tall, tilting her chin. "Nature calls."

He stared another moment, his beard almost glistening from the reflection of the flames. Then he nodded. "Well, then be quick or I'll be after you."

She turned and walked past the wagons, past the pallet made for Bess, and into the rows of trees, searching the darkness.

"Psst! Here! What took so long? Surely you haven't been jousting with your husband all this time?" A voice, thin and reedy, came from just beyond where Fiona stood.

"Bess, where are you?"

"Here!" the maid whispered again, and stepped farther into the tiny clearing.

"Ah, praise heaven. God may be a Sinclair after all. Have you anything for me?" Fiona grasped at the tiny bundle held in Bess's hands, quickly unwinding the fabric. In the darkness, she could barely make out the shapes.

"There's bread and a bit of cheese, and some dried meat. I couldn't find you any water or ale. They keep a closer eye on their drinks than their food."

Fiona nodded, wrapping the bundle back up. "Thank you, Bess. This is fine. Are you certain you've the will to go through with this? I'd not put you in harm's way without your consent."

"Aye, I've the will. But you're the one who is sure to get lost in the woods and be eaten by wolves."

"I'll face wolves of a different sort if I stay. So, let's be quick. That hairy red giant is waiting."

Bess unclasped her gray woolen wrap, handing it to her mistress and donning Fiona's green one. "And what will you tell the Frasers when you arrive on their doorstep, weary and ragged, and a Campbell bride, to boot? They'll not take you in if it means facing Cedric's wrath."

"Aye, they will. The Frasers hate the Campbells as much as we do. They'll give me aid, if only to rob Cedric of something he wants. Now stop rattling on and listen to me. You must convince them you wanted no part of this and that I forced you to comply."

Bess scowled. "That's the truth of it, close enough! But I'll convince them and do my part. Your mother would want me to protect you."

Fiona hugged her, fast and hard. "You have protected me, Bess. Always. I owe you my life."

"Have you any idea which direction to go?" the maid asked.

"Aye, I heard the men talking. We're just south of Tain. Balintore is but a few hours' walk southeast of here. With a good foot under me, I should reach Fraser's keep by midmorning, no worse for wear. Now, off with you to the tent. And stand up straight, or we're done for."

The women embraced again. "Godspeed to you, miss." Bess's voice rasped with emotion.

"May God watch over you, Bess. You've been a good and faithful servant. I could not have asked for better."

Fiona looked to the starry sky to get her bearings, and with a final kiss to her maid's cheek, she stepped toward escape.

# CHAPTER 8

M YLES HEARD TAVISH SPEAK TO FIONA OUTSIDE THE TENT and tried to rouse himself, but days of travel and the burden of getting acquainted with his new wife had taken a heavy toll. When moments later she returned, he fell back into blissful slumber knowing his men were on watch, his wife was back in the tent, though needlessly wrapped in her green cloak, and all was right with the world. When the birds called their morning salutations, there she nestled at the very edge of the bed, her hood tucked firmly over her head.

With bleary eyes, Myles slid over and nudged aside the green woolen fabric, lightly kissing Fiona's temple. A trickle of alarm crept through his sleep-drugged limbs. Her skin felt peculiar, rough and loose, and the fragrance of vanilla and nutmeg he'd come to associate with his wife was replaced by something sour, a repellent combination of lye and old age. Like Pandora opening her box, Myles slowly pulled aside the cloak and let loose a bellow fierce as Lucifer's fury. He jumped from the pallet, pushing the woman away as he leapt. The form unfurled on the ground, bones creaking.

"What sorcery is this?" he snarled. "I lie down with a goddess and wake up to an old hag?"

Bess quaked where she landed, eyes watery and fearful.

Outside, the men stirred fast to action by their master's shout, ready to defend their lords. In seconds, his father and Tavish burst into the tent.

Bess struggled to sit up, but Myles reached over and grabbed her bony shoulder.

"Where is my wife?"

Bess blinked, saying nothing.

Cedric stepped to the tent flap and murmured to a man-at-arms, who nodded and quickly moved away.

Myles jostled the old woman, setting her teeth to rattle. "Answer me, you conniving witch."

Tavish stepped closer, regret thickening his voice. "They must have switched places."

Myles cast a scathing glance at his uncle. "'Tis obvious, Tavish! But where is Fiona now?"

"Gone," answered Bess.

Anger and dread mingled as one inside Myles's chest. "Gone where?"

The man-at-arms returned. "She's not on the maid's pallet, my lords. Shall I have the men search the area?"

Cedric nodded and took a step toward Bess, towering over her, hands fisted on his hips. "Where is she, woman?"

Her lips clamped, and Myles poked her with his foot. "You think she's unsafe with the likes of us? How will she fare in the forest with the wild creatures and the wicked terrain? Or the cold rain? Do you hear that thunder? A mighty storm is coming."

"I told her not to go," she said faintly. "She commanded I take her place. 'Twas not my will."

His lungs felt full of peat bog. "Where is she off to?"

Bess ducked her head, as if to avoid a blow, though not one of them had raised a hand. "She forbid me to tell."

Myles bent closer still. "You do her no service by keeping this secret. She's sure to come to harm in those woods. If you care for your mistress, you'll tell me where she was headed. Home?"

Bess shook her head and eyed him warily. "Will she come to greater harm if you find her?"

Myles grit his teeth in frustration. "I will treat her with care. I cannot promise the same for you if you do not answer. Where has she gone?" He pressed upon her shoulder.

"To Our Lady of the Immaculate Heart," the maid spit out.

"The convent?" the men exclaimed in unison.

"Aye. She has an aunt there. Her mother's sister."

"Where is this convent?" Myles asked. Surely no destination could be less suitable for his disobedient bride. Then again, perhaps a life of discipline and penance might be just what she needed.

Tavish spoke. "In Ludlow. I know the place. But 'tis a full day's ride from here. She'll never make it without a horse. She didn't steal a horse, did she?"

Bess rose up straighter. "My lady is no thief!"

Myles snorted. "No thief, perhaps, but a troublesome she-devil. And you"—he pointed a finger at Bess's nose—"you should have awoken me last night."

"She cannot have gone far in the dark," Cedric said. "And clever as the lass might be, she no doubt left a trail wide as Loch Ness."

Myles moved to the bed of blankets and shoved one foot into a boot. He bent to lace it. "I'll deal with this, Father. You be on your way. I'll find her quickly and catch up to you."

Cedric nodded. "The carts keep our pace slow enough, but if we reach Inverness, we'll stay and wait for you. Take ten men on your search. More eyes will make the task easier."

Myles wanted to argue and insist he could find her without aid. 'Twas disgraceful enough she'd left him while he slept! Christ Almighty! What kind of a soldier was he, to let the enemy slip from his grasp just because he was content and sleepy? But then again, who could have imagined the chit would be so foolish?

"Tavish, choose the men," Myles ordered.

Tavish snapped to attention. "'Tis done. And if it suits you both, I'll count myself among them. 'Twas I who let the girl out of sight." He turned to leave the tent, nearly tripping over Bess. He nudged her none too gently with his toe. "And what shall we do with this sack of gristle and bits?"

"Tie her to a tree and leave her for the wolves." Myles wasn't serious, of course, but let her think he was, by God. Then she'd tell her mistress not to cross him again. If he ever found her. An odd sensation twisted in his gut. It took a moment to recognize it, for the feeling rarely visited him.

It was worry.

The earl regarded her a moment. "Put her in the cart. She goes with us to Dempsey. And, Tavish, don't judge yourself too harshly over this occurrence. After all, the lass is pure Sinclair."

The brothers exchanged a look that Myles didn't wholly understand, but he'd press his father on that issue later, after his bride was found.

Tavish nodded and hauled Bess from the tent.

Myles tugged on his other boot, avoiding Cedric's gaze. Sinclair or no, the girl had duped him with her compliance. He jerked the laces tight and finished tying them.

"You mustn't judge yourself too harshly either, son."

"I had that old crone in my bed, Father, without even realizing. Marriage has me addlepated, and it's only just begun." Frustration rasped in his voice.

Cedric's easy laughter filled the tent, his good humor in stark contrast to Myles's own. "Truer words were never spoken.

Women have a way of complicating the simplest of things. And desperation makes them stranger still. Don't fret on it. Just find her and bring her home."

"Desperation." The word stung on the tongue. "That's what I don't understand, Father. Why was she so desperate to leave she'd rather face a future full of calamitous repercussions?"

"Because her father filled her head with lies, lad. You know I didn't murder Aislinn Sinclair, but this lass certainly thinks I did. It's up to you to convince her otherwise."

Myles picked up his belt, taking note of his missing dagger. At least the girl had the sense to arm herself, but he'd be wary of that blade when he found her. She'd stabbed his father with nothing more than a brooch. She could do real damage with his knife. His thoughts trigged a question that burst forth unbidden. "How is it Aislinn had your brooch, Father? Was it stolen?" His father's expression turned somber in that instant. "It was given freely. 'Twas meant to be proof of a promise I made."

"What promise?"

His father shook his head. "Your wife awaits you in the woods. We'll talk on this another day."

His father was coy as a courtesan when it came to Aislinn Sinclair. But he was right. Every moment that passed took Fiona farther away from the protection of the Campbells and closer to certain danger—a wild boar, perhaps, or worse yet, forest brigands. Myles picked up his own cloak and left the tent. Rain started in earnest, and thunder rumbled like an omen.

The pelting rain stung Fiona's eyes, slowing her progress to a pathetic pace. With no idea how far she'd come, she knew only that she'd walked for hours and was irretrievably lost. She had struggled to keep her path due east, but the night stars played cat and mouse among the clouds until at last the sky was so heavy with rain she saw nothing but darkness. It was morning now, but still the rain fell.

The best she could hope for now was to eventually hit Moray Firth and then decide if she must go north or south. Or perhaps she'd wade straightaway into the frigid waters and be done with herself. She'd been drowning slowly for hours now, her limbs already shriveled and pale as a corpse. How much worse could a swift death in the ocean's raging tide feel compared to this elongated death?

The rain doubled the weight of her garments, and despondency bore down on her spirits heavier still. She'd made a mistake. A horrible, irreconcilable mistake. She knew that now. Twice during the night, she'd heard such a wicked howling in the woods she'd climbed a tree trying to hide from it. Her dress was in tatters, torn by brambles and branches, and it was quite possible she'd broken a finger when trying to break her fall after tripping over a bulky tree root.

Her plan, which seemed plausible when whispered under a dry cloak with Bess, now revealed itself to be utterly absurd. She had panicked and run, convincing herself she could simply disappear with the help of her Fraser kin. The marriage had been consummated, so the truce would hold and Margaret would be safe. But with the dawn, logic had replaced desperation, and Hugh Sinclair was cursing her from the heavens for her impetuous failure.

The Frasers held more hatred toward the king and Campbells than most. But even if she made her way to their stronghold, would they offer aid? Would they house and clothe and feed her, and then, God willing, see her safely to Glamis Castle and her Douglas cousins? Even if they did, the likelihood of her husband relinquishing his claim on her was improbable, and her family would very well suffer the consequences of this night's misadventure. Oh, what a stupid, foolish coward was she.

She should've killed him. She should have sliced his throat like a pig to slaughter and pulled out his heart for soup. Then she should've turned the knife upon herself. 'Twas the only way to purge her soul of his stain and save her sister from the same fate as herself.

But what now? She could not go back. She knew the type of punishment Cedric Campbell could dole out. Her mother's battered body had been evidence enough. The memory of that hateful day bore down on her, heavier and colder than the rain. She'd been just ten years old when they'd laid her mother on a trestle table in the great hall so that every Sinclair might see the damage done at the Campbell chieftain's hand.

Aislinn Sinclair, beautiful and once so vibrant, bruised and tinged by death's gray palette. A villager admitted to having seen Cedric near the spot that day. And if that testimony was not great enough, there was the brooch, pinned through her very flesh, a brand, a flag of victory.

Seeing her mother cold upon the table, Fiona plucked the pin out, thinking in her childish mind that, once it was removed, her mother might come alive again. But she did not.

'Twas John who led Fiona away soon after, drying her tears and vowing to avenge their mother's death. But he'd lied. His recent betrayal wounded her far greater than Simon's, for Simon was a brute, all instinct and strength with little insight. But John knew her loneliness. He shared the ache of missing their mother, and still he'd done nothing to stop Simon from sacrificing her to the Campbells. The last remaining shards of her heart splintered. Yes, she had escaped her husband, but now it seemed she had no brothers left to return to.

Lightning cracked, reminding Fiona of more immediate dangers. There, in the distance, she spotted a dwelling. Blessed heaven. 'Twas a small, abandoned hut, but a palace to her eyes. She hurried to it and stepped inside. Searching in vain for any food, she realized the mice had long since cleared the place of even the tiniest crumb. But still, there was a dry spot on the floor, and she sank down on it like it was a bed fit for the pope himself. Weariness collapsed her limbs, and fitfully, she slept.

For an hour or more, Myles and his men headed toward Ludlow and searched the forest in the dismal rain, looking for any sign. They found none. No footprints or bits of fabric left behind. No broken branches or strands of deep-red hair twisted in a thicket. And all the while, questions rammed against the doors of his mind. What if he could not find her and never learned her fate? Or what if he found her too late, after some evil of the woods had done its worst?

The rain let up, and Myles signaled to his uncle. Leaning forward from his saddle, he spoke the words quietly. "'Tis clear the old nurse lied. These Sinclairs are a duplicitous lot."

Tavish nodded. "I've been thinking the same thing. Fiona could not have come this far without a horse, and all of ours were accounted for. But if not to Ludlow, then where?"

Myles looked around, as if she might be waving from a distance just to taunt him. What would he do to dupe an enemy? "If it were me, I'd send my pursuers opposite of the way I was headed. Fraser land is east of here. Do you suppose she'd go to them?"

Tavish scratched at his red beard. "There's no telling what the foolish thing might do. But she's not come this way. That is certain."

"We'll return to last night's camp and start again. We know she's not gone west. And Father is traveling south. So we'll divide and search east and north. She really cannot have gotten far."

"Unless she had help."

Myles looked at Tavish, cold dread spiraling in his gut at the notion. "Help? Do you think this was prearranged?"

His uncle rolled his wide shoulders and spit on the ground. "'Twas a bold move to wander out into the forest alone at night. She's either brave, mad, or planning to meet someone."

The idea clutched at Myles like a sinewy claw. If she'd had help, then only God Himself would know where to look. He rose up in his stirrups and whistled to his men.

# CHAPTER 9

RESTARTING FROM LAST EVENING'S CAMP, MYLES AND half his men headed east. Within a mile, they picked up her trail. He sent one man to gather those heading north, and soon they were a party of ten once more. His anger, simmering since finding the nurse in his bed that morning, now scalded. His wife's foolishness was beyond comprehension, her actions leading them straight into enemy lands. Pride stung like a nettle on his collar as they trailed bits of fabric, broken branches, and footprints in the soft forest floor. His men knew him to be resourceful and wise, but his wife seemed hell-bent on making a fool of him. He'd not tolerate such disobedience, and when he found her, he'd make certain she understood as much.

The girl had taken a circuitous route, either getting lost or perhaps trying to cover her way. She was clever enough to think of that, while he'd not been clever enough to realize the nurse had lied. He'd not make such a mistake again. Duplicitous Sinclairs.

For the next few hours, they followed her trail, and as the sun tipped the crest of the mountains, they came upon a tiny shack. Myles knew deep in his gut she'd been there, and perhaps lingered still. He motioned for his men to approach silently.

Tavish leaned in for a whisper. "Perhaps we should circle the place. She's likely to slip into a rabbit hole if we're not paying full attention."

"If she does, 'twill be you I send in after her."

"Best be a very large rabbit hole, in that case." Tavish ran a thick hand over his belly.

Myles halted his horse and slid from the saddle, landing on the ground with practiced ease. He reached for his dagger, remembering then that the little wench had swiped it. Not a thief, indeed!

"Give me your dirk, Tavish. If I need a blade, I cannot wield a sword in so small a dwelling."

Tavish had the nerve to look indignant. "Where's your dirk?"

Myles looked to the sky in a plea for patience. "Where do you think?"

"Ah, she is a pesky little menace, that wife of yours. Here." He handed him the dagger. "Please try to see that I get it back, would you?"

"As surely as you make certain she doesn't sneak off again in the night."

Tavish's ruddy complexion took on a deeper hue. "'Twas a clever trick."

"Indeed." Myles nodded once and made short work of getting to the door of the hut as his men circled it at a distance, still on their horses.

He listened for a moment and heard nothing. Holding the dirk in one hand, he eased open the door with the other. And behold, there she was, asleep in the dirt. Filthy, bedraggled, her hair tangled in knots, breathing soft and innocent as a newborn babe.

All day he'd stewed over this moment, and now he'd caught her. His hands itched with the need to throttle that slender white neck. Lord knew she deserved it. But at the sight of her, an odd relief coursed through him. She was found, safe and whole. She had not perished in the forest, or worse, found sanctuary with the Frasers. But relief soon gave vent to his pent-up frustration.

He bent low, gripping her shoulder and jostling her awake.

She gasped in surprise, and before he knew what she was about, she swung her arm around and pain sliced at his leg.

*Curse the little hellion! She just slashed me with my own dagger!*

He flung himself against her body, pinning her between himself and the hard ground. Breath woofed from her lungs as he twisted one hand into that damnable red hair and caught her wrist with his other. He squeezed, making her gasp again, and his blade fell from her fingers onto the dirt.

Ire and relief mingled. He wanted to pummel her. And shake her. And kiss her. The shocking combination disoriented his senses. She was a foe like no other, using guile against which he had no weapons.

"You found me?"

"You thought I wouldn't?" He pulled her arms up over her head and pinned them with one hand as she grunted from his weight.

"You should be halfway to Ludlow." Her voice rasped for want of air in her lungs.

The wench knew no humility. He had her trapped like a rat in a bucket, and she had the audacity to make accusations?

"No, I should be halfway to home, but your capriciousness brought me here instead." He pulled a cord from inside his jerkin and began to twine it around her wrists, his face stern. "Girl, you try my patience. You've cost me hours in the saddle, worn out my horses, irritated my men, and put us all in danger. And for what? Your stubborn Sinclair pride? You are a Campbell now. You answer to me. 'Tis time you learned that."

And then he kissed her.

Fiona was dazed and bewildered. She'd been in a dream, a hideous, harrowing dream, being chased by long-armed demons. Suddenly, one reached out and grabbed her hair, but she had a spear and threw it. Only, it was no dream. It was Myles, pressing down on top of her, smothering away the last of her breath with his mouth.

She tried to move, but the binding cord twisted the tender skin of her wrists, stinging in contrast to the warm melding of his lips against her own. How had he found her, when she herself didn't even know where she was? All those awful hours, wandering, searching for the Fraser keep, and all her efforts for naught.

As suddenly as his kiss began, it was over. But he was angry still. She saw it in the glow of his eyes, felt it pulsing from him as he weighed her down.

Fear and cold took hold, and she shivered despite his warmth. Or perhaps, because of it. "I've done my part for this truce," she whispered. "My brothers cower under your dominance, the king is satisfied, and you mighty Campbells have claimed another Sinclair woman. Must I sit at your feet like a hound? Let me go, and I'll speak of your mercy. Of how you spared my life in repayment for my mother's."

He grabbed hold of her face with one hand, still pinning her wrists with the other. "'Tis a bold lie, Fiona. My father did not kill Aislinn Sinclair. Say it again, and you will suffer for it."

Fiona trembled at the severity in his voice, at the violence coiled beneath his surface, and realized how mildly he'd treated her until this moment.

A gentle tapping sounded at the door, and the red giant's head poked in, his eyes bright with mischief. "Have you subdued her, then?"

"In a manner of speaking." Myles scoffed as he rolled off and sprang up, pulling her with him so fast her head spun with dizziness.

Breath hissed from her lips as the cord binding her wrists cut deeper. Her finger, still bent at an odd angle, had long since turned purple. Fiona bit her lip. She'd not cry out in his presence, no matter the pain.

"You're bleeding, lad," Tavish said, nodding at his leg.

"Aye, she sliced me, the little witch." He winked at Tavish before leaning down and pulling a strip of fabric from her already shredded skirt. He dabbed at the wound. "'Tis a scratch."

Tavish bent to peer more closely at the wound. "Still, I should tend to it."

They stepped from the hut, Fiona pulled by her husband, and she found herself surrounded by glaring Campbell men, their hair wet and hanging down, their horses soggy and foaming round the bit. She was the reason for their discontent, and well she felt it in their stares.

"Lads, she is found." Her husband raised her bound arms in a mild show of victory.

A grumble of acknowledgment followed. A particularly shaggy man with brown eyes and an unkempt beard stepped forward. "The skies are clearing, my lord. Should we ride to catch your father or make camp?"

Myles looked to the heavens. Fiona watched his shoulders rise and fall with a sigh. The rain had indeed stopped, but the sky darkened with the coming evening.

"It'll soon be too dark to travel. We'll make camp. Taggart, take some men and see what you can scare up for food."

The men dismounted and went about their various tasks. Myles nudged her toward the side of the hut, where she sank down and remained largely ignored. Before long, fire crackled in a hastily dug pit and a few rabbits turned upon a spit. How the men had found dry wood or caught the hares in so short a time she could not imagine. But soon enough, the smell of cooking meat made Fiona's stomach scorch with want. The meager supplies Bess provided had long since worn away, and she quivered with hunger and thirst, but her last shred of pride prevented her from asking for anything.

Her husband let Tavish minister to his wound and said nothing more to her, nor did he spare her a glance. His disregard was oddly unnerving, for without seeing his face, she could not read his mood. But when the hare finished cooking, he took a hearty section of it and came to sit near her, neither smiling nor scowling in her direction.

He ate loudly, smacking his lips and commenting to no one in particular about the meal's deliciousness, while offering her none. She closed her eyes and breathed deep, as if the smell might nourish her. But it only made her stomach clench and her mouth water. She twisted her hands beneath the binding, hoping the pain might distract her from the hunger. It didn't.

*Curse him and his rabbit-tainted breath. God have mercy, may he choke on a stringy sinew and cough it all up.*

Tavish approached her, his hand outstretched. She stared down at her feet, covered with thick mud and nettles she could not work loose.

"Would you like some bread, my lady?" he asked, his voice solicitous.

She looked up. Lord knew that girth of his could spare a bit without suffering. She nodded once, the smallest of concessions.

But he stuffed the bread into his mouth with a chunky fist and talked around it, crumbs falling. "More's your sorrow, then. Think of that next time you sneak away on my watch."

"Tavish," Myles chided, shaking his head.

But the big man looked less than remorseful. He turned and walked away, his big body shaking in mirth.

Defeat, utter and complete, battered her defenses. If she had that dagger now, she'd use it on herself. She lowered her head against her knees and succumbed to weeping.

Myles sighed. "Oh, come now, none of that." He tapped her leg and handed over his plate, still piled high with meat and bread. "Here you go, you silly girl. 'Tis better than you deserve, but none of us will sleep if you're keening with hunger all night."

She looked at the food and then to him, and saw an easy smile, not a glower or boast or trick. He seemed in earnest.

Slowly, she reached for the food and saw his pleasant expression change to dismay. He looked to her hands, where welts from the cord oozed blood, and her purple finger still bent to the side.

"What happened to your finger?" He set down the plate and moved to unlace her bindings.

"I fell." She gasped as the air stung like salt against the wounds on her wrists.

He frowned, leaning in to examine her hand. "You could've been hurt much worse, you know. But I need to straighten that finger. Are you ready?"

She nodded, but could not bite back a cry as he set her finger back into position. Her head swam, but she willed herself to stay upright.

Myles tore another strip from her dress, which was disappearing with the hours, and tied the fractured finger to its neighbor, along with a small stick to keep it straight. His ministrations were efficient but gentle. Then he fetched a bit of clean cloth from one of his men and wrapped each of her bloodied wrists separately, tying the cloth off in a bow. Two neat little cuffed bandages and, just like that, her shackles turned to bracelets.

And her mind turned to confusion.

He was the strangest enemy she could imagine. When he should rail and torment and break her bones, he set them instead. He made no sense at all. He was a terrible soldier, aiding his combatant at her weakest point.

He sat back once more, picking up the plate and passing it into her unbound hands. She ate, and after a moment, he said, "I am a simple man, Fiona. It takes little to please me and great effort to bring me to violence, yet you seem hell-bent on doing the latter. But for every Goliath, there are a hundred dead Davids who could not defeat him. I will always win. Remember that."


Darkness fell and Myles helped his men settle the camp for the night. His wife ate her food and drank her water, saying nothing, but not glaring or crying anymore either. Sometimes victory must be measured by one arrow at a time.

After giving his instructions to the watch, Myles pulled Fiona back into the hut, spreading out his mantle for them to lie on and using her maid's thin wool cloak for their covers.

"You, little wife, have peculiar tastes. Last night, we slept in a cloud of blankets and wanted for nothing. Yet tonight, because of you, we lie in dirt like dogs. Now, must I tie you to me, or will you promise not to run again?"

"I will not run." Her words came on a sigh.

"Or walk, or skip, or slither either?"

A wan smile, pale as the moonlight, passed over her face. "I'll stay put. Another night like last, and there'll be nothing left of this dress."

The thought of taking the remainder of that rag from her danced wickedly in his mind, but just as quickly danced away. Even he was not brutish enough to take her in a place like this.

Instead, they lay down on the cloaks, positioned like the night before. Myles gripped his arm around her, perhaps more tightly than necessary, but she did not resist. And within moments, her breathing evened out and he knew she slept.

Inside the tiny hut, with wind whistling and moon shining brightly overhead, he heard his wife mumble something incoherent, and he relaxed his hold.

Her face, awash in the moonlight, was lovely as she slept. Her soft lips moved slightly as she whispered within her dreams. The warmth and softness of her body teased him. In spite of all the unpleasantness that had occurred between them, in spite of her harsh words and foolish actions, he felt his heart opening up to pull her inside. And quite suddenly, like a flint ignites a spark, he understood how his father had come to make a promise to Fiona's mother.

Though Cedric Campbell had not spoken the words aloud, Myles knew with certainty his father had once been in love with Aislinn Sinclair.

# CHAPTER 10

WANDERING ABOUT IN THE DARKNESS LAST NIGHT HAD been unduly miserable, yet this day was equal torment for Fiona. Riding astride in the rain, her legs chafed, her muscles burned in protest, and she could not fathom worse discomfort. Her finger, tied in the makeshift splint, throbbed relentlessly. Yet, despite thunder and rain, Myles insisted they press on. It was his aim, she'd heard him tell Tavish, to rejoin the other half of the Campbell traveling party and his father with all due haste.

Her desire was the opposite. Fate awaited her in the form of Cedric Campbell, a man she had blatantly defied. A man wicked enough to squeeze the life from her mother's throat. Though Myles was magnanimous with his forgiveness, she was not so naive to imagine her father-in-law would be similarly swayed. She straightened in her saddle. But whatever punishment she faced, she would accept it. She'd not run again. Myles would only recapture her, and last night, in the cold and the dark, she'd come to a sobering realization.

She was not prepared to perish for the sake of family honor. She was no martyr, nor a hero.

Onward they rode, mile after wet, stretching mile, but as morning gave way to afternoon, the rain stopped and they came over a crest to behold a scene so devastating it shocked her to the core.

Fingers of black smoke clawed toward the sky, the acrid scent of spent flames lingering in the air. Carts lay singed and overturned, their charred cargo cascading into the muck. And bodies, a dozen or more, splayed open by brutal weapons, were strewn about in bloodstained heaps upon the road. A few men milled upright, tending to the wounded, though they themselves appeared injured and exhausted.

"Christ Almighty!" Myles spurred his horse to motion, and his men quickly followed. Commotion erupted as they entered the scene, and in that instant, Fiona realized this was what remained of the Campbell traveling party.

Heart thudding like a gong, she nudged her mount forward, not wanting to be any part of this, yet pulled inexorably onward. Somewhere in that horrible mayhem was Bess. A peculiar numbness flooded her limbs, and she felt as if she were trying to move underwater. Sounds muted in her ears, and the smell of blood created a foul taste in her mouth.

Myles took charge, and soon the air was filled with questions and shouts.

"Where is my father?"

"Who sees the chief?" another called out.

And the dazed answers from the men remaining.

"They came upon like hounds of hell, my lord."

"We were outnumbered, my lord, but fought them off."

The battle had ended, but recently. Flames still licked at one of the carts, and two men worked frantically to extinguish the last bit of fire. A few others searched among the fallen for their Campbell kin. Fiona heard Tavish call to Myles, but their voices blended in the screeching discord of alarm and she knew not what they said.

Sliding from her saddle unassisted, Fiona called for her maid, but her voice was thin, lost amid the chaos. "Bess," she shouted again, sweat prickling at her skin like bee stings. And then she saw her. A narrow form, twisted in a fearful fashion inside a green cloak. Her cloak.

Bile rising, Fiona ran to the spot and sank as if her limbs were made of water. A fervent prayer spilled from her lips, but for naught. Fiona eased the hood away from her nurse's face and gasped. A foul gash cleaved along the side of her head, blood darkening her gray hair. Horror, hot and red, filled Fiona's mind. What villain would do such a thing?

She looked up and around, and was surrounded by dead enemies, their blank eyes staring into a void of nothingness. None near could give her any answers. They were on their own dark journey. Looking back to Bess, she dabbed at the wound, trying to press the sides of flesh back together, but it made a sickening sound, and Fiona's stomach rolled with nausea.

It was her fault Bess was in this mayhem. She should not have escaped and left her nurse to fend for herself. She should not have even allowed the old woman to leave Sinclair Hall in the first place. Were it not for Fiona, Bess would be safe at home, playing nursemaid to young Margaret.

Tears scalded her cheeks. All around, the view was a macabre painting, with colors too vivid to be real. But the smell was real enough. Death and fear had its own stench, and her head filled with it. The sounds began to separate, and she heard each voice more clearly now.

"Where is my father?" her husband called again.

"We've been searching, my lord! We cannot—"

The man's words were cut off by a distant cry. "Here! I have found him. He is wounded."

A sensation, like steam rising, thin and indistinct, built inside Fiona's chest. Cedric Campbell was wounded. She should be glad, and yet she felt nothing but morbid curiosity and the faint hope that she'd awaken from this nightmare. An odd stillness overtook her senses, as if she watched from a faraway place.

Overhead, the birds twittered gaily, the wind whispered its love song to the budding trees, and the sun shone bright as Mother Nature, perfidious once more, ignored the horrors of men.

Myles rushed to his father's side and dropped to his knees next to him. Cedric's ashen face, marked with mud and worse, bore no expression, and Myles's heart ripped asunder.

"He lives, but barely," his man Benson said, his voice husky with concern.

Blood, dark and sticky, covered the earl and the ground around him. Myles could taste its metallic sourness on his tongue.

A series of wounds shredded his father's garments, along with the fragile flesh beneath. White bone protruded from a broken arm, stark in contrast to the puddle of burgundy blood it rested in. On one side, a gash, deep and jagged, tore through from rib to hip, and another small gash laid open a gouge on his temple.

Tavish joined them, intoning a fast prayer.

"Father," Myles called softly, grasping his father's unbroken arm, "can you hear me?"

Cedric gave no flicker of response, but a telltale pulse thrummed on the side of his neck. He was alive, and for that, Myles must have hope of saving him still.

He and Tavish went to work, cleaning the wounds and setting his father's arm as well and as gently as they could manage.

"What happened here?" Myles asked Benson as they scrambled to bind cloth around Cedric's midsection.

"'Twas an ambush, my lord. About an hour ago, we came over that rise and into the valley, and suddenly, they were all around us, screeching like banshees. A dozen, I'd say. We fought as best we could. We killed many, but a few escaped."

"You did well. I counted eight of theirs among the dead," said Tavish.

"Yes, my lord, but one more thing. They knew who we were."

Unease twisted Myles's gut.

Tavish's hands clenched into fists. "What makes you think that?"

"In the thick of it, I heard one shout, 'We need the Campbell, dead or alive.' They nearly got him too, but for Seamus, God rest his soul. He fought alongside your father, my lord, and took down three of them before he fell."

Such news as this was worse than bad. If they had been a simple band of thugs out for whatever they might steal from travelers, then the marauders would be far away by now. But if they had a purpose, if they sought to harm the Campbells in particular, then his father and the rest of them were in more peril every moment they tarried. They needed to leave and be away from here as fast as possible.

"I thought you'd be in Inverness by now. Why are you still this far north?" Myles asked, frustration scratching in his voice.

"We lost a cart wheel, and the rain left so much mud we moved at a slug's pace. I think your father might have pushed harder too, but he was waiting for you."

Myles looked to Tavish, anger washing over him like burning oil. Had he not dallied in the hut last night with Fiona, or lost her in the first place, if he'd pushed his men back into the saddle, they might have reached his father sooner and prevented this attack.

Tavish shook his head, guessing at his nephew's expression. "'Twas not your fault, lad. We had no choice but to retrieve your wife."

His wife? Indeed! His wife! 'Twas she who forced a separation in the traveling parties. Had they been at their full number of twenty men, no brigands would have dared to attack. Yet they'd been split, and his father sprawled near death's door because of Fiona's reckless selfishness. And his failure to keep track of her. A twig cracked, and garments rustled behind him. Like a silent demon, his wife appeared. Her dress, already torn and filthy from the night before, bore fresh blood, and her pale face, streaked with grime, displayed no hint of emotion, as if this day's events meant nothing.

"Is he dead?" she asked, her voice flat.

Her indifference lit the cannon of his temper. He reached out, like a falcon snatching at a rat, and grasped her shoulders. He pushed her to her knees next to Cedric. "He lives, no thanks to you. But do you see what has been done? Because you led us astray and divided our forces! Was that your Sinclair plan all along?"

She made no sound, only stared at his father's inert form.

Myles leaned low and growled into her ear. "This is your doing, woman. If he dies, it will be your soul he torments."

He released her shoulder, and she crumpled, pressing her palms into the muck and staring at Cedric with blank eyes.

Myles's fury fell with her. She was his wife. She was his burden. He should help her. But he stood upright and turned away.

Tavish caught his arm and whispered, "Go easy, Myles. She's had a time of it, and now her maid is dead."

"So are six of our clansmen, Tavish. Our sacrifice was greater than hers."

He had no ill will toward the nurse. She was as loyal to her lady as he would expect from one of his own servants. But he'd not offer words of concession to his wife, though they burned in his throat. Sinclair devils or no, his men had been attacked, and had they not divided forces to search for Fiona, his father might now be safe and whole. Still, he was not without heart.

He motioned to young Darby and spoke quietly. "See to my lady. Keep her from my sight, but be sure to keep her in yours."

Darby nodded and helped Fiona up from the mud, leading her away.

The men finished bandaging Cedric and moved him into the only cart not smashed or burned. Someone had lined it with the blankets. The wounded were tended to, while others set about digging graves for their dead.

"Who do you suppose did this?" Myles whispered to Tavish moments later as they readied the horses for travel.

Tavish spit in the dirt and scratched at his beard. "Hard to say. We're past Fraser land here, but they could've come this far south."

Myles nodded. "Perhaps. This is MacDougall territory, and they've no quarrel with us. But only the Sinclairs knew when we traveled."

Tavish shook his head. "We were within their grasp for days, both to and from Sinclair Hall. Attacking us here makes no sense."

He walked to one of the dead assailants, rolling him over with a booted foot and peering at the silent shell as if it might yield some clue. "I don't recognize any of them. They've no clan markers, nothing to distinguish them or who they belong to."

"My lords!" called out a man-at-arms from twenty paces away. "This one's alive!"

Myles and Tavish rushed over, kneeling on either side of the injured enemy. Myles grabbed the front of his jacket, hauling him up to a sitting position, and noticed a fierce wound on the man's leg.

"Who are you?" Myles growled.

The man's clouded gaze cleared for a moment; then he laughed, a horrid, gurgling sound. "Kiss my arse, Campbell."

In an instant, Myles ground his elbow into the open leg wound, and the man's laugh turned into a cry, until he clamped his lips together. Sweat and blood mingled on his brow.

"Who sent you, and what did they want with my father? Answer, and I'll show you mercy. Refuse, and I'll slice you open and leave you to the vultures."

The man said nothing. His head turned. His gaze drifted away from Myles and caught on Fiona. She was leaning against the cart's wheel, her arms wound around her knees, her dress in tatters.

"My lady is worse for wear by your hand, I see."

Myles's gut churned. *His lady? What game is this?* He flung the man back to the dirt and strode over to his wife. A more pathetic sight he had never seen. But he pushed aside those gentle thoughts and grasped her by the wrist, hauling her up and over to the wounded man.

"Is this your lady?" Myles demanded.

Her expression remained blank.

"Aye," the man murmured, "my lady."

His wife blinked, like one coming awake after long, deep sleep, looking to Myles and then to the man on ground. She shook her head and frowned.

"He lies," she said. "I don't know him. But whoever he is, his men killed my maid." She leaned forward and spit in the man's face.

Myles's grasp on her arm tightened. More than anything, he wanted to believe his wife had played no deliberate role in this day's events. Yet why would the man claim false allegiance to her? Unconvinced, he prodded the man with his foot.

"Tell me her name, you wretched cur, and I'll show you mercy yet."

The man wiped the spittle from his cheek, glaring. "She was the Lady Fiona Sinclair. Now she's nothing but a Campbell whore."

The words burned his ears, engulfing Myles in anger. He pressed his boot against the man's throat, for the bastard insulted both his clan and his wife with such a statement.

"Myles," his uncle spoke softly, "have a care. We can gain information from him yet."

Myles looked at the man writhing on the ground beneath his heel. He could squash the life from this wastrel like a bug. Enjoy it, even. But his wife had seen enough of death this day.

He pressed a moment longer to make his point, then stepped away.

"He'll last a day or more with such an injury. That leg is sure to fester. But that gives him time enough to tell us all he knows. Bind his wound and put him on a horse."

# CHAPTER 11

Her husband turned guarded eyes her way, confusion and anger at war upon his features. "You'd best tell
me all you know of this as well, Fiona. I'll not be duped by you
again."

His voice was calm, too calm, for she could see the muscle twitching in his jaw. The thinly veiled rage he'd shown the
wounded man could just as easily be turned on her. Still, he
seemed willing to hear her speak, though she'd given him no
reason to trust her.

Her limbs quelled. "The man is no Sinclair. I swear, I know
him not."

"Then why did he say he was?"

"He knew my name, nothing more. And he called me a whore.
No Sinclair would besmirch my honor in such a manner." God
save her, she had enemies from every angle. "Ask him another
question, Myles. Something only a true Sinclair would know."

The man rolled to the side and spit blood upon the ground as
Myles stared at her, hard and unrelenting.

The sky went white before her at her husband's silence, but
she would not be cowed. She cast her gaze to the dying man and
nudged him with her own foot. "Tell me, you wicked liar, in

which ear is my brother Simon deaf? That should be easy enough to answer."

She looked back to Myles, who glanced from her to Tavish to the enemy on the ground.

After a moment, Myles pressed his sword tip into the man's leg. "Answer the question."

The man flinched and cried out, "The left!"

*Thank God.* "Wrong. My brother Simon isn't deaf at all. 'Tis John who's hard of hearing."

"The light is waning, Myles," Tavish interrupted. "And the longer we delay, the better chance they have of coming for us still. Let me fling this piece of shite on a saddle and we can question him as we ride."

Fiona scanned the woods at Tavish's words, and her belly twisted tight. Whoever these marauders were, they'd likely show her the same mercy they'd shown Bess. And for the first time, she found herself wanting to stay very close to her husband's side, in spite of the mistrustful way he glared at her now. She could see he knew not what to make of the man's accusations. And in truth, neither did she. Without doubt, none of those men lying dead on the ground were hers. She'd never seen any of them before. But why the man had said she was his lady, she could not fathom.

Myles nodded. "You're right, Tavish. Finish readying the horses. Benson, see that the cart with my father is ready to go." Then his eyes met Fiona's, full of doubt.

"Darby!" he called after moment's hesitation, and the squire appeared as if from nowhere.

"Yes, sir."

Myles sighed, and she saw resignation claim him. "Bind the lady's hands and help her to a horse. But keep the reins to yourself. Understand?"

"Yes, sir."

"And when we ride, stay close to me or Tavish."

Darby nodded, solemn as a bishop, but his cheeks blushed apple red as he held his hands out to take Fiona's.

"Why am I to be bound again? If we are attacked, I'll not be able to defend myself."

Myles stared another moment, as if weighing the choices before him. "Then that shall be your misfortune." He turned and strode toward the cart to check on his father, while unease lodged deep within Fiona's chest.

'Twas not her fault they'd been attacked. And these were not her men. No Sinclair would insult her, nor would they have harmed her dear Bess. These evil deeds were the work of some other force.

She watched her husband climb into the cart to adjust the earl's covering, and a great sadness enveloped her once more. She should not care if the old Campbell died. 'Twas just as he deserved. His suffering should be her joy, but gladness was long absent. Death lingered at this scene, its cold finger pointing this way and that, claiming too many souls today. And at Demspey Castle, half a dozen women would learn their men were never coming home. They were her enemy, true enough, and though she should be glad, she was not.

They loaded up a short while later, after the Campbell dead had been hastily blessed and buried, Bess along with them. They'd left the other corpses in the road for their enemies to come and claim.

They traveled as fast as the muddy roads would allow, eating what little food they had while staying in the saddle. Fiona was hungry and tired and sore. But little did that physical discomfort compare to the heaviness of her heart. She could feel it breaking, bit by tiny bit, with each jarring step of her horse. She left a trail of broken shards along this path and knew, if she made it all the way to Dempsey, she'd have nothing left in her chest save an empty void.

Darkness was full upon them when they reached Inverness. Reining in next to a building loud with revelry and glowing with light, Myles called instructions to his men.

"Tavish, see to getting us rooms. Benson, find a physician and bring him here. Nigel, choose a man and go arrange for the boats. We must set sail at first light. But, men"—he lowered his voice—"use caution. If our enemies are near, it won't do to have them realize we are here."

Tavish nodded. "Wise thinking."

The men went on about their business, and Fiona fought to keep her seat in the saddle. Overwhelmed by fatigue and sadness, it seemed she'd lived a lifetime since her wedding just two days ago. She was beyond caring what came next, or so she thought until Myles dismounted and walked her way. She realized she did indeed have room for a little fear. His expression was darker than the sky above.

"Get down."

She struggled off the horse's back, for her hands were still bound, and her legs buckled as she touched the ground. Her husband caught her with one arm to keep her from collapsing fully onto the cobbled street, but there was no tender care in his touch. Instead, he pulled her to the side of the road, setting her upon an overturned cask pushed up against a wall of the building.

"Stay."

Her eyes closed of their own volition. "Wherever would I go?" When she opened them moments later, Myles was gone and Darby stood before her, weapon drawn and at the ready in his slender, trembling hand.

"My lord Myles said I should see that you stay put."

She smiled at the bran-faced boy. "How old are you, Darby?"

"Eleven. But I'll be twelve soon enough." He lifted his chin as if to add to his height.

"Will you stab me if I move?" she asked.

He straightened his narrow shoulders. "Best not tempt me to find out."

She closed her eyes again with a resigned smile. "Ah, another scrappy Campbell. Even the little ones are mean."

It seemed hours but was only moments when Tavish returned and they saw the earl safely transported into a room. The innkeeper let them use the back entrance—for a fee, of course—so that no prying eyes might see who lay upon the makeshift stretcher.

The surgeon came shortly thereafter, joining Tavish, Myles, and his father in a tiny room lit by lanterns and a crackling fire. He was a diminutive man by the name of Drummond, with beady eyes, a balding pate, and apparently, a great thirst, for he took a mighty swig of whiskey before he started.

Tavish looked over the man's head at Myles and shrugged his thick shoulders.

In spite of the drink, Drummond was efficient and knowledgeable. He cleaned the wounds and sewed the angry gash along the earl's torso. Battle-hardened though he was, Myles blanched at the sight of the thick needle and cord jerking though his father's skin. When the surgeon set the broken arm, Cedric jerked awake and cried out. But after a long pull of whiskey from a metal cup, he passed out cold again. Mercifully, the head wound was minor compared to the rest, and a bandage soon covered it.

"If you're willing to travel with us to see to this man's well-being, I'll make it worth your while," Myles told the physician as he gathered up his tools. "We'll pay well for your service and discretion."

The little man eyed the money purse Tavish dangled in front of him. He licked his lips. Myles could nearly taste the man's craving for ale.

"Where are you traveling to?" Drummond asked.

"Sail with us down Loch Ness as far as Invermoriston. Depending on how our man fares, you could return then or go with us farther. I cannot say to where. Too many ears in a thin-walled inn."

The doctor nodded. "I'll think on it. Let me tend to your other wounded first." He picked up his bag and stepped toward the next room, where several injured Campbell men awaited his attention. He hesitated for a moment, then reached back to the table and grasped the bottle of whiskey. He nodded at Tavish with a wink. "'Tis the finest medicine."

After the surgeon left, Myles stared at his father lying so still in the bed. The earl's breath was shallow and fast.

Tavish turned away, scratching his beard. He sat down heavily in a chair near the fireplace. "That doctor had some mighty interesting tools in that bag. Just the kind of implements to bring forth truth from a man's lips."

Myles wiped a hand across his jaw, whiskers scratching against his palm. His eyes felt full of sand when he blinked, and it seemed he had not rested in a month. He had no taste for torturing men, but they had a prisoner to question, currently bound and gagged and guarded in a stable next to the inn. He'd told them nothing of use during their ride to Inveraray. "Find out from him all you can. If we have enemies so bold, I need to know who they are."

Tavish nodded. "Leave it to me, lad. I can be very persuasive. In the meantime, you might try asking your wife once more."

Myles's mouth went dry. Fiona was in another room, hands tied to a bedpost and two men on guard outside her door. She'd not once pleaded her innocence while they traveled from the ambush site to the inn, nor had she spared a glance at the prisoner. Whoever he was, she was not in the least concerned over his well-being.

"'Twas no secret who I married, Tavish. He could have known her name without being a Sinclair," Myles said.

"True enough. And he knew nothing about her brother's hearing."

Myles scoffed at that. "Nor do we. She could be lying. Do you know if either of her brothers has a bad ear?"

Tavish cleared his throat. "I've heard the younger son, John, took a blow to the head as a lad and lost half his hearing then. And then there is the maid. I cannot think even the Sinclairs are so brutal they'd kill off their own maid."

"Especially one wearing my wife's cloak. And they would have known to send more men. They could not plan on Fiona being able to divide our group, and Benson said they were attacked by a dozen. Sinclairs would have sent a larger force."

"True. I had not thought of that. But one thing is for certain. If they were not Sinclair, they took great pains to convince us that they were."

"So it would seem. Perhaps an enemy hoping to draw us back into conflict with them? Someone opposed to the truce, perhaps?"

"That hardly narrows it down. Half the Highland chiefs have issue with us, and the other half despised Hugh Sinclair." Tavish stood back up. "I guess I'd best be visiting our guest in the stables while you question your bride."

She might survive this journey, but as sure as the sun rose each morning, her wrists would be scarred forevermore. Fiona twisted on the bed, straining against the bindings keeping her in place.

It wasn't Myles who had bound her thus, but rather, one of his men, and obviously one who had no wish to fail. She could not even roll to her side. She lay on her back, silently counting the cobwebbed rafters up above and the stone-hard lumps in the mattress beneath, trying with all her might not to think of Bess. Guilt was a stone in her chest.

An hour passed before she heard the door latch lift. She slammed her eyelids shut and feigned sleep, thinking perhaps avoidance was the better part of valor.

The edge of the bed creaked and lowered. "You're not asleep, minx. I'm on to your tricks."

Reluctantly, she opened her eyes to find her husband perched near her feet. She could kick him in the face from that angle, but for what gain?

"How is your father?" The words popped out unbidden. She did not care, so why she asked was a mystery.

Myles regarded her a moment. "He lives. For now. Does that disappoint you?"

"Not so much as you might think."

The smallest of smiles crooked a corner of his mouth. "Did anyone bring you food?"

She shook her head. "I could not have eaten if they had. These bindings are clamps of steel."

Myles rested an elbow upon his knee and his chin upon his hand, seeming to take a moment's pleasure at her captivity. He sighed, deep and slow. "'Tis the first time in three days I'm not worried about what you're doing. I rather like you trussed up like a game hen."

"I promised you I would not run again."

His eyes narrowed. "You promised to love and obey me as well. But you, my dear, are a liar. And one I dare not turn my back on for fear you'll sheath my own dagger in it."

She flushed and felt her face burn hot. His tone was teasing enough, but truth lay behind those words. And though that band of murderous vandals may have done her a service with regard to Cedric Campbell, she'd support no coward who dumped the blame upon her family. "I could have stabbed you in the tent that first night of our travels, if I had a mind to. But I didn't."

"Generous of you."

Her frustration grew at his tone. "That man is no Sinclair."

"Why would he lie?"

"I cannot imagine. But he did." The bindings felt tighter still.

Myles ran a hand over his jaw. "Dying men are prone to tell the truth, while you have been anything but forthright. And yet, I do begin to think we have a shared enemy. One that opposes the truce between our families. Who would be against such a thing?"

She could think of several clans in the north surrounding Sinclair Hall that had no desire to see the Campbells' strength and holdings increase. But he would know that too. She'd give him no specific names, for anything she might offer would be conjecture and might lead him to doubt her even more. "I stay out of men's politics," she said instead.

His jaw set sternly. "Whoever they are, we will crush them. We have the might of the king's army on our side. With James on the throne, none can vanquish us. They are fools to try."

A shiver traversed Fiona's body. He was arrogant, like his father, but what he said was true. Though she was loath to admit it, perhaps this alliance was in the best interest of her clan. Although she might live among the Campbells, eat their food, even sleep in Myles's bed, her heart was forever Sinclair. She owed that much to her mother's memory.

Myles stood up and pulled out his knife. She gasped at his intent. But he merely leaned over and slashed the cord holding her to the bedpost. She lay still a moment longer, willing her arms to lower, but they were numb. "Could you help me? Please?"

His dark brows rose considerably. "Please? My lady has said please?"

*He isn't clever. He is tedious.* All she wanted to do was sit up. Must he make an example of her weakness? But he reached down and gently lifted her by the shoulders until she was upright. Her arms lowered, and the blood rushing back was one thousand needles poking. She shut her eyes as they watered with pain.

Myles crossed the room and opened the door, speaking to the men standing guard. "Have someone bring us food and at least two buckets of hot water for washing. Tell Tavish to arrange for a few of the men to watch over my father for an hour or so until I rejoin him myself. And send someone to find me a dress."

"A dress, my lord?" The man's voice squeaked with bemusement.

"For the lady, you sodding fool."

An unexpected chuckle bubbled up inside Fiona at Myles's exasperated tone. That she could leap from irritation to humor in the present circumstances only proved how overwrought she was. She was giddy with hunger and thirst and exhaustion, for the idea of hot water and food nearly made her leap from the bed to kiss her husband in gratitude.

Her heart clutched at the notion, and she opened her eyes fast.

Yes, for certain, she needed food and rest before her addled emotions wreaked havoc on her actions.

# CHAPTER 12

A SERVING GIRL OF TWELVE OR SO ARRIVED WITH A TRAY bearing roast pork, bread, cheese, and wine. Myles let his wife fill her plate, then took his own and tore into the food without ceremony. No king's banquet had ever tasted so fine. Before they finished, the lass was back with two wooden buckets filled to the brim with steaming water, and with them, washing cloths and soap.

His wife eyed the water with unabashed longing, her gaze so full of want Myles could not help but think he'd like that look to come his way one day.

The servant set the buckets down and made her exit, while Fiona continued to stare.

"Would you like to bathe?" He cleared his throat, embarrassed by the huskiness.

Eyes wide, she paused with bread nearly touching her lips and nodded reverently.

For that moment, she looked so innocent and eager he could think of nothing but brushing aside that bread and plundering her lips with his own, fool that he was. It seemed distrusting her had no bearing on his want of her.

The room was little bigger than a stable stall, with a narrow bed against one wall and a tiny fireplace on another. No table or chairs adorned the place, and so they ate their feast while sitting on the bed. How easy it would be to simply push her back against the pillows and pull that scrap of dress from her body. Her hair was ragged, tied back with a simple cord, and dirt smudged her temple. But even so, she was tempting as a juicy plum. He took a drink of wine.

"Kiss me," he said.

"What?" Her spine straightened as her eyes met his.

"Kiss me, and you shall have the bathing water."

*Damn him and his devil's bargains.* "I'd sooner kiss your horse's arse."

"My horse can find his own kisses. It's me that's between you and that bucket."

Her happily full stomach quaked. She'd never kiss him willingly, for it went against every promise she had made to herself. But the steam beckoned, and her skin itched for want of soap. "What if I refuse?"

He shook his head, dipping it in a show of false sadness. "Then you shall have no bath, m'lady." His posture was relaxed, as if he had not a care in this world. But his eyes were direct, like he thought to devour her as he'd devoured this meal. With messy abandon.

"I'm no whore to sell my kisses."

He chuckled. "Whores aren't interested in baths. But you are. Look at that steam. You could even wash your hair."

Her breath drew in, sharp as an arrow's tip. Touching her head, she felt bits of mud clinging to the strands. Disheveled as she was, how he could even want to kiss her was a mystery. But men were base. Far be it for him to let a little thing like cleanliness interfere with his desires. And far be it for her to let his want of a simple kiss stop her from bathing.

"One kiss?"

"Aye. But a real one. A kiss meant for a husband."

She quivered inside, not entirely certain what he meant. But she had her suspicions.

"One real kiss and then you leave me alone to bathe in private."

His brows furrowed. "One real kiss and I help you wash that filthy hair. Then I shall leave you alone to…finish with the rest of you."

Is this what marriage to Myles Campbell was to be like? Full of persuasion and persistence?

"I can wash my hair by myself."

"You'll make a mess and use up all the water. I'd like one of those hot buckets for myself, you know. And the longer you argue, the cooler that water gets. So, come on, now. Yea or nay?"

Oh! This man was infuriating. "Yea! Yea. Fine."

One eyebrow rose. "Really?"

"Yes." It wouldn't be that bad. One simple kiss, be it real or not. She'd been through worse. She tossed the last bit of her bread onto the tray and plunked the tray upon the floor. "Where do you want to do it?"

His smile went wide. "Well, I was planning on the lips, but if there're options…"

"You're a dirty swine."

"And you're my very dirty little wife." He smiled at his victory. "Now, hush up and be still. Let me savor this moment."

Her arms crossed in pointless self-protection as he moved toward her. She leaned back, bumping up against the wall, and still closer he came. Shallow breath fluttered in her breast, flickering like candlelight.

His smile faded as his eyes went sleepy and dark in a gaze that stirred her somehow, somewhere deep within. She could not look into his eyes and keep her bearings. She glanced away instead and saw the water buckets tantalizing her in much the same way. With promises. Washing her hair would be pure joy, worth any price. But his hands, working the soap through her curls, caressing her scalp, would be too much. She tingled at the thought and slammed her eyes shut against it. She'd made a mistake. She should tell him to stop. Kissing was a dangerous game. Yet no words came forth. With eyes closed, she felt the heat of his face near hers. Felt his breath and knew his lips hovered near her own.

And she waited.

His hand cupped her jaw, the calluses of his palm at odds with the soft caress.

A tiny gasp escaped her, and her eyes went wide once more. She halted his wrist. "I never agreed to touching."

But his hand stayed. "Touching is part of a real kiss."

She sighed, frustrated and edgy. She should have gotten more details before she made this trade. Her heart thumped, knocking hard against her ribs.

Myles's gaze floated toward her mouth. She felt a puff of his breath, and his lids shuttered closed.

And still he did not kiss her.

Instead, he grazed his cheek along hers, running his thumb across her bottom lip, and her own eyes fluttered shut as if too heavy to hold open. Sweet Mother Mary, he needed to kiss her and be done with it. This anticipation was too sweet a torment. She tried to remember all the reasons why she should push him away and could think of none.

He lingered, poised so close a raindrop could not find its way between them, teasing her with the scrape of his whiskers and his hands upon her face, until at last she betrayed herself and turned to meet his lips of her own volition. He growled low in his throat and deepened the kiss with the pressure of his mouth, the welcomed invitation of his tongue, until they both gasped with the pleasure of it.

'Twas he who pulled away, blowing out a lungful of air as if the kiss had shocked him.

She pressed fingertips to her heated lips and waited for the shame to flood her senses.

It didn't. She wanted him to kiss her again, but he stood up and quickly turned away. He scooped up one bucket without looking back at her.

"I'll have the serving girl assist you with your hair. I know nothing of such things. I'll be staying with my father, but you have men on guard outside your door, in case you should need anything. Good night, Fiona."

And then he was gone.


Christ! The girl was ivy twining round his gut, weaving into his thoughts and squeezing away all common sense. His father lay at risk in the very next room, yet all he could think about were her dark-lashed sapphire eyes and lips so sweet he could taste them still. He wiped the back of his hand across his mouth. Even Odette's kisses had not stirred him so, and he had loved Odette. Hadn't he?

This grimy, mischievous chit was more his nemesis than his lover, wife or no. And he'd do well to remember. That kiss had come too easily, meant to distract him from all her offenses. But by God above, he was no fool. He'd not be ruled by his prick like some randy peasant boy. The girl was a Sinclair and full of deceit.

He opened the door to his father's room to find two of his men—Dermott and Benson—sitting at a tiny table next to the bed. These were souls he could trust, not that slip of a wench next door.

"How fares my father?"

Benson stood, ducking his head under the low beam of the ceiling. "He is quiet, my lord. Breathing steady. No fever yet. Pray that holds."

Myles nodded and gestured for Benson to sit back down. "Has the doctor been back?"

Dermott shook his head. "Not yet, sir. But he's nearly finished with the others."

"And Tavish?"

"Still with the prisoner."

Myles held the bucket in his hand. He'd forgotten to grab any of the cloths or soap in his haste to leave Fiona's side, but there was extra bandage swaddling near Cedric's bed. "Take this water and clean my father's face and hands. You may use the rest for yourselves."

"Will you go first, my lord?" Benson asked.

Myles looked down at his own hands. He'd rinsed them with cold water before eating, yet still they were stained with brown blood and dirt ground layers deep. But the hot water in that bucket suddenly held little appeal. Better to use it on his father.

Cedric should be first in his thoughts, but he'd been entranced by his bride, seeing to her needs before that of his own men. He'd gone in her room to interrogate her, not barter for her kisses.

He set the bucket down so fast and hard, water splashed to the floor.

"I'll wash later. First, I'll see what Tavish has learned. Stay with the earl until I return."

Myles made his way quickly down the back staircase and across the yard, meeting his uncle at the doorway to the stable.

"Any news?" Myles asked, crossing his arms against the night's chill.

Tavish wiped something dark and sticky onto a cloth twisted in his fist. "He recanted his kinship with your bride, but that may have been as much due to my influence than the truth of it. He spewed hatred of the Campbells and our king, and claims he was a mercenary, along with the others."

"A mercenary hired by which clan? If that's the case, it could lead us right back to the Sinclairs."

"Aye, it seems that way to me as well."

Questions crashed inside Myles's mind, clattering like hooves against a cobbled street. And each led back to his wife. Had she betrayed him from the start? Been complicit in some scheme of her brothers? It could not be so. Her kiss still tingled on his lips, and even as his judgment warned him against trusting her, he felt his heart giving way to tender emotions, as dangerous as any enemy.

This was not the time to follow his heart. 'Twas his brain he must use now. He'd not let that lass sway his way of thinking.

Tavish turned, and they walked back toward the inn, speaking in hushed tones. "I was rough with him, Myles. As rough as I could be without killing him outright. He'll be dead soon, and well he knows it. I even offered to send word of him to his family if he gave me more, but..." His voice trailed off.

"Maybe another night of suffering will loosen his tongue."

"He may not last the night. And I'm not sure he even knows who hired him."

Pain, dull and thick, lodged inside Myles's lungs. Having enemies was nothing new. But none before had acted with such singular malice toward his father. Their purpose, he could not fathom. For if, God forbid, his father perished, Myles would take his place as chieftain and the Campbell clan would continue to thrive. And if not him, then his younger brother, Robert. That could only mean one thing.

If one of them was in danger, so were they all.

# CHAPTER 13

JOHN SINCLAIR DRAINED THE ALE FROM HIS CUP, THE CONTENTS
sour on his tongue. His head ached from too much of the stuff
and from the incessant scrape of Simon's voice against his ears.
From the moment the last Campbell's horse disappeared from
their view, his brother had done nothing save plot and rant.

"The Sutherlands are sure to side with us. They lost a third of
their holdings to Cedric Campbell when King James claimed his
throne a decade ago. And for what? His *valor*?"

Simon spit out the word like it tasted of piss. He slammed his
own cup down upon the rough-hewn table, splashing the contents without care.

The two brothers were in the hall surrounded by a half dozen
of their most trusted men. Sinclair cousins, mostly, each devout
in their hatred of the king and Campbells. They lounged indo-
lently near the fireplace, legs flung over chair arms, cups ever
present in their hands. They'd spent the evening drinking and
boasting of the victory sure to come.

Simon scowled and blinked into his empty mug. "Where is
that girl? Say, you there! Bring us more drink."

John sat at the far end of a trestle table—a bit away from the
others, as usual—and turned to see the girl Simon had beckoned.

Her eyes narrowed at his brother's tone. But she ducked her head with a nod and moved toward the buttery, where the ale was stored.

"That's a bonnie piece, aye?" Simon asked the group, licking his lips and staring after the girl's retreating backside. "Ripe as a melon, that one. I've a mind to split her open, have a taste."

Cousin Darrin, sitting closest to Simon, grunted his approval. "She's a widow. They're the finest. Trained and left wanting."

John's fingers clenched into a fist, and angry words stung his throat. He'd not defend her, though, no matter what sludge Simon flung her way. His attention so would only bring her more harm.

She was Genevieve from the village, with hair so thick and blonde a man could wrap himself in it and imagine it was starlight. Her eyes were green as the moors at dawn and just as lonely. She was John's woman and had been for months, but none save the two of them knew it.

She was back fast as a hare, filling the mugs and deftly avoiding each man's hungry stare. Except for John's. She winked at him when none could see and bent lower to fill his cup than for any of the others. John's heart ached at the sight of her. He'd take her far from here if he'd a way. But the second son of an exiled lord had few options. Simon's was the cloak he clung to for his daily bread now, and he himself had nothing to offer.

But if Simon's plan went their way and they defeated the king in battle, the Sinclairs would be in power once more, and John would take his place among the reinstated nobility. But news had come of late that gave him pause and made him wonder at the necessity of their scheme. Cedric Campbell could not be trusted, for he was a conniving murderer, and yet at the wedding, he'd pulled John aside and spun a tale for him so fantastical it very nearly might have been true. And if it was, John had more options than ever he'd had before. Perhaps his fate might change. But only if he had the courage to set things into motion, for once he pushed this boulder from the cliff's edge, there'd be no stopping it.

"John!" Simon growled. "You are silent today. What say you about the Sutherlands? Will they stand with us or cower like maidens?"

John met each man's gaze before speaking. "My sister's marriage has bought us time to forge those necessary alliances and to build our army. If we strike too soon, without the support of the other Highland chiefs, they'll turn us over to the king and we'll hang as traitors. For once, we must be patient."

Simon laughed and wiped away a dribble of ale upon his chin. "Patience? Bah! Patience is nothing but lost opportunity. No, John, in this, you are wrong. The king will sail around the Highlands in just a few months' time. Pompous bastard that he is, he thinks to command our fealty just by asking. But when he arrives in Gairloch, we'll be waiting with a fierce Highland welcome. One of steel and might." He smacked his hand against the table.

The men turned back to Simon, grunting their collective approval like sheep bleating in unison. John watched his brother's chest swell with their acceptance, and Simon spoke once more.

"Even the king's stepfather, Archibald Douglas, is on our side. Though he is exiled in London, he is anxious to reclaim his post as Scotland's regent and knows well we can get him there."

John swallowed down his sigh. God, these men were so simple. Not one of them could think more than a few days into the future.

"So you'd ally us with England just to rid us of James?" Darrin asked, getting a sharp look from Simon.

"I ally us only to our own freedom," Simon stated. "I want back all that King James took from the Sinclairs when he claimed his throne these ten years past. I want our lands, our homes, and the honor of our good name. We sided with Douglas when he held the boy king captive. He owes us now. And when this king is dead and Scotland is a regency once more, I will sit upon the board and rule beside Douglas, just as my father did."

John drained another cup, motioning to Genevieve to fill it once more. His brother could boast like this for hours. It was thirsty work, listening and nodding.

Genevieve ambled to his side, her hips swaying in a way that made him think of meadow grasses blowing under a warm sun.

"You drink too much, my lord, and too often," she murmured quietly so none might hear but him.

He let his eyes travel up her body slowly, lingering on the curve of her breasts before reaching her face.

Her cheeks flushed pink, the way they did when he pressed her against the pillows.

He held out his cup, his fingertips extending to touch her wrist discreetly. "I'm thirsty."

Her lashes sank in a slow blink. "Perhaps you're lonely too."

He looked to Simon, fearful his brother might be watching, for Simon was greedy as well as jealous, and if he thought John favored this girl, he'd take her for himself. Just because he could.

"I am," John whispered softly. "Will you come to me?"

She tilted her chin and filled the cup halfway. "I will. Best you sober up a bit."


When she arrived in his room that night through a servants' passageway, John was waiting. He kissed her, hungry and urgent. She met him with equal fervor, pulling at his clothes and biting his shoulder when he squeezed her breast. Their coupling went fast, so fast he had no time to fully undress her, though long enough to leave them both spent and well satisfied. When it was done, he savored the task of removing her garments, exploring the lush treasures he found beneath with still more kisses.

"Simon makes me uneasy," she admitted sometime later as she pressed against John beneath his covers.

Her words made him pull her closer, so tight she giggled from it.

"How so?" As if he did not know the answer.

"He watches me, but no more so than he watches the other women. Bertrice is fond of him, so we usually send her his way."

"If he makes a menace of himself, you must let me know."

She nodded, her tresses tickling his nose as she did so. Then she rolled onto her back to look him in the eyes. The light was dim, but candles and the fire lit their faces. "It's not my place to ask, I know. But could you tell him now that I am yours? And save me the risk of his attentions?"

How he wished he could. "You know Simon well enough, Gen. He covets most what others have. But he's the laird now, and were I to ask permission for your hand, his interest in you would only grow more intense. Keeping us a secret is the best way to keep you safe. Rest easy, though. Things are happening, and when the summer is over, my place will have changed one way or another."

"I don't understand," she whispered.

"I cannot tell you more, Gen. Not just now."

She sighed and rested a soft hand against his cheek. "So many secrets with you, John. I cannot keep them all straight."

He turned his face to kiss her palm. "But you know the most important truth."

"What's that?"

"I love you."

She sighed and slid her hand down between them, wrapping it around the length of him. "Show me," she whispered.

# CHAPTER 14

OVER THE FINAL CREST THEY RODE, FIONA AT THE BACK OF the pack, with Darby leading her horse. The last two days had been arduous, first traveling by boat down Loch Ness, then obtaining more horses and riding the rest of the way, stopping rarely. They'd slept outside again last night, and she'd not had Myles's body to keep her warm, for he'd said little to her since leaving her room that night at the inn and seemed intent on avoiding her in every way. She had no inkling why his manner had changed so thoroughly, but could only assume the prisoner had spewed more falsehoods.

As they journeyed, Cedric clung to his miserable life, passing in and out of awareness. Or so she gathered from the murmured comments she overheard from the men.

As the sun began to settle on the mountaintops, Fiona caught her first site of Dempsey Castle. Both relief and trepidation rippled through her. The place was monstrously large, with whitewashed masonry walls and brightly colored pennants flying high from every turret. Two massive guard towers flanked the entrance, with a barbican reaching forward and ending at a stone bridge. A moat surrounded it, and outside of that, the village hummed with evening's activity.

Down the final hill they went, the horses' ears pricking up, as even they recognized home. Her palfrey nickered and stepped more lively, prancing and pulling at the bit. Fiona gripped the pommel in her hands and clenched her tired legs against the eager horse's sweat-soaked sides.

Darby turned and smiled, his freckled cheeks pink with anticipation. "'Tis a grand place, isn't she, my lady? You're a lucky one to live in such a palace."

Fiona bit her lip. Lucky, indeed. Perhaps the dungeon would be warm and dry in a place such as this.

Avoiding the main avenue of the village, they circled around and passed over the bridge and under the first arch of the barbican. The wooden grid of the portcullis raised, its iron-tipped spikes looming overhead like snarling teeth. What her future held beyond this gate, God only knew. And He seemed averse to sharing information.

The cluster of weary travelers clattered into the bailey to a symphony of joyous voices calling welcome. But it hushed away as those within the castle yard took in the disheveled appearance of their traveling clansmen. In seconds, Fiona and the others were surrounded by an undulating sea of arms reaching up to assist them. What a commotion it was as men jumped from their saddles, kissing the women who ran to their embrace.

Fiona waited, perched upon her palfrey, well above the fray. Darby, bless him, stayed by her side, and for that, she was grateful. He was small, but he'd been her champion these last few days, seeing to her needs after Myles had forsaken her.

Her husband swung down from his saddle, and her chest went tight, thinking he might come her way. He didn't, and an odd weightlessness overcame her, as if she were in this moment and yet played no part at all.

He strode instead toward an older woman who'd come down the impressive stone steps. His mother, surely, for she was dressed as fine as a royal in a satin gown of deep burgundy, with slashed sleeves revealing a plum-colored girdle beneath. Gold thread weaved through the trim of her French hood and glinted in the fading sunlight.

The woman pulled Myles close, clutching him tightly, and another flood of emotions washed over Fiona. A mother's love. How long she'd been without. Seeing Myles with his own mother should have kindled her anger anew. But she only felt bereft.

"That is Lady Marietta," Darby said, his voice reverent.

The woman's expression of concern deepened as Myles spoke. Then fast as a blink, she took charge, calling out orders and instructing the men to find a stretcher so they might move her husband into the hall. There was a set to her jaw that Fiona recognized, for she'd seen it on Myles's face. Quickly, the men-at-arms went to work, with Myles and Tavish by their sides.

As Cedric was moved from the cart, Myles finally glanced over at Fiona. She sat up taller. But his mother paused beside him, following his gaze, and Fiona could not help but look to her.

Steel-gray eyes pierced her, and Fiona felt the icy coldness in that sharp look. Like the point of a blade, it cut through. Fiona fought the urge to smooth her hair, for little would it do to improve her appearance. She was a frightful mess, wearing a dun-colored dress purchased from the innkeeper's daughter and dirt embedded in her skin. She could see Myles's mother had already made her judgment.

Marietta scowled and turned away, picking up her skirts and following her husband's broken body into the hall. Myles's face softened slightly, so slightly Fiona thought it might just be her wishful fancy, for then he turned as well and went with Cedric.

Darby twisted off his horse and slid down, his feet landing with a soft thud in the dirt. "Can you manage off that mare, my lady?"

Fiona, left breathless by the wordless dismissal from her husband, nodded. She managed to swing her leg around and maneuvered downward. Her skirt caught up in the stirrup, and Darby gave it an overzealous tug. Had he not, she'd have met her new kin by giving them a view of her all and sundry.

His cheeks burned red as coals. "Come this way, my lady. I'll find someone to tend to you."

"Darby!" a feminine voice called. "Here."

"Mother!" He ran toward the voice, and Fiona took one step to follow but stopped short, for never was there a more beautiful woman than Darby's mother. She was dressed as fine as Marietta but was younger, with straight black hair and eyes so pale a blue they nearly seemed silver. Her smile was full as she raced to gather her son into her arms. Fiona felt that ping again, for the loss of a reunion she would never have.

"Darling, I've missed you so. My goodness, did you roll in the mud?" She hugged him again, paying no heed to the dirt he smudged on her finery.

"Not roll, exactly. But I slept in it a night or two. Come, meet Lady Fiona." He pulled her by the hand, and she came willingly, stopping mere inches before Fiona. Slowly, those silver-blue eyes perused her, from filthy foot to ragged hair. Fiona had never felt more bedraggled in all her days. She braced for another look of hatred, the same as she'd received from Myles's mother, but none came.

"You are Myles's new bride?" There was a chuckle in her voice, and the hint of a French accent.

Fiona nodded.

"You look dreadful. What a journey you've surely had." She reached out both hands to clasp Fiona's. "Blessed Mother, your hands are like ice. Come with me, we'll warm you up and clean you off. My nephew will have his hands full for a bit and won't miss you."

"Your nephew?"

The woman laughed. "Aye. Myles is my nephew, though we are nearly the same age. I'm Vivienne. Lady Marietta's youngest sister."

"You are his aunt?" Did she sound as addlepated as she felt?

Vivienne laughed again. "More like a cousin." She motioned to a servant, who instantly came her way. "Tell my sister that I'm seeing to our guest, but she should send for me if she needs me. And bring me word of my brother-in-law's condition."

The servant nodded and rushed away. All around them, others scurried to unharness the horses and linger over their greetings. This beauty seemed unfazed by any of it. She smiled at Fiona once more and started walking toward a small set of wooden steps leading to a tower. Fiona followed.

"Mother, shall I come too?" Darby asked, trotting along beside them.

"Yes, we'll set you to bathing in my chamber after we've gotten Lady Fiona settled."

Darby frowned. "I'm not so very dirty. I could wait another day or so."

She squeezed his shoulder. "Today, my pet. And you shall tell me all about your grand adventure."

*'Twas anything but grand*, Fiona thought, making her way behind them, but at least they had arrived and the traveling was behind her. And it seemed she was to have a real bath. Praise be to God. The last had been only partially cleansing, and the memory

of it made her lips tingle at the thought of her husband's kiss. She'd actually waited for him to return to her room. Wanted him to, even. But she'd come to her senses since then. 'Twas shameful what a simple kiss could do to a girl's emotions, and she'd be certain not to make that mistake again.

They made their way up a narrow turret stair, which opened into a spacious corridor. Elaborate tapestries and portraits covered the walls.

Darby chattered to his mother, and Fiona wondered at Vivienne's age, for certainly she could not be old enough to have a son of eleven.

"Here we are. This is your chamber," Vivienne said, pushing open a mammoth wooden door and stepping inside.

Fiona hesitated on the threshold, gazing in wonder, for the room was so fine she feared it a mirage and she might fall through the floor.

The walls were covered in paneled wood, with medallions of the Campbell crest adorning each corner of the fireplace. To one side was an enormous bed, the posts carved with intricate vines and berries and draped with red velvet curtains. Dozens of pillows rested at the head, and opposite the bed sat two cushioned chairs beneath a mullioned window, with a table in between. The fireplace burned, cozy and bright, though night had not yet fallen. Never had she seen so fine a chamber. She stepped inside, glad to discover the floor and room were real.

"Darby, scoot back to the kitchen, would you, love? And get our Fiona a tray of food. Eat something for yourself too, if you're hungry," Vivienne told him.

"I'm famished," he answered, clutching his belly.

She smiled and kissed him atop his messy hair. "Then eat, but hurry back with something for the lady."

"Yes, Mother." He smiled at Fiona and shot back out the door, quick as a mouse.

Vivienne looked after him, smiling.

"He's a wonderful boy," Fiona said, awkwardness overtaking her.

But Vivienne offered yet another smile, one warm and without guile. "Yes, he is. I'm lucky to have him."

"You must have been very young when he was born." She stepped farther into the room and lightly touched the velvet curtain. Her hand, with its soiled, broken nails and a pinky still tied to its neighbor with filthy cloth, looked like a hag's against the sumptuous fabric, and she snatched it back to hide behind her skirt.

"He was born of another, the product of my husband's rampant indiscretions. But when his mother died, we took him in, and he's been mine ever since."

"Then it's he that's fortunate."

Vivienne tipped her head, graciously accepting the compliment. "We were both fortunate, for soon after he came to live with me, his father met with a tragic death, though one I'm sure was not nearly as painful as he deserved."

A gasp of humor escaped Fiona at this woman's bold words, and she eyed her more carefully. Beyond the expensive clothing and sweet smile lay something more. A resilient will. She'd not turn her back on this one, nor cross her. In that instant, Fiona knew they were destined to become either the dearest of friends or the most violent of adversaries.


They laid his father on the bed, and Myles noticed his father was not so large as he'd always thought. Suddenly, the earl looked frail and mortal.

Myles's mother went to work cutting away her husband's tattered garments. "Send for the surgeon, Tavish. And the priest."

"Already done, Mari. They'll be on their way soon."

She nodded once and then gasped as she peeled away her husband's shirt and bandage, revealing the long, angry slash along his torso. "We need more light. Myles, bring the lamp. The rest of you, give us privacy. But send up water and fresh bandages."

"Aye, my lady," one of them said.

The men filed out silently as Myles grabbed a lamp and lit it with a stick from the fireplace. He set the lamp upon the table and helped his mother and uncle finish stripping away the last remnants of his father's clothing.

The bandages were red with seeped blood, and the earl's broken arm was bruised from well above his elbow all the way to his wrist. Even his hand looked swollen and discolored.

'Twas his sword arm that was broken. Losing it would be worse than death.

Father Darius arrived along with a servant bearing supplies, and soon after, the surgeon joined them too. They worked in unison, bathing and rebandaging the wounds. Myles's mother flinched each time his father made a sound.

At last, the surgeon wiped his hands on his apron. "The rest is up to God, my lady. I'll cauterize the wound on his side in the morning, but the arm will have to mend itself. His fever is low, but we must pray it doesn't rise. And that gash upon his head might cause some confusion when he awakens."

Marietta pursed her lips, her face pale in the warm room. "Open the windows. We should cool this chamber."

The surgeon nodded. "Let's try to get some broth into him as well. He'll need all his strength."

"I'll see to it," Tavish answered before Marietta even had a chance to ask.

113

She clenched his arm in gratitude. "You and Myles have taken good care of him, Tavish. He owes you his life, I should think."

"He's my brother," Tavish answered, as if that explained all.

She turned to Myles, eyes bright with fresh tears. "You've done well, Myles."

He thought to argue. To tell if he had not lost his bride, perhaps none of this would have come to pass. But he kept silent his tongue and merely nodded.

He turned from her and realized with a start it was not her opinion of him that rankled. No, it was Fiona he worried over. His mother was shrewd and not without her own faults, prejudice being one of them. She'd been against this marriage. He knew this, though she had not shared her reasons why. And if she thought any Sinclair had been involved in this attack, his wife would bear the brunt of her resentment. So it must be he who shared the details of their journey, not Tavish or any other. For his bride's sake, whether she be deserving or no, Myles would paint her in a better light than all the facts might lend to. His mother would make her own assumptions, but if he could pave an easier path for Fiona, he would.

# CHAPTER 15

Fiona soaked in the tub until the water cooled and her skin was wrinkled as a raisin. A maid had come, Ruby was her name, and she'd scrubbed Fiona's hair, and feet, and even her hands, taking gentle care of her broken finger. She'd bustled around, built up the fire, and finally toweled off Fiona, bundled her in a dry linen sheet, and now worked to comb the snarls from her hair.

"'Tis a pretty color, m'lady. But Lordie me, what knots ye've got. We'll get them out, though, don't ye worry. I've a skilled hand with hair. Now, Lady Vivienne takes no more than a brushing to make her hair shine. I need a few more tricks with Lady Marietta." Her cheeks flushed. "She's a fine-looking woman, though. Don't misunderstand."

"Most of us are not so blessed as Lady Vivienne." Fiona nodded. She'd not reprimand the maid for so small a slight against her mother-in-law, especially considering the welcome she'd received.

Ruby smiled, continuing with her monologue, which had begun the moment she'd entered the room and seemed in little danger of ending. No matter was too trivial or obscure, and though Fiona longed for peace and quiet, she knew the information could only help acclimate to her new surroundings. Though the girl's manner was nothing like her own Bess, somehow it soothed Fiona's aching heart.

"Robert is serving at court right now. He's three years younger than Lord Myles. A wicked scamp, that one. Could charm the feathers off a goose with just a wink. Then there's Alyssa. She's just turned fourteen."

"Alyssa?" Fiona asked, her eyes watering from a particularly harsh tug of the comb.

"Aye, she's the youngest. And a prettier little filly you never did see. Sweet as honey, too. You'll adore her."

Siblings? Fiona had never considered the idea that Myles had brothers or sisters. Even the fact that he had a loving mother was difficult enough to fathom, for back at Sinclair Hall, they'd often joked that Campbells were spawn and hatched from eggs. A foolish bit of childish humor, for certain, yet the thought they were a family just like her own gave her pause.

Homesickness washed over her, flooding her with a great longing to see Margaret's face. Or even John's. He'd betrayed her at the last, and yet she missed him still.

The maid prattled on, but Fiona drifted back to Sinclair Hall and a warm spring day when some lambs had just been born. Simon had brought one to the yard for her and Marg to pet and giggle over. They'd put the little thing on a lead and walked it round the orchard until their mother discovered them.

She'd scooped it up and took it away. "A lamb needs its momma," she'd said.

How right she was, for she was dead a week later, leaving her own children to fend for themselves against Hugh Sinclair.

Simon had fared well enough, for he'd been a lad of fifteen and already matched their father boast for boast. He was not bowled over by Hugh's unpredictable temper. But John had suffered enough for the lot of them. 'Twas not long after when Hugh boxed his ears and damaged his hearing, and forever after treated him more as a stranger than a son.

Tears welled in her eyes at the memory, but she brushed them away.

"Am I pulling too hard, m'lady?"

"No, Ruby. It's fine. But I'd like to dress and have you finish with my hair after."

"Yes, m'lady. But I'll have to go find your things. No one has brought your trunks yet."

Fiona stood up, pulling the linen towel more tightly around her middle. "I have no trunks. They were left by the wayside when Cedric and his group were attacked. Just give me my old dress. I'll don that."

Ruby's mouth formed a perfect circle. "Oh, no, m'lady. Ye canna wear that. 'Tis nothing but a filthy rag. I'll borrow ye a dress from Lady Vivienne."

"I'd just as soon wear my own dress."

Ruby's eyes flicked toward the fire.

Fiona looked to the flames and saw a scrap of brown muslin. "You threw my dress in the fire?"

"Lady Vivienne told me to." Her lips began to tremble.

Fiona's mind raced. Either Vivienne was kind and would indeed loan her a dress, or she'd just maliciously left her with nothing at all to wear.

"It's all right, Ruby. But could you go and find me something to put on?"

"Aye, m'lady. Perhaps you want to eat while you wait?" Ruby gestured to the tray Darby had brought soon after she'd gotten into the tub. It was laden high with delectable food. At least they did not intend to starve her.

Blissful silence fell after Ruby departed, but Fiona soon realized the chatter had been a helpful distraction. Left on her own, her thoughts raced hither and yon. She plucked some almonds from the tray and wandered about the room, picking up objects and peering out the window. She could see the inner ward from this chamber, but there was little activity there at the moment, for the hour had grown late.

Between the chairs and the fireplace was a small door. She opened it to find a storage room full of personal items. She stepped inside to look more closely. Cloaks of wool and velvet, embroidered jerkins, a doublet of brocade and ermine, and boots of various styles. But these were men's clothes! She turned, this way and that, looking around. Everything in the room suddenly took on certain masculinity. The maps lying on the table, the portrait hanging over the fireplace, and the massive size of the bed. Good Lord. This was Myles's chamber. But of course it was. Where else would she sleep?

The linen wrap she clutched around her suddenly felt transparent. But what was she to do? She had no clothes. She ran to the fireplace, hoping against hope she might pull that rag from the flames, but she was far too late. She sat down on the chair, deflated. Frustrated, she plucked a biscuit from the tray and looked around—for what, she was not sure.

The biscuit was good, and so she had another. Her stomach responded eagerly, and soon she was eating her meal.

And waiting.

'Twas a different affair altogether, waiting in this room, than it had been waiting at the inn. She wasn't bound to a lumpy mattress. She was fresh and clean and full. And sleepy. She finished her wine and looked to the satin-covered bed.

Night was full upon the castle now, and she heard voices rising and falling as Campbells strolled past her chamber door. Or rather, Myles's chamber door. And still, no Myles. No sign of or word from her husband. No clothes to wear either, for Ruby had not returned. Perhaps she was to languish here for all eternity. Perhaps that was the punishment befitting whatever crime that prisoner had accused her of. At least he'd served his own punishment, for he was dead the morning they left Inverness. She knew, for she'd seen Tavish dump his body in Loch Ness.

She could not be sorry for him, though. He'd murdered her Bess and six of the Campbells. She cared nothing for their souls, of course. But still, any such carnage saddened her, regardless of the target.

She drank another cup of wine, and drowsiness overtook her senses. The bed beckoned, but she'd not slide under those covers naked as a newborn. Instead, she went into the little room and hesitantly selected a shirt. It was soft, clean, and enormous, falling halfway down her shins. But it was superior to wearing nothing save a drying cloth. Then she took the top coverlet off the bed, wrapped it round herself, and lay down. Surely, Ruby would be back any moment with something more suitable.

Cedric's condition worsened. He thrashed about until they bound him to the bed for fear he'd do himself more harm. He mumbled and shouted and opened his eyes. But they were glassy with fever, and he knew none of them by name. Myles sat by his side, with his mother and Tavish. The priest was there, and the surgeon too. Eventually, Vivienne joined them, sitting next to Myles's mother and holding her hand. Through the night, they waited and prayed.

By dawn, his father was little better, sleeping in fits and starts, but at least the agitated mumbling of his dreams had stopped.

As sunlight brightened the room, Myles's mother turned weary eyes to him. "You should get some rest, darling. I'll send for you if anything changes."

"I'm fine, Mother. 'Tis you who needs to rest. I can stay a bit longer." He squeezed her shoulder.

But he was in sorry need of freshening up. At her further insistence, he relented and made his way to his chamber and some clean clothes. Wiping a hand across his tired eyes, he pushed open the door and stepped inside. Then he rubbed his eyes once more, for the sight upon his bed stopped him in his tracks.

Fiona, half wrapped in a coverlet, her head resting in a puddle of red curls, lay sound asleep upon his mattress. Why hadn't someone put her in a chamber of her own? His teeth ground together. 'Twas Vivi's ploy, no doubt. She was forever playing silly tricks. He ran a hand through his hair, cursing his aunt silently. He stepped lightly toward the bed. Lord Almighty, his wife was a sight, though, enough to stir a eunuch, with one slender leg stretched out from under the covers. If only she were truly as innocent and soft as she appeared. He wondered briefly why she'd not slipped under the bedcovers, but then again, everything about the troublesome wench was a mystery to him.

She turned then, rolling to her back, and he smiled. She was wearing his shirt, the sleepy temptress, and beneath the fine linen, her breasts, pink-tipped and impudent, taunted him like a prize. His body stirred. Christ, even in her sleep, she roused him.

He'd avoided her well enough while traveling those last two days, the task made easier by simply keeping the wench behind him. And thinking of his father. But here she was, snuggled in his bed. There'd be no avoiding her now. He shook his head, trying to dispel the vision of his wife's breasts and failing. He strode silently into his storeroom to gather fresh clothes. He'd not wake her up by bathing in here. Lord knew the last thing he needed was to strip naked while she reclined in his bed. In *his* bed! He'd not considered sharing a chamber. Lord, she'd be ever underfoot, touching his things, leaving her fragrance upon his pillows. Troublesome girl.

He grabbed at a shirt and doublet, and a few other items to complete his dressing, and moved back through his chamber toward the door. He did not spare her a glance, for all his thoughts were circling toward desire and she'd not welcome him, filthy as he was.

Stepping into the corridor, he nearly collided with Ruby.

"Oh, good morning, m'lord. I was just going to check on your wife."

Myles felt his face flush, as if the maid could see the lusty images he'd conjured in his mind. He looked back into the room to see Fiona still dozing, that slender ankle sticking out from the covers. He should pull her from his bed at once and send her to a room of her own, before she settled in further, like a tick under his skin. But the sunlight caught her red-gold hair, burnishing it like molten copper.

"Let her sleep, Ruby. Come back later and see to her needs then."

Ruby dropped low in a curtsy, a mistakenly knowing glint in her eye. She thought he'd exhausted his bride with good loving. Hah, hardly.

"Of course, m'lord. Is there anything I can do for you?"

"Yes. Set up a bath for me in Lord Robert's room."

"Very good, m'lord." She bobbed her head and turned away, humming as she went.

He looked at Fiona once more. Still asleep, lounging like a cat in a shaft of sunlight. He pulled the door closed.

Later.

Later, he'd remind her of her vow to love and obey him.

# CHAPTER 16

F IONA AWOKE AND STRETCHED, HEAD FOGGY FROM SO DEEP A slumber. The sun streamed in through the mullioned window, casting beams across the bed as she rubbed sleep from her eyes. The coverlet was twisted round, and she flushed to realize Myles's shirt was tangled up betwixt her legs. She pulled at it and looked around as if someone might see. And there was Ruby, chubby-cheeked and smiling.

"Good morning, m'lady. I thought ye'd never wake. I've been sitting here nigh on an hour."

Fiona pushed a tangle of curls away from her face and pulled herself into sitting. "Good morning, Ruby. What time is it?"

"Nearing midday. Are ye hungry?"

Fiona's stomach rumbled, but more from nerves than hunger, for lunch could well mean dining with her enemy in-laws. Meeting Myles's mother face-to-face was a frightful thought. The woman despised her. That much was obvious from yesterday. But Fiona had faced Cedric with her chin high. She'd do the same with this woman. But not while dressed in naught but her husband's shirt.

"Did you find me a gown?" She pushed out of the bed, about to put her feet on the wool rug.

Ruby sprang up. "Oh, wait, m'lady. Let me stoke the fire and warm the room."

What lavish treatment she'd received thus far. She must enjoy it while it lasted, for there was sure to be a reckoning soon, once Myles shared the story of their travels from Sinclair Hall to here.

"Thank you, Ruby. And about the dress?"

Ruby's cheeks went pink, and her eyes seemed to land on everything except Fiona.

"Yes, m'lady. About that. Well, ye see, Lord Cedric has taken a dip in his health. Seems he has a powerful fever raging, and my cousin—she works in the kitchen—she heard tell that Lady Marietta ordered him tied to the bed on account of all his thrashing about. So I can't ask Lady Vivienne, since she is with her sister, sitting vigil at the earl's bedside." Ruby made a hasty sign of the cross and bowed her head a moment before adding, "Likely that's where your husband was getting off to in such a rush too."

"My husband? When did you see him?"

"When he left yer room, m'lady. Just a few hours ago."

"He was here?" She clutched the coverlet up to her breasts, as if that might undo whatever he'd seen. He'd been there and made no attempt to awaken her. His persistence in pretending she did not exist pricked her pride. Not that she wanted his attentions, for surely she was better off when he left her alone. A sigh passed through her lips.

"What shall I do, Ruby? I cannot prance about Dempsey in some old shirt of my husband's."

A soft knock sounded on the door, and Ruby went to answer while Fiona tried to smooth her hair and cover herself. Never had she been less prepared for a visitor.

"Is she awake yet, Ruby? I've been waiting ever so long." The voice was soft and sweet, as was the visage that came with it. This must be Myles's sister—Fiona knew at once. The girl stepped inside with a tentative smile. Her light-brown hair was styled with intricate braids, and a white pleated cap sat atop her head. Her gown was bright yellow and made of the same quality satin as Marietta's and Vivienne's. The sleeves folded back with wide cuffs of turquoise, embroidered with gold thread. And in her arms she held another garment. This one of deep blue and lavender.

"Good morning. I'm Alyssa. Did you sleep well?"

Fiona was befuddled once more. Kindness at every turn. "Um, yes, I did. Thank you. But I've only just awoken. I must look a fright."

"You look fine. I'm sorry to burst in before you're ready to receive. But I must return to my father, and Vivi asked me to bring you this." She held out the gown, and Ruby quickly took it with a curtsy.

"Thank you, Lady Alyssa. We were just speaking of what to wear," the maid said, relief evident in her voice.

Alyssa walked closer to Fiona and held out both hands.

Uncertain, Fiona lifted her own hands slowly, until Myles's sister grasped them gently.

"I'm so glad you've come to live with us. I do hope you'll be happy here. We're sisters, now, you and I." She leaned over, kissing Fiona softly, first on one cheek and then the other. "I'm sorry I can't stay. I'm off to sit with my father. Ruby, let us know when Lady Fiona is dressed. Mother wants to meet her."

And with a flip of yellow satin, she was gone.

*Mother wants to meet her.* The words clanged like warning bells inside Fiona's mind.

Even if the prisoner had said nothing damning at all, her own actions condemned her, for she'd run away like a coward and put them all at risk. Surely, Lady Marietta would be aware of this and treat her accordingly.

Fiona straightened her shoulders and pushed up from the bed, pushing those fears away as well. She'd not tremble in front of her, even if she was Myles's mother. If anything, she should mock her for being married to such a man as Cedric Campbell, despoiler of women and lackey to the king. These past few days had worn Fiona down, softening her resolve, but now she was fed and rested and reminded that her purpose was to show them the strength born of every Sinclair. She was a warrior and they her enemy.

"Are ye feeling unwell, m'lady?" Ruby asked, shaking out the gown and frowning at Fiona's face.

"Yes, Ruby. Let's get me dressed quickly."

Fiona made fast work of her ablutions, and though she had not the luxury of a chemise or stockings, she let Ruby style her hair and secure the gown around her. Her feminine side called out to appreciate the silken beauty of it, for she'd never owned so fine a garment. The colors were rich, with tiny pearls and rubies sewn along the neckline in silver thread. It hugged tight to her body, for her figure was curvier than Vivienne's, and the skirt swished against her legs like a breeze.

She should spurn a dress bought with Campbell wealth. Her loyalties could not be swayed by petty things like a gorgeous dress. But she peered into the looking glass Ruby had pulled from the garderobe, and the reflection startled her. She'd never looked so lovely, with hair done up in the front with twists and tiny braids and the back cascading down in red-gold ringlets. And the gown! Oh, the gown. It was the height of fashion, and for the first time in her life, Fiona felt herself a woman grown, and not a reckless scamp of a girl. Curse their wealth and where it came from, yes. But she could not fault the garment.

When a maid came to say Lady Marietta was ready for her audience, Fiona was ready too. As ready as she'd ever be, at least.

Like a faithful Christian led to the lion's den, she walked with Ruby down the corridor until they came to another wide wooden door.

Ruby knocked, and a servant opened the door, prompt but silent, gaining them entrance.

Fiona took a breath and concentrated on blowing it out.

Lady Marietta's antechamber was decorated in pastel hues, with a broad tapestry covering one wall nearly from floor to ceiling. It depicted a garden scene, with a man and woman strolling together and tiny forest creatures all about them. Two large windows let in sunlight, which danced upon the floor. And underneath those windows sat her mother-in-law, in a chair so ornately carved it nearly looked alive.

She was resplendent in an emerald-green dress, with her dark hair pulled back under an elegant French hood covered in jewels. Her face was pale, and dark circles that had not been present yesterday now made her eyes seem even more unnerving. No smile lightened her expression.

Fiona suddenly felt tawdry in her borrowed gown. This was no pliant matron but instead an equal warrior, and one to be reckoned with.

She stepped closer to the chair and curtsied, though her legs trembled in a ridiculous manner. She was grateful they were hidden by her skirt.

Still no smile from the matron. "So, you are my son's wife." Her French accent was more pronounced than Vivienne's.

"Yes, my lady."

Marietta's eyes traveled over her, slow as melting ice and equally as cold. "You look better when not wearing half the road upon your face."

'Twas no compliment, really. Nor much of an insult. "Thank you, my lady."

Her mother-in-law perused her another moment, then gestured for Fiona to sit in the other chair, one much less regal, with shorter legs so that the occupant must look up to meet Marietta's gaze. Or more importantly, so that Myles's mother could look down. That was a clever trick, and though it put Fiona at a distinct disadvantage, she silently commended her opponent's tactics.

When Marietta spoke, her voice was soft, but laced with strength. "It should come as no surprise I was against this marriage. I still am, but what's done is done. One doesn't argue with the king, nor with my husband. But you must understand my son's happiness is of paramount importance to me. He could have made a grand match, one that would have brought him great joy. He could have married someone French, but for James's whim, Myles is instead married to you."

Fiona felt her palms prickle with perspiration. She'd escaped twenty clansmen with more courage than she now felt. But she straightened in her chair. She'd not be intimidated, not by any Campbell. Even a woman such as this who would know how to wound the emotions and yet leave no mark.

The lady continued. "Myles has told me of your escapades, your attempt at escape. Now you must tell me with your own words. Why did you run? What was your intention?"

Fiona swallowed, her throat dry as week-old bread. "I ran to free myself. I thought to make my way toward Moray Firth and find a way home from there." She'd not mention her plan to land at Glamis Castle, where her Douglas cousins lived. No sense implicating them in something in which they had no hand.

"I see. And what would you have done once you arrived back at Sinclair Hall?"

Fiona felt heat infusing pink into her cheeks. "I had not thought that far ahead. 'Twas an ill-conceived plan. Doomed to fail."

"'Tis wise you see that now. Does that mean you will not try a second escape?"

"I will not, my lady. I promised your son I would stay put."

"My son doesn't believe you."

Fiona offered a small shrug. "I cannot change his thoughts on the matter. He must choose to trust me or not. It makes no difference to me what he thinks."

Marietta's lips puckered into a frown, and Fiona knew she'd insulted Myles with her disregard and tried to make amends.

"It cannot be a secret I had no wish for this marriage either, my lady. No disrespect to you, I know our betrothal was formed during a time of friendship, but considering all that has passed between our clans, it's foolish to think your son and I would make a great match. As you said, this was the king's whim. James should have known better."

A tiny gasp of amused disbelief escaped Marietta's lips. "You will not last a day at court, girl, with words such as that. You must learn to tread more carefully."

"I do not imagine I'll spend much time at court."

Marietta tilted her head. "James has magnificent plans for my son, in spite of this detour in the path. You may be certain you will spend some time at court. So I suggest you rein in that unpredictable nature, or you'll be tucked away in a hamlet somewhere with nothing but servants to entertain you."

A tapping sounded on the door, and the maid quickly answered. Vivienne entered, smiling at first her sister, then Fiona.

"Ah, Mari, I see you've met the bride."

"Yes." Marietta's tone was neutral, betraying nothing.

Vivienne sank down into a third chair next to Myles's mother, graceful as a wave upon the shore, and winked at Fiona. "And having a lovely time of it, no doubt. My, Fiona! How fine that dress looks on you. Consider it yours."

"Thank you, my lady. It seems my other dress fell into the fire."

Vivienne laughed. "It didn't fall. It was pushed. We cannot have Myles's wife gallivanting around in rags, even if she is as naughty as a thief."

Fiona's cheeks burned once more. Vivienne was either gracious or mischievous. Or somehow both. "I fear my own clothes were lost during our travels. I have nothing."

"Oh, well, we'll see to that, then, won't we, Mari?"

Marietta gave a small, stiff nod. "Of course."

"I'll have the seamstress come to your room straightaway. What splendid amusement, to plan a new wardrobe."

A thrill of anticipation thrummed through Fiona, but she tried to shoo it away. It would indeed be a splendid amusement, but one more thing to distance her from her own family and her resolve to remain separate in every way from this new clan.

The door swung open just then, pushed by a hand from the other side, and Myles stepped into the chamber. He ducked his head under the frame and seemed to fill the doorway.

Fiona felt his presence like a burst of warm air, her lungs squeezed by some unseen hand robbing her of breath.

The last time she'd seen him, he'd been covered from head to heel with dirt and blood. Even on the day of their wedding, he'd been four days in the saddle, dusty from the road, with hair unkempt and clothes made for travel. But now he was fresh and clean, looking like a royal emissary in a jerkin of rich brown, trimmed with ermine. She wondered how the hue might affect the shade of his eyes. But he never looked her way. Instead, he walked straightaway to his mother. Once again, it seemed she was dismissed without even being seen.

# CHAPTER 17

H IS MOTHER SAT IN FRONT OF THE WINDOW, THE MUTED sunlight from the window making her a silhouette so he could not see her face.

"Forgive my interruption, Mother," he said, crossing the room swiftly and giving her a fast kiss on the cheek, "but Father is awake. He's asking for—"

His words faded away like the smoke of an extinguished candle, for in the chair opposite his mother sat Fiona. But not the one he'd known, with the mud and the wild hair. Or even Fiona from the chapel steps wearing a threadbare gown years past its prime. This Fiona was magnificent in a bejeweled gown of satin, with her hair fashionably styled and her face free of grime. He stole a quick glance at the hands resting in her lap, checking for an emerald ring and a bandaged finger, just to be certain it was indeed her.

It was.

He stuttered a moment, for she'd caught him wholly unawares. "Uh…you, Mother. Father is asking for you."

His mother rose at once, murmured something to Vivienne, and then moved toward the door. "You'll excuse me, Fiona. Vivi will look after you today. Myles, are you coming?"

Myles looked to his bride. She was lovely, he must admit to that. And what man would not be befuddled by cleavage such as hers? But now was not the time to ponder such a question, for his father waited. He gave Fiona a nod and could have sworn he saw a hopefulness in her face, but it was gone as fast as it had come, and she quickly looked to the floor.

He hesitated, for he owed her a greeting and was not so swayed that he could not carry on a simple conversation.

"Are you faring well, my lady?" His voice scratched a bit in his throat, and he coughed to clear it.

She didn't look at him again, only lifted that stubborn chin of hers. "Well enough, my lord."

Damn the girl. Only she could make so simple a phrase smack of insult. You could scrub her clean and polish her up, but she still hissed like Fiona Sinclair.

He turned to his aunt. "Vivi, see that Lady Fiona's things are moved to her own chamber."

Vivi smiled, humor curling in her voice. "To which things do you refer, Myles? All she has is my dress and your fine Campbell name."

Christ. He hadn't thought of that. The girl's trunks were abandoned, left by the road to make room for his father in the cart. He scowled at Vivi. She was enjoying his discomfiture far too much. That one needed a husband of her own to torment. He held his voice steady. "Will you see to it that she gets some *things* and then keeps them in her own room?"

"There is no other room. But I shall be most pleased to obtain for her all the items a lady needs," Vivienne answered.

'Twas obvious his aunt meant to make a plaything of his irritation. Ignoring her was his best plan. He stepped closer to Fiona.

"My father's health is precarious," he said to his wife, "and I must see to his needs. Vivi will help you settle in. You understand, of course."

"Of course."

He paused. There was more he thought to say, and so much more he needed to ask, but his mother was out the door and halfway to his father by now. Fiona would have to wait.

He turned and strode toward the door, calling over his shoulder, "Behave yourself, Vivi."

"I mean only to help, Myles," she called after him.

He snorted as he stepped from the room. His aunt was as duplicitous as his bride. He could fight two men at once on the battlefield and be certain of his victory. Defeating two women was another thing entirely.

Entering the antechamber with his mother, Myles crossed himself and whispered a prayer. God willing, his father would be hale and hearty again soon, but for now, he'd settle for having him awake and lucid.

The room was full, with both the surgeon and priest in attendance, along with Tavish and a handful of servants.

"He's been asking for you, Marietta," Tavish said, meeting them at the threshold of the door. "I told him you'd be right along."

She nodded and crossed the room in a rustle of satin, sitting gingerly upon the bed. She pulled Cedric's hand into her own and kissed his fingertips.

His eyes opened at the touch, and the faintest of smiles graced his lips.

"Mari," he said in a voice so faint it was nearly swallowed by the room.

Myles watched his mother lean closer toward the earl. "How are you feeling?"

He sighed and closed his eyes once more. "Like the horse rode me."

Mild relief tapped Myles upon the shoulder. His father had maintained his sense of humor, though he must be in the gravest of pain. "What happened?" Cedric whispered.

Myles stepped closer and sat down in the chair near the bed. "There was an ambush, Father. A few miles north of Inverness. Do you remember?"

Cedric's face twitched, as if drawing up the memory inflicted more pain. His eyes opened once more. "I remember leaving Sinclair Hall. And the girl running. Did you find her?"

"Aye, we did. She is here at Dempsey."

His father drew in a long, rattling breath and eased it out, coughing a bit.

"Get him some water, please, Tavish," Marietta said. "Cedric, you mustn't trouble yourself about the girl."

Myles prompted gently, "Father, do you remember anything about the attack? Few of them escaped and only one captive lived, though he was useless for confession."

His father's eyes floated shut once more. "My arm's a little sore," he murmured, and drifted back to sleep.

Myles saw his mother dash a tear from her cheek. He squeezed her forearm just above where her hands clasped his father's. "He'll be fine, Mother."

She nodded, dabbing at a second tear, and rose from the bed. "Father Darius, I wonder if you might join me in the chapel. I should like to pray while my husband rests."

"Of course, my lady. Let me escort you."

She took his arm, and they left the chamber. Myles stood and joined Tavish near the fireplace.

"We cannot wait for his memory to return, Tavish. Even if it does, it seems there will be little he can tell us."

"Aye, it would save us a world of speculating if he'd recognized one of them, but I doubt he can add to what we already know."

"Which is nearly nothing. And we cannot wait for answers to come to us. The time to act is now." He was laird while his father was incapacitated, and he must think like the leader of the Campbells. 'Twas a heavy burden, but one he'd trained for all his life. "The king must be informed. Choose your men and ride to Stirling at first light."

He nodded. "My pleasure. Lord knows it's better than sitting here on my arse while my brother sleeps and our enemy plans another attack."

Myles smiled. "Or you could stay here and pray with my mother."

A rolling snort came from his uncle. "Prayer is for women and old men, lad. God put a sword in my hand for a reason. He knows I do my praying on the battlefield."

# CHAPTER 18

FIONA STOOD UPON A STOOL IN A BORROWED CHEMISE, HER arms stretched out on either side. Vivienne was there, and Ruby too, along with the seamstress. Bolts of fabric were strewn all about the place, with trims and ribbons and strips of ermine and fox scattered over the bed, as if a milliner's shop had suffered a windstorm in this very spot. And if indeed a windstorm could be captured and possessed, it would dwell inside Vivienne.

She was a dervish, twirling the sumptuous cloths around Fiona, giggling with delight over suggestions made by the seamstress.

"I think the gold, with a burgundy kirtle beneath, don't you agree? Your hair will look stunning next to the gold." Vivienne's smooth cheeks were pinked by enthusiasm.

"Oh, so lovely," Ruby breathed, pressing both hands against her own ruddy cheeks.

"And you've a fine figure." The seamstress nodded.

Fiona was breathless from the gluttony of it. So many silks and satins and brocades. There were velvets and linens and furs. Vivienne insisted she needed a dress for every event. Gowns for riding, for walking, for morning and afternoon. And of course, there were the gowns for special occasions, such as visits with the other nobility, and even the king.

"Surely I'll not be meeting the king," Fiona protested.

Vivienne's finely arched browed furrowed. "But of course you will. One day soon, we'll visit Linlithgow or Falkland Palace. You'll meet him then."

Fiona felt blood pooling to her feet, leaving her woozy at the thought of being face-to-face with that ruthless sovereign. What words might she spit in his face if given the chance? But just as quickly, Marietta's words of warning sounded in her memory. *Rein in that unpredictable nature.*

*That* was as unlikely as the possibility of Fiona ever being allowed within earshot of Scotland's ruler. Vivienne was misguided in her optimism.

"I think we've chosen enough dresses. As it is, I cannot imagine wearing them all," Fiona said.

Vivienne looked over the piles of fabric. "These aren't so very many. But fine, if you grow weary, we need only choose your bedclothes and we'll be finished." She picked up a bolt of white linen so sheer it looked like frost upon a windowpane. "This should do nicely. Take off that chemise and let's see it against your skin."

Fiona blanched. She'd do no such thing. Take off her chemise, indeed. She clutched it close to her chest.

Vivienne laughed at her modesty. "Oh, come now. We're all women here. We've got the same bits as you."

"Aye, though mine have sunk a good deal lower," added the seamstress, chuckling.

"Mine are a good deal more plump," Ruby giggled. "But my husband loves a fine cushion."

The others laughed, while Fiona felt her cheeks grow hot. In fact, she felt hot all over. The idea of Myles thinking anything of the like was embarrassing. She should shoo Vivienne and

Ruby from the room and choose the most opaque fabric of the lot. Perhaps a somber gray to dissuade her husband's interest. Although his interest seemed to have dissipated through no effort of her own.

"Oh, girls, we've made our maiden bride blush," Vivienne teased, which only infused more heat into Fiona's tingling skin.

"I don't need any such impractical nightgowns. Just something serviceable."

Vivienne's laughter filled the air, with Ruby and the seamstress's quick to follow. "Serviceable? That sounds as enticing as a case of the pox. Of course you need something impractical. A flimsy little something, thin as a spider's web that tears away just as easily."

Ruby and the seamstress both nodded emphatically.

Fiona gripped the chemise more tightly. "Tears away? What good is a shift such as that?"

Vivienne doubled over in her laughter. "My goodness, what a lot my nephew has to teach you. Are you a virgin, still?"

*What a rude, invasive question.* Fiona scowled. "I assure you, I am quite thoroughly married."

"Then shame on Myles if he's left you to wonder about the joy of *impractical* nightgowns. Although, you have been traveling, and you can't do much rending of things when you're on the road. And I suppose last night he sat vigil with his father, but once Cedric is on the mend and Myles is not so distracted, I do hope you obtain a different view on the matter."

This was quite enough. Vivienne had proven kind, but this went far and beyond any business of hers. Fiona would not stand there, naked before them, while the seamstress draped her in fabric so sheer that mist from the loch would serve as better cover.

Vivienne smiled again. "Oh, Fiona. I don't mean to tease. You're so beautiful you could be clad in sackcloth and he'd want you still. I saw the way he looked at you this morning. But there's no shame in adding a little sweetness to the pot, is there?"

Fiona's mind turned to fuzz. The way he'd looked at her this morning? She'd averted her gaze when he'd come into the room, and when she'd finally met his eyes, he'd looked nothing save annoyed. Vivienne was making sport of her once more.

"He looked at me in no such manner. And I wouldn't want him to." Avoiding his attentions was her goal, not beckoning them.

Vivienne crossed one arm over the other. She raised one fisted hand and rested her chin upon it as she perused Fiona. After a moment, she said, "Can you best him with a sword?"

"What?"

"On the field or in the yard, could you beat him with a sword?"

*What riddle is this?* "No, of course not. He's far too strong."

"Could you outdrink him? Until he's passed out on the rushes?"

Fiona felt the tremors of a smile tapping at her lips. "'Tis unlikely."

"Mm-hm." Vivienne began to pace in the small space in front of Fiona. "And what of strategy? 'Tis clear you cannot evade him in the woods. But could you outwit him in a game of chess, perhaps?"

Chess had never been Fiona's forte. She was ever too impatient to master its nuances. "I fail to see what chess has to do with my choice of nightdress."

"This is your battleground, Fiona." Vivienne's hands swept round the room and ended by pointing at the bed. Myles's bed. "This is where you best him. This is where you sway him to obey your whims. If you hope to ever take an upper hand with Myles, this is where that begins. Make him want you, and soon enough, he'll jump to do your bidding at every turn."

Fiona crossed her own arms. "You mean seduce him to obtain what I want?"

"Exactly."

"But what if what I want is for him to leave me alone?"

Vivienne's eyes narrowed. "You want more than that. I'm certain of it. And to win the war, you must start with tiny victories. Remember, men are like their horses."

"Big and sweaty and fun to ride?" Ruby chimed in.

Vivienne smiled at the maid. "Yes. But in addition to that, they are drawn to whomever dangles the most enticing carrot."

Fiona frowned. "Didn't you say your husband was faithless?"

Vivienne's shrug was nonchalant. "Yes, but my husband was an idiot, and I had long since put away my carrots. Myles is another type of man altogether. And he wants you, Fiona. I saw it in his eyes. Use that, and you'll both be better off."

This put a wrinkle in her plans. Seduction. The very thought of it panicked her. She had no comely wiles to trap a man. She had nothing but a sharp tongue and a tenacious disregard for his family. She'd never trick him into compliance, no matter how diaphanous the gown. And even if she could, what good would it do her? She had sealed the truce. She was here. All she wanted now was to keep her family safe and for him to let her be.

"Take the pretty nightgowns, Fiona," Vivienne said softly. "Leave them in a chest, if you've a mind to, but some evening, you may have need to put one on. When you're ready, they'll be waiting."

Lord, the woman could tempt a sinner into church the way she prodded. Those Campbell traits of persuasion and persistence must have rubbed off.

"Fine," Fiona said at last. "But I only need one cut from that transparent bit of nothingness. Make the rest of sturdy linen."

"Make her three of the sheer," Vivienne instructed the seamstress. "And two of the linen. And add some ribbons and pearls."

Fiona looked to the ceiling and shook her head. "'Tis another frivolous waste. Pearls, indeed."

"Hush up, Fiona. By God, you are unruly." The words might scold but for the laughter in her voice. "My nephew deserves such a wife as you."

Fiona flushed once more, heady from the statement though not sure why. "Unruly?"

"Aye. One who will put him through his paces. Thank God he did not marry that simpering Odette."

A dizzy sort of tremble ran through her. "Odette?"

The seamstress and Ruby began unrolling the sheer material, though Fiona kept her chemise firmly in place.

"Aye. She had her hooks sunk deep, but marriage to her would have bored my nephew silly. Pouty little French thing. She'd never last a winter. She'd drop over dead as sure as the king's first wife."

"Were they betrothed? Myles and Odette?"

Vivienne shook her head and stepped closer to push up the hem of Fiona's shift.

Distracted as she was by the thought of some woman in love with her husband, Fiona raised her arms and soon was stripped bare. Ruby winked at the seamstress, and they spun the pale-white linen around her torso.

Stepping back, Vivienne answered, "They were not formally betrothed, for Myles has always been betrothed to you. Since the day you were born. He meant to seek James's permission, though. Of course, Cedric would have none of that."

"Why?"

For the first time since they'd met, Vivienne fell silent. She looked away and fumbled with some ribbon. After a moment, she shrugged and turned back to Fiona with the brightest of smiles. "Oh, who knows why men do any of the things they do?" She took one step farther back and tilted her dark, glossy head. "Oh, my Fiona. You are a temptress. If I were a man, I'd bed you myself."

Fiona's gasp of surprise quickly turned to laughter. And soon the four of them were giggling like a gaggle of geese.

Outside his chamber door, Myles halted, his hand poised to knock. He quickly admonished himself. 'Twas his room after all. He should not have to announce his entrance. And so he grasped the latch, about to lift it and push his way in, until a sound came through the wood. A sound that stopped him like the edge of a cliff and triggered a ripple of surprise.

Laughter.

Feminine laughter coming from *his* bedchamber. What in heaven's name where they doing in there, chortling like fishwives?

He listened for a moment, his ear pressed to the door like a snooping dowager, but he could not hear their words. Only more giggles. The sound pricked at him, to know his wife was in there, sharing her good humor with others, while all he got from her was frowns.

He pushed the door open with more force than necessary, and it thumped against the wall with a bang.

The women's laughter stopped abruptly, and his wife let out an ungracious squawk before leaping from a stool to crouch beside the bed. A cloud of white fabric puddled in her wake, and her reaction to his entrance set the other women to guffawing once more.

He stepped inside, annoyed as much from their presence as by their laughter. Women did not typically irritate him, but he was exhausted and not interested in their silly antics. Nor was Fiona, it appeared. She wasn't laughing either. Instead, she peeked from the edge of the bed, just high enough that he could see her face and her bare shoulders. So, the lass was naked, was she? His irritation decreased by the smallest degree.

"Don't you knock?" she demanded.

"'Tis my room," he tossed back, and crossed to a table where a tray rested, the remnants of her lunch, no doubt. He picked up a glass and emptied the wine inside.

"But I'm not dressed!"

He tipped his head, as if to get a better look. "I can see that."

Her face went crimson, and she scuttled back closer toward the wall. She looked to the maid. "Ruby, give me my dress."

Myles relinquished the cup and cleared his throat. Half his work was done if the girl had on no clothes, for he'd come to find her with every intention of enjoying his marital rights. "Ruby, that won't be necessary. Ladies, clear your things. This room is far too crowded for my liking."

"Myles." Vivienne took a step in his direction.

But he shook his head, not taking his eyes from Fiona. "Thank you for your attentions toward my wife, Vivi, but you've done quite enough. Leave us."

Vivienne cast a glance at Fiona and started to speak, but Myles cut her off.

"Now," he said.

The women jumped to action, scurrying like mice to scoop up the fabric and trims and baubles strewn across his bed. He bit back a smile. With one simple request, they did as he asked. No arguing, no defiance. Just calm obedience. 'Twas good for Fiona to see that. Perhaps it might teach his bride a thing or two about proper respect.

Ruby picked up a bit of tan linen from the floor and moved closer to the bed, letting it slide from her hands into Fiona's.

Well. So much for respect.

Fiona pulled the garment over her head. It appeared to be nothing more than a shift. That should not slow him down by much.

It took only moments for the others to gather their items and leave the room. Vivienne was the last to exit. She paused at the door.

"Remember, Myles, if you crush a flower, it cannot be undone," she whispered.

He looked to her and saw something vulnerable in her gaze and wondered at her words. But she was gone before he could ask.

And then his wife stood up, turning all his thoughts her way.

She was indeed clad in nothing but a shift, her arms crossed over her breasts like an impenetrable shield, her cheeks and throat flushed pink. "I should very much like to get dressed."

He paused, letting his eyes take a brief journey over her curves. "And I should very much like to take you to bed."

She took a step back. "But…it's the middle of the day."

He chuckled. Women were so illogical. As if the time of day had any bearing on desire. In afternoon light such as this, he'd be able to see her face and her body. He could watch the red-gold strands of her hair glimmer and watch her skin flush beneath his touch.

His mouth went dry as his palms went moist. Yes, it was the middle of the day, and never so fine a moment to be her husband.

He would enjoy this, taking his time and savoring her like a fine meal, for her body was a banquet to be lingered over. His own body responded, tightening in arousal and realization. This was how he'd tame her. By teaching her of all the pleasures he could bring.

Perhaps he'd not taken enough time with her that first night. Virgins were a different breed altogether, and he should have considered that. But now the barrier had been breached, and there was nothing denying her of satisfaction, save her own stubborn will.

He took a step closer. "It *is* the middle of the day. And you should be well rested, for I watched you snoring on my bed 'til the sun was high in the sky."

"You watched me?"

"Briefly." He hadn't really, but no sense telling her that. Let her mind stir with the implications instead.

She crossed her arms more snugly. Her pert chin tilted upward. "I don't snore."

He walked closer still. She took a step back, and another, until she bumped up against the wall. His hands went out on either side, corralling her inside his arms but not touching. She looked up, her frown ferocious as a kitten's, and his need to taste those lips doubled.

He leaned forward, staring at her mouth. "You needn't be embarrassed," he said softly. "'Twas a very ladylike snore. More of a…huffing sort of breath."

Her lips tightened, until she said, "I don't huff either."

He smiled, all his agitation upon entering this room now gone. A pale, delicate vein ran up the column of her throat. He wanted to trace his tongue along it, and would. Soon. "I'd say you're huffing a bit right now."

And indeed she was, with short puffs of breath. Her breasts swelled and retreated against her arms. His eyes drifted lower, watching. Lord, she was a prize worth earning.

She was rattled by his nearness, but not afraid, and the realization thrilled him. He plucked at the loose tie adorning the neckline of her shift. She looked to the ground, but he caught her chin with the fingers of his other hand and brought her face to his once more. "Are we back to this again? The reluctant maiden? You kissed me eagerly enough at the inn."

Her eyes went round and dark, and she smacked his hand away. "'Twas the bath I was eager for, not you."

He smiled, knowing how a hawk must feel when swooping down to catch its prey. "Ah, Fiona. More lies?"

"'Tis the truth. I want nothing at all to do with you."

He cupped her chin once more and whispered against her lips, "Prove it, then. Resist me."

Vivienne's words stampeded through her mind as Myles's lips pressed soft against her own. *Make him want you.* But every ounce of her common sense railed against those traitorous words.

Vivienne was wrong.

Of course Fiona must resist. She was a Sinclair.

She pushed against his chest with all her might and broke the kiss. "Did Odette resist you?"

His face blanked, then suffused with color. His hands dropped to his sides like anvils. "What do you know of Odette?"

Fiona turned away. At last, a chink in his armor. "I know you wanted to marry her. And the king refused. 'Tis tragic, really, that you should be torn from the one you love and left with me instead. I must be a pale imitation."

His dark brows pinched together. "Odette is none of your business."

"Oh, but she is. Didn't you promise God and the priest to love me, and me alone? For all the lies you accuse me of, it seems you've told a few of your own."

She was aiming in the dark with blunt arrows and no clear target. But she thought only to distract him from his original purpose. Anything to change the course of his mood so he might leave her alone. After all, what should she care if some foolish little French girl had designs on him?

"I've told no lies, nor made any false promises. I will honor you with the same dedication in which you honor me." He strode back to the tray upon the table, picking up the cup and tipping it to his lips. He tapped it to get the last drips of wine. Then he plunked it down again.

She'd made him angry. Good. She knew better how to deal with him when he was angry. It was his gentleness against which she had no weapon. When his voice rose and his face turned red, she could answer with her own fierce temper. But when he was kind, that was when she felt the worst sort of fear.

He ran a hand through his hair and turned back to her. He started to speak, then halted, as if the words would not form. His sword hand clenched and unclenched. At last, he spoke, his voice far more somber than she'd expected. "Fiona, I'd appreciate it if you would not mention Odette again. I did care for her. But she is forever lost to me. Now it's up to you and I to make our marriage real. I'll be a good husband to you, if you can give but an inch."

'Twas an odd method to trick her into bed, telling her he cared for another woman. She thought to say as much, but saved her words. For in his eyes passed a shadow, new to their depths. Or perhaps she'd only failed to notice it before. Either way, she didn't understand it, and what good would it do her, even if she did?

Once more, he proved himself less her enemy and more a shared accomplice to this farce of a marriage. Even while declaring his lack of trust in every word she'd spoken, he was asking for her cooperation. Not demanding it or forcing it. But simply… asking.

What fragile stuff her Sinclair loyalty turned out to be, for she heard herself saying, "I suppose I could try."

His shoulders rose and fell, Atlas shrugging off the mantle of the earth. "It's all I ask. Just try. Now, would you walk over here and kiss me?"

'Twas another request, not a demand. But even so, it was too much. Too much surrender. Too many steps between them. Too fraught with consequence.

She shook her head. "No."

That shadow passed by once more, and she could see him carefully choosing his next words. "I thought to come in here and bed you so well you'd never resist me again. But now it seems I want that resistance gone of your own accord. I want you to ask for my kisses, Fiona. And when you do, you shall have a thousand of them."

His words crackled like kindling. But she could not ask, and she never would. She was a weak and feeble foe, less a Sinclair than ever she'd dreamed imaginable. If she gave in to him, he'd absorb every last bit of her until she was no more. Her mother's murder would go unavenged, forgotten in the winds of time, and her father would haunt her from the grave for her feminine weakness. "I will never ask."

He picked up the weight of the world once more. "Then this marriage will be a bitter one."

They stared at each other, neither moving forward nor away, until an urgent rapping at the door broke the trance.

"My lord," a voice called through the wood. "My lord Myles, your father is awake and bids you come at once."

Myles took a few short steps and pulled open the door.

A freckled servant with cap in hand stood in the corridor, bobbing his head. "Oh, good. There you are, Lord Myles. Our laird has awakened and bid me to come find you with all haste. He says he must speak with you."

Myles turned to her. "It seems our conversation must wait."

"I believe our conversation has already ended."

His jaw set. She could see she'd frustrated him once more. But it could not be helped. He kept accusing her of duplicity when all she did was tell the truth. She'd never ask for his kisses, not even if they lived to be one hundred.

Though, deep within, she knew if he pressed his suit, she'd not deny him either.

# CHAPTER 19

WELCOME TO DEMPSEY, MY LADY," SAID THE YELLOW-haired priest. "I'm Father Darius. I've come to escort you to dinner. Lord Myles regrets he cannot do so himself, but I'm afraid the earl's fever has returned."

Fiona didn't like priests. Father Bettney from Sinclair Hall had the disposition of a badger and always made her skin crawl as if ants were upon it. But this one seemed pleasant enough, with pale freckles and an earnest manner. He smiled and offered his arm.

She had little choice but to take it. She could not spend the rest of her days lingering in this bedchamber. And truth be told, as unappealing as dining with dozens upon dozens of Campbells would be, she was getting restless. She'd spent the afternoon alone after Myles left. She thought briefly to venture out on her own, but decided against it when she heard men's voices streaming in from the courtyard.

"Thank you, Father. Will my husband be joining us for dinner?"

"I don't believe so. He and his mother are sitting with the earl. But I'll keep you company. And Lady Vivienne and Lady

Alyssa will join us too. You can tell us all about your life at Sinclair Hall."

As they walked along the corridor, passing a dozen Campbell portraits, Father Darius told her bits about each ancestor. Their history was rich, and Fiona had not realized how entwined their clan was with the Stewart monarchy. At last turning a corner, they came upon a narrow staircase, leading down and ending with a door.

The priest paused. "Are you ready to meet the rest of your new kin?"

No, she was not. Though she'd met a handful of Campbells, and most had been cordial, who knew what the rest might be like? Beyond this door would be the knights she'd put at risk, and their resentful wives. Or worse than that, the widows she'd helped create. But Vivienne would be there, and though Fiona was still not certain of the woman's motivations, at least she'd sit by her and not leave her to the wolves. And perhaps Darby would be there as well. That notion brightened her mood, for she missed her little champion.

Fiona nodded once. "Yes, Father."

"That's a good lass. I'm sure you'll find a most gracious welcome. Though, keep in mind, they are worried for their laird. Tensions are running a bit high, and the mood is somber."

He pulled open the door, and she stepped through into the most magnificent hall imaginable. It was huge, with blue-and-green banners bearing the Campbell crest hanging from every truss. At the far end of the hall hung another flag, larger than any of the others and displayed in the place of greatest honor. It was embroidered with the king's emblem—a crowned lion and a unicorn—for Dempsey was a Stewart holding, with Cedric Campbell serving as master of the royal household.

Underneath that magnificent flag was a raised dais, where the family would sit to dine, and throughout the hall were other tables, each covered in crisp white cloth and laden with silver plates and platters of food. Musicians sat behind a screen, playing loudly enough to be heard but not so much as to be disruptive, while servants moved about, efficient in their tasks.

Fiona marveled at the scene. 'Twas so unlike the hall at home, where everything had a dingy pallor and a rustic feel. Exiled to the far north by the king as the Sinclairs had been, she'd known little in the way of creature comforts. And once her mother was gone, Hugh Sinclair's only focus had been training his sons for revenge, not nurturing his daughters or providing a welcome hearth and home.

One could get used to being a Campbell if this was how they lived. Her mouth watered as the smell of pheasant and roasted boar wafted past, but she twitched her nose against it. 'Twas seduction of another sort. The fine dresses and the food and the big downy beds. And the kisses. All of this mingled into a potion meant to make her forget who she was. She'd eat the food, yes. And she'd enjoy it, too. But no delicious meal or velvet gown would bring her mother back. 'Twas Cedric Campbell who'd thrust her family into such dire straits, first by pitting the king against them and then by ripping her mother from this earth. She'd do well to remind herself of that.

Father Darius led her to the dais, where, as she'd suspected, Vivienne awaited with a ready smile. Darby was next to her, his unruly hair combed smooth.

"How was your afternoon, Fiona?" Vivienne asked, raising one inquisitive brow.

Judging from Vivienne's expression, the woman assumed she'd spent some time in Myles's arms. Fiona could not halt the heated blush.

"Fine," she mumbled.

"Any revelations about…proper fabric and such?"

Fiona cast a glance at the priest, but he seemed more interested in surveying the hall. Looking back to Vivienne, she answered, "None whatsoever."

"Ah, more's the pity."

Fiona took her seat, and soon Alyssa joined them, looking pale and weary.

Darius helped her to a chair. "How fares your father, child?" he asked.

"Still the same. The fever lingers, though the surgeon poured boiling oil over his injuries before applying the hot irons. He fears infection."

The puddle of tears in the young girl's eyes squeezed Fiona's heart. How very much like her own sister she was, sweet and shy and fragile. Though a Campbell, Fiona knew she would never hold this girl accountable for the sins of her father.

Vivienne reached over and caressed Alyssa's arm. "He's strong as an ox, sweeting. He'll be well before you know it."

Alyssa nodded, but the tears spilled out. "Mother would not let me stay. But I've as much right to sit with him as anyone."

"Of course you do. She thinks only to protect you. It isn't good for you to see him when he's not himself. But after dinner, we'll go to chapel, you and I, and we'll pray for him. Yes?" She tapped her hand against Alyssa's.

The girl nodded again and offered a tremulous smile at her aunt. "Thank you, Vivi. I should like that very much."

Vivienne turned to Fiona. "Of course, you are welcome to join us as well, if you've a mind to."

Sit in the chapel and pray for the swift recovery of Cedric Campbell? She'd sooner kiss the devil's backside. But she'd not say as much. These two had been kind and might prove to be the only friends she'd ever have.

"I should like to see the chapel," Fiona said. What harm could it do after all? She had plenty to pray for. No need to point out that her prayers and theirs would clash like swords in God's ear.

The hour was late when Fiona returned to her chamber and found Ruby dozing in a chair.

Fiona shut the door with a whump, and the maid sat upright, fluttering her chubby hands about her face.

"Oh, heavens, m'lady. Ye gave me a start. I was resting my eyes." Ruby wiped the corner of her mouth with the back of her hand and stood up.

"'Tis all right, Ruby. Has my husband been here?"

Ruby shook her head, her cap flopping askew. "No, m'lady. But the seamstress brought you two nightdresses and some other things. I put them away."

*What type of nightdress?* "Would you show them to me?"

"Yes, m'lady." Ruby bobbed her head and stepped away, only to return moments later with her plump arms filled with frothy fabric. Nerves of relief popped in Fiona's chest, for there was one plain linen sheath. Beneath it was another of the translucent material. She touched the latter like a bubble that might vanish at her touch. It was soft, with an almost sparkly sheen. Around the neck was a band of tiny pearls. How the seamstress had produced such a lovely garment in so short a time was a mystery. The woman must have nimble fingers, indeed. Too bad Fiona would never wear the thing.

"I'll wear the plain one," she said.

Ruby tsk-tsked under her breath, an affront that Fiona chose to ignore.

Donning the nightdress, Fiona turned to her reflection in the looking glass, and frustration, like sand in scallop, grit against her teeth. This shift may be plain and demure, but it was revealing nonetheless. And what would her husband do when he came to the room this night?

*Ask for my kisses and you shall have one thousand.* The notion made her limbs tremble and her belly hot. Surely, she had no use for kisses. Kisses would not bring her mother back, nor return Fiona home to Margaret's side. All his kisses did was confuse her, and she must do all she could to keep her faculties about her.

Still, it was growing harder and harder to despise him.

Cedric's fever returned with the vengeance of Cain, and all they could do once more was wait and pray. For hours, Myles and his mother sat near his father's bedside, taking turns mopping his damp brow with a cool cloth. Father Darius knelt near the foot of the bed, his hands worrying a rosary and his lips moving in silent prayer. The surgeon stood near an open window, conferring with his astrologers, looking for a sign to cure what ailed their laird.

Vivienne came in long after supper and wrapped an arm around Marietta. "How is he?"

Marietta wiped her own brow. "Worse. The side wound festers, and he's mad with fever."

"We prayed for him, Mari—Alyssa and I. I'm certain the Lord has heard us."

"Hearing a prayer and granting it are two very different things."

"Have you seen my wife?" Myles asked Vivienne.

"Fiona was with us in the chapel but has since gone to retire," Vivienne answered.

Myles nodded. "Thank you, Vivi. Now will you take Mother to her room and see she gets some rest? I'll sit here with the earl until morning."

"I'll stay as well," his mother argued.

"Father will be vexed with me if he awakens to find I've let you wear yourself out, Mother. Go get some sleep. If he worsens or improves, I'll send someone to tell you."

She started to speak, but he cut her off. "It's not a suggestion, Mother. I'll see you in the morning."

Vivi held out her hand, and his mother took it. Together, the women left the chamber. Myles turned away and sighed with some relief. For the past hour or more, his father had been mumbling. Mostly incoherent, but certain names had caught his ear. Names he did not want his mother burdened with. Aislinn Sinclair being one of them.

It was seven years past when word of her murder traveled down from the North and reached Dempsey Castle. Myles had been just sixteen then and recalled the weeks following were dark and fraught with calamity as clans took sides. Some chose to believe Hugh Sinclair's lies that the earl had done the evil deed. But just as many stood up with the Campbells, knowing Hugh for his spite and malice, and declared the earl was nowhere near the place and had no cause to bring her harm.

His father had said little on the matter, then or now, and refused to all who asked him to explain how his brooch had come to be in the possession of the Sinclairs. Still, Myles knew well enough his mother had heard the name that spilled forth from his father's fevered lips. He saw her own lips press together in a taut line and watched the tear slip silently down her cheek.

Though he longed to, he would never ask her what she knew of Aislinn Sinclair or her thoughts on what the woman meant to his father. He would not be so cruel. When his father awoke from this distress, he would press him and finally get some answers.


'Twas near midnight two full days later when Myles finally stumbled to his chamber, eager to sleep in his own bed. His father's fever had broken, and Cedric appeared to be on the mend. And at long last, his father had confided to Myles a wild story from his time at court, an elaborate tale about the midnight rescue of Scotland's boy king and of a passionate affair with Aislinn Sinclair.

Myles pushed the door open, and as expected, Fiona was cozily ensconced between his bedsheets. This time she'd seen fit to climb beneath the covers and, in another merciful gesture, had braided her tresses into one thick plait. He did not need her curls tickling his nose. He wanted badly enough to take his pleasure in her, but not this evening. Not when he was so tired he could barely hold open his eyes and had not the patience to woo her.

He stripped, fast and efficient, and slipped in next to her, praying his exhaustion would extend to every part of his anatomy.

It didn't.

Knowing she was there, within his grasp, relaxed and unguarded, brought his manhood to full attention. Traitorous cock. The thing had no loyalty to his brain and thought only of its own satisfaction. It cared not at all about the fatigue in his limbs or that his skull pounded with a headache days in the making. It also cared little of the foolish promise he had made to his wife.

*You must ask me for my kisses.*

Where had that plea come from? 'Twas a faulty gesture, one made in haste that he regretted the instant it fell from his lips that afternoon a few days past. For of course she would not ask. Her pride would not allow it.

He could reach out, he supposed. Lord knew his randy manhood tapping against his thigh would not relent. And yet, there was his own pride to consider. She behaved as if marriage to him had brought her low, when in fact it was an honor. She should be proud to be a Campbell bride. Proud and willing.

And so he must sway her to that way of thinking yet. He'd start by telling her about his most recent and revealing conversation with his father. The truth would not erase the wounds left by years of feuding between their clans, but it might make a difference. It would be a fresh start, a new foundation on which to build this marriage. A wave of relief and renewed fatigue washed over him.

Yes, that was the answer. Tomorrow, he'd tell Fiona how Cedric had loved her mother, that they'd met in the glen that day and he'd given her the brooch as a gift, the token of a promise. And most of all, he'd tell her that when Cedric had left Aislinn's side, she'd been joyous and well, and very much alive.

# CHAPTER 20

"ARE YOU CALLING MY MOTHER A FAITHLESS WHORE?"
Myles ran one hand across his bewhiskered jaw and fisted the other in frustration. Christ Almighty! The girl had no sense at all, no sense to see the grander scheme of what he was saying.

"She loved him, Fiona. As he loved her. 'Tis why they were together in the glen that day. My father admitted as much to me, though he doesn't want my mother or anyone else made the wiser, so you must not speak of this."

His wife's eyes flashed, the color high upon her cheeks. She was dressed in a gown of deep green, but her hair hung loose, for he'd sent Ruby from the room before she could style it.

They were in his chamber, husband and wife breakfasting together in an awkward silence, until at last he told her of his father's fevered confession.

"You must think me the most gullible of fools," Fiona spat. "My mother held nothing but contempt in her heart for any Campbell."

"Did she say as much?" he asked.

"What?"

"Did she tell you such a thing? Or were those words put in your mind after the fact? You were just a child when she was killed."

Fiona stood and began to pace. "I was ten, but I saw the brooch with my own eyes. 'Twas pierced straight through her skin, Myles. My memory is accurate." She dashed away a single tear as if it stung her face.

He thought she'd find relief at his words, but everything he said only raised her ire and her agitation.

He lowered his voice. "I was shocked to hear the details of their liaison too, but think on this, Fiona. It makes sense if you will listen. For years, our parents were friends at court, allied close enough to unite our clans by betrothing you to me. All was well between us. But when your father betrayed the king and helped Archibald Douglas hold him captive, my family became an enemy to yours. Still, that doesn't mean your mother despised us."

"So, my mother was a whore and my father a traitor? How highly you regard my parents."

He rose fast from his chair. "As highly as you regard mine. I'm not inventing these details! These are the facts. Can you deny your father sided with Douglas and opposed King James?"

She slapped away another tear. "I deny only the absurdity of your accusations. My father chose the losing side, but that doesn't make him a traitor. Nor was my mother duplicitous and unfaithful. You admit your father was the last to see her alive, yet I'm to believe he did her no harm? If not him, then who?"

'Twas the question he dreaded, for only one logical answer could be given. Who indeed would have greater cause to murder Aislinn Sinclair than her cuckolded husband?

Myles bit back his response, but the implication hung in the air like an executioner's ax.

He watched her thoughts unscramble as she pieced together the puzzle with her own deductions, and saw the light dawn in her eyes. But her expression turned just as quickly to disbelief. She shook with emotion.

"You think it was *my* father? How dare you!"

Myles felt sympathy for his wife. This was a horrid accusation, but surely she could see it made more sense than his own father being the villain. What reason would the earl have for doing such a thing? Even if he had not loved her, he'd have no cause to despise her.

Patience was essential to his mission, but also in short supply. "I know what manner of man your father was, Fiona. Can you deny he possessed a violent temper? And great malice toward the Campbells? Perhaps it was an accident when she died and he took advantage to blame us."

She sank back down into the chair, refusing to meet his eyes. "Would you leave me?" Her voice rasped. "Please?"

He wanted to stay and press his cause, but her arms crossed in front of her like a bar across the door. He had no stomach for talking in circles, and perhaps some time to brood might soften the bitter frown upon her face. With a sigh, he moved toward the door.

"I'll be with my father this morning, but I'll send Vivi to keep you company." His aunt seemed to have a way with her. Perhaps she could help his wife see reason. The notion nearly tripped him.

In his wildest dreams, he had not imagined he'd be turning to his mischievous aunt for help.

The gentle thud of the door as Myles left sounded at odds with the slamming of Fiona's heart. Her mother and Cedric? Lovers? What heinous lies! The very suggestion was as preposterous as it was insulting. This was just another Campbell ploy—and poorly played, at that. Myles thought to convince her she was wrong about his father by accusing her own? Absurd! Even if Cedric had loved her mother in his own twisted way, it was jealousy that made him brand her as his own. And never, never would she believe her mother had loved him in return.

Perhaps she had not loved her own husband either, for Hugh Sinclair was a hard man, stern and unyielding. Prone to melancholy and too much drink, but life was harsh in the North, and he'd been humiliated by his loss of position and lands at the hand of King James.

But Myles was mistaken if he thought her father capable of such a crime. She'd not believe a word of it. Perhaps it had been an accident, yes. But at the hands of Cedric Campbell. If anything, he'd killed her when she resisted his advances. 'Twas more likely than Fiona's father losing such control.

She stood and paced about the room, trying to recall her mother's words until her very head ached. She could not recall a time her mother had spoken harshly about the Campbells, but neither had she defended them. The memories were so hazy: glimpses of a smiling face with deep-blue eyes, the sound of warm laughter, the smell of her mother's hair. All had faded in the seven years, but the pain of missing her had not.

# CHAPTER 21

MYLES FOUND HIMSELF AT HIS AUNT'S SOLAR AND RAPPED upon the door.

Darby opened it, grinning wide to show a new space in his smile.

"Myles, look, I've lost a tooth." He rolled the tiny thing between his fingers.

"So you have." Myles smiled down at the lad. "You'd best go bury it before a witch finds it and casts a spell on you."

Darby looked to his mother.

Vivienne nodded, looking up from her needlework. "Bury it in the garden, and you're sure to grow big and strong. Run along now and let me speak with Myles."

Fast as a flint spark, the boy was gone.

Vivienne set her stitching upon her lap and rubbed the back of her neck. "Thank goodness for your company. This work is tedious and I've no talent for it."

Myles crossed the room and sat down in the cushioned chair next to her. Like his mother's chamber, this one was decorated in pale hues of lilac and pink. Women must prefer that to the red and gold of masculine decor, though he could not imagine

Fiona in such a soft setting, nor spending her hours at so mild a pastime.

He pulled the cloth from Vivienne's lap to examine her uneven stitches. "You do not exaggerate. This is sloppy craftsmanship."

She frowned with no heat and snatched back the cloth, stuffing it into a handbasket near her feet. "I should like to see you sitting in one spot for hours upon end, poking your finger with a needle until you bleed."

He smiled. "Well, there's the problem, then. The needle is meant to go into the cloth, not your finger."

She blinked at him several times in rapid succession. "Jesters must tremble in fear at the magnificence of your humor."

He stretched with false posturing. "All men tremble at my magnificence. And the ladies too."

Vivienne smiled at this and clapped her hands together. "Splendid news, nephew. So all goes well with your bride, then?"

The air of teasing was punched from his lungs, and he felt his face fall. He'd hoped to warm up to this topic, not surge in with no element of care. But there was no avoiding it now. She'd asked, as if she sensed Fiona was the reason for his visit. His aunt had the uncanny sense of an owl.

"No, not well. Little I do or say pleases her."

Vivienne laughed. "She seems charming to me. It must be you who is the problem."

"You see a different side of her."

Vivienne tilted her head. "Give the girl some time, Myles. She's sacrificed much, and none of this is of her choosing. But if you back a cat into a corner, it will hiss and run away. You cannot force her."

"I haven't forced her in any way. 'Tis just the opposite, in fact. I've hardly touched her since our wedding night." Lord have mercy, he hadn't meant to share as much. It certainly was no business of Vivi's. Now he'd never hear the end of it.

"Hardly touched her? What does that mean?"

"Nothing." What good were the cushions on this chair? They felt hard as mallets. He pulled one from behind his back and fluffed it to no avail.

Vivienne chuckled. "Oh, Myles, you poor little dear. You've finally met a woman able to resist your enviable charms, and you fall daunted before the challenge. Where is your courage?"

"I have courage aplenty. You know she slashed me, don't you?"

"I heard from Tavish it was a very tiny knife."

He punched the cushion once more, then threw it to the floor. "Whose side are you on?" His voice held no heat.

Vivienne folded both hands over her heart, innocent as an angel. "I am on the side of love."

A snort burned in his nose. "Love? By God, woman! You aim Cupid's arrow too high. I would settle for cordial, but Fiona and I have reached an impasse, and I fear neither of us will budge."

His aunt let loose a laugh. "You've been married now how many days? A week? And of those days, your nights have been spent either on the road or with your father. Honestly, it's not like you to give up so easily."

"I haven't given up. I'm just not certain how to proceed with one as irrational as Fiona."

"Why do men accuse women of being irrational simply because they don't understand us? It's unjust."

She was not helping. "I've treated my wife more than fairly, Vivi. 'Tis she who's run away, attacked me, and called me a liar. I fail to see how any of this is my fault."

Vivienne patted his arm. "It's not your fault, darling. And don't despair. With a little coaxing, she will fall in love with you. I'm sure of it. And you'll be a better man for having worked for it."

He bristled slightly at her words. "I'm a good man now."

Her smile was teasingly indulgent. "Of course. You're a splendid man, brave and strong and chivalrous. You are also brusque and, if I might say so, a little arrogant."

"Arrogant? Now, that's unfair. I cannot defend myself and still proclaim humility."

"No, you cannot." She shook her head and laughed again. "Didn't Tavish once call you a haughty pup with more wag than tail?"

"Not since I bested him with a sword." He sat forward in the chair. He should have known she'd be a useless ally, pointing out his flaws instead of telling him how to defeat Fiona's. "So, what would you suggest I do?" He could not keep the dryness from his voice.

Vivienne rearranged her silk skirts. "Be nice to her."

Myles paused, waiting for an elaboration that never came.

"That's it? That's your sage advice? Be nice to her?"

"Yes. And be patient. The easiest course is often the best. Once she learns how kind you are, she'll come around to the truth. You cannot force her to change her opinions, but give her time to see the error of her judgments. And until she does…just be nice."

More lopsided women's logic. "I've already been nice," he snapped.

Vivienne sat up, her posture rigid. "By using tones such as that? I saw how you bungled things with her in your chamber, shooing the rest of us out like we were flies. Is that how you want your wife to see you treating women?"

"I was shooing you out so I could be alone with her."

Vivienne sighed with feigned impatience. "Tsk, tsk, tsk, Myles. Have you never caught a fish?"

*What possible bearing could that have on this matter?* He should leave now and break with this conversation. "Of course I have."

"And did you take the bait and fling it at the fish's head? No, of course not. You dipped your line into the water with a tempting morsel tied to the end, perhaps something shiny and intriguing. And then you waited and let the fish come to you. A woman is no different. Let her come to you, and she'll be caught. But lose your patience, and you'll have to start all over again."

This was why women were not allowed on the battlefield. Such unorthodox tactics.

There was some sense to what she said, perhaps, but his patience and Fiona seemed always at odds with each other. Nonetheless, it was worth the smallest effort, for he had no greater alternatives. He picked up the lumpy cushion from the floor and tucked it back behind him. "I shall endeavor to be nice."

"Excellent. Your natural charm is sure to win her over. In the meantime, you might show her around a bit. She's seen little of Dempsey. Now that Cedric is feeling better, perhaps you could show her the gardens or take her to the village. And perhaps take Alyssa along. That should cheer Fiona."

The village. Yes, that might work. He had business there to settle, and she could go along. With his father incapacitated, it fell to him to see that all was well with their tenants. He could take her this very afternoon.

He stood, feeling more optimistic than he had upon his entrance, and set about making plans to woo his wife.

# CHAPTER 22

THEY RODE OUT PAST THE IMMENSE GUARD TOWERS, OVER the old stone bridge, and into the lush green countryside. Fiona followed on a mild palfrey as her husband guided his destrier northward, away from the village and toward the rugged shoreline of Loch Fyne. The sun was high in the sky, sending rays of warmth their way, and no swollen clouds threatened to dampen their excursion. God, who seemed forever inclined to rain on Fiona, kept a serving of sunshine reserved for His most favored Campbells.

Alyssa rode next to Fiona on a spirited, high-stepping mare. The lass kept up a constant stream of happy chatter, and Fiona was glad for the company of Myles's sister. Her presence was a welcome buffer and saved Fiona from having to converse with Myles directly.

The horses nickered and pranced as if the balmy day brought them joy as well. Fiona, Myles, and his sister ambled over the hillocks, spotting hares and deer, and an occasional crofter's cottage, until they reached one edge of Loch Fyne. They stopped a moment to admire its beauty and the dark water rippling against the rocky shore. Fiona turned her face up to the sky. The breeze was soft and sweet, with no hint of the brine often present on the winds near her home. It was a lovely day, and even Myles's constant presence and his frequent looks in her direction could not spoil that.

He'd said nothing more of Cedric's supposed confession. In fact, his manner was pure charm, as if a cross word had never passed between them. He'd been solicitous when they were still in the bailey, helping Fiona mount her horse. He had adjusted her stirrups with great care and let his hand linger on her ankle. She'd watched emotions play across his face for the space of one heartbeat and then another. She thought he had meant to run his hand up her calf right there in the yard. But his fingers had stayed put, and his smile was enigmatic when he'd glanced up at her. Now he merely rode along, that same relaxed look upon his features as he pointed out aspects of the landscape for Fiona and told her bit about their history.

After a few miles, they circled back around and headed toward the village just north of the castle.

"Myles taught me to ride," Alyssa said as they went on. She looked pretty and petite, riding high upon her saddle, and she handled her mount expertly.

"I had little choice," he responded. "'Twas either teach you to ride or let you forever clamor upon my back. My knees did not enjoy it. Nor did I take well to the switch."

Alyssa giggled brightly. "I never once struck you with a switch."

"I remember well you did. And often too. You were merciless."

"'Twas a ribbon, you silly goose."

"Well, then you wielded it harshly, for it stung like a switch," he teased.

She laughed aloud. "Forgive me, brother. I had no idea you possessed so tender a rump."

In an instant, the word brought a furious blush to Fiona's cheeks, eliciting a memory of that very same rump on their wedding night. Tender, indeed. It had felt of pure muscle beneath her hand. She coughed to clear her throat of nothing more than air.

Myles looked at her askance but said nothing.

The conversation continued, relaying nothing of import, but it struck within Fiona an acute aching for Margaret. She missed her sister more each day, but never more so than when she was with Alyssa. The girl was sweet and calm, innocent as spring rain. Even her laughter sounded so like Margaret's, Fiona could close her eyes and imagine her own sister was next to her.

How she longed to send her a note and let her know she was safe and well. But in that letter, she would also have to reveal what happened to Bess, and she could not yet put the incident into words. As it was, she was not even certain if the Campbells knew she had a sister. For some strange reason, she had kept all thoughts of Margaret to herself, reluctant to share them, as if keeping her a secret kept her closer to Fiona's heart.

She was grateful a few moments later when they arrived in the village, for thoughts of home had made her misty-eyed and sad.

All along the thoroughfare, shops of every sort lined up, with vendors out in front, hawking their wares. But at the sight of their laird's son and daughter, the townsfolk stopped in their actions and began to call out greetings. They offered broad waves and eager smiles, and soon, groups of them surged forth in welcome. As each one called out to the next, more and more villagers poured out of the buildings, followed by dozens of children. So grand a welcome Fiona had never seen. It was as if they were royalty.

Stopping at the square in the center of the village, her husband slid from his saddle and greeted each person fondly, and often by name. It seemed he knew them well, and their respect for him was evident in their deportment. They were enthusiastic but respectful, none being so bold as to touch his garment or interrupt his words.

Her own kin displayed no such warmth with one another. Doubt tapped at her senses, but just as quickly, she dashed it away. 'Twas easy to be friendly when times were good and food was plentiful. So although there may be less familiarity among her clan, their loyalty was no less fierce.

Myles continued with his greetings as he reached up to help Alyssa from her saddle. He set her lightly upon the ground, and she was quickly swallowed by a throng of friendly women.

Next, he came to Fiona's side.

"Friends," he called out over the din of voices, "please allow me to introduce my wife. I bid you welcome Lady Fiona Campbell, late of Sinclair and now one of our own."

*One of their own.* The declaration should have burned like a brand, but instead, she felt a peculiar swell of dignity encompass her. She was their lady now. Not the daughter of the laird, nor even the sister. She was his wife and would one day be the lady of Dempsey Castle. How odd that she had not considered that sooner. And more odd still that the notion should give her pleasure.

She looked over the crowd and saw their friendly faces. She let loose a breath she'd not realized she'd been holding.

"Welcome, my lady."

"'Tis grand to meet you, my lady."

"What a blessed day to meet our mistress."

The wave of bodies surged once more, surrounding her horse and reaching up to clasp Fiona's hands in welcome until Myles laughed. "Back off, now. Let my lady off her horse."

He raised his arms and gazed at her expectantly. She had no choice but to ease into his arms. He was the devil wearing a leather jerkin and her husband's smile.

And down she slid.

He could have simply lifted her from the saddle and set her on the ground, but so fine an opportunity he could not let pass. Instead, he pulled her close against him, letting her body slide down along his own. It was a mistake, he realized in an instant, for his cock sprang to life as if she were naked beneath him. The scent of vanilla wafted past, and he knew it came not from the baker's shop, but from his wife's warm skin. Her essence. Heaven help him, was this lass the poison or the cure?

'Twas little difference, really, for he'd consume her either way.

Her hands gripped at his shoulders, and he could not stop the vision of her legs wrapped around him too. Her lips were plump and parted as he lowered her farther still. The need to kiss her clubbed him like a mace. He could do it, here and now. His people would cheer and think him an adoring bridegroom.

But her reaction he could not predict, and he'd not be rejected in front of his clan.

He swallowed and set her feet upon the ground harder than he had planned, and she looked at him in some surprise.

"Sorry," he mumbled, and maneuvered her by the shoulders so she was standing right in front of him. He needed that moment to tame his wicked thoughts and rein in his stubborn erection.

"I have business with a few of you," he called out. "And my wife and sister and I should like to stay for supper."

"You can do business at my inn, my lord," called out a gruff voice. "Best ale and cleanest tables!"

A chorus of voices called out their objections and their own offers for Myles to consider.

He raised one hand, laughing again. "Thank you, Tom. Your taproom will do nicely. I thank you all for your fine suggestions."

Alyssa came to his side then. "I can lead Fiona around, Myles. I'm sure the ladies will show us the greatest of care."

"Indeed we will," added an orange-haired miss with enormous teeth and a flour-coated apron. "Come to my shop, my ladies. My biscuits are the finest this side of Edinburgh. Light as air, they are."

Fiona looked over her shoulder at him, as if to ask permission. He thought to make a joke of that but bit his tongue. Vivi had admonished him to be nice, and so he merely smiled and caught Fiona's wrist. He lifted it and pressed a tender kiss against the back of her hand. "The afternoon is yours, my lady. Do whatever you wish. If you see something you'd like to buy, you may. I'll settle the accounts when we are finished here."

She looked perplexed, as if his words were foreign, but she did not snatch her hand away. Then, just as quick as he had spoken, Alyssa giggled and pulled his wife in the direction of the baker's shop. He watched them go, Fiona's dark-red curls shiny amid the muddy browns and dull yellows tucked beneath the modest caps of the other women.

Old Tom approached, grinning wide in spite of an alarming lack of teeth. "You do me an honor, my lord. You know my place is right this way."

With a final glance toward his retreating wife, Myles turned to follow his clansmen to the inn. He hoped the business for today would be simple and quick. He was in no mood to linger over trivial matters of runaway sheep or one man's goat getting into another man's garden. He was here today to demonstrate a good show of faith, to build the clan's confidence in his wisdom and sense of justice in the absence of his father, but mostly, he wanted to be done with all that and follow his wife into the baker's shop and feed her sugared pastries.

He shook his head against the vision. That girl was a ridiculous distraction.

Settled at the taproom with a mug of ale, Myles sent out old Tom to spread the word he was ready to hear of any grievances or requests his townsfolk might have. His hope for a quick afternoon was quickly dashed as a line formed outside the taproom. He took a hearty gulp of the ale and signaled Tom's wife to pour him another. Then he called in his first case.

There were complaints about a randy bull that continued to get loose despite the farmer's best efforts to contain him, a plea for funds to repair a leaky roof over the gristmill, and a dispute over whether a man should be charged for bacon stolen by his dog. The last issue of the day was a man asking permission for his daughter to wed a Mackenzie. Myles consented, for the Mackenzies were a good sort, and he could not resist the girl's pleading eyes as she peeked at him around her father's shoulder. The father seemed relieved, and the day's business ended on a happy note.

Myles drained his cup, thanked the innkeeper, and went in search of his wife and sister.

He meandered down the lane, back toward the square, wondering how they'd spent their morning. With Alyssa as his emissary, no doubt the two of them dawdled over pretty ribbons and baubles and perhaps another gown or two. His coffers would be the lighter for it, but if it provided a means to an end and a more malleable wife, then it would be well worth the funds. This he pondered as he walked and wondered at his sudden sentimentality, for he realized it was not simply peace he sought with Fiona. He did indeed wish her happiness. It seemed, from the little she'd confessed of her past, she'd known little of pleasure or joy, while he'd had an abundance, more than enough to share. He chuckled to himself and thought perhaps the ale had taken a toll, but he'd had only a cup.

"My lord," came a voice over his shoulder.

He turned to see the goldsmith standing in the door of his shop.

"Yes?"

"My lord, I wonder if I might invite you in and show you something your lady admired. If I may be so bold to say so, it would make a fine wedding gift."

Ah, so the little minx had been looking at shiny baubles. He went into the shop and was promptly shown a gold necklace of fine craftsmanship. At the center was an emerald, much the shape and color of the ring Fiona now wore. It was an exquisite piece, and the price was beyond reasonable.

Myles looked at the clerk. "Are you sure she liked this one?"

The man nodded. "Quite certain, my lord. She even tried it on, and may I say, it looked even more beautiful on her lovely throat." He cleared his own.

"Why didn't she buy it?" Myles asked.

The shopkeeper flushed. "She said it was far too expensive, although the Lady Alyssa assured her it was not."

Myles smiled. 'Twas just the thing to bait a hook, shiny and alluring. He'd show Vivi he knew how to fish, for women were swayed by jewels. Even he knew that.

"I shall take it."

The smith's eyes sparkled like the jewels. "Very good, my lord. Thank you, my lord."

They finished their transaction, and Myles went on his way, now in search of his bride with a fine gift to offer.

He made his way to the square, and just beyond it, he could see the hillside rising up beyond the edge of the village. And there, sitting upon blankets, were dozens of women, with children all around. The sound of their chatter carried on the breeze. It seemed his lady had joined in on a picnic, for surely she was with them.

He tucked the bag containing the necklace inside his doublet, for he'd do well to save this gem until they were alone. Perhaps she'd reward his generosity with a kiss. The thought warmed him as much as the fast pace he kept.

Up the hill he went and spotted his wife, sitting on a plaid next to his sister, along with a dark-haired girl whose name escaped him. Fiona leaned back, propped on her palms with her blue skirts puddled around her like a satin pond. A little girl of six or so was weaving flowers into her hair.

His gut twisted, not from exertion, but from the vision itself. His wife, with a chubby-handed child in attendance. Fiona looked so happy, smiling at something Alyssa said, then tipping back her head and letting loose a full-throated laugh. A flower floated down from her hair to the grass. She picked it up and sniffed its aroma before handing it back to the child.

All around, children played, running in patterns and giggling, while their mothers chirped like happy sparrows. The image blessed him, for these were his people, and they were well cared for. He was proud and silently vowed that, when his time as laird truly came, he'd see that they remained as prosperous.

Fiona had yet to notice his approach, and when Alyssa caught his eye, he pressed one finger against his lips to silence her.

But his wife's words stopped him. "My little sister is so much like you, Alyssa. How she makes me laugh. At least, she did until I had to leave her behind."

Alyssa patted Fiona's hand. "Then we must bring her to Dempsey for a long visit."

He stood a moment, his chest thumping in a most peculiar fashion. She had a sister? How had he not known this?

He cleared his throat, and Fiona looked at him in surprise, her cheeks flushing red as if she'd been overheard saying something much more scandalous.

"Ladies." Myles tipped his head. "May I join you?"

Fiona licked her lips and fussed with her skirts, but his sister smiled brightly.

"Of course. Please do." Alyssa moved over, making a space for him next to his wife.

He settled down between the women and tried to catch Fiona's gaze, but his wife seemed intent upon twisting the ribbon in her hands and in no mood to welcome him. He leaned down over her lap and looked up at her so there was no avoiding him.

"How was your afternoon, my lady?" he asked, and sat back up.

"Fine, my lord."

He tugged at the ribbon she held. "Did you buy this?"

She shook her head, still avoiding him. "No, 'twas a gift from one of the children."

He looked around. "Which one?"

She pointed. "That lass over there, with the braids."

He saw the girl running circles with a scampering group of children all about her age. Seven or eight years old, he imagined. *And how old is Fiona's sister?* he could not help but wonder. But his wife had turned her head in the other direction, and so he tucked the question away, along with a list of others.

It struck him then how little he knew about his own wife. He knew her irascible temper, of course. And her impetuous nature, and the way her eyes glinted when he said something that offended. He knew how soft her lips were, and the sweet taste of that curve in her neck. And that she'd had a pony when she was a child. But other than those few things, he knew nothing of her life before their marriage.

"How did you pass the time today?" he asked instead, thinking the question so banal that surely she could take no issue with it. Then he held back a sigh of frustration while his sister answered in her stead and regaled him with every excruciating detail of their adventures. And Fiona's gaze landed everywhere, except on him.

# CHAPTER 23

R IDING BACK TO DEMPSEY, HER HUSBAND SEEMED SUB-
dued. He'd been pleasant enough when he joined them
on the blankets, yet something in his manner hinted at distress. She didn't care, of course, but his moods changed like
the weather, and with less warning. Now he rode in silence
next to her, as if his thoughts were heavy. But like their ride
earlier in the day, his eyes kept coming back to rest on her.
She felt his glances, like butterfly wings, resting and then fluttering away.

Alyssa rode a length behind them, humming softly to herself.

The sun began its descent over the mountains, turning them
purple in the distance, and clouds cushioned the sky. It would
rain soon. The horses sensed it and pulled at their bits.

"Did you enjoy the day?" Myles asked at last.

"I did. Thank you for inviting me." She could be gracious, if
she wanted to.

"Thank you for accepting," he replied with a tilt of his head.

They rode another minute, and the wind picked up, setting sail to a flower in her hair. She caught it with her fingertips,
embarrassed. "Oh, I'd forgotten about these." She reached up to
pluck the others out.

"Don't," he said. "They look lovely. You should always wear flowers in your hair."

He seemed in every way to be earnest, but she felt exposed and on display. She let the petals fall from her hand but left the other buds in place. To pull them out now would seem defiant, and they'd had such an agreeable day she thought not to shatter it with impertinence.

Another silence fell, with only the soft footfalls of the horses' hooves upon the grass sounding out, and the occasional call of a bird.

"Why didn't you tell me you had a sister?"

Her husband's question, though delivered in a soft tone, still dealt a blow. She wasn't certain until that moment if he had heard her say so.

"You never asked."

"No, I didn't. And yet, that seems the sort of detail which might have arisen without my prodding. Where was she when I was at Sinclair Hall?"

"Hidden." Fiona gripped the reins more tightly.

"Hidden? Why? Is she malformed?"

She frowned at his base assumption. "Quite the opposite. She is the fairest imaginable."

"Then why hide her?"

"Because there was no need for you to meet her." She could not keep the warning tone from her voice.

Now he frowned. It was obvious in his expression he thought her answers deliberately evasive, yet his voice was steady. "I should think she'd want to see her own sister wed. You're not telling me the whole truth of it."

Fiona took in his rigid posture and realized there was no harm in telling him now. Margaret was safe at Sinclair Hall, and he no longer posed a threat.

She met his gaze squarely. "Had you seen Margaret, you might not have settled for me."

Her husband paused, his manner lightening noticeably. "You feared I'd wed her instead?"

"Perhaps."

His lips twitched. His shoulders rose another degree. "I was betrothed to you, Fiona. But I confess, I'm flattered by your worry."

Ah, the arrogance of the man. Such a Campbell. He thought it was sisterly jealousy that had made her keep Margaret from his sight. A sour taste crept up her throat, and she could not keep her words at bay.

"There is no flattery implied, my lord. I sought only to protect my sister from your advances. I would not force her into my situation."

The humor fell away. His eyes went dark and narrow. His voice lowered to a growl. "Of course. For a moment, I forgot your distaste for this marriage and the way I've abused you. Praise God your sister's fate is not so abysmal as your own."

With a fast kick to the flanks, he spurred his horse into a gallop and rode away without a backward glance.

He was a fool. That little bit of ale from the inn must have addlepated his senses, for he'd sat upon that blanket all afternoon, pondering ways to make his wife adore him. But she was equally determined not to. *Protect my sister from your advances, indeed!* He could buy Fiona a dozen emerald necklaces, and still she'd see him as her enemy. Myles rode across the bridge, his horse's hooves clattering over the stones like warning bells. In the ward, he jumped from his saddle, tossed his reins to a groom, and strode into the hall.

"Bring drinks to the laird's chamber," he told a serving girl, for he had a strong urge to sit by his father's side and ask once more how on God's green earth the man had found himself in love with Aislinn Sinclair. She must have been far sweeter than her daughter.

He entered his father's chamber, glad to see him sitting upright in his bed. Marietta sat beside him, a book of psalms in her lap. Myles crossed the room and bent to kiss her cheek.

"Greetings, Mother, Father. You're looking well, sir."

Cedric's chuckle ended in a wet cough. "I'm hearty as a new-born kitten, but you're a loyal son to humor me."

His father's words were not far from the truth. He was wan, his color mottled at the temple where one injury could still be seen. The gash was healing, but the bruise remained. His arm was in a bright silk sling, a fanciful bit of frippery in stark contrast to its intended purpose. His other injuries were hidden beneath a fine linen shirt. Another bit of impracticality, but one must put on the appearance of having dressed in one's best. That shirt must have been his mother's doing.

"How was your trip to the village with Fiona?" his mother asked.

"Quite productive, Mother. Father, you'll be glad to hear old Bigsby's bull is still rutting his days away, impregnating every maiden cow in his path."

"Myles!"

His mother only feigned shock. He knew well enough he could not scorch her ears.

"My apologies, Mother. Perhaps you would excuse us while I tell Father about the more mundane details of my day's events?"

His father nodded. "You've sat by my side long enough, Mari, and I'm dull company. Go find something to gossip about with that sister of yours."

His mother looked about to refuse, but his father prompted once more. "Go on with you."

She rose, resting the book of psalms on the table next to the window. "Very well. I shall retire for the evening. Good night, my love. Good night, son."

After the door closed, Myles sank into the seat his mother had just vacated, and propped his feet up on his father's bed. "There is not much else to tell. Simple matters, easily rectified. The gristmill needs a new roof."

The serving girl from the hall arrived with several cups and a pitcher of wine. She set the tray on the table and then handed a full goblet to Myles.

"Can you drink, Father?" he asked.

"Of course I can. I'm not dead."

The girl handed him a goblet as well and then with a fast curtsy was on her way.

Cedric took a long draught, sighing afterward. "Ah, that's the stuff. The surgeon has me eating gruel. As if that could bring back a man's strength. What else did you encounter today? Did I hear your mother correctly? Fiona joined you?"

Myles pulled his feet from the bed, and they thumped to the floor before he leaned forward in his chair. "Aye, she joined me. And we had a pleasant day until the end. Father, do you recall all you shared with me during your fever?"

Cedric took another hearty swallow. "I do."

Myles scratched his head. "Well, I shared a bit of that news with my wife, and she is wholly disbelieving. 'Tis clear her own mother kept the secret as well as you."

Cedric sighed. "I had hoped to never tell you any of it at all. But this attack has made me ponder my mortality, and if I die before the truce has taken root, all will be for naught."

Unease clutched at Myles's gut to hear his father speak of dying. They faced it every day, of course, but never before had the earl been so harrowingly close to its edge.

"But why is this truce with the Sinclairs so important? It's little matter to Aislinn now, as she's no longer here."

"I'm here." His father's face flushed with color as he spoke. "And I vowed to protect her children. The promise is no less binding."

"And you hope to protect Fiona and the others by aligning them with us and the king?" He took a gulp from his own cup.

The earl nodded. "There is that."

Myles choked a little on his ale. "Is there more?"

His father drained his cup. "Some of my secrets I shall keep."

Blast his father and these secrets. He was being coy again, and it was frustrating. "Father, I cannot lead effectively without knowing all you have to impart. If there is more, tell me now."

But Cedric only held his cup out to be refilled. Myles picked up the jug from the table and filled the goblet.

"You know there is a chance it was the Sinclairs behind that ambush, yes?" Myles asked, irritation clear in his voice.

The earl considered this a moment. "I spoke at length with John at your wedding, Myles. He seems a sensible sort, and I trust he sees the value in this truce. He's not ruled by blunt emotion as his brother is."

"Aye, but it's his brother who is laird."

"True. But I cannot think why Simon would agree to the marriage and then seek to undo its purpose. Your mother tells me Tavish has gone off to inform King James of our attack. Mark my words, if he learns anything at all, it will be that Archibald Douglas is behind this somehow."

"But Archibald Douglas has been in London for years, since the king exiled him."

"Aye, and Douglas is a serpent whispering into the ear of England's sovereign. No two men conspire more to knock James from his throne, for if our king is indisposed, Douglas will return home and once again lead the regency ruling Scotland."

"Douglas has no true claim. He is the king's stepfather, nothing more."

"Aye, but still married to the king's mother. And since James has no heirs as of yet, Douglas is still next in line. And there are many powerful clans who would love to see him back at the helm, for it would benefit them."

"And destroy us."

"Yes, most likely."

Myles took another hearty swallow. "In that case, let's hope Tavish returns to Dempsey soon with useful news."

"Yes, and in the meantime, you must convince your wife we are not monsters."

"I confess, Father, I find myself at a bit of a loss in that regard. I've never encountered so willful a lass. I even turned to Vivi for advice."

His father burst with laughter, which ended in another cough. "What help could Vivi be?" he choked out. "She's never had to woo a wench."

"Aye, and she drove her own husband to the grave. But she seems to have a way with my wife."

Cedric raised a brow. "Birds of a feather, perhaps?"

Myles smiled against his will. "Vivi suggested I be *nice*."

"Nice?" The earl's other brow joined the first.

"Yes, nice. And so I've bought my bride a necklace."

His father nodded. "Seems the right approach. And what happened when you gave it to her?"

"It's in my pocket. She annoyed me on our way home, and I've yet to give it to her."

The earl laughed once more. "Give it to her. Perhaps you will sway her yet."

The talk moved on to other things, mundane details of running such a household, the warmth of the weather, the price of labor for the gristmill roof. The hour grew late. It felt good to simply spend time in his father's company, without worry of plots and wives and matters of intrigue. But at last, the earl's eyes began to droop, and Myles acknowledged his own fatigue.

"I'll leave you to your rest, Father. Sleep well and mend."

He left the earl's chamber and walked to his own, wondering what reception he might find there from his wife, if she was even still awake. The necklace felt heavy in his pocket. He should trade it for a kiss, if she'd give one. He chuckled as he put his hand to the door's latch, but then her words from earlier in the evening whispered through his memory.

*I sought only to protect my sister from your advances. I would not force her into my situation.*

He flushed with unwarranted shame, and it rankled him to the core, for he had done nothing to feel shameful of. He'd been patient with her, more tolerant of her behavior than most men would be. Ungrateful wench. He'd have her ask for his kisses after all. He'd not force himself on a woman who found humiliation in his touch. Protect her sister, indeed.

He took his hand off the latch and made his way farther down the corridor. He'd take his rest elsewhere and let his wife keep warm in the blanket of her own stubborn pride.

# CHAPTER 24

FIONA WONDERED WHERE HER HUSBAND SLEPT THESE DAYS. Four nights had passed since he'd left her and his sister on the road heading back to Dempsey. And during those days, he'd been cordial but cool, arriving each morning to change his clothes and then be on his way again. During meals, he might come to the hall and join them, but he just as often dined in his father's chamber. Fiona passed her time with Vivi and Alyssa. Marietta remained remote, gracious but aloof. So much so that even her own sister began whispering comments into Fiona's ear.

"Take heart. It's isn't you she doesn't like. She has always been this way."

Fiona reminded herself it didn't matter what the wife of Cedric Campbell thought, yet in some tiny corner of her mind, it did.

The ladies were together, sewing in Vivi's chamber, when a shout rang out, and soon after, a fast rapping sounded on the door. One servant opened it, and there stood another, beaming.

"My ladies. Lord Tavish has returned. And he's brought Lord Robert with him."

Alyssa squeaked with joy as she and Vivienne set their mending aside. "Oh, Fiona, you're sure to adore Robert. But you mustn't let him tease you. He is notorious for jests."

Fiona's heart gave a thump. *One more Campbell to be wary of? Wonderful.*

Alyssa was out the door, skipping down the hall. Vivienne and Fiona followed at a more leisurely place.

"You look grim," Vivi said.

"More so than usual?" Fiona had taken to her own kind of teasing with Myles's aunt, and their friendship seemed to blossom from it.

Vivienne's laugh was light as she tipped her head to look more closely at Fiona's face. "No, not more grim than usual. And certainly not so grim as that very first night."

The women walked through the hall and into the bailey, where Tavish and Myles's brother were being greeted as conquering heroes of the realm. Fiona spotted Robert instantly, for he bore the look of Cedric but with the more angular jaw afforded by youth. His coloring was lighter than Myles's, and he had a light-brown mop of curls. He tipped up his face, and his eyes met hers. She nearly faltered in her step, for those eyes of his were the deepest, brightest blue she'd ever seen, more violet than indigo. No wonder women succumbed to him.

Vivienne giggled beside her and whispered, "Mind yourself. He's an utter rapscallion."

Myles stepped up next to his brother and turned to follow his gaze. When his eyes landed on Fiona, he frowned and stepped in front of Robert, saying something she could not hear. Robert laughed and nodded.

Fiona felt color heating her cheeks, for whatever was said was most certainly about her.

When her husband turned back in her direction, the lines of his face were more relaxed, and the brothers made their way toward Fiona and Vivienne.

Robert leaned in to kiss his aunt's cheek. "Vivi, you saucy wench, you haven't aged a day. Are you some kind of witch?"

"Something like that. Welcome home, Robert." She kissed his cheek in return.

"I'd have been home sooner, but Tavish slowed me down. Age and too much ale has got to him." His smile brightened as he teased, for Tavish was right behind him.

"I could still show you a thing or two in the yard, boy. Meet me there tomorrow."

"Is that a challenge, Uncle?"

Tavish grinned. "'Tis a promise."

Robert nodded. "Tomorrow, then." He turned his gaze once more to settle on Fiona. She hoped her face wasn't bright with pink. The man had a ridiculous amount of appeal, with dimples deep in each cheek and another set in his square chin.

Myles stepped closer, reaching out to clasp her hand and tuck it close into the crook of his arm as if they were the most intimate of partners.

"Robert, 'tis my great pleasure to introduce Fiona Campbell. My wife." The word was ripe with hidden meaning. Or perhaps not so hidden.

But Robert displayed the most appropriate, impeccable manners, taking her other hand and bowing over it, quick and succinct. "'Tis my honor to meet you, Lady Fiona. I am in your debt."

Her voice was unsteady. "In my debt, sir? How so?"

He smiled wide. "With my esteemed brother preoccupied by one so lovely as you, I shall have all the available ladies for myself."

"And a few of the less available ones," Tavish murmured. "Get along with you, now. Your father is waiting."

Robert nodded once more and winked at Fiona. "I look forward to becoming much better acquainted, my lady."

Myles squeezed her hand and pressed her more securely to his side as the party moved toward the great hall.

"Robert has been at court, my dear," Myles said. "Forgive his forward manner. Now, I shall be with my father for a bit. I trust you can find some entertainment while I'm gone."

She looked at her husband's face. 'Twas more words than he had said to her in as many days. And how solicitous they sounded. She'd been left to her own for nearly a week, so why his sudden inter—ah, his brother. Of course. Myles would play the adoring husband for Robert's sake. What silly folly, for surely Robert was clever enough to know there was no love between her and Myles. Perhaps she should erase any doubt and snatch her hand away from her husband's arm.

But she glanced over at Robert and found him staring back, a keen glimmer in his eyes. Perhaps that's how things were managed at court, but she hoped her own face showed indifference, for it would do her no good to create friction between the brothers. And just as Myles was her enemy, so too was Robert. No matter that he had an archangel's face and a rogue's smile.

"I shall find some way to pass the time without you," Fiona told her husband, keeping her voice and expression deliberately bland.

Myles returned a smile that seemed both grateful and strained. "In that case, I look forward to seeing you at dinner." Then he caught her chin with his fingertips and pressed his lips to hers, so hard and fast it felt more a brand than a kiss. She knew it was for Robert's sake, but it tingled nonetheless and left a hollowness in her chest when her husband pulled away.

Myles's mother was with the earl, fussing about as ever, when the men entered the chamber. She spotted Robert and dropped the brush from her hands into her husband's lap.

"Robert! How grand!" She crossed the room fast, wrapping satin-covered arms around her son. "Goodness! You're too thin."

"I've missed you, Mother. There's been no one haranguing me for months. And I'm not too thin. I'm solid muscle."

"You are thin. Doesn't the king feed you?" She pulled him over toward Cedric.

"Mother, I've been on campaign in the borderlands, and the food was putrid, but you may fatten me up while I'm at Dempsey, if you wish."

Cedric laughed. "Come here, son. Let me get a good long look at you."

Myles stood to the side, watching as his younger brother sat down on their father's bed and leaned back against the post, his manner so relaxed it felt as if he'd never left. "Tell me, lad, how fares the king?" asked Cedric.

"Full of plans, as always. He married Marie de Guise a few weeks past and, in her honor, has renovated much of Linlithgow. 'Tis a finer place than Falkland now, though the hunting's not as good. And he plans to sail around the Highlands toward summer's end. He's asked me to join him. And you too, Myles, if Father can spare you here."

Myles felt a rush of enthusiasm. 'Twas a great honor to sail with the king. But fast on that came the thought of leaving Fiona so soon. Things were as yet unsettled between them, and he should like to be around to put them in a better place before abandoning her. The notion startled him, that he should put her needs, and even his own, before the king's. The girl was like a ripple in a pond, her every action causing movement all around.

"And what of Douglas and his ilk? Have they been causing problems?" Cedric asked. He gestured for Tavish to come closer. "Did you discover anything?"

Tavish eased into a chair. "King James has sent scouts to scour the area where we were attacked. It's not likely they'll find anything, but he has his spies and perhaps they'll learn something of some use."

Myles walked over, grasping the post behind Robert's head and leaning closer. "We were on Fraser land when we were attacked."

Robert nodded. "Just north of Inverness, Tavish told me. If that's the case, then likely it was Frasers, with aid from their Douglas cousins. Both clans are riled beyond measure because the king has accused Lady Janet Douglas of conspiring to poison him. She is Archibald Douglas's sister, of course, and suspect by association. Still, 'tis treason to communicate with Douglas, and the king has evidence they've exchanged numerous messages."

"What messages?" Cedric asked.

Robert shrugged. "I don't know, exactly, but if the king wants a reason to dispose of someone, he'll find it. Or create it, if it pleases him."

"Watch what you say, lad. Talk like that could well put you at the end of a noose," Tavish warned.

"He's right, son," Cedric agreed. "James trusts no one unconditionally. Not even us."

"So, what happens next?" Myles asked. This talk of treason made him uneasy, for even though it seemed his wife's family had nothing to do with the ambush, not so long ago the Sinclairs were a target of the king's wrath. 'Twas only his marriage that protected them now, and his father's determination to keep them safe. The fragility of the situation chilled his blood.

Robert stood up. "Next, I suggest we have dinner. If Mother says I am too skinny, she must be right."

Dinner was a joyous affair, and Fiona found herself enjoying it immensely. The great hall was full to the trusses with clansmen eager to greet Lord Robert. As they dined on roasted boar and blancmange, sweetmeats and ambrosia, he regaled them all with ribald tales of his adventures. The wine flowed like a river in springtime, and Fiona soon grew warm with drink and merriment as the boisterous din of revelers buzzed in her ears.

Throughout the evening, her husband was ever present by her side, offering bites of some delectable morsel or bidding the server to fill her cup again. His smile was ready and natural, his posture relaxed, so unlike the Myles of the last few days who'd barely looked her way. If his attention toward her was purely for show, he was a fine actor, for he played the adoring bridegroom with conviction. Or perhaps his brother's arrival had cast a spell over them all.

"You seem at ease this evening, my lord," she finally commented.

A shadow passed over his features but was gone as quickly as it had come. "I am at ease, as I should be. My brother is home, my father is on the mend, and I've a comely wife by my side." The look he sent her way was as much a challenge as a declaration, as if he dared her contradiction.

Her tongue twisted in her mouth, with no response at the ready. She smiled instead, and sipped her wine.

For whatever purpose, he wanted Robert to believe all was well, and she could see no reason to dispute it. Her own brothers were in constant competition, and so it seemed to be with these two as well. And indeed, if Robert saw a weakness in his brother's marriage, he might be the type to take advantage. She had no use for one Campbell pursuing her. She certainly did not want a second.

Myles leaned closer at her silence. "You are comely, you know, when you haven't that Sinclair scowl upon your face." His voice sank to a husky whisper as his hand covered her own. She very nearly jumped from her chair at his familiarity. "I might even confess to missing you a bit these last few days," he added.

The smolder in his eyes was undeniable. Heat from his grasp shot through her like a torch. And if she were an honest woman, she might admit she'd missed him, too.

"'Tis you whose whereabouts have been the mystery. I've not hidden," she answered.

His lips crooked in a lazy smile. "Is that an invitation? A simple word from you, and I'd be most obliged to rejoin you in our chamber."

He was as clever as a serpent, this husband of hers. He'd left her to her own devices, hoping she'd grow lonely, and well she had, but not so much that she'd encourage his return to her bed. Or at least not so much that she'd admit it.

"I find I quite enjoy the solitude, my lord. I sleep undisturbed and imagine I am still a happy maiden back at home."

His jaw stiffened as the smile froze on his face. "Imagine what you like, Fiona. The truth cannot be undone."

She had not meant to rile him, only to put him off. When his eyes went dark and sleepy in that sensual way, when he touched her hand and whispered close, she could not think past her defenses. It was as instinctual as a blink to push him away.

The night took on a different tone for her just then. Her husband turned away and struck up a conversation with Tavish, sitting on the other side of him. Fiona felt a foolish tear well in her eye, and from whence it came, she could not imagine. She blinked it away.

Alyssa was sitting to her right. "Are you well, Fiona?" she asked.

Fiona nodded. "An ash in my eye, I think. Nothing more."


Hours later, as Fiona undressed with Ruby's assistance, she thought of her husband and the gleam in his eye when he'd looked her way. Her body tingled in an unfamiliar fashion, and her mind felt equally bemused. He had made no secret about wanting her, yet found another place to spend his nights. For days, he'd made no attempt to seduce her, and she should be glad. She *was* glad, of course. 'Twas far better to keep him at a distance, for when he'd stroked her hand at dinner, she'd nearly gasped from the burn of it. The flames licked through her even now, though she fought against it. Her Sinclair strength grew weaker by the day.

"Arms up, m'lady," Ruby instructed. "Let's get off this shift."

Fiona raised her arms, obedient as a child, but as the maid eased the garment up and over her head, the fabric grazed against Fiona's nipples in a whispering kiss and she drew in breath sharp as a pin. She let it out slowly, half wanting to cup her breasts with her own hands to stop their sudden ache. Her body felt odd, hot and cold at once, like water dropped upon a hot skillet, popping and sizzling in a heated dance.

Fiona frowned at her own thoughts. She'd spent too much time with Vivi of late. The woman had far too randy a nature, always speaking about the great pleasures of physical love. 'Twas hogwash. Fiona had tried it. It had not been awful. If truth be told, there'd even been some pleasurable bits, but mostly, she recalled a lot of grunting and chafing. She had no need of that. And yet, her body seemed inclined to disbelieve her mind.

Ruby was back now with a nightdress, the heavy linen one she always wore, and when the garment floated down over Fiona, her traitorous body reacted once more. Images of her husband flashed in her mind's eye. Myles, lying next to her upon the mattress, kissing her at the inn, urgently pulling her legs around his hips on their wedding night. Lord save her, how could she long for his caress? When had she become so wanton?

Ruby came around to face her, tying the ribbons of her nightdress securely, trussing her up like a swaddled infant. But she was not an infant. And yet, not quite a woman either. She was somewhere in the middle. Of everything. No longer a virgin, but not quite a wife. No longer a Sinclair, nor thoroughly a Campbell. Tears burned in her eyes, and she nudged Ruby's hands away.

"Thank you, Ruby. I can finish the rest."

"Yes, m'lady. Is something amiss?"

Fiona managed a smile. "Everything is fine," she lied. "But my head aches a bit, and I should like to be alone."

"Yes, m'lady." Ruby bobbed into her clumsy version of a curtsy and left, pulling the door shut behind her with a final thud.

Fiona sat down at the dressing table and picked up the brush, running it through her hair. Then she set it back down and ran her fingers through her locks instead, slowly, like a lover might, and once again, her body hummed with want. Her eyes closed, and for a few luscious moments, she let herself imagine how her life might have been if she'd married for love instead of obligation.

What joy would it bring to be stroked by a man who adored her? Who cherished and respected her? A man whose kisses made her heart pound and her legs tremble and fall open. Though she tried and tried to conjure some imaginary knight, her every vision was interrupted by the image of Myles's face. She could see his smile and his eyes, could feel his hands. And his mouth.

She pressed her fingers against her lips, as if she could taste him there. Cursed man. He'd robbed her of both her virginity and her identity. Now he'd stolen her thoughts as well.

She stood up fast from the table, knocking over the chair her haste. She left it there, like a sulking child, and stomped over to the bed, blowing out every candle on the way, until the room was nearly pitch with darkness. Only the red glow coming from the fireplace remained. She climbed beneath the covers with a sigh as heavy as her heart and prayed for sleep.

Sometime later, a scratching near the door disturbed her fitful slumber. The fire was low, the room was dark, and sounds from the hall below had faded away to nothing. She guessed it to be near midnight. The door eased open and in came a great hulking shape. She thought at once to yell, but the beast passed between the bed and fireplace, and she could see it was a man. She might have demanded his identity, but the brute's foot caught the overturned chair, and he fell with such a clamor and commotion and a torrent of scandalous obscenities she knew at once it was her husband.

# CHAPTER 25

W HAT ARE YOU DOING HERE?" HIS WIFE DEMANDED, AS IF his presence needed explanation.

"'Tis my chamber!" he growled. His knee throbbed as if a cannonball had ripped through it, but worse than that, something had struck his face, and even now, he felt the sticky ooze of blood coming from his nose. "God, woman, had I known you set a trap, I'd have brought a light."

He'd been in the hall with Robert and Tavish, reminiscing about the past and strategizing about the future, until at last he'd had his fill of wine and his brother's stories. So he had bid the men good evening, and for the first time in four nights, he sought his own chamber. He'd been sleeping in Robert's lately, hoping his absence might stir some tender feelings within his wife. But Robert was home now, and Myles had decided enough was enough. She was his wife, and whether she found joy in that or not, he'd be sleeping next to her from this day forth.

All through dinner, he'd hoped to soften her with his attention. And still she would not make the invitation. Now he found himself upon the rug, clenching his teeth against the throbbing in his knee and holding a hand to stem the flood from his nostrils.

"Had I known you were coming, I'd have set the chair to rights," she said.

Christ, the girl had the nerve to sound indignant. 'Twas such a gift she had, making every sentence smack of accusation.

"Could you light a candle, please?" He strove to keep his voice mellow, and failed.

Nonetheless, he heard her leave the bed, and soon a flint sparked. The meager light of one lone candle, added to the dim fire, created shadows about the chamber.

"Are you hurt?" she had the decency to inquire. "'Twas an awful clatter."

"I am fine."

Fiona came closer then, the flickering light casting an otherworldly glow upon her translucent skin. She'd left her hair unbound and was wearing a white linen nightdress. A modest garment, yet one that set his blood to pounding. The throb moved from his kneecap to his groin.

She leaned closer and gasped. "Good heavens, Myles, you're bleeding." She set the candle upon the table and quickly lit a few more. She threw a log onto the fire. Then she disappeared into the garderobe for a moment before returning with some cloth.

"Here, sit in the chair. Let me see."

He let her pull him up and to the seat. "'Tis my nose. I must've struck it on the chair's leg."

She moved the candles closer and poured water from a pitcher into a basin, dipping in the cloth. "Tip your head back. Move your hand."

"You're a bossy wench."

"You're a bleeding sot. Now, move your hand, I said."

He let her minister to him, surprised at the gentleness of her touch compared to the harsh tone of her words. He'd not complain at that, though, for when she bent over, he could see her breasts bobbing free inside the white linen. He swallowed again and wished the candlelight were brighter and her neckline more willing. If he reached up just now, he could fill his palms with her flesh. The thought shot straight to his bollocks. Even so, his hands were spotted with his blood, and so he kept them in his lap, out of trouble and covering the evidence of his burgeoning arousal.

"Do you think it's broken?" she asked.

Thinking only of his cock, he uttered, "What?"

"Your nose. Do you think you've broken it?"

"Oh. I doubt it, though it hurts like the devil." He pressed his index fingers to the bridge, wiggling it.

Fiona dipped the cloth into the basin once more, then wrung it out. She pressed it to his nostrils. "Here, hold this against your nose."

He did as she'd instructed and tried to hide his surprise when she took his other hand and began to wipe it with a second damp cloth. He could have just as easily dipped it into the basin, but he didn't say so. 'Twas far too pleasant having her tend to him.

She did one hand and then the other, her brows pinched together in concentration as she stroked his palms, letting the moisture of the cloth clean away the crimson stains. She seemed more thorough than necessary, but still he held his tongue.

Then she wiped each finger from base to tip, slow and sure, and he thought he might die from the motion of it, as if he had ten little cocks each straining beneath the warm friction of her hands and the wetness of the cloth. She teased him without knowing. Christ, how he wanted her.

His hands were big. So much bigger than her own, and rough with calluses and scars. Not beautiful or soft, not the hands of leisure, and yet she found herself mesmerized by the strength and thickness of his palms, the sturdy bend of each finger and the signet ring declaring him a Campbell. Such hands were made for brandishing a sword and vanquishing a foe. Killing hands. And yet, she knew them to be gentle too when he'd touched her face at the inn or cut the ties from her wrists. Or when he held her hand at dinner. It made no sense that such brawny, well-worn hands could touch her with such delicacy. Yet she knew they could.

She wiped away the final bit of blood and peeked at his face. His head was tilted back, his eyes pinched closed. The injury must be causing him immense pain, for perspiration beaded on his forehead and his breathing was uneven. She noticed the pulse beating rapidly along the cord of his throat.

She let go of his hand and it fell, wrapping into a fist. She rinsed the cloth once more, wringing it out and exchanging it with the one his other hand pressed against his face. He opened his eyes and looked up at her in such a peculiar way, she thought for a moment he must be light-headed. Seeing their own blood did do that to some men, although he did not seem the woozy type.

"Are you well?" she asked again.

He tipped his head forward and pulled away the cloth. Scant traces of blood flecked it. He sniffed. "I think I'm fine."

"Well, put your head back and give it another moment."

His brows knit. "No, I'm fine. But you're a little worse for wear." He nodded toward her torso, and she looked down to find her nightdress damp with pink-tinged water from the basin. It clung to her belly, and she shivered, suddenly noticing the coolness of the room.

"You should change." His voice was gruff, and she could not imagine why, except that he was cross. This was her doing after all. Had she not left the chair tipped over on the floor, he'd not have fallen. She supposed she should apologize. 'Twas the bigger thing, after all, to admit when you were wrong.

"I'm sorry," she said, her voice barely above a whisper.

His eyes narrowed. "For which part?"

"For leaving the chair in your way. What else have I to apologize for?"

He stared at her for so long she wondered once again if he'd been dealt too hard a blow, and then he chuckled, a hollow sound with no humor in it. "What, indeed. Get yourself cleaned up, Fiona. I can manage for myself now."

His dismissal wounded her. She had tended him most gently, and now he seemed peevish. Leaving the chair in his path had been an accident. And why should she think he'd be wandering about in the dark of this room when he had not been here for days?

She strode into the garderobe and snatched another night-dress from the peg. Thanks be to God she had a second one of the sturdy linen. She'd not parade back out there with nothing but that sheer bit of ridiculousness. She pulled off her damp garment and quickly donned the other, tying the ribbon at the neckline as tightly as she could manage.

She heard Myles in the other room, emptying the basin and adding wood to the fire. It seemed he planned to stay, and so she had no choice but to reenter the chamber. Setting her chin, she walked back in and headed for the bed.

"Come sit here a moment." He pointed to the chair next to the hearth.

She hesitated, until he said, "Please. I've something to give you."

A scolding no doubt, but still she sat down as instructed.

"Wait here a moment." He strode into the garderobe and was back moments later. He knelt down by her knees, and his supplicant posture stole her breath. He handed her a red velvet pouch.

Her heart skipped, like a stone over the surface of a loch, until plunging deep beneath the murky surface.

"What is it?" she asked.

He chuckled at her unease. "You're a suspicious lass, aren't you? 'Tis nothing venomous, I promise. Open the bag."

She untied the cord and tipped the pouch, curiosity rippling through her. A gold-and-emerald necklace tumbled to her lap. She recognized the piece at once. 'Twas the one she'd admired when with Alyssa. She reached out but did not touch it.

"How did you know?" For a foolish moment, she wondered if a pendant such as this might be enchanted.

"My spies are everywhere," he answered, then chuckled when she did not smile. "The smith informed me when I passed his shop, but I was pleased to buy it for you. I thought to give it to you sooner but…but I was annoyed with you."

She looked into his eyes. "And now you are not?" He was an oddity.

Her husband took a deep, slow breath. "I am still annoyed. But I also realize you lost much when we left your trunks on the roadside, and I mean to see those items replaced. But more than that, Fiona, you've left behind your family and your home. And although you ran, and fight me still, you've never cowered. I respect that, even while I wish you'd stop."

"Stop?"

"Stop fighting me." His voice held a hint of pleading, but just a hint.

Her breath went misty in her lungs. "Why this change in your manner? You've barely seen me for days."

He shrugged. "Perhaps my brother's return has stirred in me a new understanding."

"A new understanding. Or a jealousy?" 'Twas a bold question, but she'd know the truth. If she was to be a pawn between them, best she know now.

He shook his head and gave a rueful smile. "I have no reason to be jealous of my brother. Robert annoys me too, as often as he pleases, but if fate should separate me from him, I would suffer for it. And I wonder if you suffer at the loss of your sister's company. I would ease that burden, were there a way."

Tears of surprise stung her eyes. 'Twas the first time he'd acknowledged that her coming here was anything other than her honor and a blessing she should cherish. To admit she'd made some sacrifice went far toward her forgiveness of him for being a wretched Campbell.

She picked up the necklace. It was the finest she'd ever seen. Far more expensive than any item stowed away in one of those trunks. She held it up, and the candlelight bounced off its links and danced around the walls. Enchanted, indeed.

"Thank you, Myles. It's lovely." She could not prevent the hitch in her voice.

He smiled. "Not so lovely as it shall be upon your neck. May I put it on for you?"

Ah, she should refuse this gift bought with Campbell wealth, riches gained at the loss of lesser clans like her own. But she wanted nothing more than to put it on and gaze into the mirror. She turned in the chair, and he stood up. She pulled her hair aside and held it as he positioned the chain, bringing the ends of it behind her.

He fumbled for a moment. "This clasp is made for daintier fingers than mine."

She imagined those fingers just then, the ones she had just stroked clean, and pressed her legs together tightly beneath her nightdress.

At last, he was successful in linking the necklace. He rested his hands briefly upon her shoulders, giving them the slightest squeeze. She let loose her hair and it fell against his forearms in a whoosh. She heard his breath expel.

She turned to face him, running her own fingers along the fine metalwork. "How does it look?"

"Stunning. Look for yourself." He reached over and pulled a hand mirror from the table, and then knelt before her once more, holding it aloft so she might peer at her reflection.

Her cheeks were warm, and she could not hold back a smile. "'Tis too dark in here. I wager you cannot even see it."

"I can. It glimmers against your skin like gold dust."

She reached out to adjust the mirror he held. Her hand brushed against his, and she felt a great jolt, as if their hearts aligned to beat in rhythm.

She glanced into the glass for a scant second, noticing the gold and the emerald and the glow of her skin. But it was the heat in her eyes that captured her own attention. They were wide and dark in the dim chamber, and it was not the necklace that made them so. She looked to Myles, and he set the mirror aside, his own eyes full of longing.

She wanted to despise him. 'Twas her Sinclair duty to do so. But she had tried, and it was too hard. His presence muddled her thoughts and clarified her desire. He had awakened in her a knowing that could not be unlearned. Her husband wasn't cruel or harsh or wicked or any of the things she'd thought all Campbells were. Instead, he was kind, and patient, and generous, and sincere. And he asked for little more than for her to be his wife in every way.

"'Tis a fine gift," she murmured.

Had he reached out just then and touched her, she would have slid into his arms, for she understood now how a blossom turned toward the sun. Her body seemed pulled in his direction, primed for his kiss and his plunder. But he did not reach out. He kept his hands to himself. His pride was as great as hers.

He clenched his fists, the need to touch her like a wave pushing him in her direction. But he resisted, for he wanted her to lean his way instead.

"I meant no disrespect by keeping my sister a secret," she said at his continued silence. "I think you would have taken care had you wed her instead. But I was frightened. I didn't know you then."

He pondered this a moment and saw a weakening in her defenses. "And do you know me now?"

"A little. Enough to know you are not cruel."

A compliment coming from her.

She was lovely in the firelight, staring back at him with those long-lashed eyes. She'd left her hair unbound. He could not resist. He moved his hand and twined a lock around his finger. She did not move or voice objection. From her, that might be as much an invitation as he could hope for. And if all the sons of Scotland waited for their wives to offer, his kin would die away, and his homeland would overrun with dirty English.

"'Tis you who is cruel," he teased gently. "To tempt me with your smiles and still refuse my kiss."

She stared a long moment, unsmiling. "You have not offered one in days."

His breath caught high in his throat, and his manhood sprang up with optimism.

She was sitting straight upright in the chair as he knelt before her. Her hair was silk ribbons. He twined a second curl with the first. "No, I haven't. You must ask, remember?"

She gave a delectable sigh of impatience, and he very nearly pulled her face to his to end this stubborn madness. But she fell back against the chair's cushion and looked to the fire, pressing her thumb against her lips. Her hair had pulled from his fingertips as she moved away. He sensed the Sinclair warrior within her battling against her woman's desire.

He reached down and ran his hands up along the back of her calves, inching her nightgown up as well.

"Stop that," she said without conviction, still staring at the fire.

"If I cannot kiss you, I must find some other way to pass this time."

She pushed one of his hands away with her foot, but he caught it and rubbed his thumb against the arch. Her eyes closed for the space of a breath. He moved his thumb again and saw a telltale flutter of her lashes.

Ah, perhaps this was the way to this lass's heart. Through her feet. And what a lovely route that would be to travel. He cupped both hands around that foot and squeezed, rubbing his palms against her skin.

She turned and frowned, weakly trying to tug from his grasp. "What are you doing?"

He shrugged and smiled. "Passing time."

"With my foot?"

"'Tis pleasant, is it not?"

She huffed and turned her gaze back to the fire, but did not pull away. "'Tis nothing at all, but amuse yourself, if it pleases you."

He chuckled at her transparent lie and caught up her other foot, leaning back and resting it against his thighs. Those knees of hers were clamped together, but he'd make her relax yet, and soon he'd delve between them. His chest filled with want. If she moved her foot an inch to the left, she'd know with every certainty how she affected him. As if she didn't know now. She was not so very innocent.

He rubbed her feet another moment, then moved his hands to her ankles and slowly caressed his way up the back of her calves until his fingers caught behind her knees. He leaned up then and pressed against her shins.

She sighed and caught her bottom lip between her teeth. The look she turned his way was full of indecision. 'Twas a far cry from her forbidding frowns of days past. He was halfway home.

He eased her nightgown up another inch or two, over the bend of her legs, but she caught the hem and held it steady.

"Don't," she whispered.

He was too close. His hands burned like cinders as he trailed them forward along her linen-covered thighs and brought them to rest at her waist. Even through her nightgown, she felt the heat, as if there were no barrier between them at all. He leaned forward until his face was a mere breath from hers.

She clutched at her hem and felt the muscles of his stomach flex against her hand. With her other, she pressed against his shoulder, as if trying to nudge a mountain from her path.

"'Tis enough," she said, but the quiver in her voice betrayed her.

He gave a tiny shake of his head. "No, my love, 'tis not nearly enough."

Her heart trembled at the endearment, though she knew it to be false. He did not love her, no more than she loved him. 'Twas instinct, nothing more. But when he lowered his head and ran his cheek against one breast, making it peak and swell and lift to him, she could not stop herself. She caught the back of his head and pressed it more firmly against her. He groaned and opened his mouth against her, moistening the fabric of her nightgown and branding her flesh.

His hands were fast, much too fast for her thoughts to react. His one arm reached around her waist and pulled her forward while the other hand slid past that hem and up along the outside of her thigh until his hand cupped her bare bottom and squeezed.

She cried out at that, dismayed at her unwitting concession and yet wanting nothing more than to arch against him and move her legs so he might reach between them.

His mouth traveled upward, toward the column of her throat, leaving a hot, moist trail. Her mind called out for him to cease and leave her be, but nothing came forth from her lips save wanton sighs. God, she was a helpless traitor. As useless to her clan as a sparrow.

He ran his lips along her jaw and paused, hovering over her own lips. She looked at him then, all dark and shadows in the dim light. Her heart thumped wildly in her chest. She could barely breathe for its erratic pace.

"Ask me," he whispered, nuzzling the side of her mouth with his own.

She turned her head away, not daring to speak, for nothing but permission would surely come forth.

He turned her face back toward him. "I am your husband, Fiona. Ask me, and I will show you such pleasure."

She licked her lips. She had one last arrow in her arsenal. "You are my enemy. I want nothing from you." But the words tasted bitter and sounded false.

He pulled her closer. "You're a liar."

She sighed at his accusation and could not deny it any more than she could deny him. She wove her hands into his hair and stared at him another moment. Then she kissed him, full and with abandon, welcoming the intensity of his desire.

His arm was steel around her, a welcome prison, and his other hand kneaded at her bottom. She gave in to it, to all of it. Her clan and her brothers be damned.

For delicious moments, they pressed and swayed within the confines of the chair, relief and tension building, two sides of the same coin. Myles pulled her to the edge of the seat and trailed his hand around to tease at the juncture of her legs. She pressed against his hand and felt a tremor build within.

He kissed her throat, tugging her nightgown aside with impatience, exposing her shoulder. The fabric caught on her necklace. He chuckled deep, running a finger along the gold. "God, Fiona," he sighed, "I would have given you this jewelry days ago had I known how it would melt your defenses."

His words penetrated the fog of her desire, dousing her ardor like the sting of autumn rain. She shoved against him and jerked back in the chair. Is that what he had done? Baited her with shiny baubles to sway her compliance?

"Melt my defenses?"

The look on his face went from confused to remorseful. He shook his head. "'Tis not what I meant, Fiona. I phrased that poorly."

But she would not be fooled. "You think to pay me off, like some whore? Give me a pretty jewel and watch me fall onto my back?" God, and she'd let him. She'd opened to him without even the need for a bed. They were in a chair and very nearly about to couple on the floor like peasants.

"I meant for the necklace to be a gift. Not a bribe. I had no expectations." His voice was strained. Of course it was. He'd failed in his purpose.

"Now who is the liar?" she demanded. "Can you look me in the eye and say you did not think to trade kisses for this jewelry?"

He lifted a stern jaw. "Yes, I meant to trade you kisses. But I'd have given you the necklace either way. I have not forced you, Fiona. 'Tis my earnest desire to avoid just that which has led us to this spot. I have been patient. And I make no apologies for wanting you."

"'Tis the trickery you should apologize for!" She pulled her nightdress up over her shoulder and worked to tie the neckline.

He ran a hand over his head. "I meant no trickery. If you'd be reasonable, you'd see that. Seduction isn't deception."

"Not the way you do it." She'd had one arrow more, it seemed, and this one struck its mark. He rose abruptly and turned to the fire, running a hand through his hair.

She was a foolish girl to think he cared about her feelings. If he respected her the way he said, he'd not have baited a trap with gold and emeralds. But he was a Campbell, after all, full of desire and manipulation. She'd let herself forget. 'Tis likely how her mother was deceived and found herself alone in a glen with Cedric Campbell. Fiona would not be so gullible.

# CHAPTER 26

A SOFT KNOCK SOUNDED ON THE DOOR EARLY THE NEXT morning, rousing Fiona from vivid dreams full of crimson colors. In the gray light of dawn, she rubbed her eyes and opened them to see Ruby coming in, a breakfast tray balanced on one hand. The smell of warm bread and bacon wafted through the air.

"Good morning, m'lady. I've brought ye—" The maid's voice cut short as she halted near the end of the bed. "Oh, good morning to ye as well, m'lord. I dinna—" She stopped again, her eyes going wide as Myles lifted his head from the pillow.

Still hazy from slumber, Fiona had forgotten he was there, but the night came rushing back in vivid detail. Him tumbling over the chair, the nosebleed, and the aftermath.

But 'twas daytime now, and the maid stood gaping at her husband, her expression indicating more than just surprise at Myles's presence. Fiona looked at him and gave a tiny gasp. He sat up and whisked a hand through his hair to smooth it. "What?" His voice rasped with sleep.

Fiona sat up next to him and looked back to Ruby.

"What?" he demanded once more.

"Forgive me, m'lord. You have a bit of a blackened eye," Ruby answered.

"Bring me a looking glass," he said thickly.

Ruby scurried to set the tray upon the table and found the mirror where it had been left upon the floor. She brought it to him, her lips betraying nothing, pursed together as they were.

Myles took the glass with some hesitation. He looked at Fiona first. "Is it awful?"

She shrugged. "Not so very awful."

With a sigh of resignation, he gazed into the glass and let out a huff. He ran his hand through his hair again and held the mirror higher, to see himself in better light.

"Christ," he muttered.


"Come on, now," Vivi prodded. "Tell me how you blackened my nephew's eye. A randy scuffle twixt the sheets, yes?"

"No, 'twas just as I explained. I left the chair in his path, and in the dark, he tripped." She'd come to Vivienne's solar in the hope some sewing might purge her restlessness, but the task at hand merely made her neck ache and her temples throb.

Vivienne frowned and plucked at her mending. "Have you worn your new nightgown yet?"

Fiona squirmed in her chair. "You are inordinately interested in my bedclothes. I should think you'd have more important things with which to occupy your mind."

"Well, I haven't. I cannot find a man for myself until I'm back at court. You are my only source of entertainment." She jabbed her needle through the fabric and straight into her finger. "Ach!" She popped the finger into her mouth and mumbled around it. "By all the saints in heaven, how I detest mending."

Fiona smiled despite her somber mood. "I'm sorry I cannot distract you, but there is simply nothing to tell."

That was not entirely the truth, of course. There was much to tell, but Vivi would be disappointed it had gone so poorly. As was Fiona, for Myles had not said another word after she'd pushed him away. He'd stared into the fire for so long she'd finally returned to the bed and lain awake for near on an hour, waiting for him to come to bed. At last, she'd fallen asleep and had been surprised to see him next to her in the morning.

"Oh, there must be something. At least tell me you've gotten better acquainted since your wedding night."

Fiona felt her cheeks burn bright. She ducked her head over her own sewing and offered a tiny shrug of her shoulders.

"Haven't you?" Vivi's eyebrows rose to the ceiling. Then she chuckled and fell back against her chair. "I cannot think how Myles is holding himself back. I told him to be patient, but I had no idea he'd take my advice so to heart."

"You told him to be patient? With me?"

Vivi's expression showed no remorse. "Yes, I did. And I told him to be nice as well. But it isn't very nice of him to leave his bride chaste as a pockmarked nun. And shame on you for making him wait so long."

A rush of uncertainty rose within Fiona, and yet she was in no mood for a scolding. "No shame on me. I never wanted him in the first place."

Vivienne cocked her head. "But you'd have him now, yes?"

Fiona's shrug was noncommittal. That necklace had felt like a yoke when she'd thought he'd meant to bribe her with it. But when daylight came, she wondered if she'd been too hasty.

"He's a lovely man, Fiona," Vivi said, "and a fine husband. Why would you not want him?"

Fiona's jaw tightened, even as tears puddled in her eyes. "It isn't that, Vivi. But it's not so simple. Do you forget who I am? And what pain his family has caused mine?"

Vivienne twisted her mending into a thick knot and tossed it aside. "Fiona, honestly, you carry this burden too far. I know you think Cedric had something to do with your mother's death, but I'm just as certain he did not."

"He is your brother-in-law. Of course you'd think the best of him."

"The best of him?" A delicate snort escaped Vivienne's nose. "He has been a rogue and a knave. He broke my sister's heart. And though he's tried to make amends, I have not forgiven him. Still, for all his flaws, Cedric is a lover of women, not a murderer of any."

A tingling began at the base of Fiona's spine and scuttled upward to the nape of her neck. She felt at once both hot and cold. "He broke Marietta's heart? How so?"

Vivienne stared at her, for once serious, as if she strove to choose her words with great caution. "No one is infallible, you know. Not even those we love with all our hearts."

"I don't understand."

Vivi glanced about the room, as if someone might be peeping through a crevice or listening at the door. She leaned forward in her chair, and Fiona did the same until their faces were mere inches apart.

"If Mari knew I shared this with you, she'd burn me at the stake. But I will tell you nonetheless, if only so you might stop with all this foolishness." She looked around once more, then locked her gaze on Fiona. "Cedric and Aislinn were lovers."

Fiona thumped back in her chair, frustration echoing in her chest. "Oh! That nonsense. Myles tried to ply me with the same story. They think to convince me it was *my* father and not the earl. 'Tis nothing more than rumor and Cedric's way of tricking me into compliance."

But Vivienne grasped her wrist, hard. "'Tis a good deal more than rumor. I have proof."

Fiona's breath turned to dust in her lungs. "What proof?"

"Come with me, and I will show you." Vivienne stood up, letting the rest of her mending fall from her lap onto the floor. She held out a hand to Fiona. "Come on, then."

She let Vivi pull her from the chair and out the door, down one corridor after another, until they stood outside the chapel.

Vivienne clutched her hands and squeezed. "What I am going to show you, Fiona, is not meant to tarnish any memory you have of your mother. She was a woman, same as you and me, forced to make difficult choices." Her voice was an earthy whisper. "My only wish is for you to be happy here at Dempsey."

Fiona's heart plummeted and bounced back into her throat. She had no idea where Vivienne was leading her or what they might discover. She only knew there was no turning back.

Vivienne eased open the wooden door and they stepped inside. The interior of the chapel was dim, smeared with blurry colors made by light shining through the stained-glass windows. Intricate carvings covered the dark paneled walls, and several rows of candles surrounded the altar. At the front hung an ornate cross with Jesus looking down on them in pity.

They walked down the aisle of the nave and turned to the left, toward another door. Vivi knocked softly. "Father Darius?"

Silence answered.

She turned back and motioned for Fiona to come closer, and then she pushed the door open. "Father, 'tis Vivienne. I need a word with you. It seems I've sinned again." She let out a chuckle at her joke, and still more silence answered.

She nodded then and stepped inside Father Darius's chamber.

"We can't go in there." Fiona's admonishment was barely above a whisper.

"Of course we can. It's the only way to the sacristy."

"The sacristy? We can't go in there either." What antics had Vivi pulled her into? They were treading over holy ground as if it were no more sanctified than a mucked-up stall.

But in Vivi went, past the priest's bed and kneeling bench and straight to yet another door. This one small and tucked into a corner. She plucked a taper from his bedside table and lit it. She looked over her shoulder, saucier still. "Stand there, and he's likely to discover you. Follow me if you've no wish to be caught."

Fiona peered back into the chapel. It remained empty, with no sign of Father Darius. Vivi disappeared into the stairwell behind the tiny door, the meager glow of the candle lighting her way.

With fear tapping on one shoulder and curiosity tapping the other, Fiona closed the door to the priest's chamber and scampered along behind Myles's aunt.

Vivienne lit sconces along the wall as she made her way downward. It was a short staircase and opened at the bottom into a room of cupboards, some with locks as heavy as an anchor. A ring of metal keys hung on a peg, and Vivienne set down the candle and scooped them up. She fumbled for a moment until she found the one she sought.

"They should be in here." Vivi put the key into one of the smaller locks and jiggled it until the thing fell open with a scrape and click.

Fiona jumped at the sound, for in the tiny chamber, it echoed like a slap. "I'm sure you're not supposed to open that."

Vivienne cast an exasperated glance over her shoulder. "If God didn't want me to unlock it, He'd not have left the keys where I could find them. Trust in the Lord, Fiona."

Fiona thought to ponder this but had not the time, for the cupboard door creaked open and Vivienne shuffled several items aside, at last pulling from the farthest recesses a dusty bundle wrapped in faded muslin. It was tied with a simple leather cord. She set the bundle on the floor and made deft work of unknotting the string.

"I think this is it," she said, and worked loose the last of the tie. The fabric fell to the sides, and there sat a stack of folded papers, tied with another ribbon, this one of deep crimson.

Fiona could not breathe or swallow, for though she had yet to learn the contents of those letters, she knew beyond reason that they were about to change everything.

"What are those?" Her voice cracked; her palms went moist.

Vivi looked into her eyes and held up the bundle as if it were the chalice from the Last Supper. "Letters. Love letters from your mother to Cedric Campbell."

Fiona's stomach rolled, and she felt dizzy and confused. So much so that Vivienne stood up fast and clutched her arm. "I told you I had proof," she said. Still holding Fiona steady, Vivienne leaned down and grabbed the cloth and other tie. "We cannot read them here, though. Hold these. Let me lock the cabinet again, and we can take these to my chamber."

Dazed, Fiona accepted the bundle, and even managed to wrap the cloth around it once more as Vivienne fastened the lock and put the keys back on the peg. Then Vivienne spun her by the shoulders, turning her around and pushing her back up the stairs, blowing out the candles as they went.

At the top, she grasped Fiona's elbow. "Let me go first." She stepped around and went into the priest's chamber once more. Crossing to the other door, she opened it a crack, peeking into the chapel. She motioned for Fiona to follow and stepped through.

Up the aisle they rushed, but before they reached the door leading to the corridor, it opened and Father Darius stepped through. Fiona crossed her arms over the bundle as Vivienne stepped in front of her to shield it from the priest's view.

His smile was warm, and Fiona thought once more how unlike Father Bettney he seemed. But that might change, once he realized she'd just stolen something from his sacristy.

"Father Darius." Vivienne's voice bubbled with enthusiasm. "How lovely to see you."

"And you," he answered. "I did not see you at mass this morning." His eyes crinkled at the corners. "Or nearly any morning this week, if my memory is correct."

"I'm sorry, Father. Mornings are such a sad time for me. 'Tis when I miss my dear dead husband the most, and I fear my weeping would distract your congregation."

Priests should not scoff and roll their eyes, but this one did. "Vivienne, the Lord is everlasting in his patience, but even He must be getting tired of your fibs. However, come to mass tomorrow, and both He and I may forgive you. You wound my pride when you do not listen to my sermons, you know."

Vivienne's lips turned up in humor. "Isn't pride the work of the devil, Father?"

Father Darius laughed, a rich, warm sound that echoed through the chapel. Fiona had never heard a priest laugh before. In fact, she could not recall a time when Father Bettney had done anything other than scowl and scold.

"Your wit has bested me, my lady. But I should like to see you at mass occasionally nonetheless. Now, what brings you to the chapel today? Is there something I can do for you and Lady Fiona?"

He nodded at Fiona, and she gripped the bundle more tightly still. She felt like Herod snatching the baby Jesus from his manger.

"No, thank you, Father," Vivienne answered smoothly. "We are done. We came to offer prayers for Lady Fiona's mother and father."

"Ah, yes. I'm sorry for your loss, my lady. I will add them to my prayers this evening."

"Thank you, Father." Fiona could not seem to raise her voice above a whisper, choked as it was with a myriad of emotions.

"Thank you, Father," Vivienne said as well. "That is kind of you, indeed. And I vow to make more effort to attend mass. But now we must be going." With a fast smile, she pulled Fiona the length of the aisle and out the chapel door.

Shutting it behind them, the women leaned back against the wood. Fiona's heart raced as if she'd run for miles, and the bundle of letters weighed a stone and plenty.

Vivienne took them from her. "Best let me carry these."

They quickly made their way back to Vivienne's chamber and sat upon her bed. She unwrapped the bundle once more.

"Would you like to be alone to read these? Or shall I stay?"

Fiona stared at them, as if each letter might turn into a snake and writhe around in a dark and twisty pile. She dared not touch even the crimson ribbon binding them together.

"I should like you to stay, please. But first, you must tell me how you knew of them, locked up as they were."

Vivienne rose up off the bed and poured herself some wine from a pitcher sitting on a table. She took a hearty sip before filling another cup and handing it to Fiona.

"Before Father Darius arrived, there was another priest here. A debauched old lecher, much too fond of drink. But what a font of information that one was." Vivienne's shoulders rose and fell in a delicate shrug. "One evening, when he was well into his cups, he told me of the letters. Cedric put them there so my sister might never know of them. And once the priest told me...Well, I confess the temptation to read them was far too great."

"You've read them? All of them?" It should not be a shock, and yet it was. The action felt like betrayal of the deepest cut.

But for once, Vivi demonstrated some display of shame, dipping her head and looking to the floor. "I'm sorry, Fiona. I know I shouldn't have, but I never thought to know you. It seemed like such an appealingly wicked game at the time, until your poor mother turned up murdered, of course."

Bile roiled inside Fiona at the mention. "Do the letters hint at anything about that?"

Vivienne shook her head. "Nothing that I recall. But it's been years since I read them."

"And no one knows you've seen them? Or that they even exist?"

"I have no idea who knows of them. That old priest could keep no secrets. 'Tis why I gave up confession altogether."

Breath was hard to come by as Fiona stared into the pile once more. Love letters. From her mother to Cedric Campbell. The desire to read every word equaled her fear of what she would learn. To think of her mother as a young woman, a woman longing for a man other than her husband, made Fiona's skin flush and her throat tighten. She sipped at the wine Vivienne had given her, then set her glass on the table next to the bed.

"Of course, these are only the letters Cedric received from your mother. There is no telling where his letters back to her might have gone," Vivienne added.

Fiona looked to her at once. "His letters to her? I had not thought of that." Of course she had not, for until that very morning, she'd had no knowledge of any such communication between them. And indeed was still not certain this pile of scraps before her proved a thing. She could not know unless she read them.

So she must.

# CHAPTER 27

H ER MOTHER AND CEDRIC HAD BEEN LOVERS AT COURT. OF that truth, Fiona now had little doubt. At first, she'd hoped the letters might be forged, written by another's hand for some diabolical purpose, but each one revealed the tiniest details of life at Sinclair Hall, things that only her mother might remark upon and things only she could have known. She wrote about her garden where she tended flowers and the orchard out behind the wall. She wrote of a deep abiding love for each of her children, but also of how she longed to be back at court and with Cedric once more.

How surreal it was bearing witness to her mother's innermost thoughts, the secrets of her heart, and her passionate longing for a man she could not freely love, for they'd both been married when first they'd met. It seemed Cedric had answered each letter, too, for her mother responded to questions he must have posed and instructions of where they might meet when he traveled to the North. So it seemed the affair had continued after James had claimed the throne and Hugh Sinclair had been banished. Fiona could think of few times when her mother's whereabouts were unaccounted for, but she had been a child then and had not given thought to her mother's whereabouts. Vivienne sat silently, reading the letters as they were passed to her. At first, Fiona had wanted to keep them to herself, but quickly found she could not bear this burden alone. She was glad for the other woman's presence and the way Vivienne passed her a fine linen kerchief when Fiona's tears flowed fast and steady. She knew not which aspect of the letters prompted tears, so varied and vast were her emotions.

Betrayal, that her mother had deceived her father in such a manner. Though he'd been a harsh man, no one deserved such treatment. Sympathy, for a woman who had not the freedom to live life as she would have chosen. And anger, that this secret, or the revelation of it, had somehow caused her murder. For certainly the manner of her assault spoke of anger and retribution. If there were letters from Cedric, perhaps her father had known.

And if he had, what might he have done? She thought of the brooch, Cedric's brooch, a token from a lover stuck through her mother's skin. Her belly recoiled. That was an act of jealousy if ever there was one. And yet, she could not accept that thought. There must be someone else to blame.

The last letter, dated just a few weeks before her mother's death, left Fiona robbed of breath and full of still more questions.

*My darling,*

*My heart leapt with joy for your news. How proud you must be to have been appointed James's constable at Dempsey. You've done well to earn his respect and he is most fortunate to have you as a friend, as am I.*

*Things are changing here of late. My husband grows more watchful. There are moments I fear for myself and the safety of the children. There are things I would discuss with you about the future I dare not put into a letter. The time to act is drawing near.*

*My sons grow tall and strong and I am so proud of them both. But Simon is turning away from me. I fear he may cross a bridge from whence I cannot call him back. John is ever my observer, my philosopher, but he is still so young, and more sensitive than the rest. I am not certain he is ready for whatever may come to pass. My girls are a joy, playful and sweet. I pray each night that one day things will be set to rights, and your Myles and my Fiona can be joined as we had always planned.*

*Darling, how I long to see you. I need your advice. But more than that, I need your kiss. It has been near on a year since we last met and my heart grows heavier each day. Send word and I shall count the moments, as I count the memories of our times together.*

*Yours in love,*

*A.*

The time-yellowed letter fell from Fiona's hand and floated to the bed. Vivienne looked at her, sympathy and curiosity mixed in equal measure upon her face; then she reached over and picked up the paper. She read it quickly.

"The time to act is drawing near? What can she mean by that?" Vivienne asked.

Fiona's heart fluttered like a hummingbird, frantically flapping its wings just to stay in place and not plummet to the ground. "I don't know. I don't understand any of it. Except that she hoped Myles and I would one day be married."

"Can you see now that he would not have harmed her?"

Fiona's head ached. "I can see there was love between them. Still, it doesn't explain everything that happened. Some of my clansmen said they'd seen him on our land the very day she died.

He admitted to Myles he was with her then but swears he left her alive."

"Then someone must have come upon her after he left."

"But who?" Tears swelled in Fiona's eyes. She could deny the truth until her own dying day, but everything she'd learned supported Cedric's claims. And made her father the most plausible culprit.

# CHAPTER 28

J OHN SINCLAIR SAT IN THE GREAT HALL AND LOOKED ACROSS
the scarred wooden table at the council of Highland chiefs,
each man a king in his own right, defender of his piece of rock
and willing to fight for it to the death. Each eager to hold tight his
grip on the illusionary power that came with it. Sutherland, Ross,
Mackay, and Gunn, and a few of the lesser chiefs. Those willing
to discuss their collective fate had gathered at Sinclair Hall at his
brother's request, and the arguments began before they'd even
sat down.

"Why should we trust you, Simon? You're in bed with the
Campbells now. What's to say you're not leading us into treason?" 'Twas Sutherland who spoke, his white hair bright in the
dim light of the hall.

Simon stood at the end of the table, his booted foot upon
a chair and a tankard in his fist. "I'm no more in bed with the
Campbells than I am with your wife, Sutherland."

Ross barked out a laugh, a raucous sound that scraped John's
good ear. The man's jowls flapped like a hound's when he spoke.
"I've seen Sutherland's wife. I'd not bed her either."

"As if she would have you, you louse-bitten cur," Mackay jibed. He was the youngest, and anxious to prove his place among them.

Soon they all joined in with their crude jokes and boastful insults. Like rams butting horns, they postured for dominance over nothing more important than rocky crags and empty pastures where little grew and nothing bloomed.

John let them crow, these coarse men and their pompous sense of purpose in the world. Simon had called them here to plot and scheme, but what did it matter if they swore fealty to James when he sailed around the Highlands? Here in the North, they were insulated from the politics of Edinburgh. They could promise one thing yet do another, and the royal court would be none the wiser. The king was a fool to seek loyalty here among these beggars and thieves, but they were even bigger fools to stir up trouble by refusing him.

John knew that now, for he'd thought on it in solitude these past few weeks but would share none of these thoughts with Simon. His brother had no sense at all of how his feelings had changed since the day Fiona rode away. Before the Campbells came, he'd thought only of revenge like the rest of these brutes. But now he'd had time to think about the future, his future, and all he'd learned from Cedric Campbell after the wedding.

"Stop pecking at one another, you vain peacocks. We've important matters to discuss." Simon banged his empty tankard against the tabletop. Once they settled and he claimed their rapt attention, he continued. "The king arrives in Gairloch in September. Now, who among you will fall to your knees like a whore and beg for his love, and who will stand like men beside me and my brother and fight for our freedom?"

The chiefs cast uneasy glances at one another, with none speaking up.

"Well?" Simon demanded again.

"If the king defeats us, Sinclair, he will show no mercy," said Sutherland, looking to each of them.

"Mercy?" Simon spit upon the rushes. "Mercy is for old men and wee girls. 'Tis freedom I'm talking about. He thinks to strip you of it, of your lands and your titles. And he'll not stop at that. Once James has us in his noose, he'll tighten it until we must beg him for every breath. My father would not live that way, and neither shall I!"

His passion stirred them.

"Nor will I," called out Mackay, his fist raised in solidarity. "Sinclair is right. The king plays at being generous by telling us we may keep our lands. But what right has he to grant us permission to anything? The Mackays have occupied this area since before the first Stewart planted his arse upon the throne. I'll not swear allegiance to him or any king who cannot see past the needs of Edinburgh."

"It's not enough to win the battle, you shortsighted fools," shouted Sutherland over the supportive outburst from the others. "The king will come with a moderate force, but even if we defeat them, we'll have to take his life. And then we'll have the Campbells at our throats, along with any who fight to avenge King James. We will be bringing hell down upon our own people."

"Not if we have help from London." Simon doled out the words slowly, like each one was a precious gem.

John shivered, as if a ghost had walked through him.

"What help is that?" Ross asked. He was a head shorter than the rest, but twice the width.

Simon refilled his cup, taking his time and seeming to enjoy this moment. "The help of Archibald Douglas, of course."

Sutherland scoffed. "What aid can he lend us, hiding as he is in England?"

"He knows of our trials. He respected our right of self-governance while he was Scotland's regent. And the king has no legitimate heirs. With James dead, rule reverts back to the king's mother, Douglas's wife, making Archibald regent once more. I should think he'd be thankful—grateful, even—if our efforts put him back on the throne."

"And he'd let us rule our lands as we see fit," Mackay added, his dark eyes glaring at Sutherland.

John listened to them banter and sipped from his cup. The ale was sour in his mouth. He thought to get up and find himself some wine. Good wine, not the swill they'd served to the likes of these puffer fishes. They'd go on for hours, debating every contingency, plotting and recoiling, and going through it all again. And all their chatter would be for naught because Simon always had his way. But this time, John had plans of his own.

A movement caught John's eyes, and he hid his smile behind his cup. 'Twas his Gen, peeking down at him from an archway of an upper corridor. She gave a tiny wave, and he tipped his head discreetly. He'd told her to stay far away from this mass of men, and so she had. She'd spent all morning lounging in his bed instead, letting their child grow big and strong inside her belly. How he wished he could've spent the hours there beside her. But he must be here to steer these sheep without Simon realizing.

Leaving her side was always a sacrifice. He had not imagined a woman such as she might exist. She made him laugh and burn. She raised him up and gave him courage. For her, he would do anything, which made Simon's next words that much more difficult to hear.

"Once we have ensured allegiance to our cause from the other Highland chiefs, my brother, John, will go to London. He will take a letter, drafted and signed by each of us, swearing our support to Archibald Douglas as regent of Scotland if he will join us in our plan to remove James from the throne."

"'Tis bold-faced treason to sign such a letter!" Sutherland slammed his fist upon the table. "I'll not sign such a thing."

Simon smiled, an ugly thing that twisted his dark face. "We all sign so that none of us can betray the other. And 'tis only treason if we're caught, but my brother is a clever man. Aren't you, John?"

All eyes to turned to him. He held his face steady. "More clever than any of you could imagine. I'll deliver that letter with none the wiser."

"There, you see?" Simon brushed his hands together as if the accomplishment were his and victory all but assured. "That is why we married our sister off to the Campbell pup, you dullards, so that my brother might have easy access through the whole of Scotland and straight on to London. He can plead loyalty to either side, depending where he is and who is doing the asking. We'll sew the letter into the lining of his doublet so, until he takes it out, no one will even know it's there."

"Until he's caught and someone puts a blade to his throat. He'll spill out our names rather than his own blood," Ross grumbled.

Simon leaned over and grabbed the little runt by the throat. He squeezed, just enough so John could see Ross's fleshy cheeks go red. "My brother will not offer any of us up, except for maybe you, if you say the likes of that again."

Simon pushed him back against the chair, and Ross sputtered and coughed.

"I'll not be caught," John said, his voice loud and strong. He stood up. "To all the world, we have the might of the Campbell clan protecting us. Their arrogance makes them believe we are glad for it, that we cower at their superiority. They have no idea we use them like a cloak to hide our true purpose. Nor will the king until his foot lands upon our shores and his feeble army meets our swords. Even without the help of Douglas, we would succeed, for we have surprise on our side, and the king's forces will be weakened after weeks upon the water. But with Douglas's aid, there is nothing that can stop us."

The men thumped their hands against the table and harrumphed their agreement, spurred on by John's careful enthusiasm. They were like sheep bleating for their supper, for his words had reached the target. He hit upon their own conceit, their certainty that they were the most deserving.

Simon smiled, raising his tankard to salute him.

John felt the faintest tapping of remorse knocking on his soul. He was Judas in Gethsemane, betraying one he loved. But he'd do this wicked thing for the most righteous of reasons and pray that history and all who knew him as a son of Hugh Sinclair would understand. And so that Fiona had not been sacrificed in vain.

# CHAPTER 29

"LET ME SEE IF I QUITE UNDERSTAND YOU, BROTHER." Robert Campbell's dimples deepened in his cheeks. "You did that damage to your face...with a chair?"

Myles flexed his arm and raised a wooden sword toward his brother's chest. He and several of his men had joined Robert in the bailey to train. A good long bout of thrusting jabs at his brother was just what Myles needed to clear the cobwebs from his mind.

"I told you, the room was dark," he said.

Robert leaned forward, examining the bruise with greater scrutiny. "Well, 'tis impressive, to be sure. Next time I'm off to battle, I shall leave my sword at home and take a chair instead. Although, without your bride to wield it, I'm not sure I could do such harm."

"She didn't wield it. 'Twas merely left in my path."

His brother grinned. "On purpose?"

"No." He swung his sword and clipped Robert in the shoulder. The day was bright and the air smelled fresh with blossoms, but he'd passed a restless night and his head ached from lack of sleep and too much unquenched desire. He'd stuck his foot in it with that thoughtless comment about the necklace.

But the lass had overreacted. Tonight, he'd try again. He would kiss her and cajole her and be as honest as a bishop about his intentions. With luck and patience, his self-imposed celibacy would end.

His brother returned a blow with his own wooden sword, and so they went, thrust and dodge, jab and block. The yard was alive with activity, with the men training and carts coming in laden with stores for the castle. The sound of women's laughter floated from the laundry as a few came out with baskets full of wet garments to hang on the line.

"Tavish told me of Fiona's antics during your travels. She sounds a handful." His brother's voice was relaxed as he easily deflected each stab.

"She can be. Or tame as a kitten," Myles lied.

"Things between you seem harmonious."

Robert swung wide, but Myles dipped low to miss the hit.

"Harmonious enough."

"Your words are as evasive as your footwork, brother. Answer me straight, how does it feel to be a husband?"

*It felt like being stuffed into a pickling cask and left for days on end.* "Fine."

Robert's laughter caught the attention of the other training men, but Myles cast a glare their way, and quickly, they turned back to their own sparring.

"Fine?" Robert said. "Hardly glowing words from a man during his honeymoon."

Myles lunged to strike him in the shank, but Robert sidestepped.

"We are adjusting. You know the circumstances, Robert," Myles said. "She's a Sinclair, for God's sake." He did not intend to admit so much, but Robert was putting him through his paces and the words had escaped before he considered them.

"A Sinclair, you say. Are they as wicked in bed as on the battlefield?"

This time his brother went too far. Myles swung his training sword with all his might and struck a fierce blow to Robert's thigh. The contact was loud as a thunderclap and brought his brother to his knees.

"Jesus!" Robert cursed, clutching his leg.

It was a dirty blow, and yet Myles felt little remorse. "'Tis my wife you're speaking of, little brother. You'd best watch your tongue."

"And your sword too, it seems, you miserable prick." Robert glowered at him from the ground.

After another second, Myles reached out his hand.

"Is there a knife up your sleeve?" his brother asked, his humor returning.

"Oh, stop complaining. I didn't hit you that hard. And you deserved it. When you're married, you'll understand."

Robert shook his head but accepted Myles's hand. "Marriage has made you testy."

Myles nearly nodded, for his brother was closer to the target than he knew. Still, he'd had enough of this conversation. "Do you want to stand here peeping like chicks, or are we here to train?" He brandished his sword once more.

"Now that you've crippled me, you mean?" Robert rubbed his thigh.

"Ah, I'd forgotten your spindly legs were fragile as reeds. I'll go easier on you." Myles smiled and took his stance, planting his feet wide apart.

Robert did the same, smiling in return. "No, I'll have your best and show you how inferior that is to my remarkable skills."

They fought fairly but with all their might until both were drenched with perspiration. Myles pulled his shirt up over his head and tossed it into the dirt.

"Ready to quit?" Robert teased.

"Not until you're begging for mercy."

And so they set to battling once more, back and forth, until a movement caught Myles's eye and brought him to a halt. 'Twas Fiona crossing the bailey with Alyssa on one arm and a basketful of flowers on the other. Such a lovely, ordinary thing, and yet it set his heart in a spin.

His wife looked over and smiled, her expression genuine and warm as sunshine. She gave a tiny wave, jostling the basket, and a few blossoms fell to the ground. When she bent to pick them up, the view of her backside punched the breath from him like no strike from Robert ever could.

Or so he thought, 'til Robert plowed the handle of a training sword straight into his gut.


Fiona had watched them train while she and Alyssa cut flowers in the garden. How ferociously they wielded their swords, neither giving ground to the other. She'd seen men train before, of course, but this was like a dance, for Myles and Robert moved in unison, so alike and yet so different. And when Myles pulled off his shirt, she stood gaping until Alyssa's giggle cut through her thoughts.

"Best close your mouth, Fiona, or a bee will fly in."

"That isn't very nice," she said, feeling heat that had nothing to do with the sun overhead.

Alyssa was nonplussed. "'Tis true though. You look at him as though he's a plate of marzipan."

Marzipan, indeed. Since reading the love-drenched letters from her mother, Fiona's attitude had changed. She'd fought to resist Myles's tenderness and his advances, but now, knowing her mother had wanted them together, there was less reason to deny him. And with the feud between their clans based on a faulty accusation, perhaps there was no reason to resist him at all. Perhaps her brothers had known something she didn't. The very fact they'd given her over to the Campbells was evidence they sought this truce. It seemed she'd gone about this all wrong, for now she understood. She was always meant to be his wife, from the day she was born. The thought swirled in the base of her stomach, leaving her light-headed. Or perhaps it was just the sun after all.

"Let's go inside. I suddenly find myself quite thirsty," Fiona said.

She and Alyssa crossed the bailey, coming closer to the men, and Fiona could not resist giving her husband a tiny wave. But flowers fell from her basket, and so she bent to scoop them up.

She did not see the blow but heard the grunt and thud as Myles hit the dirt. Unbidden, she rushed to his side, hauling Alyssa in her wake.

"What happened?" she asked Robert as she knelt down by Myles's inert form. He was on his side, but she rolled him easily onto his back and cradled his head in her lap. His eyes were pinched shut.

Robert shrugged and leaned upon the hilt of his sword. "I bested him."

"You've knocked him unconscious."

He prodded Myles with the tip of his boot. "He did that to himself when he tripped over his own shirt. 'Twas his rock-hard melon hitting the ground that did him in. And might I add how clumsy he's become? First the chair, now this. Maybe it's marriage that has tipped him off-kilter."

"I saw you ram him in the belly," Alyssa scolded.

Robert shrugged again and looked up at the clouds.

The other men had gathered round, some murmuring, others posturing to get a look at their chief's son taken down by a mere training sword. Fiona looked down at her husband, noticing his shirtless, sweat-soaked torso once more. She'd blush later, when she thought of that again. For now, she thought only of bringing him back to his senses. She brushed the damp hair back from his forehead and patted him gently on the cheek.

"Myles, can you hear me?"

His mouth twitched, and she felt a tremor in his shoulders.

"Myles?" she asked again.

The tremor grew stronger, and the twitching of his lips increased. What was the matter with him? Then he opened his bruised eye to peer up at her. His smile broke free, along with his laughter, and he opened the other eye.

"Oh! You're not unconscious." Irritation soon gave way to relief. It washed over her like spring rain, and her own smile could not be contained. "You're not hurt at all." She patted his cheek again, perhaps a bit harder than necessary.

"Ach, woman. I will be if you don't stop hitting me." He raised his arms up to grasp her wrists and pull her closer. And she let him.

"I thought you were truly wounded." She could not hide the concern in her voice, and his eyes caught hers, the pull stronger than his hands.

"I am wounded each time we part. But kiss me, and I'll be well again." He teased, yet she could see the longing in his expression. He'd forgiven her for her part of their discord last night. She could see it in his face. *I'll make no apologies for wanting you.* Her heart fluttered as she remembered his words, and other bits quivered as well. A kiss. Such a tiny thing, such a minor request, and yet the two of them knew how much it meant. Fiona leaned in closer. She could kiss him now, and every day after, if she wanted to. He was her husband after all.

Robert cleared his throat. "You think she'd kiss you like that, brother? With you stinking and dirty from the yard?"

The men laughed. The spell was broken.

Myles's chuckle was good-natured, but his eyes remained on her.

She bit her lip and leaned down farther still, until her lips were near his ear. "Take a bath, and I shall kiss you later."

Then she stood up fast, nearly dumping his head in the dirt, but he sat up on his own strength. Fiona smiled and nodded at Robert and the others. "Carry on, men. Please don't let me keep you."

Without another glance at Myles, she turned and flounced away, hearing Robert say as she left, "Tame as a kitten, indeed."

# CHAPTER 30

E VENING COULD NOT COME FAST ENOUGH. FIONA'S DECLARA-
tion had shot through his chest and continued south. 'Twas
only a kiss she'd promised, but her eyes spoke of more. Something
in her mind had changed, and he knew one kiss, one delicious
kiss, could light the wick of her desire.

Back in their chamber, he washed and dressed at a leisurely
pace, hoping she might arrive and forfeit that kiss immediately.
But the time passed and she did not enter. He grew impatient at
the thought she meant to tease him further. He'd be late to the
evening meal if he lingered any longer, and so he made his way to
the great hall and found Tavish, Robert, and his mother already
there, waiting and dressed in their finery.

His mother clucked over his bruised eye. "Oh, Myles. Is
it painful?"

"'Tis fine, Mother."

"Robert tells me you took some hard hits in the yard."

Myles cast a wicked glance at his brother. "Thank you,
Robert. I myself might have omitted that."

Robert's smile was banal. "I am ever the herald. Where is
your lovely bride?"

Myles turned and looked about the hall. "I thought she would be here. She did not come to change."

"Here she is," his mother said, looking toward the entryway.

And there she was, indeed.

Vivienne was next to her, dressed in bold crimson, but all eyes must have been on his wife, for she entered the hall wearing a gown of palest peach, so pale one could almost not tell where her skin ended and the dress began. The kirtle beneath was ivory trimmed in lace, and swayed as she walked. She wore the emerald necklace, and his chest tightened at the sight of it. The crowd within the hall murmured their approval.

Her hair was loose, cascading down in ringlets and caught up in the front under a beaded French hood. She was a goddess. He stood a little taller knowing she belonged to him, and tonight, he'd claim her once again.

Fiona stepped onto the dais where they waited, her smile seeming shy and less certain than her appearance would suggest. She made her greetings, along with Vivienne, then looked to him, guileless and direct. She curtsied deep as if she thought to offer him a delectable view of her cleavage. "Forgive me, my lord. I have kept you waiting for too long."

He heard a chuckle come from Vivienne and wondered at Fiona's meaning. He extended his arm, thinking just then how he'd love to press his lips against the curve of her neck. "Such beauty is worth waiting for. Shall we dine?"

He didn't want to dine. Food was furthest from his mind, but he needed this meal over and done with so he might take his bride upstairs and collect upon that promised kiss.

He was dressed in shades of blue, with his dark hair combed and his face clean-shaven. Tonight, he seemed the rogue, mysterious and dark. An air of danger surrounded him, something raw and predatory. And intoxicating.

Heat radiated from his torso as she accepted his arm and let him escort her to her seat. The others in the hall began to take their seats as well, and soon the hall was abuzz with the serving of the meal. Before them, servants set platters of roasted boar, mince pies, and breads warm from the ovens.

The repast smelled divine, but with her heart thumping in her throat, Fiona wondered if she could eat a bite. She felt conspicuous in her gown, for she'd sensed the stares as she'd entered, had heard the pause in conversation, but Myles had looked at her in such a way she'd felt emboldened, if only for a moment.

He looked at her that way again, saying nothing, only caressing her with his eyes until his gaze landed upon her lips and stayed. Her skin tingled from it.

At last, he raised his eyes to hers and smiled. A more seductive look, she could not imagine.

"You are beautiful."

"So are you," she said, then gasped at her own foolish honesty.

But he laughed, and so did she.

Sitting on the dais next to Myles, she drank her wine and toyed with her food, but mostly she observed. There was joy within these walls, a kinship she had never witnessed at Sinclair Hall. These people loved one another, and they loved Myles. She could see it in their eyes when they spoke to him, and even once or twice, she felt their warm gazes fall on her. She was becoming one of them.

An effervescent gladness bubbled up inside her breast, and she let it. For once, she did not strive to stuff it down and hide it behind querulous words or obtuse thinking. She watched her husband chew a bite of bread, the strong line of his jaw moving in a smooth rhythm, and somehow the motion made her flush all over. She looked away and smiled at her private thoughts.

"Is something humorous?" Myles asked.

"No, my lord," she said, smiling.

He took another tiny bite of bread, his gaze flicking over the gold and emerald at her throat. "You're wearing your new necklace. I'm pleased to see it."

She ran her finger over the fine metalwork. "I'm pleased to wear it."

Her husband turned toward her a little, and she heard his soft sigh. Her heart spun at the earnestness in his expression.

"'Twas a gift, you know, Fiona," he said softly. "Not a trade. I would spoil you, if you would let me, for no purpose other than to please you."

"I know."

"Then ask for something so I may prove it."

His words stoked a fire low in her belly—no, lower, even. Not because she coveted jewels or a gown or any possessions, but simply because he offered them so readily. He had been unerringly generous to her from their first moment onward, even when she'd tested his every patience. Vivi was right. He was a good man. How could she not desire him?

"I want for little." That was a lie. She wanted much. She wanted him. "Although, there is one thing I would ask for. Something you promised me once before."

His eyes lit with hope.

"I need something to ride."

His jaw went slack, and she laughed at his surprise.

"Back at Sinclair Hall, you promised me a horse of my own. Do you recall?"

He blinked once, slowly, as if to conjure up the memory. And then he smiled broadly. "Ah, yes. A horse. I do recall, and on the morrow, we shall find you one."

Christ, she was delectable, with her pale gown and her flushed cheeks. If he did not know her better, he would think she meant to flirt, the way she fluttered her lashes and teased as though she were some sought-after courtesan. Then she'd laughed and all the candles in the room seemed to dim at her brightness. The combination was beguiling. Bewitching.

He was besotted.

He'd eaten his food. He knew he had, but even now, he could not remember a bite of it, for all he could taste in his mouth was the kiss he sought to claim.

"I have been troublesome to you," she said. "And I am sorry for it. I had my reasons, though. And you know what they were."

His attention narrowed to that one small word. "*Were*?"

She nodded and licked her lips. He'd kiss her here and now if she did that again.

"Yes. But now I've had some time to think, and wonder if perhaps I've been too hasty in despising you."

No declaration of love was that, and yet from her, it felt like one. "What brought about this welcome change?"

"Does it matter?"

He regarded her a moment. "No. But I must say, I am most glad to hear of it. We must celebrate." He whispered the last, as if they shared a secret.

She hid a smile behind her hand. "Perhaps we should."

"Myles, a word, if you please." Tavish ambled up and wedged himself into the chair next to him. Marietta had been sitting there, but moments ago had left to check on her husband.

"Now is the not the best of times," Myles answered.

"It won't take but a minute. It's about the roof they're needing on the gristmill. Now, I was thinking—"

"If you'll excuse me, gentlemen, I'm sure you have no need of my opinion on this matter. But my lord Tavish, please do not keep my husband up too late drinking. Last night you did so and look what happened to him." She gestured toward the black eye.

Tavish paused, looking at her in some surprise. Then he winked. "As you wish, Lady Fiona. I shall deliver him to you myself as soon as our business is complete."

Surely, Tavish could wait with his question, but as soon as Fiona rose from her chair, he began to ramble on about the roof. Myles would listen for a moment, but no longer. Even now, he thought to stuff a roll into the fat man's mouth and hurry after his bride. Instead, he settled for listening with half an ear and watching the way Fiona's gown shimmered as she walked—nay, floated—toward the stairs. He had waited this long. He could wait another ten minutes.

Perhaps.

# CHAPTER 31

Αnd once we've fixed the roof, the entire southwest corner could use shoring up. It's near to crumbling."

Tavish took a hearty gulp of wine, and Myles took advantage of the lull in his monologue.

"Your concern is duly noted, Tavish. I'll set Benson to the task as soon as the sun is up tomorrow. We'll have the mill up and proper before the next rainfall." He stood before the man could take another breath. "Now, if you'll excuse me, I have other duties."

"What other duties? It's near to midnight."

Myles crossed his arms and looked down at his uncle.

"Oh. Oh, of course. Well then, by all means, do not let me keep you."

Myles bid the rest of them good night and made haste to his bedchamber. Yet even so, by the time he reached the door his arousal was undeniable. He adjusted the front of his doublet. This was it, then. Christ, if she played a game, it was the cruelest ever. But he'd seen her open smile and the flush on her cheeks. There was no mistaking her invitation. And if he had misunderstood, he'd simply cover her with kisses until they were in perfect agreement.

He paused outside the door. Anticipation, sweet as opening a gift, assailed him. For she was a gift, as was this night and all they were about to share. Myles gave a silent prayer of thanks and pressed against the door. It swung open easily and he stepped inside. The room was cast with light and shadows, for she had lit a dozen candles or more. Logs crackled in the fire. He took another step and closed the door, securing the latch. Then he turned, and the breath kicked from his lungs.

There beside the red-gold glow from the fireplace stood his bride. Tresses unbound and shining, she was an angel descended from heaven, dressed in gossamer, the sheerest bit he'd ever seen. In the breadth of his imagination, he could not envision any other woman looking so blessed and yet so sinful. Any doubts about where this evening might lead fled his mind. Tonight, she would be his.

"You are ever a surprise to me, woman. But this is my favorite thus far." His voice was husky, even to his own ears.

She smiled, shy in spite of her wanton appearance. "Good, for I'm not certain I can best this."

"I cannot imagine better. You are a vision." And she was. To simply gaze on her was a joy, but to touch her would be pure bliss.

He walked close, until she was just an arm's reach away, and still he did not lift his hands from his sides. He wanted to memorize her, to drink her in and not disturb the perfection of the moment.

Her lips parted, her pink tongue ran along them, and he nearly buckled at the knees. Oh, how he wanted her. He wanted that tongue on his lips and those pale, slender arms around his neck. But mostly, he wanted her crying in release at his touch. She was ready this time. No longer the tender miss she was on their wedding night. Now she'd had time to grow accustomed to him, to decide for herself what she wanted. And she wanted him.

His chest ached as all his breath and all his blood rushed to his groin. Her next words were nearly his undoing.

"You are overdressed, my lord."

When had her voice become so sultry? Who was this luscious vixen? "So I am. Will you undress me?"

She looked uncertain, and for a moment, he saw the Fiona from their first day, skittish and tentative, but the look passed, and she blinked, slow and demure.

"If that would please you."

"Oh, it would."

After another brief hesitation, she reached up to the button near his throat. He saw the tremble in her hands. She was nervous. But tonight, he would take his time and show her the true measure of desire, for in bringing it to her, he'd find his own. He'd explore every curve and every valley, and lavish her with kisses and sweet words. He'd linger at the sweetest spots, tasting where neck turned into shoulder and waist turned into hip. He'd do all the lovely, wicked things he'd been dreaming of since first he'd seen her walking down those steps at Sinclair Hall.

Fiona's heart fluttered so erratically she could scarcely keep her breath. She knew nothing of seduction, and all of Vivi's instructions muddled in her mind and slipped away like sand inside an hourglass. But her moment was now.

It was no easy task to push the button through the thick fabric of his doublet, and when at last the first one popped free, she exhaled in relief at her tiny victory. Encouraged, she moved to the next. This doublet was long, reaching almost to her husband's knees, but the buttons stopped at his waist. A good thing, for she could not imagine reaching lower. She was not that bold.

All the while she made her way down the front of him, her husband stood silent, watching her. Not touching, as she longed for him to do, but simply…looking. His gaze branded her skin.

When she managed the last one, she eased open the edges of the fabric, exposing his shirt underneath. Then she met his gaze and challenged him. "Am I to do all the work?"

His eyes darkened. He smiled and shrugged the garment off his shoulders while she pulled at the sleeves. It fell away from his arms, and he plucked it from her hands to toss it aside.

Then he caught her face in both his broad hands and tipped it up. His grip was made of steel and yet gentle as a breeze. His lips hovered near hers. They drifted over her cheeks and eyes as if he could breathe her in.

Her eyes fluttered shut at such sweet torment. She wanted his kiss, and yet he teased. She stood before him, all but naked beneath his gaze. It was too much.

"Look at me, Fiona." He breathed the words against her heated cheek and then leaned back so she might see his face. "What do you want of me?"

And so it came to this. He would make her ask.

"All of you," she answered. And it was true. There was no point in denying it, and no reason to either. She lifted on her toes and slid her arms around his shoulders. "All of you," she said again, and pressed her lips to his.

She meant to kiss him lightly, to tease and hint. But there had been enough of that. She clung to him instead, and opened her lips beneath his. He held her face in his hands and kissed her, urgent and hungry. The dam had burst, and so she gave in to it, tilting her head and welcoming his tongue, his lips, the pressure of his hands. 'Tis what she'd been longing for, though she'd denied it, even to herself.

He wrapped his arms around her waist, pulling her tight against his chest. She could not get close enough. His kiss only stoked the fire burning low inside. She thought of all the times he'd been patient and the times he'd looked at her with such heat it struck the breath from her. All that came to this. This moment. This embrace. This kiss.

Clumsy, frantic hands, both his and hers, pulled away his shirt, and she rejoiced in the feel of his skin and his heat burning through her thin nightgown. He ran his hand down her back and cupped her bottom, pressing her closer still. He kissed the curve of her neck, and she arched to grant him access. His hands and his mouth seemed everywhere at once, and yet in none of the spots where she needed him most. The bits of her that burned the hottest.

Emboldened, she slid a finger into the waist of his trunk hose and tugged. He growled deep in his throat and caught her earlobe in his teeth.

"Still too many clothes, my lord."

She tugged again, and he groaned louder, twisting his hand in her hair and tugging in return. He kissed her mouth again, hot and hard, plundering it with his tongue until she was breathless from it. He moved down the column of her throat, grazing his teeth along her flesh and biting softly until she shivered with need. She had not imagined such a hunger could exist.

He pulled her toward the bed, kicking off his shoes as they went. He reached out and flipped the covers down, then turned back to face her. She stood, weak-kneed and flushed with heat. He looked at her as if she were made of gold, more precious, even. Not breaking their gaze, he crouched low and gathered up the hem of her nightgown. Slowly, so slowly she almost yanked it off on her own, he inched the garment up, leaning in to kiss her hip once it was exposed. She could not hold back a breathy sigh. At last, he pulled it up and over her head. "This thing is made for sin," he murmured. "You must wear it every night."

She felt shy suddenly, with nothing between them but flesh and air, and yet his hands on her body were so divine she soon gave up her hesitation and leaned back against the bedpost, arching to grant him access to her bare skin. He filled his palms with her breasts, nudging them together so he might kiss them both at once. Her nipples peaked, as if reaching for him. She knotted her hands into his. If this was Campbell sin, then she would willingly burn for it.

She felt free and reckless, tugging at his hair and trailing her nails down his broad back. His muscles flexed beneath her touch, and she felt his tremor.

His hands moved up, and he held her face once more, looking deep into her eyes.

"I cannot think what stars have changed to bring you to my bed, but I shall thank them every day," he said.

He did care for her. She could not deny it, for even in her innocence, she knew his words were not spoken lightly. She'd not deny him either. In this moment of raw tenderness, she must admit she cared for him as well.

"The stars were always aligned. I just couldn't see them."

"You see them now?"

"Yes."

"You come to me willingly?"

Her heart felt near to bursting. "Yes."

He kissed her mouth. She strained against him, wrapping her arms around his neck and rising on her toes. He bent and caught her up beneath her bottom with his forearms, lifting her from the floor as though she weighed little more than a flower. Then he twisted and they fell together to the bed.

He spread fervent kisses along her throat and nudged his thigh between her legs to press against that moist, heated core. She moaned and gripped his shoulders, urging him on.

"Patience, my love." He chuckled against her collarbone. "We have all the night to discover one another. Do you trust me?"

She trusted none of this, for it was too lovely to be real. Still, she nodded. "Yes, I trust you."

He kissed her again and trailed his hands along her torso, moving slower than the moon, but scorching like the sun. His lips followed, kissing her here and there, the scrape of his jaw soothed away by the caress of his tongue. He teased at her breasts, sending ripples outward, but still she ached for more.

She pressed her hands against his back, marveling at the feel of soft skin over taut muscle. He was heat and passion, and she sighed with gladness. At last, his hands traveled farther, landing right between her legs. Easy and certain, his fingers parted her most intimate folds and slipped between them. Relief and tension coupled as something new and wonderful began to coil within her.

Following the same tantalizing path as his hands, he kissed his way down along her belly, stopping for a moment to explore her navel and circle it with his tongue before continuing. What luscious, carnal delight. So improper, yet she had no mind to stop him. He kissed one hip and then the other, teasing and tickling. Then he moved his face between her thighs.

She gasped and twisted against him, suddenly embarrassed, but he was immobile. She twined her fingers into his hair and pulled, but he did not relent.

"Myles." She thought to stop him from such indelicacy. He could not mean to—oh, but he did. As his fingers stroked her most sensitive core, he kissed her there, right upon the spot that cried out for it most. Her body arched, no longer hers to control.

She closed her eyes as if the darkness might conceal her wicked thoughts, but nothing could disguise the way she moved against his mouth. Her chest was tight, as if her heart might burst, and breathing seemed a chore. But still, the rolling flutter continued. Sensations came in lovely waves, building with each lap against the shore. And just when she thought she could not bear another second, a languid sort of spin began, like sliding over ice. It started in her toes, surging upward until it hit her middle and burst forth like a shooting star, shattering her awareness. White light, like heaven's gate, blinded her.

She floated on it for eternity, and then she was in the darkness, drifting downward, graceful as a feather.

She felt her husband shifting upward, and she could not meet his eyes. So unbridled, she should feel ashamed. But he caught her chin with his palm and turned her face toward him. He offered a most roguish grin. She buried her face into the curve of his neck and kissed him there, tasting salt and the manliness of him, breathing in deep as if to collect his essence. His pulse, rapid as her own, thrummed against her lips.

"I didn't know you could do that," she whispered, and wrapped her arms around him, wanting him closer still.

"I told you I could." He chuckled hoarsely. "You just didn't believe me." Then he moved again, the fine hairs on his chest grazing seductively against sensitized breasts. Her heart thumped. Or was it his? They were so close there was no way of knowing.

"There's more, yes?" she asked.

"Yes." His breath was a sigh, or a prayer, perhaps. He moved his hips, found his mark, and filled her to the hilt. He moaned into her ear, a wordless plea of yearning.

She rose up to meet his thrust, pressing her feet against the mattress. Ah, she had not remembered this part of it feeling so delicious. The ebb and flow, the mingling of breaths, and the glorious sensation of him sliding in and out. This was better, so much better than before. No pain, no fear, no hesitation. Just the two of them in a timeless rhythm.

Their bodies moved together, the muscles of his chest flexing against her breasts, until at last he caught her bottom with his hands, pressing into her deeper and faster until she gasped from the pace. Swirling tendrils snaked over her limbs once more, and suddenly, her nerves coiled and sprang, in a burst more powerful than the last. She cried out in pleasure as Myles drove onward toward his own fulfillment. Seconds later, his body tensed and arched, his breath rasped in her ear, an inarticulate endearment. She clung to him and rode the storm until he relaxed against her with a long, sweet sigh.

Their breathing slowed, and Fiona became more aware of her surroundings. He was heavy, but his weight was a fortress meant to protect. She felt bereft when, moments later, he rolled to his side, but he pulled her with him and kept her in his arms.

"I believe that's how it's meant to be," he said at last, and kissed her on the forehead.

She could think of nothing to say to that, so she pressed a kiss against his chest and rested her head on his shoulder. But surely he was right. She could not imagine it being better.

# CHAPTER 32

FIONA BRUSHED AWAY A TICKLE ON HER EAR, BUT IT WAS BACK in an instant. She scratched at it, and heard her husband's throaty chuckle. Even with her eyes shut, she could feel the daylight upon her face, but it seemed as if she'd only just gone to sleep. Memories of the night spread over her like honey from a comb, warm and golden and remarkably sweet. Her body ached in delicious ways, and she stretched to ease her muscles.

"Good morning, fair damsel," Myles said, ticking her ear once more.

She slapped his hand away in jest. "Stop that. Haven't you poked at me enough already?"

He shook his head. "Not by half." He pulled her back against his chest, pressing his arousal to her bottom.

He was a randy buck now that she'd set him free. But little did she mind, for he'd shown her there'd be pleasure in her part of it. Nonetheless, she feigned a feeble struggle, thinking it the proper thing. "'Tis morning, you hound. Time to rise and begin the day."

He pushed against her buttocks firmly and wrapped a solid arm around her waist. "I have risen. See?"

She laughed and tried to wiggle free, but his lips upon her shoulder silenced any false complaints. His kiss was a tonic to her senses as he nipped her skin and soothed away the tiny injury with his tongue. Trailing a finger down her side, along the curve of her hip, and landing on her thigh, his touch sent ripples of anticipation through her body. Warmth flooded through, draining any will to resist. She gave in to it, willingly, wantonly, sighing into the pillow. He ran the finger up to the side of her breast, then down once more to her hip, his touch soft as a feather.

She reached her arms up toward her head, granting him full privilege to stroke her body at his leisure. He groaned softly into her ear, and the pressure of his hand increased. He cupped her breast and ran a thumb across the tip until it tightened. Her breath hitched in her lungs, hot and thick. She'd never thought to know such indolent pleasure. Dewy with want for him, she pressed her buttocks back against his erection, longing to be closer, to be one.

Gentle as a whisper, he pressed her belly down upon the mattress and nudged her thighs apart with his own. Contentment spread throughout her limbs when his hand slid beneath them both and delved into the curls between her legs to tantalize that tiny bud. His fingers circled and teased, creating sensations so enticing a moan rose unbidden from her throat. And she sighed with gladness and relief when at last he sought the entrance to her femininity and sheathed his body deep inside of hers.

He rocked slowly, his chest upon her back, rolling like an endless wave caressing the shore until her own hips began to set a faster pace. Her breasts rubbed against the sheets, adding a delightful friction to the smoothness of his strokes. She pressed down upon his hand, bold in her desire.

And so they rode, until she thought she could not breathe from the pressure building inside, but with one final gasp, her lungs burst free and she tumbled into white-hot bliss, and seconds later, Myles joined her. They lay spent and breathing hard, until at last he rolled onto his own back.

"I may never leave this bed." His words came on a sigh.

"We will get hungry enough, eventually." She lifted up onto her elbows and looked over at him. His hair was wild, his jaw covered in stubble. And yet he'd never looked more handsome. His face was wondrous to behold, all angles and shadow. His torso and arms were thick with muscles. Yes, he was impressive, this husband of hers. He turned to gaze at her and gave a smile hot enough to melt a frozen loch.

Her heart clenched inside her breast, and tender feelings, so foreign for their newness, threatened to overwhelm her. Her mother had died over such feelings of longing. Fiona would do well to try to keep her head about her. She was free now, to care for him a little. He was her husband, after all, but she'd not be so foolish as to give him her whole heart. Perhaps just a sliver.

"I am hungry, now that you mention it," he said. "Shall we have breakfast and then go find you that horse? We could ride to Killean, or even Oban, but that would take a day or two."

"You need not purchase a new horse for me, Myles. Just let me choose one from the stables."

"If we have one you've set your fancy on, then fine. But I should enjoy a little sojourn with you. And you've not seen much of the countryside around here. Now that I think on it, a trip to Oban is a grand idea."

Once her husband had made his decision, it seemed there was no stopping him, and the very next morning, she found herself upon a borrowed Campbell horse heading toward the Firth of Lorn and the town of Oban. Six Campbell men-at-arms who rode a ways ahead, keeping watch, accompanied them. Robert and Vivienne insisted upon joining them as well, and they made a joyous foursome. It was a pleasant journey, with fair weather. The conversation as they traveled was robust and often bawdy, with Vivienne and Robert each determined to provide the most scandalous anecdote.

"At least King James's new bride has a sense of humor," Robert told them, taking a bite from an apple he pulled from his pocket. "She was wooed by Henry of England, you know. But when he offered for her, she refused. 'Tis rumored she said, 'I may be a big woman, but I have a very slender neck.'"

The others laughed, yet Fiona put a hand to her throat. "Did King Henry truly chop the head from his last wife?"

Robert nodded and took another bite of apple. "He did. But she plotted treason against him and deserved such an ending."

"It's so brutal." A cloud dimmed the sunshine as if in agreement.

"Aye, it's brutal. But treason must be dealt with harsh and swift. If allowed to fester, it can infect an entire country, and no king will risk that."

"Marietta told me of Janet Douglas," Vivienne interrupted. "What punishment will King James bring down on her, do you imagine?"

"Janet Douglas?" The question popped before Fiona could think to bite her tongue, for Janet Douglas was the distant cousin with whom she thought to ask for refuge when running from the Campbells.

Myles answered, "There is talk she conspired with her brother Archibald Douglas to poison King James. Have you heard anything of that?"

Fiona's blood frosted, though she'd answer with the truth. "What could I possibly know? I have not seen her since I was a child." And that was true enough, but had she managed her escape, she'd be with the woman now. Suddenly, she was glad to have failed in that mission.

Her answer seemed to satisfy her husband, and Robert answered Vivienne's question.

"I cannot think he'll tolerate her disobedience. She can hope for prison, but I think he means to set an example of her. It's hard to say. She's his aunt, though only by marriage."

The talk moved to other, more pleasant things, but the day had turned gray for a moment, and Fiona could not shake the sense that something evil tapped upon her shoulder.

Oban was a modest town, set upon the shore and dotted with buildings of every shape and size. There were alehouses, milliners, blacksmiths, dry goods stores, and various other establishments, each with colorful signs hanging from their doorways. People milled about the streets, stopping by market booths to buy fish and dried beans and bolts of cloth. The smell off the firth blended with that of roasting meat and too many people.

"Darkness will soon fall," Myles said. "Let's get some food and find a place to rest our heads."

"'Tis early yet. The town's just waking up," Robert protested.

Myles nodded. "Aye, but my wife is near asleep in the saddle. See?"

She was, at that. For the last hour, she had struggled to keep herself upright and maintain some understanding of the conversation. Only entering the village had rallied her strength once more.

"I am fatigued, I must confess."

"Why so sleepy, miss?" Vivienne murmured so that only she might hear. "Good reason, I hope, and not the product of a lumpy mattress."

Fiona felt her cheeks grow hot and glanced around to ensure no one might hear. Robert and Myles seemed in a conversation over where to lodge, and the other men had scattered once they'd reached the edge of town.

She let her lips curl into a smile, her voice equally low as she answered, "The mattress was puffy as a cloud. But oh, what thunder and lightning."

Vivienne's laughter caught the attention of the men, and Myles's lips twitched.

"Thank the heavens, Fiona," Vivienne said, "I could not last another moment knowing you two were at odds. But given how your husband cannot keep his eyes off you, I fear you're in for another sleepless night."

Fiona would not mind so much, although she was powerfully hungry and just as tired.

Myles instructed his men-at-arms to find their own lodgings for the night, and then he arranged for three rooms at the largest inn for Robert, Vivienne, himself, and his wife.

"Tomorrow, we shall find you a fine horse, Fiona," Myles said as they supped later over fragrant rabbit stew and crusty bread. They dined in the inn's main room, along with Robert and Vivienne and a dozen others in Oban for one reason or another. The place was well-appointed, with cloths upon the tables and fresh rushes on the floor.

"There are two equally fine stables toward the north of town," Robert added. "Though, for truly excellent horseflesh, you cannot beat the stables near Stirling."

"I don't care much for Stirling," Vivienne said, dipping her bread into the gravy. "My dead husband had far too many mistresses in that hamlet."

"I should not say as much, Vivienne, but I fear your husband had mistresses in every hamlet. He was more of a goat than a goat often is. I'm glad you're rid of him," Robert said.

"I suppose I am too. But I am in the mood for another husband."

"To marry, or just to entertain?" Robert teased.

If Vivi was insulted, it did not show. "I think perhaps I should like one of my own. But a good one, this time. Less a goat and more of a lapdog. But fierce with a sword, of course. And he must be handsome."

"You cast a small net with such a list of wants," Myles said.

Vivienne nodded and took another bite of stew. "I know, but I've the luxury of beauty and riches. Until both are spent, I intend to wait for just such a man. And it is not so far-fetched an idea. Just think of our Fiona here. She was pledged to Myles on the day she was born. But for the grace of God and the king, she could be married to some fat, old drunkard now."

Fiona felt her cheeks grow warm. The fates had indeed twisted oddly in her favor, for her husband was all the things a maiden could want. And in that moment, her fatigue waned as her wish to go to bed increased.

Myles stretched his limbs, his feet sliding out from the covers and draping over the edge of the short bed. The inn was clean enough, and the food palatable, but the beds were far too small for his big frame. All the more reason to press against his bride, he supposed.

Fiona sighed in her slumber. Two nights of vigorous lovemaking were bound to tire a lass, but she'd held her own against his lust and matched him kiss for kiss. He counted himself most fortunate. His wife was a beauty, and her temperament over the last two days had matched that. She had told him of the letters from her mother, and so it seemed the tide had turned. She no longer considered him an enemy. Far from it. Instead, she'd wrapped her velvet limbs around him and whispered words of pleasure when he plunged into the warmth of her. His body quickened at the luscious memories.

The need to please her swelled his chest. He'd find her the finest horse this land had ever seen. If not here, then Stirling or Edinburgh. Christ, he'd go to London if that's what it took. He'd pamper her and show her all the joys of being a Campbell bride.

At last, she woke, and though his cock stirred, for once he ignored the thing and told her to get dressed. The morning was waning away, and they had business—other business—to conduct. They made their way downstairs, to find Vivienne and Robert already there. Bits of bread and cheese left upon a plate between them gave evidence of their breakfast.

Robert shook his head and stretched within the chair when he spotted them. "It's about time you left your burrow, you busy rabbits. I thought to order another ale if you did not appear soon."

Myles thought to scold him for being crude in front of Fiona, but she laughed and answered, "Rabbits are dreadfully fast, Robert. Is that how you think it's meant to be?"

Ah, yes, she was turning into a fine wife, indeed.

Myles and Fiona breakfasted with haste, and then the four of them ventured out into the streets of Oban. They strolled at a leisurely pace, the ladies with their heads together, giggling and pointing out items to each other as they passed each market booth. Myles lagged behind, with Robert at his side.

"You are happy this morning," Robert said.

"What's not to be happy about?"

"Indeed." They walked along in silence, but in another moment, Robert said, "That was a powerful reaction yesterday, when your wife heard of Janet Douglas."

His tone was casual, yet Myles caught his meaning.

"I believe they are cousins from some generation past. Lady Douglas was born a Fraser, long a Sinclair ally. 'Tis only natural Fiona would be alarmed."

Robert spit into the dirt as they kept walking, and said no more. But Myles knew his brother well enough.

"Speak your mind, Robert," Myles prompted after they'd walked a few more yards and let the ladies get farther ahead.

Robert frowned and tilted his chin. "There is nothing on my mind, Myles, save bawdy songs and loose women."

Myles stopped in his spot. His brother did as well.

"My wife has nothing whatsoever to do with Janet Douglas."

"I did not say she did."

"You implied it."

Robert shook his head and scoffed. "Honestly, brother, forgive me. I've spent too many days of late dallying over royal intrigues. It makes me suspect hidden purpose where none exists. Think nothing of what I said." He began to walk again, whistling merrily.

Myles thought to prod him for more, but what would be the point? His brother was foolhardy if he thought Fiona had knowledge of any such nefarious business. Robert had indeed spent too much time at court if he could even ponder such a thing.


Arriving at the stable, Fiona's heart took a skip and a leap. So many fine horses, some regal and tall, while others were dainty and sweet. They passed down the row of stalls, admiring each horse, stroking a velvety nose now and again. But at the end of one row, she found a soft, gray mare, so much like her Gwynlyn Fiona knew at once she must have her.

The horse stood fifteen hands high, the perfect size, with white stockings and a blaze. Fiona leaned against her neck, murmuring soft words, while Myles ran a hand down the mare's rump and patted her flanks. This was not the horse of Fiona's childhood, of course, but still she possessed an endearing disposition. She butted Fiona on the shoulder, looking for a treat.

"Do you like this one?" her husband asked.

Fiona nodded, blinking back a ridiculous tear. Of all the things she'd had to cry over in her life, especially these last few weeks, she should not get weepy over finding an average little mare. But something sang inside her when she looked into those limpid brown eyes. And if she was to have a horse, this must be the one.

Myles waved to the groom. "We'll take this one into the paddock. I'd like to see her gait."

The groom was tall, lanky as a pelican, with a beaklike nose to match. "Yes, m'lord. But this one's spoken for."

Fiona's heart squeezed.

"Spoken for?" her husband asked.

"Aye, m'lord. A gentleman who come by yesterday took a shine to this one and half a dozen others. Told me he'd be back in a day or so to make his payment."

"If he's given you no money, then this horse is still for sale."

The groom swept his hat from his head and twisted it in his grimy hands. "Uh, well, m'lord, that might be true in a manner of speakin', but he was powerful persuasive and told me not to sell them without his consent. Unless you've a mind to buy all seven, I'd not want to lose the rest of his business. Begging your pardon, sir."

Robert joined them. "That's a shoddy method. What if the man never returns?"

The groom pinked up under all his dirt. "As I said, m'lords, he was a might insistent. Seemed the type to not take no for an answer."

"It's all right, Myles. I don't need this horse." But her heart broke a little to say the words. She knew this mare was not her Gwynlyn, and yet for a moment, she had let herself remember a sweeter time at Sinclair Hall.

But her husband was not finished with this groom. "Tell me the man's name, and I'll convince him. If my wife favors this horse, then she shall have it."

She flushed at his tone, both flattered by his will to please her but also uncomfortable for the sake of the groom.

"Really, Myles, I can choose another."

"What's the man's name?" Robert prompted the groom as well.

The groom looked from brother to brother, sweat beading on his forehead. "Sir Goodman, m'lords. Late of Ballengeich, or so he says."

Myles's jaw clenched shut, while Robert's head tipped back and he gave such a guffaw the gray mare flattened her ears and took a backward step toward the wall.

"Who is Sir Goodman?" Fiona asked. Any man who wrought such varying degrees of response from these two Campbells must be an intriguing fellow.

Vivienne joined them then, her eyes sparkling. "Did I hear you mention Sir Goodman? Is he on the prowl?"

"It seems he's here in Oban," Robert sputtered in amusement. "And he's laid his claim on Fiona's filly."

"Who is Sir Goodman?" Fiona asked again, louder.

Myles shook his head and lowered his voice. "Suffice it say he is an influential man who prefers to keep his affairs private."

Robert snorted. "Affairs, indeed. I'm sure he has several going on at this very moment."

"Shh," Myles hushed his brother and spoke to the groom. "Thank you for your assistance, lad. We'll call you back if we have need."

The groom bobbed his knobby head and stepped away.

Myles waited until the lad was far from hearing before he spoke. "If Goodman is here, he wants no one to know it. That groom will double the price if he knows who he's dealing with. But what the devil is he doing this far west?" Myles directed the question to his brother alone.

"I cannot presume to know. Perhaps investigating the port in preparation for a journey?" Her husband frowned and ran a hand through his hair. He looked to the mare and then to Fiona. "Sir Goodman is an acquaintance who is at times most generous, but he can also be most contrary. Whether we can purchase this horse will depend entirely on his mood."

Fiona felt ill at ease, creating such a stir over something as inconsequential as her choice in mare. She'd fallen in love with this one in an instant, but she could easily make a sacrifice and chose another. Lord knew she'd lost loved ones of greater consequence. This sting would pale compared to that other grief.

She touched her husband's arm. "Truly, Myles, I can find another."

His scowl softened at her tone, and he covered her hand with his own. "We will seek out Sir Goodman. Perhaps he'll be amenable to some sort of trade."

"Splendid idea," Robert said, clapping Myles on the back. "I suggest we trade him the filly for Vivi."

# CHAPTER 33

OBAN WAS RIFE WITH ALEHOUSES, AND ROBERT WAS certain they'd find Sir Goodman imbibing at one. Still, locating him proved no easy task. Fiona's feet ached from walking on the cobbled street, and still they searched, poking their heads into establishment after establishment.

"Everyone seems to be drinking except for us," Robert grumbled as they made their way into a stone pub with wide green doors. The place smelled of wet sheep. Vivienne sneezed.

'Twas there that they discovered him, sitting at a battered table and surrounded by a bevy of wenches. He was tall, red-haired, and about the same age as her husband. She'd expected someone older.

He spotted Robert and Myles and offered a lopsided smile and a wave. "Why, what fortune shines on me this day? 'Tis the brothers Campbell, I see. Join me, my fine fellows." He smacked his hand upon the table and nudged a lass aside with his elbow. "Make room, you bonny maidens."

The girls were reluctant to forfeit their spots. Some eyed Fiona and Vivienne with malice, while others looked over Myles and Robert in much the way the men had looked over the horses.

Fiona half thought one might step up and run a hand along her husband's rump. She slid her arm through his and squeezed.

Sir Goodman blinked as if to clear his eyes, and a slow, curving smile took over his face. He stood up then and walked to them. "Why, this must be your bonny bride, Myles. Well done. Your king has done right by you, yes?"

His manner was altogether too familiar. He should not address her husband so casually or make remarks about her, but Myles seemed not to notice.

"Greetings to you, Sir Goodman. May I present you with my wife, Fiona Campbell. And yes, the king has my full gratitude. He is wise in every way."

Fiona met the man's eyes and found all cloudiness of drink had disappeared. He stared at her, shrewd as a hawk and with a predatory gleam. In an instant, she understood the groom's hesitation to displease him.

She gave the slightest curtsy.

He took her free hand in both of his, rubbing his thumbs across the back. "Lady Fiona, 'tis a pleasure. When I was young, I had the delight of meeting your mother, and now I hope we can be friends as well."

No other words could have surprised her more, but he let go of her hand and instantly turned to Vivienne. All of Fiona's questions stuck in her throat like a clump of dried figs.

Vivienne curtsied deep and long, and batted her lashes like a coquette.

Goodman smiled. "You have not changed a whit, Lady Vivienne. How I've missed your smile. You must come to visit me again very soon."

"Nothing would please me more, Sir."

Sir Goodman smiled, his voice growing ever louder. "Oh, come now. No standing on ceremony on this fine day. Sit with me awhile." He turned to the tavern wenches, waving at them like flies. "Enough now, be gone with the lot of you." He gestured to the barmaid to clean away the soiled cups.

Myles spoke as they took their seats just vacated by the sullen-looking wenches. "Sir Goodman, I hope this day finds you in fine health."

"It does, Myles. And speaking of health, how fares your father?"

Fiona wondered at the question. It seemed news of the earl's attack had traveled far.

"Improving by the day, Sir. Eager to be back in the saddle and resume his duties. I've attended to things in his stead, however, and all is well at Dempsey Castle."

Fiona heard the pride in her husband's voice and sat a little straighter in her own seat.

"Excellent. Your efforts will be rewarded."

Fresh cups filled to the brim with foamy ale were set before them, and Robert scooped his up and took a hearty gulp. Fiona sipped her own and wondered at this stranger.

"Bring us a meal as well," Sir Goodman instructed without bothering to ask if they'd recently eaten. Or if perhaps they had made other arrangements. They had not, of course, and Fiona was famished. Still, this man was beyond presumptuous, and something was amiss, for Myles and Robert behaved as if he were a noble of the highest order. The sparks of her curiosity burst into flame.

Sir Goodman took a hearty gulp of his ale and sat back. "That's an ugly business about the attack," he said, setting the cup back down. "Our enemies will stop at nothing to see Douglas back at the helm. But I'll not stand for it. The traitorous cowards shall suffer for it."

"Have you heard any news of who might be behind it?"

"News aplenty and not a lick of it reliable."

Her husband nodded and stole a glance her way.

The serving girl returned and loaded down the table with plates of stew and bread. The conversation turned to the weather and other mundane things while they dined, but Fiona's mind was whirling and it seemed to make her stomach whirl as well. She grew more certain by the moment that this Sir Goodman was something more than they pretended him to be. He dressed like a lowly farmer, and yet if he knew her mother, he must have spent some time at court.

It suddenly felt a lifetime since she'd read her mother's letters. In some ways, it was another life, for her mother had rarely spoken of court. Or if she had, Fiona had been too young to understand. Yet, this man had known her and called her a friend. A desperate yearning to learn more filled Fiona with a long-buried ache, a need to understand who her mother had been and all that she'd been through.

Perhaps this Sir Goodman had some answers.

Myles had waited until the meal was nearly ended to bring up the mare, and he sensed his wife's growing anxiety. When the conversation lulled, he made his move. "We were at the stables today, Sir, to find my bride a fine horse. That is how we came to know you were in town."

Goodman took a drink from his cup. "Is that so? I intend to make a gift of a new horse to my wife as well."

A thumping started in Myles's temples. "Yes, I've heard your wife is a most accomplished horsewoman."

"She is. You shall have to come and meet her when your father is well enough to travel."

"We would be most delighted. I know both Mother and Father would be pleased to spend the time with you. Ah, there is another matter, Sir, I wondered if I might speak upon."

Goodman tipped his head. "Speak, then."

Myles rubbed his hands together under the table. "I must ask if you are set upon the mounts you've chosen from the stable. The groom informed us you'd chosen seven fine beauties."

Sir Goodman wiped his mouth. "That groom's a chatty fellow, nattering on about my business. Nonetheless, I've chosen seven, indeed. Six are matched to pull a carriage, and the other is for my wife."

This did not bode well. Obviously, the gray was for his bride. He sensed Fiona gazing at him from the side, waiting for him to say more.

It must seem such a simple request to her, but Myles knew this man, and when it came to him, no request was trivial. Still, he'd promised her a horse, and that was the one she wanted. "I wonder if you might reconsider the gray, Sir."

Vivienne and Robert stared down at their plates, while Fiona directed her gaze toward the man across the table.

Goodman sat back, a frown furrowing his brows. "Reconsider? I'm not prone to changing my mind. I should think you'd know that."

"I know, sir. Of course. But my own wife has taken a liking to that horse as well."

Goodman swung his gaze to Fiona. "Has she, now? You like that filly, aye?"

Fiona straightened her spine, the telltale lift of her chin a warning sign. Myles's gut twisted. His bride was wholly capable of saying the most inflammatory things, and this was no man to toy with.

"I do, Sir," she answered, calm and direct. "I had one just like her when I was a child. Were you truly friends with my mother?"

Everyone, save Fiona and Goodman, shifted uneasily in their seats at her abrupt question, and Myles wondered if they'd lose the horse and more.

Myles covered his wife's hand and murmured. "This is not the time to speak of such things."

But Goodman raised his own hand and leaned forward, his voice low but commanding. "Nonsense. I'll not refuse the question." He smoothed the front of his plain cotton doublet and took time refilling his cup with a pitcher from the table.

Myles stole a glance at his brother, and Robert offered a discreet shrug to indicate his shared bewilderment. Goodman took a hearty swallow and returned his stare to Fiona. She sat still as a statue.

"Indecision is a weakness. So I shall buy all seven horses, as I planned."

Disappointment knocked at Myles's heart.

But Goodman continued speaking. "However, I am also generous to a fault. And therefore, Lady Fiona, if you desire that horse, consider it yours, a wedding gift from me to you."

Fiona gasped and pressed a hand to her throat. "Sir Goodman, there is no need to make a gift of her. My husband has the means to pay."

Myles squeezed her hand to silence her.

A chuckle tumbled from Sir Goodman's lips. "Has he, now? Then he should consider himself most favored. But I assure you, lass, I have the means as well. And as for your mother, yes, she was a most true and loyal friend. In fact, one might argue that had she not risked her life on my behalf, I might not now be king of Scotland."

# CHAPTER 34

FIONA SAT BEFORE SCOTLAND'S KING IN A HUMBLE ALEHOUSE, surrounded by wenches and drunkards. She had never dreamed to meet him, and most certainly not under such unassuming circumstances. She wore a simple woolen dress with not a jewel or an adornment, save her emerald wedding ring. She fought the urge to smooth her hair, for little good would it do other than to display her sudden agitation.

This was the man who banished her family to the North, who ensured they were the enemy of many, and who stripped her father of his titles and his wealth. Yet this was also a man who professed to be a friend to her mother. Who allowed a marriage and a truce between her clan and the Campbells. What divergence in his nature allowed such contrary behavior?

Perspiration prickled at her skin, and Myles squeezed her hand again.

"I see I have surprised you. I'm glad." King James chuckled into his cup. "I love a good surprise. As to details about your mother, that shall have to wait until another day. The drink has made me drowsy and I've need of rest." He directed his next words to Myles, leaving Fiona feeling hollow and dismissed.

Surely he could understand her eagerness to learn more? But the king was done with her.

"Myles, I shall send my man with instructions to the groom. Take the gray whenever you wish. I'm heading toward Ballachulish in the morning, but after my visit there, I shall stop by Dempsey before heading back to Linlithgow. I shan't make a long visit of it, for my new wife awaits me. Tell your mother not to make a grand fuss."

Myles smiled, yet Fiona sensed some tension in his posture. Still, his voice was smooth and easy. "I will do as you command, Your Highness, but well you know my mother. You might expect some fanfare."

The king laughed, along with Robert and Vivienne. It seemed they were all jovial once again, but Fiona could not join them. Too many questions, too many mixed emotions, churned in her gut. If he left on the morrow, when would they discuss her mother?

She looked to Myles, her eyes imploring him to press on her behalf. But he gave his head a tiny shake. There would be no more answers on this night.

"Why didn't you tell me?" Fiona demanded once she and Myles were alone in their tiny room at the inn. Her nerves were frayed as an old rope, and she could not begin to decide how she felt about any of this.

"He travels incognito of his own choosing, Fiona, and I'm not at liberty to reveal him. To do so is treason." Myles sat down and began to unlace one boot.

"The rest of you knew his identity. It did not seem such a secret among you."

"Robert and I have both traveled with him in such a manner. And Vivienne seems privy to much information with no obvious means of obtaining it. I am quite certain I don't want to know her methods."

"He is the king, Myles," Fiona persisted. "What if I'd said something that offended him? And why does he go about dressed one step above a peasant?" She paced to the window and then back to the door, chewing her thumbnail to a nub.

"James has an odd sense of humor, I'll admit. But it's far easier for him to slip about and do his business without the royal trappings. It's a game for him and helps him understand the common folk. He's beloved by the people, you know." He unlaced the second boot and let it fall to the floor with a thud.

"Beloved by the people? You see only what you choose to see. Where I am from, he's much maligned, for he thinks nothing of snatching land away from the northern clans. By his own admission, my mother was a friend, and still he sent her to a place with nothing but rocks." She stopped her pacing to stare at him. "And what business was that about her risking her life?"

Myles's chest rose and fell in a heavy sigh. "Fiona, he could have thrown your father into prison, or worse. The king spared his life for your mother's sake. And now he's given you the horse. Perhaps it's you who only sees what she wants to see."

He sat in the chair in his stocking feet, calm as a loch at daybreak. Of course he was calm. He'd known all along they were in the presence of the king. He'd not had a rug pulled out from under his feet, as she had.

He'd not spent his life listening to a father constantly railing against King James's ferocity and malevolence either. Tears burned at her eyes, but she would not shed them.

"I don't know what to make of this."

Myles stood and crossed over to her, sliding his hands up her arms. "Accept it. He is the king. What's done is done. And at least he had the wisdom and grace to marry you to me." His tone was as teasing as his touch. He squeezed her shoulders, and she fought the urge to step closer.

"'Twas my mother's wish we marry. The king had nothing to do with it."

Myles closed the narrow gap. "Then commend his generosity of spirit for agreeing to it." He wrapped his arms around her waist. "Truly, Fiona. Think on it. James could have smote your father from history, and yet he chose to let him live. He did not even banish him from Scotland, as he did so many others. True, James is not merciful in all things, and perhaps your father had good reason to despise him, but in the end, it could have been much worse. So now the decision falls to you. Will you be your mother's daughter, or your father's?"

"I am both," she whispered, letting the tears slip down her cheeks unhindered. "I cannot turn my back on everything Sinclair. I was raised to loathe this king."

"And yet your mother sought to see him on the throne. Surely, any man she'd risk her life for deserves some respect from you."

"But how was she at risk? What happened?"

He tucked an errant strand of hair behind her ear. "I know nothing of that. But I shall ask my father when we return home. Perhaps he knows. Until then, will you withhold your Sinclair judgments?"

His words confused her, and his nearness made her body relax, even when her mind remained in turmoil. His chest pressed tight against her breasts, and he leaned down to murmur against her throat.

"Honestly, Fiona, I don't care what you think of this king. But if you choose to harbor ill will, hide those thoughts. He'd turn on his own mother if he thought she disrespected him."

She tilted her head, the warmth of his breath melting her defenses. He pressed a kiss below her ear, and she sighed, the edge of her frustration softening. "You ask me to pledge loyalty to a man who'd turn on his own mother?"

Myles lifted his head and smiled down at her. "His mother is English. 'Tis reason enough."

A soft chuckle bubbled up from her throat. She could not stay angry when he smiled at her and teased like that. His desire was a tangible thing, weaving a web around her. She had neither the will nor the inclination to fight it. "Well, perhaps I am gracious enough to admit he provided me an adequate husband."

Myles frowned. "Adequate? Is that all you think of me?"

She gave a tiny shrug, a smile playing at the corners of her mouth. "At the moment. But with some effort, you might change my mind."

His furrowed brows relaxed. "Mm. And how might I do that, Lady Fiona?" His voice became a husky whisper.

She turned her head to kiss his mouth, but he tilted away and locked his hooded gaze on hers. "No. Tell me. How might I please you?"

Her cheeks flamed hot, lust bridled by embarrassment. The list of naughty things she hoped he'd do with her, and to her, was long and sinful. Thoughts of the king evaporated like mist, replaced by bold images of her and Myles tangling in the sheets. But she could not explain such things.

Instead, she pulled him toward the bed and whispered, "Surprise me."

# CHAPTER 35

I N THE WEEKS SINCE RETURNING FROM OBAN, MYLES'S WIFE
had blossomed. Vivi and Alyssa adored her, and even his
mother had taken to using a less frosty tone in her presence.
Fiona's smiles came as fast and easy as her willingness to tum-
ble into his bed. The thought made his head spin and his groin
tighten. His wife was a vixen and an angel melded into one enticing form.

Now, nearly a month since getting her the pony, they had
finally received news the king was soon to arrive at Demspey.

His mother had left no detail to chance. Every nook and
cranny of the castle was free of grime, every horse brushed to a
sheen, and each Campbell within the bailey walls dressed in his
or her finest.

Banners waved and heralds trumpeted as James passed
under the gate and rode to where Myles and his family stood.
The earl stepped forward using a cane and greeted James warmly
after the king dismounted.

"'Tis good to see you up and well, Cedric. You look fit and
hale to me."

"I am, Your Grace. Thank you for saying so. Welcome back
to Dempsey."

The king made his greetings to each of them, pausing in front of Myles and Fiona. He took her hand and raised it to his lips.

"We meet again, my fair Fiona. How is your horse?"

Her color rose, and she smiled. "Spirited, Your Grace. We are a fine match."

James laughed and nodded. "I am glad to hear of it. We shall speak more later, you and I."

He moved on, but Myles watched his wife's face. He knew she was thinking of her mother once more.

His father had been reluctant to discuss with Fiona his involvement with Aislinn. And as to the rest, he would only say it was the king's story to share, and so she must wait for his visit. And now it had come.

This evening, they would dine and dance, and be regaled by minstrels and musicians. His wife's eyes sparkled in anticipation, and he felt a swell of pride that he could provide her with such a life. She was one of them now, with no trace of past hostility lingering in her nature.

Still no word had come of who'd been behind the ambush in the forest, but Myles felt confident her brothers were no part of it. Over these last few weeks, Fiona had shared with him more stories of her youth, revealing her relationship with Simon and John. The elder sounded simple and brutish, but by all accounts, her brother John was sensible. 'Twas Myles's hope that, without their father's malice to nudge them toward revenge, perhaps a time of peace between their clans had truly come. But the situation was tenuous at best, for there were murmurings of unrest stirring in the North.

The view before Fiona was spectacular. The great hall glimmered with banners and fine linens. Gold plates adorned the tables, which groaned beneath the weight of so much food. Musicians played a lively tune from behind a screen while every member of Clan Campbell displayed manners befitting such an auspicious visitor.

King James sat between Cedric and Marietta, with Robert and Myles on either side of their parents. Tavish was there, and Vivi and Alyssa too. Even Darby, his unruly hair combed into place, sat dressed in a fine new doublet. He looked quite the young man, but tugged at the collar as if it were a noose.

Fiona leaned closer to her husband. "Has the king said how long he plans to stay?"

Myles turned and met her eyes. "A day or two. James moves about on a whim unless he has some purpose in mind. He said you'd speak, and so you shall. But you must wait for him to ask."

She was impatient for an audience. She'd waited weeks now, and curiosity of how her mother had helped this king claim his throne gnawed at her. She took a bite of venison, but suddenly, it tasted sour. She swallowed anyway and washed it down with wine.

The evening went on with jugglers and troubadours and more food and talk, until at last the king indicated he was finished with his dining. With a whispered word from Lady Marietta, servants cleared the tables with practiced speed, and soon the hall was transformed for dancing.

Fiona wiped her hands across her lap, suddenly nervous. Over the last few days, she'd practiced with Vivi and Alyssa, who had found it delightfully funny she did not know how to dance. But there had been no teacher at Sinclair Hall, nor any occasion for such a frivolous pastime.

Perhaps it was the king's presence, or just the idea of being on display for all the Campbells, that made her palms moist and her stomach quell. Regardless of the reason, a surging wave of nausea rolled through her. She swallowed down the bile and reached for her husband's hand.

He leaned in close and whispered in her ear. "Are you unwell? You're pale as a ghost."

Fiona gave a tiny shake of her head and took a deep, slow breath. Her stomach settled after a moment. "No, I'm fine. I think the sauce on the venison was a bit much."

He pressed a glass of wine into her hand. "Here, drink this. I will take you upstairs if you've a need to lie down."

She was not feeling so unwell she could not take that bait. "How wicked you are, trying to seduce me away from an evening with the king."

Myles chuckled. "I should let you enjoy a dozen such evenings with the king if that was your wish, but you were green as moss there for a moment. Are you truly fine?"

Fiona took a sip from the cup and let the warmth of the wine spread over her. "Yes, much better now. I cannot let my dancing lessons go to waste."

Myles offered a dubious expression, and she was wounded. "Don't you think I've mastered any steps? Alyssa is a fine teacher."

"Then perhaps she should have spent some time with me." His cheeks flushed pink, and she smiled. It was not often her husband had a cause to blush. Or admit to any inability.

She reached beneath the table and squeezed his thigh. "We shall manage this well enough."

A smile, full and sweet, spread across his face. He cupped the back of her head with his hand and pulled her close to place a lingering kiss upon her lips. 'Twas wholly inappropriate in front of such a crowd, not to mention the king, but Fiona gave in to it. When her husband released her, she saw James watching them, a crooked smile upon his regal face.

"I have done well by you, Campbell," the king said loudly enough for most to hear.

Myles turned around and nodded at his liege. "Yes, Your Highness, and I am most grateful."

"As you should be. And now you must share that bonny bride of yours. But only for one dance. Lady Fiona, would you do me the honor?" He stood and held out his hand.

Fiona felt light-headed once again, but fended it off with another deep breath. It would not do to swoon when asked to dance by the king. She nodded and rose from her seat.

"I should like a coranto," the king said over his shoulder.

Lady Marietta quickly whispered to a servant, who rushed to instruct the musicians.

Fiona stiffened her spine against her trembling. He was a man, nothing more. She had faced down and outrun twenty Campbells, hadn't she? Well, nearly. She could certainly take a turn about a dance floor with just this one man. Even if he was the king of Scotland.

She placed her hand over his outstretched arm and let him escort her to the center of the room. The musicians began the lively tune, and after a nervous moment, she became enthralled by the dance itself. If she missed a step, he did not falter, but merely led her to the next. It was difficult to converse, so focused was she on not treading upon his toes, but at the end, they faced one another and the king gave a slight bow of his head.

"If you should like to hear of how I am indebted to your mother, perhaps you would join me for a turn about the gardens in the morning," he said.

Fiona hesitated a moment longer than was proper, then dropped into a curtsy. She briefly met his eyes. "I should like that very much, Your Highness."

She rose, and he took her arm, tucking it into the crook of his elbow as they walked back toward the dais. "Wonderful. Then I shall return you to your husband before I say something untoward."

"Untoward, Your Highness?" Her chest fluttered and compressed.

The king leaned closer. She felt his warm breath upon her ear as he whispered, "Your husband's kiss is still upon your lips, my dear. I find that quite enticing. Best go get another from him."

The next day was warm, the air moist with the scent of fertile fields offering up their bounty as Fiona joined King James among the flowers. He was dressed in casual togs again, like Sir Goodman rather than the royal highness he'd been last evening.

"Do you travel today?" Fiona asked.

He gave a nod of his red head, his bright eyes intense. "I do. My wife awaits me at Linlithgow, and I confess I find myself longing for some feminine companionship."

Fiona looked to the ground, not certain how to respond. He was by turns overly forthright and frustratingly vague.

"I am sure the queen will be most glad for your affection," Fiona murmured.

The king chuckled, although she did not intend to be humorous. Indeed, she could not think why that was funny.

"Yes, perhaps she will. And it's quite obvious you will not."

"Your Highness?" She looked at him, startled.

"Would you kiss me if I asked you to?"

Heat rose from her belly to her cheeks. "No, Your Grace, I would not."

"But I am your king."

Fiona heard the teasing lilt in his voice. "Yes, but not my husband. Still, you may rest assured that, when I am old, I am certain to regret having refused this opportunity."

He laughed out loud at that and pulled her arm through his. "You have the look of your mother, my bonny Fiona, and her wit. Walk with me and let's enjoy this sunshine before I must be on my way."

They strolled in silence for a moment, the only sounds being the birds in the trees and the *shush-shush* of her gown as it swayed against her legs. Her mind spun, and she wondered if she might speak next or if protocol demanded she wait for him.

"How old were you when your mother died, Fiona?"

She nearly stumbled at his abrupt question. For a king, he had little finesse. "Nearly ten, Your Highness."

They stopped walking, and he turned to face her. "If I ever learn who killed her, you have my word, he'll be drawn and quartered and left upon a pike."

The image was too much, and Fiona struggled for her next breath. She swayed closer to remain upright, and nausea rolled over her once more, as it had last evening.

The king braced her with his hands on her shoulders. "I'm sorry, lass. I didn't mean to be so colorful. I only meant to say I'd see her murderer brought to justice. Come now, sit on this bench over here a moment."

Fiona could not think what made her feel so faint. She was stronger than this. She was still a Sinclair after all. Not by name any longer, but still by blood.

They walked to the bench and sank upon it. "Forgive me, Your Highness. I fear the warmth of the day has left me lightheaded."

"Hm…perhaps." He sat down next to her and looked at her with a measured stare. Then he chuckled. "What do you know of me?"

That was a fearful question if ever there was one. "You are the king."

"And?" he prompted when she said no more.

This cat-and-mouse charade was tiresome. He asked one question after another, and all she wanted was answers to her own. Her stomach rolled. "You are the king. And you know I'm desperate to hear about my mother and yet have not offered even a sliver of information."

His brows rose, his eyes went round, and Fiona nearly clapped a hand over her foolish mouth. He'd see her dropped into a pit for such insolence. But instead, a boom of laughter rolled forth from his chest, and he slapped his thigh in humor.

"Your mother's wit and her temper. You are right, of course. How ungallant of me to taunt you so." He shook his head, as if her words had made him dizzy. "Your mother served my mother at court, a ladies' maid to Queen Margaret. You knew that, yes?"

Fiona nodded, her heart giving a flutter now that it seemed he was at last to offer something of value. "Yes, but she rarely spoke of it—to me, at least."

The king continued. "She was favored by many for her smile and her cleverness. She was exceedingly beautiful—more beautiful than you, even, and you are quite breathtaking."

Fiona heard only the compliment. 'Twas no insult to be found wanting when compared to her mother.

The king took a breath and settled himself more comfortably on the bench. "When I was a boy of eleven, my stepfather, Archibald Douglas, strove to keep me captive at Tantallon Castle. Being young, I did not realize at first I was not free to leave. I had the run of the place, but little in the way of entertainment."

Fiona folded her hands in her lap. It seemed he would make a tale of this and interrupting would not serve her purpose.

"'Twas a quiet life, but many days, your mother came to talk with me. I had other visitors too, but only a few sought to keep me informed of what was happening outside my prison walls. For it was a prison."

His cheeks flushed, and he stared off for a moment as if struggling with the memories. His voice was heated when he next spoke. "Five years, I lived like that, all but shackled within my own property, knowing all the while that Douglas was lining his own coffers with my gold and stealing land from those loyal to me to bestow upon his own clan."

She swallowed against a tide of unease. Her father had been loyal to Douglas until the day he died. She knew better than to remind the king of that now.

"But your mother was always honest with me, and so it was to her I turned when I devised a method of escape. Have you heard this tale before?" He eyed her with fresh speculation.

Fiona shook her head. "No, never."

Now he smiled a tiny smile. "Well, as I grew into a young man, some of my lady visitors were, shall we say, less savory than your mother. Douglas thought to keep me occupied with trollops, thinking the distraction would keep me satisfied and not longing for my throne. It did not work, of course. By fifteen, I yearned to grasp the reins of the country I was born to rule. And so, one evening, your noble mother dressed herself like a lowly wench and came into my room. She brought me a whore's outfit, with a wig and rouge and powder to disguise my face." He chuckled now. "I made a fine-looking wench, if I do say so myself."

Fiona could not imagine his appearance, for the man before her now was anything but feminine. She murmured a noncommittal response, and the king went on with his tale.

"Once disguised, your mother helped me sneak past all the guards and into a cart Cedric had waiting in the courtyard. We rode out of there and straight to Stirling, where the Campbell army waited, along with many of those eager to see me wrest my throne from Douglas's greedy clutches. Had it not been for Cedric and your mother, there is no telling how history might have been written."

Fiona had heard rumblings of how the king had escaped those long years ago, but nothing quite like this. She'd had no idea her mother had been so intimately involved. How was that possible? She wiped her fingertips across her forehead.

"Your Highness, may I speak my mind?"

"You may." He crossed his arms.

"My parents must have been married by this time, yes?"

The king nodded. "They were. You and your brothers were born as well. Have you no memory of being at Tantallon?"

Fiona had the vaguest recollection of moving into Sinclair Hall but none at all of where they'd been before. She shook her head.

"'Tis no surprise. You would have been a wee lass. You lived there with your mother, but your father was often away, tending to Douglas's dastardly business."

A cloud passed by his face. "Your father was a traitor to the crown, Fiona, but I have no quarrel with you or your clan so long as they prove their renewed loyalty to me. I admit, when Cedric asked me to enforce this betrothal between you and Myles, I hesitated. He assured me that with Hugh gone, the Sinclairs would once more become faithful servants of Scotland. May I have your word on that?"

Fiona swallowed, and perspiration dampened her gown once more. This was what her brothers wanted. They had given her over to an enemy just to prove their devotion to King James. She realized now that John had been right all along and that her sacrifice guaranteed the future safety of her clan.

A surge of certainty and pride swelled within her. She nodded. "Yes, Your Highness. I pledge to you our faith and loyalty. We are your humble servants."

The king smiled and patted her hand. "Good. Then I shall be most happy to make Sinclair Hall a stop along my grand tour in a few weeks' time. I'll set sail at the end of the month." He set his hands upon his knees and looked her over. His eyes assessed, but not leeringly; rather, it felt as if he were seeing her for the first time. "I believe your mother is smiling down on you right now. She would be most pleased that we are friends."

Fiona felt tears of gladness swell in her eyes. "I believe she is, Your Highness. I am honored that you would consider me as such."

"Good, then since we are to be friends, you will not be too peevish when I tell you I have need of your husband at Linlithgow for a few weeks."

"My husband?" What an odd, hollow feeling the thought of his absence brought forth.

"Aye, I want the Campbell men to travel with me, but I'll return your beloved soon enough. Matters of the state must take precedence over matters of the heart."

"Travel with you? Today?" She could not hide her surprise and dismay, and the king chuckled.

"I see I have distressed you with my haste. Perhaps I could stay another night, but we leave at first light in the morning. And do not hint to anyone that you have swayed me. I cannot have every pretty face thinking she can lead me by the nose."

He rose from the bench and held out an arm. Fiona took it, thinking there was more she should ask, more she wanted to know about her mother and that night of escape, but suddenly, all her thoughts were of Myles and the fact that he would ride away in the morning. He'd go to court and be surrounded by intrigue and dazzling beauties.

Blood rushed through her veins, and once again, the nausea overcame her. This time it could not be stopped. She pulled away from the king to lean over the bench and promptly retched up all her breakfast.

She felt the king's hands upon her waist, steadying her. He pressed a linen handkerchief into her hand.

She dabbed at her mouth as nausea gave way to humiliation. Lord, have mercy. She had just vomited in front of the king. Could anything be less appropriate?

He patted her back gently. "Better now?"

She nodded, but could not meet his gaze. "Forgive me, Your Grace."

"Nothing to forgive. Does your husband know?"

She frowned and glanced his way. "Does my husband know what?"

The king chuckled. "Why, that you're breeding, of course."

# CHAPTER 36

MYLES PACED INSIDE THE GREAT HALL. HIS WIFE HAD BEEN with King James for far too long. And in the garden, no less. He was probably pressing her up against a tree at this very moment, trying to steal a kiss. James had no boundaries when it came to other men's wives. He collected them like a boy collected pretty stones, admiring them, then slipping them into his pocket to be forgotten.

Myles turned and paced in the other direction. Fiona did not deserve such treatment. She was ignorant of courtly culture and its licentious ways. He should have refused when she asked to speak with James alone, but her blue eyes had pleaded, and she was so eager to learn more about her mother. Still, he'd been tolerant long enough.

Turning on his heel, he strode out the door and into the sunlight. The brightness blinded him but did not slow his pace. His boots cut marks into the ground until a wall of sultry fragrance from the garden halted him. And there he found them, his wife and the king.

Fiona had her back to him and turned at his approach. She looked stricken, guilty as a thief, and had a lace handkerchief pressed against her lips. It seemed His Majesty had given her a token. Perhaps more.

The king's eyes sparkled in amusement. He loved nothing more than getting caught and flaunting his superiority. He knew no man would challenge him, for any who did found themselves on military campaign in some far-off land. Myles would not risk that. Not because he was a coward, but because he would not leave Fiona to fend for herself.

"Myles," said the king, "you've arrived just in time."

Fiona's eyes were wide and round as saucers. Good Lord, what had James done to her?

The king put a possessive hand on her elbow and steered her forward. "She may need to rest a moment. But I suggest you find a different bench. It's malodorous near this one. Come find me when your wife no longer has need of you. We need to talk."

The king tipped his head to Fiona. "I look forward to seeing you this evening, my dear, when you are feeling well again. Good afternoon."

With that, he left them.

Myles's mind raced. It hurt to breathe, as if he'd been lanced in the gut. How casually the king cast her aside and went on his way. Myles looked to her face and found emotions he could not name. Not distress, but more an expression of bewilderment.

Perhaps it was not as Myles had suspected. Perhaps the king had merely shared something unexpected about her mother. He fought the urge to demand to know what had happened, for whatever had occurred, it was not of her own doing. He caught her elbow where the king had just released it.

"Would you like to sit down?"

Fiona nodded, and they walked to a second bench, not far from the first, but secluded in the shade of an apple tree. The scent of lilacs and honeysuckle swirled around them. Fiona dabbed the cloth along her forehead.

"You look distressed. Did the king say something unpleasant?"

She paused and then shook her head. "He told me how your father and my mother helped him escape."

Myles had long known of his father's involvement in that escapade but had no notion Aislinn Sinclair had been involved. But that explained much. "What else did he say?"

Fiona's eyes met his, and a flush crept over her pale cheeks. "It seems he has no quarrel with my family now that my father is no longer laird."

"That's good. Then the truce has served its purpose."

She nodded and the hand in her lap moved to her abdomen. "Yes. It seems it has."

The king must be mistaken. She could not be with child. Not this quickly. But as she sat upon the bench next to Myles, she counted back the days silently. It had been a month since they'd gone to Oban. And heaven knew they'd made randy use of that time. Nearly every day, they'd lain together, and not once in all that time had Fiona given thought to her monthly flow. Indeed, now that she did think on it, she'd not had it since before leaving Sinclair Hall. Mother Mary! Had it happened on their wedding night?

It was possible, she supposed.

If the king believed she carried a Campbell in her womb, he was not likely to keep that secret to himself.

She looked up at the trees, bursting forth with their tiny fruit, and felt a kinship. Fertile and blooming. Inside her, a new life blossomed.

"It seems there is something else as well." She met her husband's eyes once more and felt moisture build within her own. "Myles, I think I may be with child."

He stared at her a moment as if he had not heard, then a smile, rising slow and shining like the sun, lifted all his features. A single puff of laughter escaped his lips. "Are you certain?"

She shook her head. "Not quite. But it's a possibility."

He looked down at her belly and gently pressed his hand against it, as if that might give a clue, but his eyes were quickly back upon her face. "Fiona, I...I am overjoyed." He hugged her to him and tried to kiss her mouth, but she turned so he might kiss her cheek instead.

He stiffened at her reaction and loosened his hold. "Are you unhappy about this?"

She chuckled softly and pressed the handkerchief to her mouth again. "No, I am equally overjoyed. It's just"—the nausea rolled once more—"it's just I should have known a Campbell child would cause me such distress."

Then she leaned to the side and daintily retched once more.

"The four of you will ride with me to Linlithgow," the king said from his chair next to the fireplace. He sat with his legs splayed out before him, but his harsh tone belied that indolent posture. "I want every strategic mind determining how best to chop off the head of this beast. Douglas grows too bold. He thinks to strike before I beget an heir. I want this dealt with before I sail north."

Myles sat at the table with Tavish and Robert, while his father paced before them.

"We are humbly at your service, Your Grace. I wonder if you might wish for one of us to stay behind and guard Dempsey in case there is unrest," the earl said.

Myles wondered if his father spoke of him. The captain of their guard was wholly capable of maintaining order in their absence, so it would seem the earl sought to give Myles an excuse to stay with Fiona.

The king stared into the flames and paused with his answer. "I should think Dempsey will be safe enough. You'll be back in a month or less."

Disappointment lodged in Myles's chest, and he tried to ignore it. 'Twas a great honor to be called to court, and he'd been anxious to return. Until he'd brought Fiona home. Now it seemed all he wanted to do was play and lounge about with his wife. She'd tamed the warrior in him. Perhaps the king had sensed that and thought to remind him of his duty.

"Have you decided on the matter of Janet Douglas?" Cedric asked, filling a cup and handing it to the king.

The king grasped it and took a sip, casual, as if they spoke of mundane things, the weather or this evening's menu. "She burns at the stake in two weeks' time." He glanced their way to gauge their response. "She meant to poison me. Her own sons testified against her. I see no way around it."

Myles tried to keep his expression bland. It would not do for James to see his discontent over this news.

"What of her accomplices?" Tavish asked, shuffling his feet beneath the table.

The king shrugged. "Other than Douglas, I have no proof of who they are. Her sons would say nothing against anyone save their own mother. Still, news of her execution will travel fast and serve its purpose."

Myles turned to the window. He knew little of Janet Douglas, and until his marriage to Fiona, he would not have cared a whit about some treasonous woman. Perhaps she did deserve to die, but James could just as easily imprison her. Instead, he sought to manipulate the nobles with the ferocity of this punishment. If he would execute his own aunt, what foe would dare to challenge him? It was brilliant strategy of course, meant to warn the Highland chiefs, but it made Myles's blood run cold. This was news he must keep from his wife.

He stole a glance at Robert, and his brother gave a tiny shrug, as if this were just another whim of the king. Myles knew it was good fortune and the king's grace that had brought him and Fiona together, but now James would prove he could just as easily pull them apart by calling Myles to court. James played with lives as if they were wooden chess pieces. Myles and his bride were the lucky ones. Janet Douglas was not.

Dinner that evening was another grand event, with fine food and rowdy entertainment, but as soon as the king finished dining, Myles turned toward Fiona. He could not sit there through the dancing and the idle chatter when his Fiona was beside him, leaning close and inadvertently brushing her breast against his forearm. Not when he must leave her in the morning.

"You are looking pale again, my dear," he said. "Perhaps I should escort you to our chamber."

Fiona looked back, her eyes clear and sparkling. "On the contrary, my lord. I am feeling most energetic. The nap this afternoon did me a world of good."

Myles did not take his gaze from her, but sipped his wine before speaking again. She did look well, with a rosy blush to her cheeks and a gown that accentuated the creamy hue of her skin. He wanted to peel that dress off with his teeth. "In that case, might I suggest I escort you to our chamber?"

"But why? I am—oh." The color bloomed on her face, and her smile was quick.

He leaned close. "I leave in the morning with much regret. I should like to spend each moment until then showering you with my affection."

The shy dip of her head was nearly his undoing. She looked up at him through thick lashes.

"Now that you have mentioned it, my lord, I am feeling a bit light-headed. You should rush me straightaway to bed."

Blood shot to his groin so fast he was nearly light-headed himself. He glanced over his shoulder to where his mother sat.

"Fiona is feeling unwell. I'm taking her upstairs."

Marietta leaned forward to look at her daughter-in-law and frowned. "She looks well enough to me."

"Mother," he admonished.

She rolled her eyes and waved him off with the back of her hand. "Oh, be off with you. I'll make your excuses to the king."

Myles chuckled and helped Fiona from her seat, squeezing her shoulders as she rose. They strolled from the great hall with measured steps, but once free from observant eyes, they rushed up the stairs and down the corridor, until at last they burst into their room. He caught her round the waist and leaned her up against the wooden door, kissing those soft lips that parted in invitation. He intended to make the most of this night, and it began now.

She trembled in his arms and tilted her head with a sigh.

"Myles." She breathed out his name like a prayer and clutched at his back. "How shall I bear it while you're gone from me?"

Her words caught his heart like a net, scooping it from his chest. He lifted his head to gaze at her face. "Will you miss me?" he whispered.

Her eyes were big and dark, as if she had not meant to make such an admission, but then she nodded and placed her hands on either side of his face. She kissed one corner of his mouth and stole his breath away.

"Yes," she whispered.

She kissed the other corner.

"Yes."

His body felt loose and light, floating on a breeze and anchored only by her velvet palms upon his cheeks. She ran a thumb over his lips and stared at his mouth until he thought that he might die from want of her.

"Yes," she said once more, and then she kissed him.

His soul melted into her lips and her tongue and the arms she wrapped around his shoulders. Wherever her body met his was where he was alive, and so he must press all of himself into her. He urged her up against the door, hard, as if to forge them into one, and still he could not get close enough.

He snaked his arms around her waist and lifted, carrying her to the bed. They fell together and began at once to pull off one another's clothes. In moments, they were breathless and joyful and naked, free from the hindrance of fabric or modesty. He lavished her with kisses, cherished her with his hands and mouth. She was his journey and his destination. That first day at Sinclair Hall, he'd thought her a thorny rose, but she was not. She was an orchid, rare and delicate, blooming for him alone.

He pressed her back against the covers, but she pushed at him instead, urging him onto his back. He rolled over and chuckled. God, what sinful delight. Her hair trailed down his chest, a sultry tickle, as her hands stroked every expectant inch of him. And when she took him in her mouth, the hot sweetness left him overwhelmed. In all the realm, there could be no other wife such as this.

And later, as they lay spent and satisfied, Myles lifted his head to gaze in wonder at this woman he'd been blessed with.

"I love you, Fiona."

She touched his face and smiled.

"I love you too," she said, and he knew that it was true.

# CHAPTER 37

"MY LADY, COME AND LET SOFIA TELL YOUR FORTUNE." The gypsy's accent was as thick and coarse as her black hair. She tugged insistently on Fiona's sleeve.

Fiona laughed and shook her off. "No, thank you."

She was enjoying an afternoon visit to the village with Vivi. They'd seen the colorful carts resting on the nearby hillside and the gypsies' shaggy horses grazing on grass. Not too far from the edge of town sat a collection of tents, the patchwork fabric shimmering in the sunlight.

In the weeks since her husband and the others had departed with the king, Fiona battled incessant nausea and overwhelming fatigue. It seemed the child was determined to make his presence felt. But yesterday, she'd awoken with a fresh bout of energy and no sickness to speak of. She had eaten everything they set before her, and today, she felt well enough to join Myles's aunt for an outing.

The late-summer sunshine was a delight upon her face, and even the persistent gypsy could not mar her fine mood. And though she missed her husband with an aching heart, each day brought him closer to returning.

"Pretty lady," the gypsy said again, "I will share with you such wondrous words. I have amazing gifts and much to tell you. Yes, you come with me."

There was something most compelling about her, this woman, with her dark, exotic eyes and thick braid tied with a scarf.

Vivienne laughed. "She'll steal your coins and tell you lies."

The woman stepped in front and offered Vivienne an enigmatic smile. "You have heard many lies in your life, my lady, but none from me. Come to my tent later, and Sofia will tell your future. But first, this one calls to me."

She took hold of Fiona's arm and pulled her forward. Fiona laughed and let herself be led away. She was in the mood for an adventure. This might do.

"I'll find you when I'm finished," she called over her shoulder to Vivi.

The gypsy guided her to the closest tent and pulled the flap aside. Fiona stepped inside onto a thick rug and blinked in the dim interior. The sweet smell of jasmine and cloves assaulted her nose. Nervous excitement thrummed through her.

Two chairs and a table sat in the middle of the tent. The gypsy nudged her toward one chair and said, "Sit there. Wait."

Fiona sat down gingerly, expecting the gypsy to take the other chair, but she did not. Instead, she held one finger to her lips, as if to warn Fiona to silence. Then she stepped to the other side of the tent and slipped out past another flap.

Moments passed until Fiona began to wonder what had become of the woman. This was most odd. Uneasiness rustled through her thoughts like leaves in a breeze. Then the flap opened once more, and a figure emerged. Not the gypsy, but a man. He was tall and hooded in a brown homespun cloak. Fiona stood abruptly, her heart skipping a beat.

But he pulled back the hood, and the gaze of his familiar sapphire eyes pierced through her, splintering her lungs like shards of glass.

"John?"

His smile was tight and uncertain. "Fiona, 'tis good to see you."

A dozen questions crowded into her mind, so many she could not think of where to start. His appearance rattled her senses like a squall on the sea, and she thought at once of his stern farewell the day she'd ridden away from Sinclair Hall. She'd been angry with both her brothers for casting her to the enemy, but John's betrayal had cut the deepest.

Yet here he was, arriving with no warning, like some angel of gloom in a dark, filthy cloak. Her surprise gave way to agitation.

"What are you doing here?" she spit out at last.

"Shh, lower your voice. Fabric walls lend little privacy." He stepped closer, indicating she should sit again.

She did not want to. She wanted to stand. Or more than that, she wanted to run, for whatever his purpose here, Fiona sensed no good would come from it.

He put a hand upon her shoulder, gentle but insistent, and she reluctantly sank down on the chair. He sat down opposite her, moving his seat so that the table was not between them. She stared at him and wondered if perhaps this was a dream. He was pale and tired, with dark smudges beneath his eyes. For a moment, she felt sorry, but she pushed those kind thoughts away.

"If you're concerned over fabric walls, why accost me in a tent and in such a surreptitious manner?" She spoke low, but accusation gave her tone a breathless edge.

John's face was serious. "We have much to talk about, Fiona. I am sorry for my methods, but I could not be certain what reception I would get from the Campbells."

She frowned. "You would get your due respect if you arrived honestly. If they catch you here like this, they'll think you are up to some ill purpose. As do I."

He leaned forward and rested his elbows on his knees, his hands draped between them. He shook his head. "I cannot begin to hope you'll understand me, sister, but hear all I have to say and save your judgments until I have finished. Will you do that?"

Good sense told her to bolt from this chair and not listen to a word. And yet he was her brother still and had been her ally in the past. She nodded with a grudging spirit.

He leaned back in his chair and sighed. "Then, tell me, how is your life among this clan? How do they treat you?"

She thought for a moment to tell him they were of the most brutal sort, for it was John who had given her over to them with no concern for her well-being.

"It is too late for such a question, don't you think? Any damage would already be done."

His cheeks flushed with heat. "I know. I have carried that burden with me since the day you left. Though I'm sure you do not believe me, I've worried for you every moment. So, answer. Are they wicked or kind?"

He looked earnest, more so than she had seen him look in years, and her spite cooled.

"They are kind, John. More gracious than you could imagine. They have welcomed me as one of their own."

A whisper of relief passed over his features. "And what manner of man is the earl himself?"

Fiona hesitated, wondering how much she might impart. Not so long ago she had despised Cedric for cruel deeds he did not commit. But John knew nothing of his innocence.

She reached out and took her brother's hand. "He is not the monster we thought, John. In fact, I have great cause to think he was not responsible for what happened to our mother."

John pulled his hand from hers, and his eyes narrowed. "What makes you say so?"

He would not believe her. He'd spent a lifetime, like her, thinking the worst of Cedric Campbell.

She must choose her words with caution. "It seems he and our mother were friends, even after James claimed his throne. They...corresponded."

"Did the earl tell you that?"

"No. He'll not speak to me of her. But I've seen her letters."

His eyes opened wider at this admission. "What letters?"

Fiona pressed her hands together. Such news would be a shock, but telling him was her best course.

"Though it would seem impossible, I believe our mother cared for him. And he for her. The letters spoke of love."

John remained unmoving in his seat, his face devoid of surprise or judgment. As if he'd known. Fiona looked into his eyes and saw relief.

"He told me something similar on the day of your wedding. At first, I thought he wove a tale for some purpose of his own, but over these past weeks, I've grown to wonder at the truth of his words. And things that mother herself told me before she died. Things that made no sense at the time."

"What things?"

"She said I wasn't like the rest of you. That I was different, meant for something grand."

A restlessness overcame Fiona. "*I am not certain he is ready for whatever may come to pass,*" she whispered.

"What?" he asked.

"Mother wrote that in her last letter to Cedric. Have you any idea what she meant?"

John ran his hands over his close-cropped hair and stewed a moment, as if his thoughts were too muddled to formulate. Then his breath came out in a huff.

"She meant that Cedric Campbell is my father."

His lips stung at the words, but John felt such relief at finally setting the truth free. He was Cedric Campbell's son. When the earl had told him as much on the day of the wedding, disbelief had governed him. But the more he pondered the matter, the more sense it made. Snippets of advice his mother had whispered in his ear, his height, so much greater than any other Sinclair. Even the way Hugh Sinclair had treated him after Aislinn was murdered.

He watched astonishment splash across his sister's face. She fell back against the chair as if pushed, and pressed both hands to her chest.

"Cedric is your father?" She spoke slowly and precisely, as if she had not heard correctly.

He nodded. "He told me so himself, and though I was as shocked to learn of this as you are now, I can see no just cause why the earl would invent such a lie. It does him no good." He stood and paced, unable to keep his seat a moment longer. Time was slipping away, and he had so much more to say. "I think our fath—I think Hugh may have known. About me, even."

Her eyes went rounder still. "What makes you think so?"

"Do you remember, days after mother died, Hugh beat me so soundly my ear bled?"

Fiona nodded mutely.

"He struck me for daring to suggest 'twas not Cedric who harmed her. Mother had confessed their friendship to me, you see, though I had no idea how long it had gone on or to what depth." He paced about as he spoke, trying to evade the bitter memories. "But when I said as much to Hugh, he called me a wicked liar and said if I ever breathed such falsehoods again, he'd drown me in the loch." Passion gave his voice a thickness. He coughed it away and faced his sister. "He knew it wasn't Cedric. He was just looking for a reason to kill him. And now I suspect mother was preparing to tell me about my paternity. Cedric gave her the brooch to pass to me."

"Why?" His sister's voice was faint, her cheeks flushed.

"He said he'd claim me as his own and that the brooch would grant me safe passage through any Campbell land if I chose to join him. He didn't realize I'd never gotten it, nor that mother had never had a chance to tell me any of this, until you jabbed him with it on your wedding day. He thought I knew and had made my choice to remain a Sinclair."

He sighed and sank down in the chair. Unburdening this tale had not made him lighter after all. Instead, it made him bone-wrenchingly weary. And only half his work was done.

"I saw no pennants flying at the castle when I rode into the village. Does that mean the earl is not in residence?"

Fiona gazed at him as if her eyes were blurred. "Cedric is with my husband and the king at Linlithgow."

Disappointment sank like a stone inside his heart. He must meet with the Campbells before the next leg of his journey. The letter signed by all the Highland chiefs was sewn securely in the lining of his doublet, yet burned against his back like a branding iron. He was anxious to be rid of it, even though it would seal his fate, along with Simon's.

"When will they return?"

"Not for a week or more."

His sister rose from her chair and pressed a hand against her belly, pacing. He wished he had the luxury of letting this revelation take hold. But time was running out.

"Fiona, there is more."

Her face went pale, and she sank down in the chair once more. "How could there be more than this? Please, John. Please do not tell me Hugh Sinclair did something awful."

He had long wrestled with that same fear, but shook his head. "I honestly do not know, Fiona."

"But surely you have some idea who the culprit was, don't you?"

John frowned. How could he make her understand that justice for their mother might never be met, and in this moment, with what was certain to come next, it hardly mattered?

"Fiona, listen to me. We are running out of time. There is a plan afoot which I must tell the earl about at once. And something you must know as well."

Her hands fell limp against her lap. "What more?"

"The truce was never meant to hold. Your marriage was a ruse."


"A ruse?"

The garish colors of the tent walls blurred. She saw John's face and heard his words like one underwater. His hands clasped hers, too warm and tight. They felt like shackles heated in a forge. She shook them free.

"What do you mean, a ruse?"

"A decoy planned by Simon, meant only to buy us time so we might ally with the other Highland clans. The Sinclairs have united with the Sutherlands, the Mackays, the Gunns, and more. When James sails north and lands at Gairloch, an army thousands strong will be there to slice him into bits. They mean to kill the king."

Those harsh words cut through the fog of her distress. She stood once more. "Kill the king?" Distress surged through her veins. "You traded my future to be used as nothing more than a…a distraction?" Her hands fell limp to her sides. "Did you know that was Simon's plan?"

There was shame in his expression. Yes, he'd known and was sorry for it, but she had no use for his remorse. He and Simon had gambled, with her body as the prize. 'Twas unforgivable. The Campbells could have been the worst sort of fiends, and still her brothers would have tossed her into that pit to suffer on her own.

John stood and grasped her by the shoulders. "Be angry with me, if you must, but there are more lives at stake here than our own. I can stop this, Fiona. If you tell me you are devoted to the Campbells, I will side with you and confess this plot to them. If warned, the king's forces can almost certainly fend off this attack."

She broke free of his grasp. "Why should they trust you now? Why should I?"

"Because I am your brother. I know I failed in that before, but I am trying to protect you now." He paused, as if weighing his words, and blew a shallow breath between his lips. "Fiona, I have a document signed by all the Highland chiefs. Proof of their treason. I'll turn it over to your husband, and he can do with it what he will."

Fear and agitation scorched her skin. She stepped away from him. "How have you come by such a document?"

"I am the messenger, tasked with delivering it to Archibald Douglas. The clans believe he will assist them in murdering the king."

Her stomach fell like a boulder off a cliff. "Is Simon's name on it?"

John nodded.

"You fools! The king would see you burn for having any part of this."

Regret twisted his expression. "I cannot undo what we did to you, Fiona. That die is cast. And I would see Simon's way clear of this if I could, but the plan of the Highland chiefs is doomed to fail and only suffering will come from it. Perhaps if I am the bearer of this news, the king will see fit to offer clemency. If not, then better Simon and I be sacrificed than all of Scotland put to war."

Fiona pressed her fingers to her temples, but nothing could stop the clamoring inside her head. This was too much. Simon had followed his father's path of vengeance, like any loyal son. Now it seemed John was similarly swayed by this knowledge of his Campbell bloodline.

She could not resist the question. "If Cedric had never told you he was your father, would you be taking that letter to Archibald Douglas instead of bringing it here?"

He held her gaze, and she saw the sadness in his eyes.

"Do not ask."

"It could have meant a dire end for me, you know. It may still. For both of us." Her breath hitched at the thought of Myles turning away from her.

John came quickly to her side. "You had no part in this. I will swear to that upon my life."

She thought of all her childish behavior on the journey here from Sinclair Hall and Myles's enduring patience. It seemed she must put him to the test once more, with a flaw of such magnitude his love might not withstand it. How proud she had been to be a Sinclair. Now she felt only shame.

"You say they will be a week or more?" John interrupted her thoughts.

She nodded.

He rubbed a hand across his jaw. "I cannot wait that long. I must reach the king before he sets sail."

"You think to simply ride up to the gates of the palace and demand an audience? He will not see you."

"I have no other choice."

"I can get him in," said a feminine voice.

Both Fiona and her brother jumped and turned toward the sound. The tent flap slid to the side and in stepped Vivienne.

"You're right," she added. "Tent walls offer little privacy."

# CHAPTER 38

"FIONA, I CANNOT SIT IDLE WAITING FOR YOUR HUSBAND AND the earl to return. I must leave at once for Linlithgow."

Her brother paced around his tiny room at the inn where he'd taken lodging. She and Vivienne had joined him there after leaving the gypsy's tent.

"But it's possible we could miss them in the crossing. There is more than one route between Linlithgow and here." Vivienne sat upon the bed in a garnet-colored dress, the deep, rich hue a contrast to the dim shades of the chamber.

"We?" John's brows rose. "There is no *we*, my lady. I make this journey alone."

Vivienne rose elegantly from the bed. "Nonsense. You cannot gain entrance without me. You need me."

John's jaw clenched. "Your offer is most gracious, but I can think of few things I need less on this journey than a woman. You'll only slow me down and cause me worry."

Vivienne smiled, and Fiona knew she would not be dissuaded.

"I can travel by horse just as a man would," Vivienne said. "You'll waste more time loitering by the palace gate if the king will not see you. And if you make a fuss, the guards will clap you in irons and tote you to the stocks, but I can get you inside the walls in an instant."

John's eyes narrowed. "The stocks will be the least of my problems if I arrive too late to stop the king from setting sail. Truly, my lady, I appreciate your offer, but I must go forth on this quest without your assistance."

The three of them had been arguing for nearly an hour, talking round each other and stewing over what to do, of how they might prevent this battle and still save Simon from the noose. John's mistrust of Vivienne was palpable. And logical, considering she'd damned herself by admitting to eavesdropping on their conversation in the tent.

"Vivienne is right, John," Fiona said. "It does no good to rush if you cannot get in, but perhaps I should go with you and beg an audience. The king was most gracious to me during his visit."

Vivienne rolled her eyes. "Fiona, forgive me, but you are naive. The king may very well think you were a part of this plot all along. I, however, will testify I heard your brother reveal his tale to you." A smile turned up the corners of her mouth. "And certainly, I'd be more adept than either of you at finding my way into the king's chamber."

Vivienne had little shame and few morals, advantageous traits for one undergoing such an excursion.

Fiona smiled in spite of her unease and looked to her brother. "She is right again. I see no point in beleaguering this issue further, John. We must go with you."

"I do not like it. This is my cross to bear, not yours," John said. "And I would not have the king and the earl think I hide behind the skirts of women."

Fiona's smiled broadened. "The king once hid behind a woman's skirt himself, only he was wearing it at the time. We might remind him of that, if necessary."

Against all of John's arguments, they set out the next morning with ten Campbell men-at-arms, each one chosen by Vivienne for his valor and discretion.

John eyed each one with caution. "She seems highly unpredictable," he whispered to Fiona, staring at Vivienne from the back of his horse.

Fiona adjusted the reins of her gray mare and followed his gaze. "Do not underestimate her. She is amazingly resourceful. We are lucky to have her on our side."

"But *is* she on our side? Are you certain?"

"She is a loyal Campbell, John, but now so are we, remember? So, yes, I am certain. Unless you have some other purpose which you have not confessed?"

The idea sent a chill through her, but her brother's expression gave her ease.

"You know everything. No more secrets. I cannot bear the weight of them. I only wish I could see clear some way to keep Simon from this mess."

Fiona nodded and dashed away a tear. Their brother was boastful and impetuous, and never one to give her ease. Yet she'd not betray him or sacrifice him if there were any other way to serve their cause.

They rode hard for six days, sleeping only a few hours each night. Fiona managed well enough, pushing through exhaustion and the occasional nausea in her eagerness to see her husband. The child seemed to tolerate the journey as well, and she was grateful for that. Yet always present in her thoughts was her concern that the message they carried would make Myles turn away from her. If he thought she'd known of this all along, what might his reaction be? Still, it was a risk she must take. The future of the country rested on the success or failure of this endeavor.

At last, they reached Linlithgow. The palace sat in a hollow on the edge of an indigo loch surrounded by fruit trees. Though the sunshine bode of good tidings, fear pressed tight against Fiona's chest. She prayed, as she had each day of their travels, they'd be welcomed by the king and commended for their haste. Most of all, she prayed John's new loyalty would be rewarded with mercy for both him and Simon.

They rode through the cobbled streets of the village, past spice shops and vintners, milliners and silversmiths, until they reached the palace gates. As expected, guards halted their progression.

"Leave this to me," Vivienne murmured to Fiona and John before nudging her horse forward. "Greetings, I am Lady Vivienne Ramsey. This is Lady Fiona Campbell and her brother. We bid an audience with the king at once, on a matter of the utmost importance."

One guard stepped forward, patently unimpressed. "The king is seeing no callers today, my lady. Please return again another time."

Her horse pranced sideways, as if annoyed by their dismissal. "The king will want to see us. We possess information most imperative to his future travels. Please send a messenger to him at once and tell him we are here."

He looked away from her. "No callers today, my lady, by the king's command."

Vivienne looked down her nose. "Tell him we are here. That is by my command."

Fiona squirmed in her saddle. How imperious Vivienne sounded! Still, the guard hardly blinked, and Fiona began to fear their failure.

"I obey the king, my lady. Be on your way."

"What is your name, boy?"

The guard's chin lifted. "Seamus Mackenzie, my lady."

She leaned low over her horse's neck so that her face was very near his. "Well, Seamus Mackenzie, I hope you crave infamy, for your name will be synonymous with a blunder of the greatest magnitude if you do not let us pass."

Fiona exchanged a wary glance with her brother. Vivienne had warned John not to make a fuss, but this had all the makings of one. Still, when John opened his mouth to speak, Fiona gave a discreet shake of her head.

The guard's lips pressed thin. He turned his head to glare at her a moment, then gestured to another guard. "Show these three into the courtyard, then take their message to the king's chamberlain. He can decide what to do. Your men must remain outside the gate." He spoke this last bit to Vivienne and tilted his solid chin in the direction of the Campbell men-at-arms.

Vivienne sat up, her smile demure. "Thank you."

They dismounted and walked together under the gate into a courtyard crowded with people. Women in elaborate gowns of silk and satin, and men dressed in equal finery, and even grander accoutrements. Stares came their way, some discreet but others blatant in their perusal. Vivienne held her head high, and Fiona tried to mimic that confidence, though she was quaking inside. John's brow showed a sheen of perspiration.

The guard instructed them to wait next to a large stone fountain intricately carved with ogres, dragons, mermaids, and unicorns, and wait they did. It was a full thirty minutes before he came back.

"My ladies, my lord, the king commands you come at once and join him in his chamber. Come this way."

Vivienne's smile to Fiona was triumphant as she smoothed the front of her dress.

The guard led them through the great hall, past an enormous three-sectioned fireplace, and down a maze of corridors, until at last they came to a set of wide wooden doors. More sentries were posted there, and their guide murmured something into the ear of one. He nodded and pounded his staff against the floor twice, announcing them.

The doors swung open, and Fiona peered into the opulent room. She saw the king sitting at the head of a long table with a dozen other men gathered around him. She spotted Cedric and Tavish and Robert. Then joy burst free inside her heart, for there stood Myles, anticipation and curiosity painted on his face.

His smile broke wide when he saw her, but he glanced at the king.

James nodded. "Go greet your wife, man."

Fiona bit back a cry of gladness as Myles strode to her side and pulled her tight against him. Relief seeped into her tired limbs. She clung fast, saying nothing. Once he knew the purpose of their mission, he might be angry, but for this moment at least, he was happy to see her.

The king and the others moved closer, and Vivienne pressed past Fiona to charm them with her smile, greeting several by name and maneuvering the group back toward the head of the table.

Fiona was grateful for Vivi's intervention and hugged her husband for another full moment until he leaned back to cup her face in his hands. His eyes were keen with questions. "What are you doing here?"

She paused, wanting to weep at the import of what she must share, but she blinked those useless tears away and harnessed all her courage. She looked to John. "You must recall my brother."

Myles glanced his way, and his expression grew wary. He loosened his grip on Fiona and offered a slight bow of his head.

"Of course. 'Tis a pleasure. Although these are most peculiar circumstances."

John bowed low. "They are, indeed."

Cedric joined them then, coming to stand next to John, eyeing him with both caution and vulnerability. Fiona could not help but look from one to the other, searching for resemblance. She could see it now, in the curve of their jaws and the tilt of the nose. Subtle, but there to anyone who might wonder.

"My lord," John said stiffly, bowing to the earl.

"John, I am most pleased to see you."

John's shoulders relaxed the most miniscule amount, and Fiona blinked back another tear. How odd this moment must be for them, yet there was no time to wonder over it.

She grasped her husband's arm. "Myles, my brother brings news which the king must hear at once. We need a private audience."

"What is this about, Fiona?"

"I cannot say until the others are gone. Please, Myles. It is most imperative the king be informed with all due haste."

He searched her face. "I will ask."

She watched, along with John and Cedric, as Myles left her side and went to speak quietly with the king. John and Cedric exchanged another wary glance with each other.

James seemed more interested in Vivienne's backside than whatever Myles might impart. Still, he waved a hand and drew the attention of them all.

"Gentlemen, leave us."

Soon Fiona and Vivienne were left with the king, Cedric, Myles, and John. Fiona's nausea seemed determined to return, though undoubtedly more from nerves and fatigue than from the child she carried. Still, the walls of the chamber wavered before her eyes, and she moved to grip the edge of the table. Myles returned to her side and pulled her arm through his.

"Come, sit here." He guided her to a chair not too far from the king, but the others remained standing.

Vivienne moved forward. "Your Grace, may I have the honor of introducing Sir John Sinclair, Lady Fiona's brother."

James rose from his chair and now stood with his hands behind his back, his eyes hawkish in their perusal, looking every bit the powerful sovereign. He took John in, from his well-worn boots to the dingy brown cloak.

John shifted on his feet a moment and then stepped forward to kneel down before the king. "Your Grace, I am your humble servant. I pray you forgive this interruption and hear my message."

The king turned and walked back to his chair. He sat down heavily. "I hope for your sake that this news is worth my time."

John remained on one knee, his head bowed. "I believe you will find the information useful, Your Grace. Distressing, but useful."

The king sat forward. "Distressing, you say? 'Tis poor judgment to bring me distressing news, don't you think? Then again, Sinclairs are not known for demonstrating sound judgment, are they?"

Fiona could tell by his tone that he taunted, and John's ears burned pink. She could not help but intercede. She rose from her chair. "Your Grace, we are most grateful for the friendship you have offered our clan. It is the spirit of friendship and loyalty which brings us here today to warn you of impending danger."

The king's gaze met with Fiona's, and he relented, waving his hand toward her brother.

"Get up, Sinclair. Tell me what you've come to say."

Fiona thought to step over toward John, to weave her arm through his, but she stood motionless, nerves rooting her to the spot. It seemed he was on his own with this tale of treason.

"It is no secret, Your Grace, that Hugh Sinclair sought to keep you from your throne." John's voice was strong, and Fiona felt a surge of pride at his courage, even while wincing at this reminder of their family's faulty allegiance. "At his knee, I was taught to wish for the same. However, as a man, I would have you know I pledge my loyalty to you, and you alone."

James tilted his head, his expression bland. "As well you should. I am your king."

"Yes, Your Grace, and I know you for a wise and gracious sovereign. However, there are those in the Highlands who seek even now to purge you from the throne and bring Archibald Douglas back to power."

James stood in an instant, all pretense of relaxation gone. Her brother flinched but held his ground.

"Who among those Highland curs panders to Douglas? Give me their names."

John swallowed. "I offer you better than that, Your Grace. I can give you their signatures." He stepped back and removed his doublet while the others watched in curiosity. He laid it on the table, but when he pulled his dagger from its sheath, the other men moved toward the king, as if to guard him, until they saw John's intentions.

Fiona's pulse throbbed at her temples, and she sat back down. The king was furious, of that there was no doubt, and she whispered a silent prayer that God might watch over her brother.

John slipped the tip of the blade into the lining of his garment and tugged. The sound of rending fabric filled the air with an ominous hiss.

Myles looked to Fiona, and her heart fractured at the unease in her husband's eyes, for the doubt she saw there was not for John alone. It was for her as well.

At last, John pulled the paper out from inside his garment and, with a trembling hand, passed it to the king.

James stared at him for a long moment, his lips a thin, harsh line. Then as if to dismiss the rest of them, he eased back in his chair to read the document. His face flushed a deeper hue. His nostrils flared, and Fiona wondered if steam or fire might come out next. "Who has seen this?" James demanded, looking back at John.

"Only those whose names are on the page, Your Grace," her brother said. "I offered to deliver it to Douglas myself so that I might bring it to you instead."

The king rose and shoved the parchment into Cedric's hands. "Upon my crown, I swear, every name on that list belongs to a dead man."

Myles had witnessed the king's temper before, but this was something more. His bloodlust to vanquish Archibald Douglas and his allies showed in the snap of every movement.

"And how came you to know of such a plot?" James asked.

John's shoulders sagged beneath the burden of this question. His head dipped. "I will not have a lie upon my soul, Your Grace, and so I must confess. I was once one of them."

Every movement ceased for the space of a heartbeat at this stunning revelation. Myles heard his father groan, and Fiona pressed both hands to her chest. Myles's lungs went hot and hollow when he looked her way, for her expression spoke of heartache but not surprise. She had known of this plot. But for how long?

The king walked a full circle around John, his eyes unblinking as a snake. "You were a part of this?"

"I was, Your Grace, but briefly only. I quickly saw the error of my judgment and beg mercy for myself and my brother. My sister's marriage was a ploy and the truce with the Campbells was not meant to hold, but upon my life, I pray it stands. I would see no victor vanquish you, for you are the true and rightful king."

"How magnanimous you are to offer your endorsement of my reign." The king's tone sliced at the air, and Myles heard his wife draw in a sharp breath.

Their marriage just a ploy? Was that why she had resisted so?

She dipped her head over folded hands as if she prayed. And indeed pray she ought, for there was little hope that either of her brothers could escape this debacle now. What foolish arrogance had led to this great folly? The king would see them drawn and quartered for such blatant treason.

Myles's gut twisted with dread. If his wife had had knowledge of this scheme, she'd given no sign of it, and yet she'd duped him time and again. Since the moment she'd descended those steps at Sinclair Hall, he had been blinded by her. Was it possible she'd known of this plot since the day of their wedding?

Christ, was it possible she hadn't?

He looked at her, and her head rose. A tear spilled over one pale cheek, and his chest turned to lead, for every line of her face spoke of guilt and regret. She had lied. She'd used him like a toy, and he had let her. Memories, too bright and suddenly bittersweet, ran through his mind, tripping over one another as his heart did battle with his mind. She could not have betrayed him so thoroughly.

And yet, it seemed she had.

"The weight of my regret cannot be expressed, Your Grace," John said, kneeling once more.

The king looked down on him as he might excrement on a royal shoe. "You Sinclairs are more trouble than you are worth."

Myles's father stepped forward. "He is not a Sinclair, Your Grace. He is a Campbell—my son—although he has not known of this for long."

The air pressed like a vice against Myles as he looked to his father. Surely he had not heard correctly. Or perhaps this was a trick meant to protect Fiona's brother?

But the earl laid a hand on John's shoulder and nodded down at him in a show of encouragement.

The king seemed as flabbergasted as Myles felt. He stepped backward and sat down in the chair again, his gaze going from the earl to John and back again.

The floor wobbled beneath Myles's feet. And still his wife showed no surprise, only culpability. She'd known about her brother too, it seemed. What an untapped well of information she had been. If only he'd sought to prod her with the right questions.

"I don't like secrets, Cedric," the king said after a moment.

"Forgive me, Your Grace. I kept this secret only to protect the dignity of my wife. I would not have her mocked for my indiscretions."

Agitation weighed in Myles's throat like an anchor. 'Twas bad enough his bride had lied and committed treason, but now it seemed his father had been duplicitous as well. The affair with Aislinn was an insult to the earl's wife. But never once had there been any indication that Myles had a bastard half brother. And one who, until very recently, plotted to assassinate the king of Scotland, no less. Any moment, God was sure to fling bolts of lightning from the rafters down on this unholy mess.

Fiona watched her husband's expression change from confusion to shock to anger. How she wanted to embrace him, to ease his mind and promise her loyalty, but the look he cast her way shattered whatever hope she'd carried. His eyes were dark with mistrust and contempt. No matter that she had no part in this. He held her guilty by association, just as she had done when first they met.

The king exhaled a mighty breath. "Your son or not, Cedric, he sought to see me dead."

The earl replied with confidence. "Yet he risks his life to bring you this warning. He puts the Clan Sinclair on trial, the only family he has ever known, his own brother, so that he might now protect you."

The king's expression soured further. "If Janet Douglas had, at the last moment, chosen not to pour the poison in my cup, would you expect me to forgive her?"

"I would if she drank it, Your Grace. This young man—" Cedric's voice hitched. "My son could have gone straight to London. He'd be safe in the English king's house, but instead, he sacrificed much to come here. I implore you, give the lad a chance to prove himself."

The king's chest rose and fell with his rapid breaths, and Fiona felt her own lungs were near to bursting with anxiety. John kept his head bowed, and she could sense his defeat. She could not sit idly by, doing nothing while John's destiny swung in the balance.

"Your Grace," she said, rising and moving to John's other side. She caught Cedric's eye, his expression wary. "Your Grace," she said again, clearing her throat, "do you recall our conversation in the garden at Dempsey?"

The king's forehead wrinkled in a scowl. "I have no time for girlish riddles, Fiona. Make your point, and make it quick."

She felt a flush stain her cheeks. "By your admission, it was the earl and my mother who helped you claim your throne. My brother is a product of their union, without a drop of Sinclair blood in his veins. He knows that now, and I attest you will not find a more faithful subject."

James's ruthless chuckle held no hint of humor. "And what role did you play in this grand charade, miss? Besides the blushing virgin bride, I mean."

The stab of his words pierced her chest. Her fate was tied to John and Simon's, but her greater concern was that Myles might think the worst of her.

John's head lifted. "She knew nothing, Your Grace. We sought to keep her far removed from any plans."

"By putting her into a Campbell's bed? If you are as loyal a subject as you are a brother, then I'd best watch my back."

Fiona's mind worked furiously, trying to formulate what she might say to ensure her brother's safety and proclaim her innocence to her husband, but before she could utter another word, the king continued.

"Guard!" the king called, and one appeared in an instant. "Escort the ladies to a chamber where they might wait in privacy."

Fiona looked to Cedric and saw concern upon his face. She thought to speak again, but he gave a tiny shake of his head. She must trust him alone to come to John's defense. How odd it was the bond between King James and Cedric Campbell that would decide her fate and that of her brothers. Though not so odd, perhaps, for in a way, it always had.

The guard gestured toward the door. Fiona turned and faced her husband. The wounded look upon his face tore at her soul. 'Twas as if he doubted every moment they had shared, yet there was nothing she could say just then that might explain her part or her remorse.

Vivienne, however, seemed bent on trying. Sidestepping the guard, she moved toward the king instead. "Lady Fiona had no role in this at all, Your Grace. She knew nothing of the plot to harm you, nor was she in collusion with her brothers regarding the truce. I heard John confess it all to her just days ago."

The king's reaction was but a flicker of acknowledgment, but it was Myles's face that Fiona hoped might change. The softening was subtle, almost resistant, as if he strove to believe the worst.

"Is that the truth?" Myles murmured to her alone.

"You know it is. For all my faults, I have never lied to you."

She wanted to beg and cry that he might be swayed, but she held her voice to a whisper.

The space of a lifetime passed and yet was over in an instant. She stared into his eyes, hoping against hope he might see her love shining there or give any indication he believed her, but he cast his gaze back to John, and she knew his sense of betrayal ran deeper than her actions. This was bigger than just she and Myles.

The king waved his hand in dismissal. "Leave us, I said."

Fiona pressed her hand against Myles's arm, but his eyes remained on John. There was nothing she could do, it seemed, and so she let the guard escort her from the chamber.

As they walked, Vivienne wound her arm around Fiona's waist. Suddenly, all the traveling and the worry converged, and Fiona became dizzy from the pressure. She clutched Vivienne's hand as they moved down the corridor.

The guard showed them to a gilded room full of velvet and brocade furnishings, and Fiona collapsed upon a chaise.

"Bring us wine," Vivienne ordered a servant waiting at the door, "and some food." There was that imperious tone again.

Fiona tried to smile through her exhaustion. "You would do well in a royal palace."

"I deserve one," Vivienne answered. "Now rest awhile. There is no telling how long the men will be."

"Is there nothing more we can do?"

Vivienne, for once, looked worried. "We can pray."

# CHAPTER 39

DO YOU SWEAR UPON YOUR SISTER'S LIFE, AND ALL WHICH you hold dear, that what you've said is true?" the king said to John, who still knelt upon the floor.

"Yes, Your Grace. Every word."

Myles watched John's shoulders sway, for this interrogation had gone on some time.

"And do you swear you have told the whole of it, with no omission?"

John nodded. "Yes, Your Grace."

His voice never quivered, and he did not plead for mercy. For that, Myles was impressed, but perhaps it was naïveté that stilled John's limbs, and he simply did not realize how close he was to the chopping block.

The earl remained steadfast, standing next to John, and Myles felt oddly bereft watching from the side.

"Stand up," the king said at last, and John rose to his feet.

James stepped close, so close John leaned back, but held his footing. "You will aid us in capturing each man on that list," said the king. "You will testify against each one, even your own brother. When you have done this, and only then, will I decide upon your fate."

John nodded and nearly buckled, but the earl's hand reached out and held him steady. "And what of my sister?" John asked.

A frost invaded Myles's veins and traveled to his heart. This was the question he had longed to ask, yet feared the answer.

The king's eyes went round, and a breath came fast between his lips. "Your boldness knows no bounds."

"I mean no disrespect, Your Grace. I only wish to ensure her well-being. She had no part in this, and I would not have her suffer for my actions. Or Simon's either."

The king stared hard, as if hoping to read all the secrets in John's mind, and then he turned that glare on Myles. "Your wife has caused a bit of trouble on her own, has she not?"

The frost in Myles turned to ice. "Only at the start, Your Grace. She has become a most loyal wife."

"Would you trust her with your life? And mine?"

The king's words twisted like a dagger to the chest, and Myles's heart split in two, for though he loved Fiona with his entire being, he could not in that moment guarantee she had been honest. His hesitation was enough to cast doubt.

"Just as I thought," said the king. "You are wise, Myles, to withhold your trust from any woman. Especially a daughter of Hugh Sinclair."

Panic seized him. No matter her offenses, imagined or real, Myles knew in that instant he would never give her up. "I do trust her, Your Grace." His voice came out strident, burning in his throat.

King James shook his head and cast a glance toward the earl. "You Campbells have a peculiar weakness for Sinclair women."

"I trust the lass myself, Your Grace," answered Myles's father. "Though we did not get on too well at first, I am convinced her loyalties follow those of her mother."

"Then she shall have a chance to prove it. Now, take your seats. We have much to plan."

The hour was late when Myles arrived at the chamber where his wife and Vivi waited. Fresh relief washed over him at the sight of her reclined upon a chaise. Vivienne held a finger to her lips to silence him.

"She only just fell asleep," she whispered. "Let her rest, for she is overwrought with worry."

But his wife sat up at the sound of his footstep. "Myles?"

He crossed to where she rested and sank down on a knee before her.

"What news have you of my brother?"

"He is fine, for now, but the king has set conditions. When they are met, John's fate will be determined."

"So the king has yet to trust him."

Myles tipped his head. "Do you blame him?"

"No." She gave a tiny sigh. "'Tis justice, I suppose. I would not see John punished, but he made this bed, he and Simon."

Her words brought some relief to the pressure in his chest, and he moved to sit beside her on the chaise. Vivi sank down into a nearby chair.

"There is little hope for Simon. You must prepare for that." Myles spoke the words with great regret, for he would spare her of that knowledge if he could.

Her lips trembled. "I know. It was no easy thing for John to turn him over to the king. Nor I. His actions may be wicked, but he is my brother, still. He sought only to serve my father, even after Hugh's death."

"Save that sentiment from the king, Fiona," he whispered as if the ears had walls, for indeed they might in a royal palace such as this. "Sympathy for any traitor is a crime in James's eyes. And your fate is not yet set."

Fear and surprise in equal measure played upon her features. "The king doubts me as well?"

"He trusts few, and this news has left him reeling." He squeezed her hand but said no more.

"And what of you? Do you despise me?" she whispered.

He held himself back for no more than a breath, for in his heart of hearts, he knew she was innocent. She might have fought and run and led him on a chase when first they met, but for all of that, honesty had been her cloak and her weapon. She had professed to love him, and he believed her.

"Despise you? You, who I adore? You, who are giving me the greatest gift of all?" His hand slid forth to caress her abdomen and their child. "Fiona, this has been a rocky path we've traveled. But whatever forces brought you forth to me, I am sincerely grateful." He pulled her closer still. "And if it's truth we are professing, I'd have you know, if given the chance to change the past, I would wed you still."

"You would?"

"Aye, if you would have me."

A tear ran down his wife's pale cheek, and he brushed it away.

"I would," she whispered.

He kissed her then, soft and sweet, and would have pressed for more had Vivienne not offered an exaggerated sigh from her spot in the other chair.

"Ah, you two make my heart weep. I should go find myself a husband."

Myles turned to his aunt. "Well, you may yet have a chance. We travel north tomorrow, but you may stay at Linlithgow until we return."

"North?" his wife asked. "Where in the North?"

"Sinclair Hall."

She had thought never to see her home again, and her heart leapt at the notion of reuniting with her sister. "And I'm to join you?"

Her husband nodded, but did not smile. "The king has use of you, my love. Though I voiced objections as fiercely as I dared, he would not be swayed. He thinks to send small armies to each northern stronghold and apprehend every chief who signed that paper."

Simon would be one of them.

"But what has that to do with me?"

"John told us of a passageway at Sinclair Hall leading from the chapel to the shore. Do you know of it?"

She nodded, her stomach growing queasy. She had only ventured once into that dark place. As a child, she and her brothers had gone there and dared one another to go to the end. It was moist and foul and full of things with many legs, and she had not gotten more than a few feet in before turning around.

"I know of it," she said.

"'Tis the king's plan that you should enter Sinclair Hall first, acting as if you are there to visit with your sister. But once inside, you must go to the passage and unlock the gates. That will allow our men inside before your brother is the wiser."

The room before her shifted, and she leaned back against her husband's arm. Dark tunnels and centipedes be damned. She could not faint at such a request.

# CHAPTER 40

Y OUR MOTHER DID ME A GREAT SERVICE ONCE, LASS. I EX-
pect the same from you. Complete this task, and the
Sinclair name will be restored. Fail, and I will know you for
a traitor." The king handed off his reins to a waiting man-at-
arms and turned toward Fiona. John and Myles stood beside
her at the edge of a thick forest on the western slope of Sinclair
land. Inside that cluster of pines, the royal army was effectively
hidden from any who might be watching from her old home.
They'd traveled fast and hard to reach this spot, and now success
depended on her.

Worry was a worm inside her chest, but she could not show
it. "I will not fail, Your Grace."

"Good. Then I expect you to unlock the iron gates inside the
passageway as soon as possible. At dusk, John and Myles will
be at the outer entrance of the tunnel to lead some of my men
through it and into the chapel. Then I shall lead the rest of my
men through the front gate. Understood?"

Fiona nodded, her heart in her throat. Tears of trepidation
blurred her vision, and she blinked them away.

John stepped forward and put a gentle hand upon her arm. "I wish that I could join you, Fiona, but Simon believes me to be in London."

She covered his hand with her own. "I'll be fine, John. I have practiccd what to say, and Simon has no cause to doubt me."

"Still, be cautious, and remember to look for my Genevieve. She will help you."

The king cleared his throat. "Get on with your good-byes. Time is wasting."

Fiona embraced her brother, fast and hard. It would not do to linger over this, for it would only stir her fears and undermine her certainty. 'Twas a bold plan they'd hatched, her strolling into Sinclair Hall as if all were right with the world, but it was the most expedient way to get her inside.

John stepped back. "Godspeed to you, Fiona."

She nodded once. "Until we meet again."

She turned to Myles then, the unshed tears pooling deeper in her eyes.

He pulled her hand and led her to a more secluded spot, away from the king. He cupped her face and kissed her lips with reverence, but anguish darkened his eyes. "I begged the king to change his course, but his mind is set. Still, listen to me. Do not put yourself in harm's way. If you cannot find a way to unlock the gate, do not fear. We will come in from another way and win the day, no matter what."

"And the king will call me a traitor," Fiona said.

Myles shook his head. "He threatens out of habit, but he would have me to fight if he thinks to accuse you."

Fiona smiled at her husband's impassioned defiance. Her gaze darted toward King James, who was too far away to hear their hushed words.

"You've spoken treason now, husband. Perhaps my bad Sinclair heritage is rubbing off on you." She tried to tease to ease his mind, but his frown increased.

"Be on guard for Simon. You say he has no cause to be wary of you, but he has much to hide and may grow suspicious. Avoid him if you can."

"Simon thinks me nothing but a silly girl with no care at all for politics. If I tell him I despise you, he'll believe me. He may even brag he does me a great justice by attacking the king."

Her husband gave so great a sigh it ruffled her hair. "Avoid him, Fiona. Keep yourself and my child safe. Do you hear me?"

She rose up on her toes and pressed a kiss against his lips. She would not leave him with such concern etched in his face. "Do not fret, my love. Have you forgotten all my courage on the night I escaped you? You know I am most clever."

"You got lost in the woods and I caught you. How is that clever?"

She smiled, though it felt false. "I slipped from your bed without a sound, duped Tavish with a lie, and had it not been for the rain, I'd have made it much farther."

Her husband tilted his head and thought on this a moment. "You are prone to trickery. Perhaps I should be worried about reuniting you with your treacherous brother after all."

This brought a real smile to her face, for she knew he teased. "Do you love me?" she asked.

"You know I do."

"Then you must trust me and keep your promise."

He pulled her closer and tightened their embrace. "Which promise is that?"

"One day, in our chamber back at Dempsey, you offered me a thousand kisses. When this ordeal is over, I should like to go home to Dempsey and collect each one."

Fiona rode her beloved gray palfrey through the crumbling gates of Sinclair Hall, her heart a pealing bell inside her ears. 'Twas just as she had left it, yet everything seemed changed, as if each slant had a greater angle or the sun cast more twisted shadows. She made her way no farther than the bailey when a gaunt young man approached. She knew him as young William.

"Lady Fiona?" he asked, his voice full of surprise.

"One and the same. How are you, William?"

His eyes darted around before coming to rest on her horse. "I am well, my lady. Thank you for asking." He took the reins and led the horse to a mounting block so Fiona might dismount. "Forgive my impertinence, my lady, but what brings you to Sinclair Hall, and all alone, at that?"

"I would ask the same."

That voice came from behind and set a trembling to her limbs. 'Twas Simon.

She fisted her hands, but with some effort, unclenched them. The drumming in her ears banged louder. She focused on her breath and hoped he might not sense her agitation. Forcing a smile, she slid from her horse onto the block, and descended the two short steps. Not until she reached the ground did she trust herself to look toward her brother.

"I've come to visit home while the Campbells play at court. I've a longing to see my sister. Is she well?"

Simon frowned. He was bulkier than she'd remembered; the cords in his neck seemed even more pronounced. "She is fine. Where are your men? Certainly you're not alone?" He looked toward the gate and grabbed the hilt of his sword.

Fiona brushed past him to walk toward the great hall. "I left them in the village, the foul goats. They think to find some willing lasses, though I've said no Sinclair woman would have them." She pulled off one riding glove as she went forward, hoping to appear nonchalant, though her legs had turned to mush.

Simon followed after her. "How many men are with you?"

She worked on the other glove and kept her pace. "What? Oh, I don't know. Six, perhaps? I try not to pay attention to any of them." She moved quickly up the steps leading toward the hall. "Where is Marg?"

"I don't know." Simon's voice was a grumble. He took a step and grabbed her arm, jerking her to a halt. "Fiona, I find it odd that you arrive here with no warning and no men to speak of. Is your husband truly so careless?"

She flicked the gloves against her palm. "My husband"— she let the word drip with disdain—"is busy playing politics in Edinburgh and has not the slightest notion that I'm here. Dempsey is an awful place. Full of Campbells, you know. I'll not forgive you and John for forcing me among them." She tugged her arm from his grasp and prayed for strength, walking again.

"Where is John, by the way?" she asked, trying to imagine how Vivi might sound in such a circumstance. "I've a scolding for him, I must say." Fiona stopped a few paces ahead and turned to gaze at Simon when he did not answer. "Well?"

He glared back, measuring her, and a chill ran up her spine.

"What is the matter with you?" she demanded.

"Nothing," he finally said. "But John isn't here."

"Where is he? In the village?"

He glowered another moment, then shrugged those massive shoulders. "He's away. Now, if you've a mind to see Margaret, then do so, but I've important tasks to attend to. I haven't time to play the gracious host."

She frowned and made certain he saw. "One would never expect you to be gracious, Simon. But this is still my home, and I can manage for myself."

She turned away and nearly buckled at the knees. He'd leave her be so she might seek out her sister and Genevieve. It was less than two hours until dusk. She hadn't much time.

Moment after moment slipped away as she sought her sister. Fiona had not been at Sinclair Hall for months, and every person whom she passed stopped her, wanting to offer her their greetings, yet none seemed to know of Marg's whereabouts. On and on Fiona went, cordial to each, for she did not want to seem exasperated, but time was slipping away like water through her fingers.

At last, she came upon Margaret, tucked up on a bench under a window in Fiona's old chamber. Needlework lay unattended in her lap.

Margaret's smile spread like sunshine. She leapt from her seat, and Fiona gathered her into a warm embrace. Joy burst within, and she kissed her sister's cheeks.

"Marg, how I've missed you! You cannot imagine."

"I have missed you too. Desperately so. It's been so different here without you."

"I know, sweeting. I know." She brushed the blonde hair back from her sister's face. "I thought of you every day. But you must listen to me now. We have much to talk about, and some of it is very serious. But first, do you know the servant, Genevieve?"

"Genevieve? Yes, she works in the kitchen, but why?" Margaret's eyes sparkled with curiosity.

"We must find her and make our way to the chapel. I shall explain everything once we are there."

Margaret tipped her head. "'Tis an odd request. Can't we visit for a minute here first? You've only just arrived."

Fiona went back to the entrance of her chamber and peeked out. Seeing no one in the dim hallway, she closed the door and returned to Margaret's side.

"I know this makes little sense, and I'm sorry to burden you with it so quickly, but our brothers are plotting something. Have you heard of their plans?" Fiona asked.

Margaret's smiled dimmed. "Plotting? No, but they seem to be training often. And John has been gone for weeks."

Fiona nodded. Her anxiety grew as she noticed the golden glow of a waning sun. She tugged her sister toward the door. "Come with me to find Genevieve. I will tell you both an amazing tale once we are all together. But, Margaret, this is not for Simon's ears. He is planning something most heinous, and it is up to us to stop him."

"Stop him? How?" Marg's feet skidded on the floor. Fiona had forgotten her sister's persistence, but for once, the girl would simply have to wait. She tugged her toward the door.

"Patience, Margaret. Please, just trust me and do as I say. Understand?"

Margaret nodded and followed, but reluctance marred her pretty face.

Fiona opened the door and stepped into the corridor, glad it was still empty. They made their way through the hall and toward the kitchen. All about them, Sinclairs moved in and out, attending to their daily chores. Another ordinary day, just as her wedding day had been.

The sisters reached the kitchen in a matter of moments.

"Do you see her?" Fiona whispered.

"There"—Margaret pointed discreetly—"that one is Genevieve."

Fiona recognized her, the lovely widow whose husband had been lost in a raid last year. She'd come to Sinclair Hall just months before Fiona had left. But when the girl turned, Fiona gasped. She was petite as a pixie, yet there was no mistaking the rounded curve of her abdomen. Fiona's hands went to her own belly in solidarity, for Genevieve was clearly with child, yet John had said nothing. Leave it to a man to omit such a detail.

There were few others in the kitchen. Still, discretion was necessary. She and Margaret wound their way closer, as if they had no specific aim, but when Genevieve looked up and saw them, she stepped back from her task in apparent surprise.

"Lady Fiona."

What a beauty this Genevieve was. No wonder John's eyes had gleamed with adoration when he spoke of her. Fiona smiled, hoping the girl would see an offer of friendship in the gesture.

"Are you Genevieve?" she asked, just to make certain.

"I am, my lady." She curtsied and tried to brush the flour from her apron without success.

"I have need of you. You must come at once."

Genevieve's eyes rounded.

Fiona leaned forward, casting a glance over shoulder to make sure none of the others might hear. "I have word from John," she whispered. "Have no fear."

Walking fast, the three women reached the chapel, and Fiona nearly collapsed in relief at having not encountered Simon on the way. Inside, the building was dim and stank of old rushes and tallow. She was struck by the contrast, for the loving care with which the Campbell servants bestowed upon their place of worship showed. No such dedication was lavished upon this sad little spot. Perhaps 'twas why God never visited here.

Fiona peered around, shivering at the thought they might yet encounter Father Bettney. Time away had not mellowed her dislike of him. Fortune prevailed, for he was nowhere to be seen.

"What is this about, Fiona?" Marg said, crossing her arms. It seemed she had been patient long enough.

"Come and kneel with me. If Father Bettney enters, I would have him think we pray. I must explain things to you quickly,"

Fiona instructed. They walked toward the altar, and she lowered to a kneeling bench between the other two. She looked to the mullioned window to gauge the setting sun and knew her words must be swift and persuasive.

As quickly as she could, Fiona whispered the details of Simon's plan and John's change of heart. She spared nothing, for if each knew the whole of the situation, they could take her place in case she somehow failed.

"John is safe and near?" Genevieve whispered, her eyes glimmering with tears.

Fiona nodded. "He is most anxious to see you."

The servant's taut face relaxed a bit, though tension still radiated from her being and the hand rounded over her belly.

Unbidden, Fiona did the same, as if to make certain her own babe was safe.

Genevieve saw the motion and smiled. "You too, my lady?"

Fiona nodded, but Margaret paid no heed, still rattled by the other news.

"I do not understand," she said. "John has been a Campbell all this time? And now he means to betray us? We are still his family."

Her voice trembled, and Fiona clasped her hand.

"We are John's family, Marg. And Simon's too. I would do anything to change this if I could, but our brothers have put themselves on opposite sides of the crown. One of them will lose. There is no avoiding that fact now. I side with John, not only because his way is more certain to keep our clan safe, but also because he is on the side of right. Simon seeks to kill for vengeance only. John aims for peace with our king."

"Are you certain? Perhaps it is the Campbells who make you believe such a thing. They are the enemy, you know," Margaret said.

Fiona wrapped an arm around her sister's shoulders and gave a squeeze. "No, sweeting. 'Tis man's pride which is the enemy. We are merely caught up in it."

Margaret still looked doubtful, but Fiona had run out of time to convince her.

"Listen, I must go into the passageway and unlock the gates. Will you come with me and hold the lantern? Genevieve can keep watch for any who might enter the chapel. We cannot fail at this."

Myles, with John pointing the way, led the king's men along the rocky shoreline until they reached the outer entrance of the passageway. They had come on foot and left the horses back with the king, so progress was slow. But at last they found it, hidden among huge stones and covered by thick branches that appeared to have been growing there for ages.

John drew his sword and swung at the thick wood, the metal of it clanging against the rock.

"Be quiet," Myles said, "or you give them warning."

He did not trust John fully, no matter that he was Fiona's brother, or indeed, even his own. But now it seemed they must work in tandem. Myles pulled the branch up, and John swung so that the blade missed the rock and struck the wood. It snapped in two, and they moved on to the next.

"See you do not slice me by accident," Myles warned.

John cocked one brow, as if to say it would be no accident at all. Perhaps his brother did not trust him so much either.

The sun set as they hacked at the remaining branches. Finally, the door was clear, and Myles leaned forward to tug the handle. Locked, still. He hoped Fiona was having success on the other side. With nothing to do but wait, Myles told the men to sit and rest while they had the chance, and so they settled upon the rocks.

"How many gates line this passageway?" Myles asked John after another moment had passed.

"Three. This one here, one at the very entrance near the sacristy, and one about halfway in between. It's near two hundred paces from here to the other end. If I had thought of it, I'd have unlocked the gates before coming to Dempsey. 'Twas a foolish oversight and would've kept Fiona from this task."

"She seems up to the challenge," Myles answered, though his breath came shallow as he thought of her and their child inside those walls.

John met his gaze. "She is up to any challenge. But I should not have allowed Simon to force her into marriage. I failed her in that."

Myles bristled at the implication he was not a worthy husband, but John continued.

"Yet it seems you are well suited. And I think she cares for you."

"We are well suited. And she does care for me."

John's gaze was earnest. "Do you care for her as well?"

"I do." He could say more on the matter, but now was not the time.

"Then be true to her. Truer than our father was to his wife."

The words were spoken softly, but Myles felt the sting of John's discontent. It must be no easy thing to learn you are a bastard son. And Myles himself had struggled with the disappointment he'd felt in hearing the earl's confession. He'd thought his father above such things, flawless in his judgment and deportment. But it would seem even the Campbell chieftain harbored mortal flaws.

"What are our options of entry if this fails?" Myles asked, bringing his thoughts to the matter at hand.

"Our options?" John replied.

"Yes, if Fiona cannot open the gates, what other method have we to get inside? Besides the front gate, of course."

John looked in the direction of Sinclair Hall, although not much could be seen from their vantage point.

"There is a weak spot in the north wall. It's half-crumbled, and perhaps it could be scaled. I cannot say for certain. It may have been shored up while I was away. But Fiona will not fail. As long as she can get past Simon, all will be well."

His words were confident enough, but his tone implied it was himself he sought to convince. Myles reached out and tried the door once more.

"Perhaps we should try to pick the lock from this side. It would give us a head start if Fiona is delayed."

John nodded, and they set to work trying to dismantle it.

"She'll not fail," John said again, but both men knew she might.

# CHAPTER 41

T HE ENTRANCE TO THE PASSAGEWAY IS BEHIND THE SACRISTY," Fiona whispered, trying to mask the tremor in her voice. "John said the keys would be in a jar near the door. Margaret, we will search while Genevieve keeps watch within the chapel."

"What if I see someone?" Genevieve asked, hands crossed over her chest.

Fiona had no useful answer. "Distract them any way you can. And be loud about it. I'll let you know when we are entering the passage."

She turned toward the sacristy, and a chilled finger of dread trailed up her spine. That tunnel had been a place of ghosts and fear when she was young, and in truth, she felt the same way still. The only saving grace was that Myles waited at the other end.

She and Margaret walked quickly past the raised altar and into the room behind it. It was dark, with no windows, and a musky scent permeated the air inside. Fiona found a small lantern sitting on the floor. It was grimy with age and, once lit, gave off scant light, but she'd not thought to bring another, and she needed what little light it could offer.

She held it up inside the sacristy. Shadows danced on the gray stone walls of the tiny room, exposing cupboards lined up in rows and the priest's robes hanging on a hook. The thought of secret love letters skittered through her mind, those written in Cedric's hand and hidden by her mother, but Fiona dismissed that thought as quickly as it came. The Sinclair priest was a bitter man and would've had no part in that. If her mother had hidden letters, for certain they'd be somewhere else.

Apprehension filled her chest, and she sighed. At the sound of it, Margaret's hand slid into hers.

"What do we do now?" her sister whispered.

Fiona looked over and met her eye to eye, for in the months they'd been apart, Margaret had grown nearly as tall as Fiona herself. Bess had been right. She was a child no longer.

"We must find the keys. The entrance is behind that rug." She pointed at the opposite wall, to a tapestry, faded and moth-eaten. She walked over and pushed the fabric gently to the side to expose a small door, but the age-worn bar from which the fabric hung gave a crackle and a snap, and suddenly, the tapestry crumpled to the ground.

Fiona's stomach plummeted with it, for now anyone who came into this room would know someone had entered. But it could not be helped. This journey had begun, and she must keep moving forth.

She pulled at the latch of the door, and it twisted easily in her hands. The door creaked as she pushed it open, but did not resist. Perhaps this would not be so difficult after all. But the entrance loomed, dark and forbidding. A smell of mildew assaulted her nose. A cobweb wafted out. This tunnel had not been used in some time—at least not by anything with just two legs.

"I found them," Margaret gasped, "right where John said they'd be." She had stepped to the corner where several jars and baskets sat. She raised her hand and held the keys aloft. "They're heavy."

Heavy as Fiona's fear, no doubt. She took them from her sister's hand. "Fast work, Margaret. Thank you. But we'd still best hurry. I'll tell Gen—"

Fiona's comment was cut short by the sound of Genevieve's voice.

"Oh, good evening, Father."

God have mercy, Father Bettney had come. Fiona tucked the lantern into the corner and then moved to peek into the chapel.

There he was, striding toward the maid, the ever-present frown marring his face.

"What are you doing here, girl?"

Genevieve knelt once more upon the bench. "I am praying, Father. Will you join me?"

The priest's eye twitched. "The hour grows late. Do your praying somewhere else."

"But Father..." She paused and took a trembling breath. Her glance darted to the sacristy door before she cast her stare back to him. "My dear mother lies dying. I must pray for her soul, and is this not the holiest place?"

Fiona made the sign of the cross from behind the sacristy door. Lying to a priest, especially one as censorious as this one, did not bode well for their mission.

"If she lies dying, you should be by her side. Scat with you now. Back to the village."

Fiona saw the indecision play over Genevieve's features, and her own thoughts rioted in turmoil. What to do? Duck into the tunnel and hope the priest did not notice? Or step out and distract him from her purpose in the hopes he'd leave them be. Fear twined around her limbs and squeezed the breath from her lungs. She glanced at Margaret. The girl was pressed against the wall, eyes wide in the semidarkness.

"Please, Father," Genevieve said, "surely the Lord will pay greater attention to your pleas than mine. Pray with me for just a few moments. Then I may return to my mother knowing I have done my best."

Time spun faster. Night would fall with relentless certainty. Fiona must act. In moments, the men would be at the gate. She could not fail them. Reaching over, she snatched the lantern back up and gripped the keys tightly in the other.

"Hurry," she whispered to her sister. "She cannot hold the priest back for long." She moved, fast but cautious, to the entrance of the tunnel and stepped inside. Margaret hesitated for only a moment, then joined Fiona over the threshold. Fiona reached back and pulled the door shut. With any luck, the priest might think the tapestry fell on its own.

The lantern offered little glow. They could see but a few inches before them. Fiona tried hard not to imagine the myriad of creatures scuttling away from the light. She felt a cobweb brush her face, like the hand of a ghost.

"We'll be fine, Margaret. There's nothing here but shadows and a few spiders." She lied to her sister. Inside, she prayed silently for courage. Her heart beat like a rabbit's, so fast she could scarcely breathe. Still, she put one foot in front of the other, and they inched their way forward. But only a moment passed before the door swung open and Father Bettney shouted.

"You there!" the priest's voice boomed, echoing like thunder. "Come out at once. You've no business in this passageway."

He loomed, a stark silhouette against the dim light in the sacristy. His reedy form filled the doorway like a leafless tree in winter.

Fear and frustration collided in Fiona's lungs. What had become of Genevieve? There was no sign of her.

"Father Bettney, 'tis I, Fiona." She held the lantern up to her face.

"Fiona?" His scowl deepened. He came forward a few feet and grabbed her by the wrist. "I heard you had returned. But you have no business in this tunnel."

She tried to wrest her hand free, but his grip was made of iron. Quickly, he pulled her back into the sacristy, and Margaret followed.

"What antics are these?" he demanded, glaring from her to Margaret. The pockmarks on his cheeks stood out in contrast to the flush of his skin.

Fiona's mind went painfully blank, and in the panic of the moment, she could think of no story to offer but the truth. It was her only hope of getting back into that tunnel in time.

"I am on a mission of mercy, Father. Please understand, it is imperative I unlock the gates of the passageway."

"Why?" The question wheezed from his chest.

Lord save them, she did not have time for explanation! But surely a man of God, even a man as vile as this priest, would be on the side of saving lives.

"Do you know of Simon's plans? To fight the king?"

His eyes narrowed. "If I did, what matter is it of yours?"

"'Tis a war we will lose, Father. Our good, brave men will perish. But the Campbells await entrance into Sinclair Hall. If we let them claim Simon, no Sinclair blood need spill."

His face suffused with color. Words sputtered from his lips like spittle. "You stupid girl! What have you done? You would let our enemy in?"

His anger was an oppressive burst, smothering her with its intensity. Margaret moved behind her, and Fiona extended her own hands as if to calm the irate priest.

"They are not our enemy, Father. 'Tis a great sacrifice to hand over Simon. It breaks my very heart to do so. But if we forfeit him, the truce will hold and Clan Sinclair will regain its rightful place among the great families of Scotland. The king has promised."

"Lies! All lies, you foolish chit! I warned your brothers Cedric Campbell would turn you into one of them. Just as he did your mother." He spit on the floor as if mentioning her left a vile taste in his mouth.

Fiona's blood thickened in her veins. "What do you know of Cedric Campbell and my mother?"

Sweat beaded, slick and bright, upon his face. A rivulet ran down into the crease along his cheek. "I know she used this passage to sneak out to meet him, the conniving whore." His voice sliced the air, the edges sharp enough to cut. He reached out and twisted the keys from her hand, throwing them to the corner. Fiona's fear doubled at his accusation. "My mother was no whore."

Contempt twisted his expression; his eyes blazed. "I know differently. Time and again, she traversed this tunnel to lie with him. I watched them, rutting like animals in the woods."

Margaret gasped into Fiona's ear, and the priest kept talking. His rage built with every word.

"Your mother was an adulteress! A faithless Jezebel!" He waved a knobby finger at their faces, his words coming fast and furious. "She had no loyalty to husband and none to her clan! And you, it seems, are cut from the same filthy cloth."

And as he railed, a realization formed within Fiona's mind, like frost creeping across a windowpane one tiny fragment at a time. 'Twas the priest who'd seen her mother last. 'Twas he who carried her body into the hall the day she died.

"Was it you?" Breathless, she could scarcely form the words.

Father Bettney sneered, a madman gripped in disillusion, his movements jerky and uneven. Froth gathered at the corners of his mouth as he spoke.

"She had no shame, that one! No remorse." He waved a fist, his words sizzling in the dry air.

Margaret's breath was fast upon her neck.

"Such immorality demanded purification. I gave her every chance at absolution, but she'd not repent. She laughed in my face and called me a fool. Until I held her to the water." He twisted back to them, his frenzied expression triumphant and certain. "Then she begged for forgiveness, sure enough."

"The water?" Bile rose, hot and fast, but Fiona tamped it down. She reached behind to grasp Margaret's hand. Her sister pressed closed against her, and Fiona felt her trembling.

"Aislinn Sinclair tarnished her soul with sin most grievous, but my grace brought her back to purity. 'Twas I who slew the demons of her lust. My prayers and intervention which allowed her death without sin."

Fiona's tongue, numb inside her mouth, could scarcely form the words. Yet she forced herself to form them, certain now at his answer. "You killed her."

The priest snorted, a crazed, choking sort of laughter. "I saved her! I baptized her in that creek so her soul might be free in the kingdom of heaven! But for me, she'd be writhing in the fires of hell."

Fiona's throat scalded at his boastful confession. "'Twas murder, you vile monster. And nothing less! 'Tis you who God will punish." She pushed at him, heedless of the danger.

He swung back, flinging her against the wall. Her head bashed against the stone. The impact drove the breath from her lungs. Dazed but determined, she tried to get up. Margaret ran to her side, but the priest knocked her away as well and stood upon Fiona's skirts.

"I see they've made a Campbell whore of you as well." His voice rasped, hot and rough. His eyes went glassy with rage and his twisted notion of morality.

Dread, heavy and dark as death itself, pressed down upon Fiona. Margaret rose slowly, looking from Fiona to the door as a commotion sounded in the bailey. Shouts from every direction began to echo outside the chapel.

The priest bent over, his breath a fetid stink upon Fiona's face. "If Campbell bastards breach our gate, the soul of every dead Sinclair will be a curse on you. You led us to this!"

The disturbance grew louder. Fiona could not tell who shouted, or even from whence it came, but she prayed the king's men had found their way in.

The priest grabbed her chin and pinched with one bony hand. "You are as worthless as your mother, you traitorous whelp."

He reached back and grabbed the lantern with his other hand. In one swift motion, he flung it down against the tapestry piled on the ground. The old fabric smoldered but a second and then burst into flames. Margaret screamed and jumped to stomp it out, but Father Bettney rose and slapped her hard, knocking her to the ground once more.

Fiona scuttled to the side, away from the fire, but thought only of getting close to Margaret. Fear replaced her anger. He meant to kill them both, and none would save them, for she had failed in her duty. And her child would perish along with them.

The shouts outside grew more distinct, closer and more urgent. The priest cast a glance into the chapel. He turned back and picked up the keys up from the floor, and his hateful gaze came back to Fiona. Her heart nearly paused. She could not breathe or call for help. And where was Genevieve?

He pulled the extra robes from the wall and threw them to the burning pile. "'Tis fitting, I suppose, that you should die by flame."

He stepped out of the sacristy and slammed the door. The metal scrape of lock and key scratched the air. The sound of something heavy crashed against the wood, and Fiona wondered if he'd tipped the altar over toward the door. Smoke began to fill the room as the robes ignited. She jumped from her spot and shoved with all her might against the door. It would not budge. They were trapped.

"She should have reached us by now," John said, rising up to stare toward Sinclair Hall. They'd worked on the latch from their side for nearly an hour to no avail. The door stood firm, and they were no closer to reaching the chapel.

Myles's agitation mounted, his worry growing as the sky darkened. "We cannot wait any longer. The king will storm the front gate soon. Take us to the place where we might climb the wall."

He signaled to the men. In seconds, each was on his feet and running toward Sinclair Hall.

"'Tis there." John pointed as they ran. "See the spot that's lower than the rest?"

Myles could just barely make it out in the dusk and shadows, but sure enough, he saw a dip in the stone wall. They ran until they reached the closest corner of the keep and then moved silently along the wall. No shouts of alarm sounded from overhead, and Myles offered up his thanks to God that they had reached this point. On they went until they stood just below the crumbled spot of the curtain wall.

"What lies directly on the other side?" Myles said to John.

"The granary. If a handful of us can get to the roof, we can wait there until we hear the king's men at the gate," John answered.

Myles eyed the wall. There was no way to get all of them up and over, but standing on the shoulders of another, a few could scale it. The rest would have to move along back to the gate and enter with the king.

'Twas no easy venture with their weapons and desire to remain undetected, but after several attempts, six of the men joined John and Myles upon the granary roof.

Myles peered into the bailey. Naught seemed amiss, no men positioned for battle. Perhaps Fiona had not succeeded with the gate, but it was obvious the Sinclairs had no notion of what was to come.

The sound of horses quietly on the move drifted up from the ground, so faint he was not sure he had heard it. But soon after, a hue and cry arose, and a crashing at the wooden gate rent the air.

"'Tis time!" Myles called out. He jumped down from the granary roof and moved quickly toward the hall. Chaos erupted and cries filled the air as Sinclair men scurried forth, unarmed and ill prepared, for who would bother attacking a worthless pile of rubble such as this?

The bailey filled with royal guards on horseback and a hundred more on foot. The air clamored with the clash of swords and the angry shouts of men.

"We must find Simon!" Myles shouted.

"Check the hall," John replied over the din of clanging steel. "This way!"

John pulled Myles back to press against the wall. They moved in unison, unchallenged by any, for all the Sinclair men with weapons had moved toward the gate to battle with the king's men, while John and Myles moved quietly along behind the fray.

"Here, through the kitchen." John pushed him past a doorway amid the strident cries of maids. Running past the tables and the oven, John called out to them. "Do not be alarmed! Stay hidden and all will be well. If you see your men, tell them to surrender."

They moved on, past other flustered maids running to and fro.

John grabbed one as she passed. "Bertrice! Have you seen my brother?"

Her eyes went wide as if he were a spectral vision. "He ran toward the bailey when the first shouts sounded. I thought you were in London."

"I'm back. Now go to the kitchen and wait there."

Myles followed fast on John's heels as they sprinted across the great hall entrance and out to the steps. There, John paused a moment to absorb the scene. Mayhem sprawled before them, with men fighting in every corner of the bailey, some using blades, but just as many defending their spot with torches or pitchforks.

"Do you see him?" Myles asked.

John's face was strained, and sympathy flowed over Myles. These were not John's blood kin, but they'd been the only family he'd ever known. Had he himself been in John's place, he might not have been so brave.

"John," a faint voice called.

Both men turned.

'Twas Genevieve waving from the steps beneath. Her dress was torn, and blood trickled from the corner of her mouth.

"Genevieve!" John raced down the steps toward the maid, and Myles followed.

"John," she cried, "come quick! The priest is with Fiona and Margaret in the chapel."

John hugged the girl to him with one hand and wiped away the blood with his other. "'Tis good, Gen. Run along and join them. You'll be safe there, and when the fighting is over, I'll come find you."

She pulled frantically on his arm. "No! No, you don't understand. 'Twas the priest who killed your mother. I heard him say so, and now he means to burn the chapel down with them inside!"

Fear, more powerful than the sun itself, burned over Myles. Without a word exchanged, he and John sprinted toward the chapel. His legs felt leaden. They moved too slowly. Even now, Myles could see smoke seeping from the windows and willed his body to go faster. The king had ordered him to capture Simon at any cost, but Fiona's life was more important.

They reached the door and yanked it open, with Genevieve just behind them. The stench of smoke was strong, but only a whisper of it filled the chapel, and Myles gave a quick prayer of gratitude. They were not too late.

But Genevieve's cry cut short his relief. "They're in the sacristy!"

His gaze followed hers, and his heart lurched once more, for clawing out from the seams around the sacristy door came tentacles of thick black smoke. At the base of the door, the altar was tipped on its side, blocking the way.

"I tried to move the altar, but it was too heavy," Genevieve sobbed.

Once more, the men sprinted, grunting as they pushed aside the altar. Myles pulled upon the latch, but it was locked. He pounded on the door.

"Fiona!" he shouted. "We are here!"

"Myles?" came her muffled call from within. She coughed, along with Margaret. "Hurry, please!"

She had not perished. He would save her yet. If he had to break through the stone walls with his own body, he would see her rescued from that room.

John unsheathed his sword and, with the hilt, smashed apart the lock. It took a dozen blows, but at last, it fell away. Myles yanked open the sacristy door. Smoke, thick and wicked, poured forth like a vaporous monster. Flames licked at one side of the tiny room, but he plunged in, heedless of the danger.

Just inside the door, he found them, Fiona and her sister, huddled near the floor. They coughed and cried, but were alive. Praise be to God. He scooped Fiona up into his arms and quickly moved her from the room. John stepped in behind and did the same with Margaret. They carried the women down the aisle and set them on the pew closest to the door and the fresher air.

Though her face was stained with soot and streaked by tears, his wife was safe and whole. The flames had not reached her. Joy burst within.

"Where is the priest?" Fiona rasped. "You must find him. 'Twas he who killed my mother."

"He meant to kill us too," Margaret sobbed, tears pouring from her red-stained eyes.

"I should have known." John's head dipped low as if the fault were his alone. "How did we not see it?"

"You did not see because you are fools! Blinded by your mother's sins!" Father Bettney shouted from the chapel door.

Myles leaned back to draw his sword as the priest strode toward them with a pointed dagger in his fist. And next to him came Simon and a dozen Sinclair men.

Fiona's lungs seized once more, finally free of smoke but clogged by fear. They were outnumbered, trapped once more inside the chapel. Simon's eyes were ablaze and bore into John like hot irons. His loathing pulsed against the air.

John stood fast, but when he reached for his sword, his hand grasped at nothing. For he'd set it down when he picked up Margaret and was now unarmed.

Simon spit upon the floor, his sword out and at the ready. "I see no fools! Only traitors. And you, John, are the greatest of them all. You call yourself a son of Hugh Sinclair?"

Pungent smoke wafted from the burning sacristy, acrid and bitter. The wood above the room began to hiss and pop. And in the space of that moment, Fiona watched as John's expression of despair transformed to quiet confidence.

"No," he answered calmly. "I call myself a son of Cedric Campbell."

Simon's angry eyes went wide, then narrowed to slits. The Sinclair men around him murmured their surprise.

"You! I knew it!" Father Bettney wheezed, pointing a gnarly finger at John. "You are the spawn of their wicked union."

Simon took another step and raised his blade with menace. "What are you saying?"

Fiona's husband stepped closer to John, brandishing his own weapon, and her heart lodged in her throat.

"'Tis as it sounds," John answered, the tilt of his jaw defiant. "Cedric Campbell is my father, and so I side with him. But before you wave that blade at me, know this. The king possesses the signature of every Highland chief who vowed to kill him. Each will be arrested, and he shall mete out punishment as he sees fit. Spare us, and he may yet spare you. I will beg him for your life. But if we die, so shall you."

Myles moved closer still and aimed his sword at Simon. Two Campbell brothers against one Sinclair.

Simon ran a hand across his jaw, his eyes darting swiftly from one man to the other. Smoke continued to sting the air. The timber ceiling began to smolder.

"Kill him," the priest cried. "He is a whoreson and a traitor. He has cost you Sinclair Hall!"

"Shut up!" shouted Simon. "Let me think."

A primal growl erupted from the maddened priest. He shoved Simon to the side and bolted forward, aiming his dagger directly at John's heart.

Fiona screamed. Her husband stepped in front of John, knocking him away, and plunged his weapon deep into Father Bettney's gut. Flesh gave way to steel, and the priest's gurgle of surprised agony made her stomach heave in revulsion.

Myles twisted the sword, jerking it upward toward the priest's ribs; then with his booted foot, he pushed the writhing priest from the blooded tip. Father Bettney clutched his wound. Blood spurted forth, some splattering on Margaret's cheek, and the priest crumpled to the ground.

Simon lunged back, swinging his blade at her husband, who deflected his strike.

In an instant, shouts rang from the entryway. A dozen men or more, all dressed in royal colors, raced inside the chapel. The king commanded them amid the fray.

Fiona gave another cry and pulled her sister and Genevieve away. The three of them pressed against the wall as a battle broke out in earnest. The haze of smoke increased as men swung their swords or used their fists and daggers.

Fiona looked for an exit, but there was no easy path from where they were to the door. And in truth, even had there been, Fiona was not certain she could look away.

Steel upon steel and the grunts of men, striking and falling, competed with the sound of Margaret crying softly, and the crackle of wood around the altar igniting. Fiona hugged her sister close and used her smoke-stained sleeve to wipe the blood from Margaret's face. Genevieve pressed against them, never letting her gaze waver from John.

Off to one side, Fiona's brothers waged a battle of their own. Faces flushed, the sheen of exertion and anger bright upon their foreheads. They raged, now the fiercest of foes. Fiona's heart split asunder at the travesty of them pitted against each other.

"Forfeit, and live to see another day, you fool," John said, striking a blow toward Simon's shoulder. "I will plead for clemency on your behalf."

Simon weaved and ducked. "Another day of James's rule? I'd rather die, you filthy bastard. How could you do this to me?" He swung and missed.

"To you?" John cried. "You gave no thought at all of sacrificing Fiona. This is no different."

They battled in a circle, moving round pews and over kneeling benches, coming ever closer to the women. Fiona looked about for a weapon of her own. She'd join this fight and see it end. She plucked an iron candlestick from its hook upon the wall.

Simon jumped a bench and huffed from the effort. "Fiona is nothing but a girl," he cried. "You were my brother!" He lunged, slicing John upon the arm.

John winced and clutched the wound, nearly slipping on the rushes. Simon smiled with deadly intent, sensing triumph. He thrust with all his might toward John's chest.

Genevieve screamed and tried to jump forward, but Fiona held her back and watched the blow fall short.

A sudden look of amazement claimed Simon's face. His weapon clattered to the floor, and he clutched his own chest. Between his fingers, the tip of a blade protruded through his ribs. He'd been skewered from behind.

The king stepped around him, breathing fast, a smile of victory upon his face. "He may have been your brother, you traitorous cur. But I am your king."

The battle had ended. Simon and the priest lay dead upon the floor, along with far too many good and loyal men. Fiona brushed a tear from her cheek and searched the faces of those still standing, though it was hard to see through the haze of thickening smoke.

At last she saw him, standing on the far side of the chapel, battered but alive. Her husband!

He seemed to be looking through the smoke as well. Then he turned and caught her eye. A tired smile tipped the corners of his mouth. She stepped away from Margaret as Myles hurried across the room. His arms, wondrous and steady, pulled her tight against him.

It was over. The fighting and the plotting and the fear. She could hardly breathe from the relief of it. Tomorrow, she would grieve for Simon and the men they'd lost, but in this moment, all she would do was cling to Myles and thank the Lord for finally listening to her prayers.

The king approached, clasping John upon the shoulder. "'Twas no easy thing you did, young Campbell. But you have proven your loyalty. Your father will be proud."

John nodded once, solemn. "I pray he is successful in capturing the Sutherland chief this night."

"I have no doubt all the traitors will be vanquished."

"And what will become of the Clan Sinclair?" John asked.

The king looked around the smoke-hazed chapel and at the flames licking up the wall and along the roofline. "I'll think on that. But for now, let's leave this place before it burns around us."

Fiona's brother turned away and spotted Genevieve. At last, he smiled and held out his hand. The maid gave a tiny cry and moved forward to clasp it.

Myles pulled Fiona toward the door as John gathered Genevieve and Margaret to his sides.

"Out, one and all!" the king shouted.

They filed from the chapel, and fast as tinder turned to flames, word spread among the clan that Simon Sinclair was their laird no more.

Fiona stood between Myles and the king and watched the fighting in the bailey cease as each man laid down his weapon and picked up a bucket to help extinguish the flames of the chapel. They worked in unison, Sinclair next to Campbell, united by a common purpose. Tomorrow, there would be still be wounds to heal, hearts to mend, and sadly, dead to bury, but the feuding was no more. This time the truce would hold.

Fiona turned a smile toward her husband and felt her joy grow, much like their child within her. A Campbell-Sinclair union.

Yes, this time the truce would hold.

# EPILOGUE

NATURE HAD A TWISTED HUMOR, INDEED. OUTSIDE, THE winds howled like a banshee in the night, wicked and cold, with an evil bite. But within the sturdy walls of Dempsey Castle, a joyous mood rang forth. The great hall blazed with warmth and happy tidings.

Fiona Campbell stood upon the steps and searched the waiting crowd. Somewhere in the midst of all her kith and kin, she'd find her husband.

She spotted Tavish at once, stout and red as ever, laughing next to Cedric and Marietta. There was Vivi, dangling a prospective husband on her arm. 'Twas just what she'd been shopping for during her visit to Linlithgow while the others played at squashing rebellion. Or so she'd said. And there were Marg and Alyssa, heads bent together, whispering over some special secret. They'd become as close as pearls on a string in the months since Marg had come to live here. A burst of gladness swelled inside Fiona's breast. This was her family.

The Highland traitors had been vanquished, and the king sat solidly upon his throne. John, though most thoroughly a Campbell, now led the Clan Sinclair, and the people rejoiced, for they were tired of the feud and embraced the peace he'd brought their way. Fiona felt a stab at his absence, but knew she'd see him when the weather grew warm once more and he and Genevieve and their child came to visit.

Fiona turned her gaze to the other side of the hall. Ah, and there at last! Her husband. Her foot faltered on the step as he turned his dazzling smile her way and hurried to the stairs. Her breath caught in a giddy lurch, and the tiny bundle in her arms stretched and yawned.

'Twas Aislinn Elizabeth Campbell about to make an entrance to the banquet. She was four months old today and every bit as much a Campbell babe as any in this room, with thick dark hair and dimples in each cheek. Robert liked to point those out and mention how they looked like his.

But when Fiona looked into this baby's face, she saw only Myles, and hoped to have a dozen more. What strange twists and turns her life had taken, but for all the brambles in that path, she had come to a most happy destination. Her mother would be most pleased.

Fiona reached the bottom step, and Myles greeted her with an indecent kiss. He had yet to reach one thousand, but they were very nearly there. And ever so happy with the trying.

He leaned lower and pressed his lips against their daughter's soft, chubby cheek. She cooed and smiled, and Fiona wondered if ever a babe had so besotted any man. She'd break hearts, this daughter of theirs.

Myles lifted his gaze and smiled at Fiona, his eyes bright green in the glow of the hall.

"Still you keep me waiting. What took so long?" he asked.

She shook her head in mock severity. "'Twas not my fault. This girl is greedy with her meals and woefully stubborn."

Her husband chuckled and reached out to ruffle the dark tuft of his daughter's fluffy hair. "I'd expect no less from a Sinclair lass. Perhaps she needs a brother or two?"

Fiona felt a rolling flutter low in her belly and wondered if one was ensconced there now. It was too soon to tell, but she had her suspicions.

Still, she laughed and answered, "My brothers failed to tame me. Perhaps it is a fine, strong husband she needs."

Myles reached out and twisted a curl of her hair around his finger, the habit so constant now she wasn't certain he realized when he did it. "There shall never be a husband worthy of our daughter," he said, smiling.

"Ah, the bloated arrogance of the Campbells," Fiona teased in return.

He shook his head. "No, you misunderstand me, wife. It is the combination of you and I which cannot be surpassed."

She laughed outright at this, whispering back, "Such hon-eyed words, my lord. Is it your aim to trick me into bed?"

He smiled, open and sincere, and her heart tripped as it did each time he gazed at her in such a manner. If she was not carrying his child now, she would be soon enough.

"'Twas never my aim to trick you, my darling," he said. "Or force your surrender. I meant only to coax you into love with me."

"And so you have. Most successfully."

"Have I?" Her husband looked pleased.

Fiona chuckled. "Do I not tell you so nearly every day?"

He moved closer, bringing his lips tantalizingly close to her own. "Tell me again."

### THE END

# ACKNOWLEDGMENTS

WRITING MAY SEEM A SOLITARY ENDEAVOR, BUT GETTING a book published requires a legion of dedicated miracle workers. I am grateful to each and every person who helped me along this path. Thanks to Nalini Akolekar, Kelli Martin, and the entire Montlake team for believing in me and making this adventure so much fun.

Thanks to my dedicated "Three Cheekas," Jennifer McQuiston, Alyssa Alexander, and Kimberly Kincaid, for always, always, always encouraging me, and making me laugh every single day at the most inappropriate jokes.

Thanks to the Ruby Slippered Sisterhood for hosting a "Best First Paragraph" contest, and to Kath Van of Dragonphli Sanctuary for nudging me in the direction I was always meant to go.

Thanks to Ashlyn Macnamara for adding her historical expertise, and for always asking, "But how do the characters *feel*?"

Thanks to all the lovely Dashing Duchesses. I'm so proud to be among you, I fear I shall swoon.

Thanks to Kieran Kramer, Katharine Ashe, Julie London, Karen Hawkins, Vicky Dreiling, Delilah Marvelle, Romily Bernard, Margie Lawson, Michael Hauge, Patty Hoffman, Darcy Woods, and all the wonderful authors who have been so friendly and gracious with their support.

Thanks to Karen Robards for writing a swashbuckling pirate-seduces-a-maiden story that captured my teenaged imagination and made me want to be a romance writer.

Thanks to Cecelia Grant, Joanna Bourne, and Sherry Thomas for always demonstrating what extraordinary writing is. I'd like to live inside one of your books.

And finally, thanks to my dear friends and wonderful family. Without you, none of the rest matters.

# ABOUT THE AUTHOR

Born on Christmas day to an Irish mother and a Scottish father, Tracy Brogan considers herself a decidedly Celtic-American. She writes fun and sassy contemporary novels where ordinary people find extraordinary love, as well as stirring historical romances full of political intrigue, damsels causing distress, and the occasional man in a kilt.

A self-proclaimed history buff, Tracy is a contributing member of the Dashing Duchesses website, where they make history sound much hotter than it really was. She is a two-time finalist for the Romance Writers of America's prestigious Golden Heart Award. She lives in Michigan with her husband, two brilliant and beautiful daughters, and two significantly less brilliant, but equally endearing, dogs.

Tracy loves to hear from readers so please visit her at TracyBrogan.com or at the DashingDuchesses.com.